THE 'ABODE OF THE DRAGON'S PEARL'

The shoji slid back. Pev stared at the tiny bowed form kneeling in the entrance. His first impression was of a child in a garish kimono topped by glossy rolls of hair. The child murmured to Shoh and slipped gracefully into the room, eyes modestly down.

'Other women will follow but this lovely blossom is Umegawa whose home city is the same as mine. She bids you welcome to The Dragon's Pearl,' Shoh said.

'Greetings, Umegawa Sama,' Pev whispered.

Slowly she raised her heavy head. He looked down at the loveliest girl he had ever seen . . .

Yedo
LYNN GUEST

SPHERE BOOKS LIMITED

First published in Great Britain by
The Bodley Head Ltd, 1985
Copyright © Lynn Guest 1985
Published by Sphere Books Ltd, 1986
27 Wright's Lane, London W8 5SW
Reprinted 1986

TRADE
MARK

Set in 10/10½ pt Compugraphic English

Printed and bound in Great Britain by
Cox & Wyman Ltd, Reading

For Harry

Contents

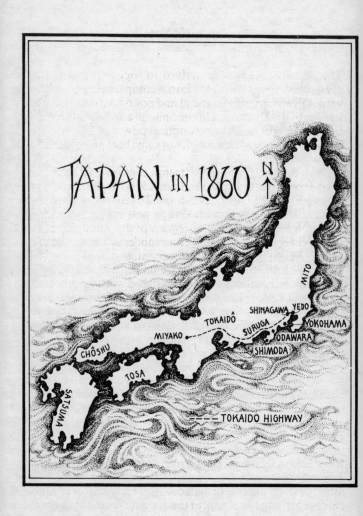

JAPAN IN 1860 N↑

MITO

SHINAGAWA YEDO

TOKAIDÔ YOKOHAMA

SURUGA

MIYAKO ODAWARA

SHIMODA

CHÔSHU

TOSA

SATSUMA

TOKAIDO HIGHWAY

Author's Note

The first foreigners who arrived to 'open' Japan in the 1850s unwittingly stumbled into a complex society on the verge of revolution. The social and political circumstances leading to the abdication of the Shogun and the restoration of the Emperor as supreme political power in 1868 are far beyond the scope of this novel, but some background might be useful to the reader.

From the twelfth to the sixteenth century civil war ravaged Japan. Naturally in such times it is the military class who rise to dominance. When the Tokugawa clan established a lasting peace in 1600 their new regime, the Shogunate, was based on this supremacy of the samurai. Yedo, as the Victorians spelled Edo, now modern Tokyo, was the centre of their government. Most contact with the outside world was broken off and Japan remained a feudal society. Although internal commerce flourished in this peace and Osaka and Yedo became rich if despised merchant cultures, the samurai themselves were generally superfluous. Some served as officials in their daimyo's (feudal lord's) administration or in the Shogun's government, the Bafuku, but many lived unproductive lives restricted by bushido, their code of behaviour. A samurai's income was a rice stipend granted by his daimyo, but when harvests were bad and the overtaxed peasants exhausted the daimyo had no choice but to cut the stipend to his diligent but useless warriors. By 1860 the class was impoverished. Furthermore, for those who were curious and ambitious their world was a narrow one. Contact with the forbidden West held an undeniable allure. The Tokugawa leaders demanded that each daimyo and a large retinue spend every other year in expensive palaces in Yedo, but even this enforced visit to the capital of the Shogunate could not have relieved the frustration of the more active samurai.

Politically the country was dividing into two camps. One consisted of those daimyo who supported the Bafuku and regarded the Emperor as too sacred to actually rule. The Tokugawa family dominated this group, running a police state which efficiently crushed rebellion until the 1850s. But other daimyo, usually from ancient clans in the wealthy south-west, wished for a larger share in the governing of the country. These men were turning to the Mikado (Emperor) in Miyako, now modern Kyoto, urging him to depose the Shogun as usurper.

When the West, by threat of its superior cannon, forced the Bafuku to accept that treaty ports should be opened for trade and Yedo opened to diplomats, the situation came to a head. The Bafuku and most daimyo reluctantly accepted that Japan could not resist the West's military advantages, however inferior they might regard its culture and religion. In the spring of 1860 Lord Ando became the unfortunate Bafuku minister charged with negotiating with the foreigners in the Shogun's name. Ironically, the Shogun himself was by then a puppet in the hands of his councillors, including Lord Ando, but the foreigners assumed they were dealing with the Emperor and called him the Tycoon or Great Prince.

Initial opposition to any contact with the West was led by Lord Mito, the ambitious head of the Tokugawa cadet branch until Lord Ando had him exiled from his fief. After Mito's death in late 1860 the Jōi or anti-foreign party had no single leader. The Mikado was a ferocious xenophobe who refused to accept the presence of barbarians in his land, but he was still too isolated and sacred to lead a party. The daimyo of Satsuma, while urging the Emperor to seize the reins of power for himself, also saw possibilities in a rich trade with the West. Other daimyo, those of Choshu and Tosa, combined their imperialism with rabid xenophobia.

The Japanese response to any crisis is to split into factions and argue. If this tendency made negotiations difficult for the first Western diplomats, it may also have saved their lives.

The characters in *Yedo* are fictitious, but Nathaniel

Jessop is based on Townsend Harris, the first American Consul, who went to Shimoda in 1856 and then moved to Yedo in 1859. Dirk Meylan is based on Henry Heusken, a Dutchman who accompanied Harris, as his was the only European language known to the Japanese through a tiny Dutch community of traders that had continued for many years in Nagasaki. Sir Rutherford Alcock was the first British minister in 1859; his fascinating memoirs are the main source for the views of Sir Radley Ferrier. The Japanese officials and place names are the real ones; however, although Lord Okubo did receive the British expedition to Fuji, his interest in Western culture is my invention.

Until the 1870s Japan observed the lunar calendar. New Year usually took place in February.

Glossary

bu	One thousand zeni.
bushi	Samurai.
Bushido	The Way of the Warrior, a code of behaviour espoused by the samurai class. A mixture of Confucist commentaries, Zen Buddhism and Shinto.
-chan	A suffix to a child's or woman's name. An endearment.
danna san	A customer in a brothel.
futon	A thick padded mattress stored in a cupboard in daytime and rolled out for sleeping at bedtime.
geta	Wooden clogs worn in rain or snow, often as high as six or nine inches.
haori	Kimono-shaped jacket often marked with a crest of family or clan.
kago	A sling seat carried on poles by two bearers; a common form of transport in pre-1870 Japan. Carriages were the prerogative of the court nobility only and the rickshaw was invented about 1869.
kami-shiro	Formal samurai dress. A sleeveless overjacket with stiff flaring shoulder-pieces combined with hakama or voluminous trousers which could be very long, over the feet, for ceremonial occasions or cut off short for daily wear. Kami-shiro are worn over kimono.
kotatsu	A charcoal heater, sometimes sunk in an opening in the floor, over which a quilt on a frame is placed. One snuggled under the quilt to warm the lower body.

Kun	A casual honorific used among male equals.
norimon	Closed sedan chair carried by four bearers.
Oba-san	Aunt; also the title given to the manageress of a brothel.
obi	A wide stiff sash worn with women's kimono. If the large bow is tied at the back, the woman is respectable; if in front, she is a prostitute.
O Bon	The Buddhist Festival of the Dead when souls visit their family altars, guided home by lanterns and bonfires. A great holiday, O Bon takes place in mid-July.
ronin	A samurai without a master either through his own choice or by mischance, i.e. the death or disgrace of his lord. Ronin were outside the tight Japanese social scheme and had to earn their rice as best they could, often as mercenaries or outlaws.
ryō	Four bu of gold.
Sama	An honorific. More respectful than San.
samisen	A three-stringed instrument, rather like a lute but played only with a plectrum.
Sensei	An honorific used for an intellectual or doctor. Sometimes used as noun.
seppuku	Also called by foreigners hara kiri. Ritual suicide by the samurai class. A man should disembowel himself, a woman cut her throat.
shinzo	An apprentice prostitute in the Yoshiwara.
shō	A liquid measurement. Approximately one pint.
shoji	Sliding screens made of light wooden frames covered with thick paper.
tatami	Thick rectangular mats covered in woven straw fitted tightly together over the floor of a Japanese room. Footwear is never worn on tatami.

torii	A tall gateway of two upright and two horizontal beams guarding the entrance of a Shinto shrine. Frequently painted red, they are a distinctive feature of the Japanese town and countryside.
Yamato	Ancient name for Japan, often used in poetry. Yamato is actually a province around Nara.
yukata	A cotton robe worn in summer or to the bathhouse.
zeni	Small copper coins, often strung together to make up a 'string of cash'.

Yedo

1
Odawara

As it neared Odawara the highway from Yedo sloped up through the riverside marshes to cross the plain rolling away towards jagged mountains and on to the far-distant Imperial Capital. Hissing through the reeds a breeze rippled the fragile rice seedlings and chilled the sweat-streaked backs bent over the fields. A burbling warbler greeted Tada Shoh as he topped the gentle rise and paused to pull off his sedge hat. Fatigue vanished as he gazed out at the landscape of his youth. Steep-pitched roofs of thatch sprouted their crowns of purple iris. The paved line of the Tokaido road plunged through a cloisonné of paddies and dikes and vegetable strips, disappearing into the distant streets of Odawara huddled in the blue foothills. Dung thickly scented the warm air, blanketing the sweetness of moist earth and the tang of the marshes.

The moment deserved a poem. But nothing came. No fleeting words to match the fleeting joy of homecoming.

A cotton merchant urging his laden ponies up from the river ford glanced amused at the dusty doctor and his servant, catching their elation of a journey finished. But the merchant must lodge that night in an unknown Odawara inn before crossing the mountains at dawn to his home in Mishima. Eager only for a bath and a jug of saké, he stepped courteously to the right of the two men and trudged on.

The servant shifted the straw box on his shoulders and leant to brush down Shoh's hakama, damp from crossing the river hunched on the broad back of a porter. 'Tada Sensei must greet Akiko Sama looking presentable or this foolish servant will lose face.'

'That is so,' Shoh muttered, knowing his venerable mother would find him unpresentable even if he arrived in black silk, carried in a carved sedan chair by matched bearers.

1

On this stretch before the big post-station of Odawara the Tokaido was lively: merchants and pilgrims and farmers pressed sleeve to sleeve, hurrying towards the tea-houses under tall cedars. A serving girl trilled out in her country drawl, 'Hot baths, good food, pretty waiting maids. Only a few zeni here. Beware high prices further on!' Hawkers offered the famous tonic brewed in the city. Their cries promised a refreshed liver and a peaceful spleen to the wise purchaser.

The shouts jangled in Shoh's head like screeching crows. The dike path between the paddies would be quieter: only the wind in the fruit trees and the splash of heron stalking the ditches in search of fish. 'Come,' he commanded his servant, 'we will leave the highway and take the shorter way home through the fields.'

He stepped quickly to the right side of the road, allowing a party of samurai to pass on the more honourable left. The bushi responded with cold formality to the doctor's curt bow.

The Tada family lived in the eastern suburbs in a lane of samurai houses behind the Inari Shrine. Long ago when the Tokugawa dynasty was young the shrine stood outside the city in the rice fields, a dark sacred place among sakaki trees. Then this ancient precinct had been swept and polished by supplicant farmers. But slowly the castle town spread over the paddies, driving out the green pheasant and meadow bunting, engulfing the shrine. Now a once gleaming red torii tilted; one old priest made lackadaisical skirmishes against weeds and sagging walls. But white prayer papers were still twisted into the drooping boughs of a dispirited sakaki. Before this sanctuary hooded by overhanging thatch Akiko had stood, heavy with child, to pray five times for safe delivery. The gods granted breath to Shoh and Masayuki but three female babies died, unlamented.

Shoh walked quickly through the torii. He poured purifying water from a stone basin over his hands and rinsed his dusty mouth. A quiet moment before the gods might calm his stomach and prepare him for his family.

A bent wraith-like figure shuffled toward him. Dingy robes and the stained yet pellucid flesh of great age

2

enhanced the old priest's commanding dignity.

Surprised to find this fragment of his childhood still in the world, Shoh bowed respectfully. 'Tada Shoh, son of Tada Teruhiko. Many harvests have been stacked to dry since I was presented at this sanctuary.'

Eyes darker than time past studied Shoh. 'I recognize Akiko Sama in her son. Your father went to his ancestors several seasons back, did he not?'

'That is so, venerable one.'

'You are samurai bred, carry two names and wear a long sword, but your hair is dressed like a doctor's. Eh? Which are you, bushi or doctor?'

'This unworthy Shoh was born bushi. Lord Okubo chose me from the castle samurai to study the arts of healing at the School of Dutch Studies in Yedo.'

'Dutch! Very partial to barbarian tricks is our lord.' The aged face twisted into a wrinkled walnut of disapproval.

Shocked at such disrespect, Shoh said stiffly. 'We in Odawara are privileged that our daimyo cares so deeply for Nippon that he encourages new ideas to lighten our darkness.'

'Pah! The ancient ways are the ways of Nippon. Lord Okubo should know that. Are you now a manipulator of needles or do you only perform western devilry?'

'This unworthy Tada has the honour to be a doctor in the clinic of Segawa Sensei, a master of the old medicine.'

'Ah. Has Segawa Sensei sons?'

'Yes, venerable one. He has a son.'

'Then he has not adopted you as his successor!' The age-etched lips pressed shut on Shoh's lustreless future in the Segawa establishment. 'Better you return to Odawara and the life of bushido. Emulate your honoured mother and younger brother.'

For a brief, rebellious instant Shoh itched to reply, but the temptation passed. What did an aged priest care for Nippon beyond these shrine walls? He bowed, determinedly respectful, anxious to escape.

But the priest had lost interest.

*　　*　　*

3

Curving between high walls of samurai compounds the lane lay quiet but for birdsong. No children played; not even an oil vendor or vegetable seller called his wares in this formidable peace – it was the kitchen gate in the back alley for them. Suddenly a stray dog, rib-thin, limped around the lane's bend. Hungrily, uneasily, as though conscious it was trespassing on a closed world, it peered at the proud clean gates. Belly down, it cringed past Shoh and plodded on towards the succulent scrap piles of the shopkeepers' yards.

Kimono flipped over his knees, the servant squatted in the bronze-leaved shade of a cherry by the Tada gate. At his master's approach he stood, hoisting the travelling basket with a grunt. Rolls of Daimaru silk for Akiko and Kanoko cotton for the others weighed heavy on the shoulders. Had it been left to him the master would have brought cakes from Asakusa temple. Good luck and light as well.

In better times, a doorkeeper waited at the barred window to admit callers, but now a bell-rope dangled outside the tall gateway. Shoh did not pull the rope. The gate itself was blistered by seasons of rain and sun but the hinges were oiled to silence. Inside, the entrance court was neatly kept: a bank of glossy camellias clipped, the stepping stones to the house swept clean.

A young boy leapt out from the camellias. Surprise caught him mid-leap, his wooden sword raised to smite an invisible enemy.

'Shohtaro? Is this tall oak sapling my Shohtaro?'

'Father! Welcome.' Flushed with embarrassment, the boy thrust the play sword away from him before kneeling on the ground. 'Our honourable father was not expected. Shall I call my mother and grandmother?'

'In a moment.' Shoh squatted down and smiled into the warrior's grave eyes. 'What was your game, my son? Yoshitsuné among the mountain demons perhaps? I played at that once.'

'No, Honourable Father. I was a brave retainer of Mito striking down the barbarians who desecrate Nippon.'

'I see. Serious affairs for one who has just bound his hair into his first top-knot.' Shoh stood and looked down at his son.

4

'My uncle, Masayuki, says no samurai is too young to die for his Imperial Grace.'

'Your uncle is a samurai of Lord Okubo, loyal servant of the Shogun. Think on that. But now, go and tell your mother of my arrival.'

Unsmiling, Shohtaro bobbed his forehead to the earth and then walked sedately past the camellias round the corner of the house.

A flurry of high voices, a clatter of geta and the latticed house door shot open, spilling out two women and a babe followed by a young servant girl. All lined up in attitudes of obeisance to greet the returned master.

'Welcome home, my honoured husband, welcome home.' Hanae kept her eyes modestly down. Her sleeves were still tied up and her plump cheeks flushed from the heat of the cooking stove. Behind her Ohisa, Masayuki's pretty wife, bowed nervously, constricted by the small girl hanging fearfully on her kimono. Little Kimi, the kitchen maid, dared not even steal a peep at the Yedo master.

'Ara, Shoh San.' His wife bowed again. 'No preparations have been made. We are deeply shamed to greet you in such confusion. All day we have been preserving quails' eggs. Ara, what confusion. Kimi, light the bath. Ohisa, bring saké. Come, Hideko, greet your honourable father.' Hanae swung her daughter on to her sturdy hip, eyes still away from her husband's face.

She was as Shoh always thought of her: dimpled plumpness with a lovely complexion that was almost too fine for her round face and thick body. A faint perfume of vegetables and wood-smoke lingered in the strong black hair. Her kimono and underskirt were of plain indigo, washed and resewed many times.

He chucked Hideko's quivering chin and bent over to breathe in sweet baby scents but the child squawked and clutched her mother's neck.

'It has been a long time, Hanae. I intended to send a message about my visit but – Are my mother and brother at home?'

'Masayuki San is at the castle but your honourable mother will be in her room.'

In the vestibule he untied his swords and, gratefully

5

easing off his geta, stepped up into the house. Despite the child on her hip Hanae swooped down to arrange the clogs neatly before scurrying after her husband.

The house was old, as old as the Tada family's service to the Daimyo of Odawara. The dry creak of the crooked corridor was as familiar to Shoh as his mother's voice. The screen frames were brittle skeletons, the paper yellowing. Reception rooms, seldom used now. His father's rooms, empty. The women's quarters, storerooms and the kitchen and bathhouse beyond.

Shoh breathed deeply: wood and dust, charcoal and damp, incense and women.

Hanae knelt before a door. Gently she slid it back revealing a glow of pale tatami and burnished cedar. The iron locks of Akiko's marriage chest glared against golden wood. A blue spiral of incense rose from a tiny bronze lotus flower on the family altar. Late sun warmed creamy paper panes, soft light caressing the age-darkened crimson of a fine sword rest. The lacquered arms gaped. The blade that should be cradled in those arms, the Chrysanthemum sword of the Tadas, was absent.

A woman knelt before the altar, fragility itself in fawn silk. Slowly, Akiko turned toward the open door. From the ivory perfection of her face, oval as a melon seed, her eyes, curved like the eyes of the Nara Buddha, met those of her elder son. Mother and son, both possessed the same sinuously shaped eyes, but there was one difference: Shoh's were warmed by love.

Maysayuki replaced the last halberd on the rack. Counted and sharpened, the curved blades glinted coldly against the dull pine wall. Only the firearms remained to check and list. He strode to the rows of muskets and matchlocks with no enthusiasm; ugly, unimaginative things, symbols of Lord Okubo's passion for anything exotic. Never to be compared with a sword.

The clerk finished rubbing the tablet of ink and waited, brush poised, for Masayuki's inventory. Outside a singing whine of bamboo sticks in the practice yard counterpointed the rhythmic clang of the castle swordsmith's sacred hammer, reminding Masayuki that he must pick up

6

his father's long sword from Zenroku, the sword-sharpener. No time for stick-fighting. Resigned, he began to examine the muskets, barking out their name and condition to the clerk.

The sun was dropping into purpling mountains when he finished but the yard felt pleasantly warm after the centuries-old chill of the armoury. Ohno Tatsuya and another samurai circled and dodged, wooden staffs held at stiff angles. Masayuki leaned against the wall, watching and wondering at Ohno's clumsy, jerking movements. Poor Ohno. A swordsman should attack with the controlled spring of a young tiger, not the lumbering sway of an ox. And yet he held his ground against his more graceful, experienced opponent.

Bout finished, the men exchanged ritual courtesies. Ohno shambled over to Masayuki. The intensity of his stare was surprising set against such clumsiness.

'Tonight at the Zen temple outside the Mountain Gate, né? Four ronin from Mito are in Odawara, former retainers of the disgraced daimyo. One is the man who cut down Russian sailors in Yokohama.' Fiery eyes burned into Masayuki, who looked away. As always, Ohno's passion made him feel a weakling, a rice seedling tossed by a storm.

'Would we not be disloyal to Lord Okubo if we –' he began, but the storm blew through his words.

'Lord Okubo serves the Bafuku. Do you know how many patriots have died by the Bafuku's command? Lord Mito at least obeys the will of the Emperor and acts against the barbarians.'

'But we of Odawara owe allegiance to the Shogun and the Bafuku. Lord Okubo has proclaimed it,' Masayuki muttered.

'Lord Okubo cares nothing for Nippon. He cut the rice stipend of his warriors and sends good samurai off to Yedo as doctors or star-gazers. Ohno Tatsuya will serve his Emperor, not the Bafuku. How stands Tada Masayuki?'

Goaded by the sneer at his brother, Masayuki said, 'I will come to the Zen temple and I will listen to Lord Mito's followers.' Ohno's face often reminded him of a bean-

7

flour bun, white and round and soft. But this awkward samurai was not soft and Masayuki even feared his implacable will. At times Ohno seemed to live in another sphere of existence, to realize ideas Masayuki could not even imagine, and at these times he almost hated this childhood friend as one hates an unnameable fear that whispers beyond the borders of one's own fantasies. Now he reasoned, but without hope: 'Your honourable father is high in the lord's councils.'

The briefest shadow darkened the bun-like face but Ohno replied sternly, 'The Zen temple. After the Hour of the Dog.'

The broad ramp zig-zagged down between lime-washed walls, through guardhouses and fortified gates and over the viscous green waters of the castle moat. Towering above, the great keep rose in six mighty tiers, each tier finished by curled tile roofs, each ridge-pole decorated by the bronze lily of the Okubo clan. Only the jagged purple, russet and snow-white slabs of the mountains dwarfed Odawara castle, guardian of the Tokaido's steep Hakone passes.

For many generations, since Ieyasu's time, the swords of Odawara men had remained in their scabbards. Now, crowded around the castle where once samurai died for the Tokugawa leader, ironworkers, goldsmiths, lacquerers, fletchers, fan-makers – all the craftsmen who serve warriors – had built their workshops and forges, huddling together like reeds on a river bank.

Masayuki stalked down the alley crowded with narrow shops and fenced yards. Children sailing bamboo boats in the open gutter scuttled out of his way with hurried bows. His two swords announced his rank and the pursed line of his small mouth warned of his mood. Resentment against Ohno, resentment against his doctor brother, resentment against a fine day spent cooped in the armoury boiled in his blood.

The steady whirr of the grinding wheel marked Zenroku's: a covered yard and two raised rooms where he lived with his wife and daughters.

Zenroku sat cross-legged, sharpening a dagger on the

wheel. One of his daughters stoo... ... crock of water. Too late Masayuki ... usually brought something – preserved ... the little girls.

'Ah, welcome to my poor quarters.' Whe... child had straightened from their bows he sen... tea for the samurai.

Thin, worn-looking, his top-knot laced wit... ...ey, Zenroku spoke with the directness of a man who knows the value of his own skill. Yet his jacket and leggings were shabbier even than Masayuki's hakama, for when times are hard for samurai they are harder still for their associates.

'This evening the Chrysanthemum sword could strike a man asunder with one blow, so perfect is its edge. Such a blade is always a pleasure. Your honourable father kept it well and so does his son.'

'The sword was the pride of my father and of his father and his father's father back to the times of Ieyasu.' Masayuki's manner was stiff, for once again he could give Zenroku only two shō of rice in payment and with the price of rice so low –

Kiku brought a tray with a pottery cup. Bowing, she offered this to Masayuki who accepted although he knew tea leaves were precious.

'How pretty Kiku grows. She is as much like Kimi as two morning glories on a fence. Zenroku San must be pleased with his daughters, beauties all.'

'Ara! May Tada San be spared the grief of six daughters. Ayamé sold to the pleasure quarter in Yedo. Oasa sold to a tea house on the Tokaido. Your gracious mother has kindly taken Kimi as a serving wench but these three little ones peep like chicks in a nest, beaks always open for rice we have not.' He passed a strong hand over his eyes. 'Forgive an old man, Tada San. But we have heard Ayamé is ill in Yedo. A wasting fever. Should the brothel owner wish his gold back, what shall we do?'

'Ah, no. The bargain was struck. You made your mark on the papers. Ayamé is their responsibility.'

'My foolish wife cries day and night for fear they will cast her out. Of course she is only a girl and should have

9

... at birth but once the chick is in the nest the ... clucks over it.'

Masayuki brightened. 'This is a problem with a solution. As you know, my elder brother is a doctor now. In Yedo.'

Zenroku nodded gravely. 'Tada Shoh San promised to be a fine swordsman. His skill was much talked over, here among the castle servants.'

'Yes, well, since my family and the family of Zenroku are tied by years of service Shoh will certainly visit your daughter. Perhaps his potions will help her.'

Zenroku shook his head. 'My child is beneath the attention of such as Tada Sensei, favourite of Lord Okubo. Too great an honour for this unworthy Zenroku.'

Masayuki's manner was commanding. 'There are obligations that must be honoured. Give me the name of her house and her professional name and I will send a message to Elder Brother by the lord's courier.'

A decision taken, his own will enforced, Masayuki left Zenroku's with an easy heart. The Chrysanthemum sword balanced well in his sash. The gathering at the Zen temple no longer seemed disloyal or dangerous.

Shohtaro was waiting beneath the cherry. Masayuki smiled at the small solemn figure, hands behind his back.

'Welcome home, Honoured Uncle. This unworthy Shohtaro hoped you would return tonight.'

'Look. The Tada sword. Come along. We'll put it on the sword rest.'

Shohtaro hung back. 'Uncle, my father has arrived from Yedo.'

'Ara, that is unexpected.'

'He brought me this.' Shohtaro took his hands from behind his back. He was clutching a straight child's bow.

'A good present for young samurai.' Masayuki flexed the small bow. 'At eight summers it is time you learned to use a bow.'

Shohtaro looked up, tragedy in his eyes although his chin was firm. 'You were to present my first bow at O-Bon. That is what my honourable uncle promised.'

'But now your father has presented this. A fine one. Box wood.' He loved this child, so like himself. Serious.

10

Eager to find the right way. He would walk though life as Masayuki did, without a glance to left or right but his heart set on the sun. And with Shohtaro he could smile and be gentle as well as stern. As he must be now.

Shohtaro stared at him stubbornly. 'It was for a bow chosen by a samurai that this Shohtaro prayed at the shrine.'

'Your father is samurai bred. His choice of this excellent weapon shows that. Now cease this undisciplined baby babbling. Run and tell Ohisa to light the bath fire and find me a clean kimono. These hakama are ripe from overwear.'

Hanae prepared the finest feast that time and her purse and the season would allow: sweet fish, bamboo shoots, young herbs and new tea. Saké she knew to be the greatest necessity to soften the stiff Tada pride and bring some gaiety to Shoh's homecoming. Ohisa went time and again to the kitchen where Kimi filled the delicate porcelain decanters from the stone crock on the wood stove.

Dressed in silk for this occasion Hanae knelt before the brothers and Shohtaro, deftly filleting their fish or picking them out the choicest morsels from the scatter of little dishes on the standing trays. Choosing to remain in her fawn kimono Akiko gracefully poured saké.

Shoh took a full decanter from Ohisa. Passing his own cup to Akiko he said, 'Honourable Mother, will you not drink to celebrate my return? Please accept some wine.'

'This Akiko bids welcome to her son.' She sipped and turned the tiny cup upside down before her to signify that she would not drink again. No wine colouring warmed her ivory skin. The Buddha eyes slid from one son to the other. Shoh's strongly chiselled cheeks and chin, his mother's eyes and his father's wide full-lipped mouth held her only a moment. She found betrayal in his soft competent hands and the good plain silk kimono of this once precious son. However, Masayuki, rigid in faded brown cotton, a black sash around his narrow hips, she studied intently. He was so much her son. The pale oval melon-seed face, a small mouth like a camellia flower. Sword practice and archery had muscled his delicate frame and

11

calloused his shapely hands, but were Akiko a man she too would have a swordsman's chest and shoulders. Only his eyes defeated her. Here Masayuki held true to his father. Eyes like narrow halfmoons. Restless. Early in her marriage she learned to ignore the panther roar of Teruhiko's words and read instead the shifting weakness in his eyes. Now the familiar worry shadowed her heart and strengthened her will to keep this son to the samurai way.

Shoh offered saké to Hanae and Ohisa who each drank a courteous cup. Kimi brought Hideko to make her good night bows. When the child had waddled away an uneasy silence fell. A gentle drizzle stirred the leaves of the damp garden. Eyes down modestly, the women waited for the men to speak or dismiss them to the kitchen so they could take their share of the remaining rice and fish.

Nervous in the waiting quiet, Shoh rose and went to the alcove. Kneeling before the rack, he reverently lifted the Chrysanthemum sword and slid it half from the scabbard. The cold beauty of its perfection moved him now as it always had: the blade that should be his, the blade that as a fine swordsman he deserved. A doctor, like a samurai, is privileged to carry a long sword, but when Lord Okubo set him aside had he forfeited the right to this one sword? The matter had never been discussed in his presence, even during the family council when the Tadas agreed they must bow to the daimyo's offer to send Shoh to Yedo.

'It is good to hold this again. Its absence this afternoon startled me.'

'The sword is the soul of the samurai. When the Chrysanthemum blade lies clean and sharp on its rack the Tada household has a soul.'

Shoh glanced back, struck by his brother's chill formality. Masayuki's face was shadowed but the candle in the standing lantern caught a glitter in the half-moon eyes. Was it possible that he and this polite stranger had once romped like puppies in the long grass behind the bathhouse?

'There is a matter I must discuss with Elder Brother.'

Shoh closed the scabbard and returned to his cushion. 'Yes.'

'Today at the sword-sharpener's I learned that

12

Zenroku's first daughter, Ayamé, suffers from a weakening fever. As the girl is a junior courtesan in the Yoshiwara –'

Involuntarily Shoh glanced at his father's memorial plaque on the family altar. Teruhiko had died of a seizure while making a dawn departure after a forbidden night in the Yedo pleasure quarter. The final one of many forbidden visits and the final humiliation for his proud samurai wife.

'–and as Elder Brother is in Yedo, I promised that Elder Brother would visit the girl.' Masayuki nervously licked his lips and said in a louder voice, 'We cannot always give Zenroku adequate compensation for his services. Despite himself, he is worried that the brothel keeper will send her home and then Zenroku must return her price and he does not have it.'

'I remember the girl. A charming little thing. Of course I shall see her. The keepers of those houses only use doctors to treat their first-rank courtesans. No doubt Ayamé has been neglected. Give me her professional name and her house so that I may find her.'

Masayuki gathered himself on to his knees and touched his forehead and palms to the tatami. 'For the honour of the Tada family, may I thank Elder Brother for taking up this obligation to Zenroku, a worthy craftsman.'

Crossly, Shoh replied, 'The honour of the Tada family is the honour of Tada Shoh.' He turned to Shohtaro, solid as a stone statue. His eyelids drooped but the young shoulders remained straight. Hanae trained him well.

'Well, my fine son. Will you come one day to visit your father in Yedo? Its size and splendour will astonish you. The castle alone covers as much ground as all Odawara from the mountains to the paddies. There are more palaces than pines on the Tokaido, more temples than stars in the sky, more shops than pebbles on the river bed, more people than grains of sand on Miho beach. Certainly the city of the Shogun is the most magnificent on earth.'

'Thank you, Honourable Father, but this unworthy Shohtaro wishes first to visit the Sacred Emperor's Capital and to pay homage before the Imperial Enclosure.'

Masayuki said, 'Such is the desire, indeed the duty, of

13

every devoted subject of his Divine Majesty.'

'Naturally. But Yedo is worth a visit too,' Shoh said dryly, aware he had been bested.

Now was the time to speak, to inform them of his new circumstances. There was every reason to be proud of the honour shown him but before Akiko's cool indifference and Masayuki's formality he felt no more important than a servant. Yet he must speak now, with all assembled. To hold back in embarrassment would only diminish him further, as though the fine line between humility and pride that should be inborn in every bushi was now blurred by the vulgarity of his chosen profession.

From the women's quarters came the muffled misery of Hideko's crying. Hanae sat very still, barely breathing. The crying spluttered to peace.

Now. It must be now.

'This Shoh has returned home today to inform his family of certain changes in his life.'

Their attention was his. Even Akiko looked up.

'As you know, Lord Okubo takes great interest in the learning of western countries. While naturally he despises their inferiority in matters of mind or spirit, their studies of this world fascinate him.'

'Unpatriotic!' Masayuki's ill-bred outburst was startling but he carried on, too angry to control his passion: 'We in Nippon have no need of western "learning". Buddha has taught us that this world is only an illusion from which we must escape to find the Great Truth. Confucius gives us laws to carry us from womb to funeral fires and beyond. A man must honour his Emperor, his lord, his father. Of what other knowledge have we need?'

'The skill of machines –'

'Machines! Intercourse with barbarian mechanics and merchants will bring us nothing. In any case, the Emperor is opposed to such intercourse.'

'That is so. His Sacred Highness has refused to recognize the treaties for trade.'

'Why does Lord Okubo fail to observe his Emperor's wishes? How can he continue to live while he defies the Divine Will?' Masayuki flushed, aware he was speaking in Ohno's words.

14

Irritated by such unseemly behaviour, Shoh said sharply, 'It is not for Younger Brother to criticize his superiors but to obey his lord. Discipline your tongue! How will a nation of swordsmen fight cannon and fast ships that breathe fire like dragons?'

'The sword of Nippon has greater power than any fire-arm.' Akiko's cool dry voice rustled across her sons' anger. 'The Shogun's ministers are weak cowards. Because the spirit of bushido has died in them, they lack heart to lead samurai against the barbarians. But the Gods will save these islands now just as they sent the Wind of Heaven against the Mongolian invaders many generations ago.'

His mother's immodesty shocked Shoh even more than his brother's lack of control, but Masayuki, although disapproving of a woman speaking on such matters, wished that those brave words had been his.

The embarrassed silence was pierced only by a night-ingale singing in the old priest's oak copse.

Finally, Shoh spoke. 'As you know, when I was sixteen summers Lord Okubo sent me into the household of Segawa Sensei, a physician. Later, at the lord's encour-agement, I studied western medicine at the Dutch School. This magnanimity shown to unworthy Shoh has brought honour to the Tada family.' He spoke firmly, knowing Akiko viewed his withdrawal from the warrior's world as another deep humiliation to be suffered and endured. The two swords his birth and profession permitted him to wear were to Akiko a mockery.

'Once again our daimyo has seen fit to honour this unworthy Shoh. The English barbarians have a physician among their number in Yedo. At Lord Okubo's command this Shoh visits the Legation to learn their tongue and their ways as well as their medicine. The English doctor also comes to Segawa Sensei's clinic to bring new cures and knowledge. It is the will of the Bafuku that this exchange of ideas takes place. I am their servant.'

Masayuki jerked to his feet. 'A samurai must die rather than betray the will of his Emperor. My brother's very breath speaks treason.'

He ran from the room. Seconds later, the crash of the

15

outside door shook the ancient walls with the violence of an earthquake.

Akiko whispered into the quivering silence, 'So. Shoh in whose unworthy body runs the blood of warriors assists willingly in the contamination of his land. If men of samurai stock can despoil themselves for the false knowledge of the barbarian, then, truly, the sword of Nippon is broken.'

Candles in tall iron candlesticks fluttered bravely against the gloom pressing down from the high-beamed ceiling. Grotesque shadows struggled across the walls. Two men with the unshaven foreheads and plain dress of masterless samurai sat on straw cushions. A little apart was a similarly attired third ronin, his grey-streaked hair silvery as a badger's pelt, his seamed handsome face closed.

Masayuki, Ohno Tatsuya and several other Odawara samurai, cross-legged on boards polished smooth by hundreds of feet, were gathered in a rapt half-moon before the three former retainers of the disgraced Daimyo of Mito. One of these was speaking, his harsh Northern accents ringing out in the barren hall: 'It is known to us that samurai of Nippon will soon sail in smoke-belching ships across the Eastern Sea to America. There they will gaze with their own eyes on the "wonders" of the barbarians. What use are these "wonders" to samurai, we ask?'

The second man was gnarled as an old wind-tossed pine. 'Think back to before the Black Ships came. Any man of Nippon who set foot on an outsider's vessel suffered the executioner's blade if he dared return to these sacred shores. Now such a traitor is praised and true patriots are beheaded or disgraced as is our former lord who dared to speak out against the desecration of Nippon.'

Masayuki shifted uneasily. Others, older samurai at the castle, muttered that Lord Mito had plotted to make his son the new Shogun against the wishes of the councillors. If this were true, if all were plotting and ambition, had not Lord Mito been rightfully reprimanded? He glanced at Ohno, wondering if he too had heard the grey-haired wisdom of the castle, but Ohno only stared at the speakers, his face rapt with admiration.

Throughout the stirring words the third ronin remained

16

still as a mountain peak. Masayuki's eyes drifted frequently from the ranting spokesmen to the abstracted face. A curious envy of this contained man filled him, the envy of the volatile for those who, controlling their passions, soar above the pettiness of emotion. Suddenly he realized the ronin was being presented by the first man: 'Kojima Sama has already set out on a path many of us in the Jōi party will follow. May the Lord Buddha lend us courage and wisdom to emulate this man we honour by calling Elder Brother.'

The words seemed to bring the ronin out of himself and back to his surroundings. Slowly his eyes travelled over the crescent of eager faces. Masayuki leant forward to catch the great man's attention and then, recollecting himself, lowered his gaze in respect.

'This unworthy ronin is Kojima Yagoro, former captain of the Right wing of Lord Mito's guards. Because a daimyo is held responsible for the actions of his retainers, actions which might draw him into conflict with his peers, this Kojima has chosen the life of a ronin. The graves of my ancestors, my family, my home, these I have abandoned that I might serve the Imperial Throne without bringing further disgrace on Mito. All who join us must make this irrevocable sacrifice.' The eyes in the seamed face burned like charcoals.

'That is so,' Ohno muttered. 'We must be free of all loyalties but that highest loyalty. To the Emperor.'

The eyes seared Ohno and then the others in turn. Masayuki's heart pounded in his breast.

'To destroy the outsiders we must walk among them in Yokohama and Nagasaki where our debased merchant class sell the silk and tea and rice of Nippon for silver –' He stopped, too angry to go on. After a moment the dry voice continued. 'This Kojima forced himself into that sewer of Yokohama and there my chance came. Four Russians, sailors from that cold nation casting greedy eyes on our northern islands, staggered in drunken stupidity through the streets. In a second my sword was drawn. One Russian oozed his life-source into the mud. The others fled but two carry wounds.'

Admiration rustled through the Odawara men as an

autumn breeze stirs the leaves of a bamboo grove. The two Mito ronin nodded their approval.

Kojima leant forward from the waist, almost as does a man preparing to drive the sword into his belly. It was his first movement since Masayuki had entered the temple. 'Other dedicated men have cut down Dutchmen in Nagasaki. Such murders strike fear into the outsiders who lack the spirit of bushido to steel their souls. Enough of these murders and they will flee! What the Bafuku has not the courage to do, ronin shall.'

The Odawara youths burst into a release of cheers.

'So be it!' the gnarled ronin exclaimed. 'To know and act are one. That is bushido. Son-nō. Revere the Emperor. Jōi. Expel the barbarians!'

With a satisfied grunt Shoh eased himself off Hanae and flopped over on to his back. Eyes closed, he heard the rustle of paper as she dabbed herself. From behind a low folding screen Hideko stirred and murmured, disturbed by her parents' coupling.

He opened his eyes. Hanae lay as though he had not loosened her sash at all, her yukata tidied firmly around solid limbs. The yukata was thin with much wear and her hands folded on her belly were also thin. Akiko worked her daughters-in-law hard, just as she had been worked hard by Teruhiko's mother.

'How do household affairs go? Is money very short?'

'Things are not too difficult. No more so than for most families since the daimyo cut the rice stipend again. The rice broker drives a hard bargain but the ryō my husband sends helps us. We need little. Fuel. Cloth. Oil. Masayuki San's tastes are frugal.'

Fearing she had been tactless, she blushed but Shoh said, 'Masayuki did not inherit my father's – interests.' Teruhiko's weakness for the night flowers of the Yoshiwara had eaten away the Tada resources. Unwilling to settle for an economical second wife or concubine, he preferred the witty conversation and variety of courtesans, and only first-or second-rank ones at that. Each year between the autumn equinox and the Great Heat he was required to live in Yedo as part of the lord's retinue.

18

Each year the temptations of the pleasure quarter caused much sash-tightening in his Odawara household. When Shoh took his pleasures in the Floating World he chose smaller houses where less silver was needed.

Hanae said softly, 'Masayuki San has not yet returned. Shall I close the rain shutters?'

'Ohisa probably has.'

'No. I would have heard her.'

He pushed off the bedclothes and sat cross-legged on the tatami. 'Tell me about Younger Brother.'

She thought about Masayuki, something she rarely did, although having eyes and ears she knew that Ohisa was more of a servant than a wife. All Akiko's scolding would not make Ohisa with child if Masayuki scorned her body.

'When he is not on duty at the castle he practises the flute which he plays most sweetly. Or he performs the tea ceremony for your honourable mother or Ohno San. Once, even for Ohisa and me. He meditates. He teaches Shohtaro-chan swordsmanship and talks with him and Akiko Sama.'

'And about what do they talk?' Shoh asked, although he knew.

'I hear them when I bring tea. Akiko Sama speaks of her childhood and the Iwa family.'

Poor mother, Shoh thought. The third daughter of the official concubine of an important official to the Daimyo of Suruga, Akiko had been married into the lower ranking Tadas. How she had been humbled. The pride of the Iwa family was one worldly illusion that Akiko neither could nor would escape.

'They read to Shohtaro from the chronicles that he may learn about the glorious past. Often they instruct him in the laws of bushido.'

Shoh laughed. 'Nothing changes. My own boyhood was the same. Reciting the teachings of Confucius and hearing the tales of the great heroes.'

'Bushido is the soul of Nippon.' Hanae closed her full lips primly over her black-painted teeth.

And poor Hanae. Disgraced by her husband too, not because he was a dissolute rake but because he had abandoned his class.

19

Gently, for he respected this grave, conservative wife, he said, 'I have been greatly honoured by the trust of Lord Okubo and the Bafuku. Some would say that Segawa Sensei's son should be the chosen physician to the barbarians. But I was selected.' For I am the far better doctor, he thought immodestly.

Hanae remained silent.

'It was not my karma to live as a warrior with no enemy to fight. Each day I am faced with challenges. All the most mystifying cases in Yedo come to Segawa Sensei's clinic. Rich or poor. Samurai or commoner. Ara! His eyes penetrate deep into a man to seek out the cause of disharmony. Subtleties of cold and heat, wet or dry, a gliding pulse, all are as obvious to him as clanging bells.'

'This is indeed great skill. Should he not serve the Shogun, preserving the health of the high ones?'

'So many have wondered. But, although certainly praise and gold are rice and wine to him, he cares for his clinic. A true physician. The same heart beats in Wilson Sensei.'

The name of the outsider doctor cut like a knife between them.

Remembering the pictures of hairy, repulsive devils she had glimpsed on display at the bookseller's shop, Hanae shuddered. 'Buddha's grace encompasses all creatures but is it not a misfortune that men should be so malformed? Perhaps those who are good are reborn in their next life as people of Nippon. Perhaps in a past life one of us was a red-faced outsider. Does this doctor sit at the feet of Segawa Sensei to learn the true medicine?'

Shoh laughed bitterly. 'They are oil and water to each other.' He looked down at his wife's apricot-smooth face. 'Ara. If only you were not a woman. How can I make you understand the confusion I live in? My head takes one path, my heart another.'

She said nothing for there was nothing she could say.

'Segawa scorns Wilson as a butcher and Wilson laughs at Segawa for a sorcerer who cannot cure a man unless he knows the stars of his birth. But our medicine probes deeply, realizing the true harmony between heaven and

20

earth and man. Illness comes from imbalance and our doctors strive to keep the proper balance. Barbarian medicine seems to concern itself only with man and then man when he is already sick. In disharmony. They care only for the surface of things. None the less, Wilson's ointments clear sores from children's eyes and his herbs drive worms from the bowels. And three times I have watched him put a man or woman into a death-like sleep. Then he takes a knife and saw, common carpenter's tools, and he cuts away a crushed limb or a diseased lump of flesh. And the patient, who I know would have died, lives.'

Hanae went pale with shock. 'But that cannot be so. If it is a man's karma to die, he dies.'

'But, wife, he lives! And he lives because of the Sensei's knife. This Shoh is sure of it. And not just this ignorant Shoh: Segawa Sensei sees it too.'

'Then it was the man's karma to live. Your barbarian has only crippled a whole man who becomes a shame to his ancestors.'

'Yes. That may be true. I tell you, my head takes one path, my heart follows another. Never will I forget the first time at the Dutch School when I cut into a corpse and saw, with these eyes, a heart and lungs and veins and channels and a liver. The makings of a man. But these organs are not as the great sages of medicine imagined them. Here the barbarian knife found the truth. Yet, when I talk with Wilson Sensei, I know that he too should look beyond this ache and that lesion. And I believe he begins to be interested, although he scoffs and praises only science. Segawa Sensei, too, reluctantly accepts that Wilson Sensei can heal but claims he heals only the symptom, not the man. Can you not see my dilemma?'

She dimpled into a pacifying smile. His problems in Yedo were so far from hers. 'My husband is torn between two teachers. One speaks with the wisdom of Nippon. One speaks in a strange tongue.'

They lay in silence. Hanae stifled a yawn, slid up the thick paper panel of the lamp and snuffed out the failing light. She said softly, 'Masayuki San has not returned. There, my husband, may lie another dilemma.'

* * *

21

Chill light filtered through the lattice window, casting grey bars on the tatami. The relentless cooing of doves in the shrine precinct stirred Ohisa from her half-dream of home, chasing fireflies through the long grasses by the stream. She shivered and dared to wish that Masayuki might speed his steps so that she could take his swords and fold his kimono. Make his tea.

Ara! The iron tea kettle! She leapt up, gasping in pain in her cramped legs, and snatched the nearly dry pot from the cooling brazier. Ma! How Akiko Sama would have beaten her!

She shuffled to the dim kitchen to fill the kettle from the water butt. On the raised wooden floor Kimi's empty sleeping pallet lay crumpled. The neighbour's cock crowed.

A step sounded. The kitchen door slid open. The maid staggered in under a load of firewood. With a dull, incurious bow she squatted down in front of the stove and began to stuff twigs into the fire-box.

The sonorous bell of the Kannon Temple boomed out over the dawn-gold city.

The day was beginning. Ohisa scooped water into a pottery bowl and stepped out to the kitchen yard to wash her face.

'It has long been in my thoughts that my honoured husband should take a concubine in Yedo.' Hanae knelt before the travelling box. Folding his striped kimono, her fingers caressed the silk appreciatively, her mind not on Shoh's pleasure but on the length of grey silk he had brought Akiko. At first the silk was rejected as too extravagant, but Hanae knew the old woman would make a kimono from the stuff. Briefly she allowed herself the ill-bred indiscipline of envy. Stretching out her hand she let her fingers brush against the smooth pawlonia wood of her own wedding chest. Pawlonia wood. A great expenditure on her father's part, but he had wished to show the Tadas he could give his departing daughter the best. How many seasons ago had coolies carried the chest to this house? How many seasons ago had she stood here, a bride, in her white and red robes, too shy to raise her eyes

22

to her new husband's unknown, unimagined face?

Now that husband sat with his pipe and tobacco box on the verandah. The partitioning walls were pushed aside making one ten-mat room. A breeze fresh with the damp richness of summer ruffled the camellia hedge and tinkled the wind bell. Somewhere, beyond the bamboo barrier of the kitchen garden, Kimi crooned a little song to Hideko.

Birdsong, the odour of the fields, the peaceful bustle of women: unchanging since his childhood. And how glad he would be to escape.

'A concubine? Well, she could be useful. I do become bored with noodles and cook-house rice.'

'Perhaps Segawa Sensei would know of a suitable girl – young and strong.'

He nodded, more to silence than to please her, for he preferred his casual affairs among professional women.

At the Hour of the Serpent Shoh went to his mother to make his farewell. Feet tucked neatly under her hips, she sat before a low table, writing box and porcelain water jar beside her, practising a poem in her flowing if uninspired calligraphy.

'May Shoh's honourable journey be an easy one. The Tokaido is long and dusty in the warm season.' The dry voice emphasized the ritual of their parting. She lifted her sinuous eyes, blind with formality, to her son's. Then a brief bow and she took up her brush.

Feeling more like a dismissed servant than a son, Shoh bowed to the stiff fawn back and turned to make obeisance to his father's memorial plaque. But the carved doors of the altar were closed, sealed with strips of heavy paper – white paper to shield the sanctuary from the pollution of a godless son.

23

2
Yedo

Peverel Fitzpaine gripped the gunwale and peered out across the shimmering water. Low emerald hills undulated in a shifting sea haze. By screwing up his eyes he could just make out lines of brown houses, charcoal smudges edging the green. Here and there scarlet roofs flamed in the sun. A city. Yes, that must be Yedo. Now his Japanese adventure would truly begin.

There had been something unreal about Nagasaki. After the penetrating stench and raw squalor of Hong Kong his first Japanese town seemed to flaunt an almost Mediterranean prettiness with its pastel go-downs and tiny houses rising in terraces through lush foliage. The toy-sized shops and bustling people were so clean, so neat compared with the crumbling hovels and hideous beggars of China. To Peverel Fitzpaine, Nagasaki was the set of an operetta. At any moment these diminutive folk in pictur-esque gowns and funny hairstyles might burst into jolly Italian song.

But of course he had spent only a day visiting with Nicholson, the Consul. When HMS *Topaz* sailed from Nagasaki Pev was aboard. The captain, a pleasant soul who had befriended him on the trip from Hong Kong, pointed to the fan-shaped island of Deshima in the har-bour. 'That is where the Dutch traders lived cooped up like chickens for two hundred and fifty years. Not even allowed a Christian church or priest. That's how badly the Japs treated 'em.'

The frigate slid past a few two-storey stone houses under a limp flag of the Netherlands. A slight shiver of excitement stirred Pev's belly but he spoke with all the authority of newly acquired information. 'The Consul told me two Hollanders were cut down by bandits last month.'

'Not by bandits. No, more likely by some of those chaps who always wear two swords and scowl upon foreigners. Samurais, they are called. You must have seen the brutes swaggering about. Give 'em a wide berth myself and so do my men.'

'I did see them. Indeed. But then what could the Dutch expect but to be despised after two centuries of servility to the natives? I found that Englishmen are treated with respect, as one would assume.'

The captain had turned away, the better to hide his smile at this lofty response. The boy could not be much upwards of twenty, fresh from his studies at Oxford, keen with his sketch pads and lists of Chinese ideographs. Although the captain regarded this mission to Yedo to deposit a student-interpreter and dispatches as an ignominious one for a Royal Navy frigate, the boy's youth was appealing. And he must be a courageous enough lad to launch himself on this peculiar land. Courageous or very naïve.

Unaware of this amused approval Pev had arranged his pencils and settled himself to capture the spiky beauty of the Japanese coast.

Now, five days later, the captain came along the deck with a jaunty step and black eyes sparkling in a weather-wrinkled face. 'Here we are, my lad. In another thirty-six hours or so the *Topaz* will be headed back where she belongs.' He laughed aloud, eager to be cruising Chinese waters again, searching out the coastal pirates in their secret harbours.

'If this is Yedo, why do we not sail in closer?' Pev waved at the wide expanse of smooth water dotted with bright-sailed fishing boats and sturdy junks.

'Too shallow. The Japs will take you in by dinghy.'

'What happens?' Pev's trunks had been packed since last night and now, in a fresh collar and his new broadcloth suit, he was anxious to begin his adventure.

'We wait.' The enthusiasm faded from the captain's eyes. 'They are peculiar such as all yellow men are. Never know if they will show up bowing in their best silk dresses or open fire with those pathetic batteries.' He pointed disdainfully at a few rocky islands. Staring hard, Pev could distinguish the metal glint of gun emplacements.

Wait they did. Through the fierce heat of morning. His collar wilted and his suit scratched like a Welsh blanket.

After noon a small junk approached. A European towered over a cluster of silk-clad 'yellow men', all with the peculiar shaved head and stiff upright queue affected by the Japanese male. The European waved a genial hand at Pev.

The sky turned from sapphire to milky grey to rose while the captain negotiated with the fluttering natives through the services of the European. Eventually, after five hours, feeling he was being presented the Freedom of the City of London at the very least, Pev was permitted to climb down to the junk.

'Your trunks and the crates for the Legation will follow shortly.' Exhausted by the afternoon's bickering, the captain held out his hand. 'I may dine at the Legation tomorrow but should the tide or these Japs prevent me, I will wish you good luck now.'

'Many thanks. Good luck to you too. Enjoy your pirates.' Pev grinned, gripped the hand and then clambered over the side.

Another hand reached up to receive him. 'Welcome to Japan. Oscar Sullivan at your service. I shan't introduce these fellows one by one but they are harbour officers – or something. Just bow a few dozen times. That will serve 'em.'

Pev giggled in sheer relief. 'I thought I should never leave the *Topaz*. Are you from the Legation?'

'That I am.' He spoke with a certain arrogance. 'You will have to accustom yourself to dithering officials. Another whole delegation will be waiting on the quay. Nothing is accomplished simply in this land.' He glanced sourly at the Japanese now folding themselves into three neat rows on straw cushions. None displayed any interest in the Englishmen but fanned themselves, gossiping in a liquid, incomprehensible tongue.

The junk was surprisingly agile for its clumsy shape and before Pev had settled they were across the bay and winding up a river between banks of feathery willows beyond which Pev glimpsed coloured lanterns and promenading natives. A boat of swaying lights and curtains drifted past in clouds of fireflies. Hideously jangling music filled the dusk.

'We are in the city now. This is the Sumida River. These banks are a sort of Cremorne Gardens, as you can see. But then, perhaps you are not acquainted with London's pleasure haunts?'

So entranced was Pev by the river scene that he had forgotten his companion. Now, sensing that he was being condescended to, he studied Sullivan: a plump man in his early twenties with curly hair and a round freckled face that should be merry – it was the face of a naughty schoolboy – and yet the mouth was discontented – or was it the eyes?

'I am a Devon man,' Pev replied stiffly.

At that moment they arrived at a primitive wooden quay where a party of surly mounted warriors, another cluster of officials and a collection of sedan chairs awaited them. After much bowing and confusion Sullivan took Pev firmly by the arm and led him to two rather miserable horses. 'Those norimons are an exquisite torture. I have *commanded* that we be allowed to ride to the Legation. You will thank me for it.' Kindness softened the superiority in his voice.

A sudden thought struck Pev. 'Are there no carriages?'

'Not the length or breadth of these islands as far as one has seen. Not even on the highway.'

Lampions on long sticks surrounded their slow procession. A city bustled temptingly beyond this wall of soft light. The straw-shod horses clopped down broad avenues and crossed curved bridges over waterways crowded with barges. Unintelligible voices, peculiar scents, doors glowing in lamplight: all these lay mysterious and tantalizing outside the official phalanx.

Sullivan rode next to Pev, pointing out a temple roof swooping like a grey bird in flight or the gate of a great lord's palace. 'We are passing the outer ring of daimyos' enclosures,' he said. 'This stretch of water is one of three concentric moats. At the heart is the Tycoon's palace but we could not cross into that quarter without permission.'

The procession halted at a solid gateway. Several armed

men scurried out to prostrate themselves before the norimon, then their cavalcade shuffled on through the opened gate. 'A barrier,' Oscar explained. 'There are hundreds of them. A very effective way of controlling a city. They can be closed to isolate a quarter in a crisis. And when the Tycoon's uncle was assassinated a few months ago the commander of the local barrier disembowelled himself for the shame of it happening in his district. They are like that.'

Pev digested this in silence.

Oscar continued, his voice slightly grimmer. '*They* are not very welcoming, you know.' He glanced back at their escort. All wore two swords. Disconcerted, Pev tensed in the saddle. He remembered the murdered Dutch sailors in Nagasaki. Sullivan continued in a low tone. 'One really never becomes used to them. They are always with us – like the earthquakes.'

'Are they for protection?'

'Ha! Guardians. Spies. Gaolers. If only one knew.'

'How long have you been here?' Pev ventured.

'Oh, for quite a year now. All of us came with Sir Radley.'

'Forgive me, but what is your position?'

'I am a student-interpreter just as you are. Basil Foxwood is the secretary. Thinks himself rather superior but he is only a lowly member of a county family in Sussex. He is with the Consular Service. North Africa before this. Not an impressive man, I am afraid.' Once again the imparter of information, he became animated. 'Then there is James Wilson, our doctor. A capital fellow, by the way. He went as a young surgeon to the Crimea but he never speaks of it. I suppose that adventure dulled the lustre of a brass physician's plate in his native Sheffield. Seems a dull prospect to me, too. As he is a Unitarian, he chanced into a meeting on China missions where the siren call of the East proved too sweet. In Canton he met Sir Radley who was a doctor too once upon a time, and came with him to Japan.'

'Sir Radley is a man of some distinction, from all accounts,' Pev said.

'Indeed. From army surgeon to Consular Service and now elevated to the Diplomatic as Minister in Yedo. So our future has promise, Fitzpaine! If we survive the monotony.'

'Monotony?' He had not expected monotony.

Oscar glanced at him, a peculiar look. 'Our lives are rather restricted, you know, and there is not a lot in the way of society or amusement.'

They were in a rural lane now. The perfume of wild rose struggled against an acrid fox scent.

'If it is not too presumptuous, may I ask what attracted you to Japan?' Pev asked.

Sullivan obviously liked talking about himself. 'A peculiarity of intellect, one might say. Languages fascinate me. After French and German at University College I fancied a change. The Far Eastern Service presented itself and –' He made a mock bow in the saddle.

'You are a Londoner then?'

'Yes, and how I miss it. You must tell me all the gossip. But then you say you are from Devon.' Pev was bristling at this worldly attitude when Oscar turned friendly again. 'What brought you to the East?'

The moist alien dusk caressed Pev. Mist veiled an early moon. It amazed him to think the same moon might hang over Exeter in a few hours' time.

'What tempted me?' he asked, almost to himself. Then, collecting his thoughts, he explained, 'My father is a solicitor. My older brother as well. It is an honourable profession but not one to stir the heart.' A memory of shelves of dusty books and the dry smell of a high-banked fire in a grate drowned the new exotic scents of Japan.

Oscar laughed. 'My father is in the Home Office. Your sentiments reflect mine.'

'My mother would not hear of India – the Mutiny, you know. My tutor suggested the Far Eastern Service exam. Here I am.'

'And languages? Are you quick with strange lingo?'

'Hm. Greek prepares one for anything, I think.'

Sullivan laughed his sharp laugh. 'You think so, do you? We shall see. Indeed, we shall see.'

The lane turned a sudden corner and debouched into a broad highroad lined with inns and wine shops. Tall lamps illuminated revellers at low tables or sprawled on the balconies. Women flitted gracefully to and fro with trays. Music and laughter and the raucous calls of hawkers filled the air. The scene was as enticing as the river bank. What a jolly city this must be, Pev thought.

'The Tokaido,' Sullivan announced. 'The highway from Yedo to Miyako, wherever that is. The chief artery of the nation but we are not encouraged to use it. As a matter of fact we are expressly forbidden it when an official entourage is due. Were a daimyo to appear now, every last traveller would hurl himself into the dust. See how they scurry away from our samurais.'

But almost immediately the procession turned from the highway down a lane and then into an avenue between old, tall trees, the boughs of which meshed over their heads excluding the weak moonlight. In this tunnel of gloom the lantern-bright inns of the Tokaido seemed a world apart.

The avenue sloped down to a stone gateway gilt with lichen. Guards, bandy-legged samurai, greeted the foreigners with sullen stares. Beyond, in a hollow among shadowed trees, Pev saw a large complex of buildings, many under those curved roofs of ornate tile. A sweet oppressive fragrance hung over the valley. It reminded him of sketching tours in Italy. Incense.

'Behold!' Sullivan exclaimed. 'The Tozenji Temple, residence of the British Legation in Yedo.'

They passed into a torchlit courtyard. Drooping in the still summer dusk, the Union Flag, that familiar banner of civilization, stirred restlessly on a bamboo pole.

And then it happened. So quickly that Pev barely caught his breath. A dark figure of a man leapt from the gateway on to the silvery gravel of the courtyard. He screamed. A sword flashed high above his head. Just as suddenly as he appeared, he vanished into a thick wall of shrubs.

'Oh, my God in Heaven!' Sullivan cried.

Pev was speechless.

The samurai grunted among themselves. One even laughed. But the pounding of Pev's heart drowned all smaller sounds.

Deathly white, Oscar Sullivan slid from his horse. The

samurai milled about. Not one moved to pursue the attacker.

Pev gasped. 'What was that?'

'An intruder!' The answer rang across the courtyard from a wide latticed door. The black outline of a man in a frock coat stood out against a lit vestibule.

'Mr Fitzpaine.' The man approached. 'Radley Ferrier. An unfortunate introduction to Her Majesty's Legation in Yedo. However, we welcome you, none the less.'

Pev woke the next morning to the steady drumming of rain on the tile roof. Without regret he abandoned his narrow bed made by a bewildered native carpenter who had never seen one, according to Oscar. Under his feet the straw matting felt pleasantly springy. It might be more comfortable, Pev reflected, to sleep directly on that matting in the Japanese mode. He crossed to the paper-paned window and slid it open on to a sodden world outside. Beyond a dim wet-slicked verandah grey sheets of water swept the lawns and banks of forlorn shrubs. A large pine tree, bent as an ancient crone, dripped over the small lake, its heavy branches trailing in the murky water. It was a most un-English scene. Now in early summer one would expect roses or peonies at least, but he could make out only trees and bushes. Everywhere was green.

His room seemed to be in the long stroke of an L-shaped wing. He had seen reception and sleeping rooms last night and knew that the entrance on the short stroke of the L faced the courtyard and it was there that the doctor, James Wilson, slept. The main temple buildings sprawled away to Pev's right. One huge structure rose above the rest and he guessed that must be the main place of worship, whatever that might entail in a Buddhist establishment. Even as he watched two men dressed in brown robes and wearing high wooden clogs darted down a path towards it. Their completely bald heads were protected from the deluge by a vast umbrella of oiled paper. Monks undoubtedly. At least they did not wear swords. He shuddered, and tried to forget again last night's incident.

Washed and dressed in his suit, which was far too warm for the day, he went down the low, beamed corridor. The dining-room, he remembered, was distinguished by a wood, not paper, door. He slid it back and peeped in, rather timorously.

A large table and some straight chairs of carved blackwood, several basket chairs and bookshelves were the only furniture. No carpets, just the local mats. Two men sat at the table looking out into the garden, which was easily done as the outside wall seemed to have vanished since last night. How did these flimsy structures survive storms or earthquakes, Pev wondered. And were the winters cold? Indeed, now rain splattered on the verandah and the fragrance of a wet summer garden filled the room.

James Wilson rose to greet him. A broad-shouldered young giant of about twenty-five, he dwarfed the room, slightly stooped under the low ceiling.

'Good morning, Fitzpaine. Hope you slept well.'

His voice had a pleasant Yorkshire warmth and Pev found himself smiling into the square face. Light brown hair with a hint of red waved back from a high forehead; the impression was one of humorous intelligence just as the large scrubbed hands were steady and capable.

'I did, thank you. But is it always so hot so early?'

The other man barked out, 'Hot! I say, just jolly well wait for summer to set in. This is only the rainy season, old chap.'

Basil Foxwood was aptly named. His narrow sharp-featured face and pale gingery colouring reminded Pev of a fox although the eyes lacked the quickness of a wild animal's. Pev had barely noticed him last night until startled by a string of questions on his family and background. His antecedents were apparently deemed uninteresting for Foxwood soon lapsed into silence and Pev would have forgotten his presence altogether but for the occasional harsh laugh. Now he waved Pev to a chair. 'Sir Radley and Sullivan have breakfasted. Afraid the bread is frightful this morning. The cook is probably sulking. Unpredictable, these Chinese johnnies.'

'I reckon the flour is mealy again,' Wilson said patiently. 'Alas, there is never any butter. That and cheese are only faint memories on my palate. But we do have eggs and smoked fish.'

32

'No bacon.' Foxwood looked gloomy. 'Never any beef or lamb. Haven't seen a kidney for eighteen months.'

Wilson's broad face split into a sudden boyish grin. 'You will find that we are obsessed with food. Sir Radley is convinced an Englishman's health suffers from lack of red meat. Medically he is quite wrong but nevertheless our thoughts do dwell on cutlets and Stilton.'

The bread *was* revolting and the tea thin and sour ('You will come to like it,' Wilson promised) but Pev, always hungry, ate his fill, watched with some interest by Foxwood and Wilson, who questioned him steadily about England and Hong Kong. Wilson said, 'You will have to forgive us. Day after day with only the four of us for conversation, it is quite exciting to hear a different voice.'

Foxwood rose languidly. 'Must be away. Finish the dispatches for the *Topaz*, don't you know. We will meet again at dinner, Fitzpaine. Stewed fowl and fish, no doubt, unless the *Topaz* has brought some delicacies.' He looked hopefully at Pev who had to admit he did not know the cargo of the *Topaz*. Foxwood left dejected.

'I sincerely hope that there is a crate of books and journals.' Wilson wrinkled his brow anxiously. 'I ordered some medical texts and Miss Nightingale's *Notes on Nursing* months and months ago.'

'You were in the Crimea, I think Sullivan told me. Did you encounter Miss Florence Nightingale?'

'Yes. After the Alma, I was with her at Scutari.' But his tone did not encourage further questions.

Pev looked out into the garden. 'Is that large building the chapel of this monastery?' he asked quickly to cover the awkward silence.

'It is,' Wilson replied pleasantly. 'The Buddha Hall where they chant and beat drums before their idol. Have no fear for your soul, however. Our monks lack missionary zeal.' He smiled.

'Are the Legations all in temples? Seems rather odd.'

'Not really. The temples are the only establishments large enough to accommodate us. As it is,' he patted his chestnut hair ruefully, 'I am always banging my head. Aha, here is Oscar.'

Sullivan appeared on the verandah shaking out an oil-

33

paper umbrella. He glanced at his muddy boots, shrugged and stepped on to the mats. 'Morning, Fitzpaine. You will have found our weather rather inclement. Monsoon season. But it is clearing now.'

Wilson walked out on to the verandah. 'Oh, dear. Here comes the sun. Now we shall all steam until it rains again. Look to your boots and treasures, Fitzpaine. Everything rots.'

Oscar poured himself some tea. 'I have just visited our guardians at the gate. Needless to say, the attacker was not apprehended. They never are.'

'Oh?' said Pev. 'Never?'

'I was given the usual story. A ronin. Probably from Mito. Slipped away in those cursed trees that close this place in. But of course they did not try to catch him.'

'A ronin?' Pev was puzzled. 'I thought they were called samurais.'

'Ronins seem to be some sort of renegade samurais. No one can control 'em or so we are told.' Oscar sneered. 'The Daimyo of Mito leads the opposition to the treaties. Well, he *was* the daimyo. Now, he is in some disgrace but his men still plague us – or so we are told. And murder government officials. But Mito might be a scapegoat. Who knows? Anyway the whole samurai class are nothing but bandits.'

At that moment the door to the corridor whispered open. Pev wheeled, expecting to see Sir Radley, but a Japanese stood silently behind him. He wore the usual long gown but his head was unshaven and his hair gathered into a short upright queue. From his sash hung two swords, one short, one long and slightly curved.

Pev gasped, clutching at his chair, but James said cheerfully, 'Welcome, Tada Sensei. Is it so late? Well, then we must be off to visit this important official of yours.' He added some words of Japanese and then turned to the bewildered Pev. 'May I present Tada Sensei. A fine doctor who wishes to learn the science of medicine.'

The Japanese bowed low. Warily, Pev put out his hand but Oscar frowned and sketched the gesture of a bow so he bobbed in ungainly imitation. The Japanese bowed again, one hand resting on the hilt of his long sword. Without so much as a smile he followed Wilson from the room.

'Was he not one of those samurais? Do they walk around the Legation armed?' Pev demanded.

Oscar laughed. 'Apparently doctors wear swords too, although I rather think Tada does spring from samurai stock. He and James are thick as thieves. Always busy cutting up some poor chap or dosing the natives with worm powder. Never know what that fellow is thinking though. To be candid, he makes me nervous. Thank heavens he does not come here all that often. James usually works at a local clinic. He is a brave man. I would not go among 'em like that.'

'But those swords! Can he be trusted?'

Oscar shrugged. 'James trusts him, I suppose. Look here, Fitzpaine, Sir Radley is busy with dispatches for the *Topaz*. Now that it has cleared I shall show you about. Most mornings we have our lessons in here, but tomorrow is soon enough to meet the dreaded Ito Sensei, our quite cretinous teacher of Japanese. Come along. We will dash over and have a look at their Buddha statue. Doubt if you will be impressed.'

As Pev stepped out on to the dripping verandah he felt a sudden overwhelming homesickness for rosy brick walls, proper glass windows and the solid Christian familiarity of Exeter Cathedral.

Somewhere a bell clattered imperiously, commanding the monks to their heathen devotions. Pev followed Oscar out into the steaming garden.

Terror glowed deep in her eyes. To James Wilson she was like a fawn facing the hounds. Try as she might to control herself those eyes and the nerve quivering under Wilson's probing fingers betrayed her. The tumour in her young bruised breast was ulcerated, a visible manifestation of the final poison ravaging her wasted body. She was still pretty, as delicate as a little fawn one would wish to cherish and protect from the hounds.

He withdrew his hands, signifying the examination was complete. In one swift graceful movement she pulled her collar closed and touched her forehead to the tatami before retreating behind a standing screen where the maidservants waited. Putting a safe modest distance between herself and the barbarian giant, he thought wryly.

Wearing an expression of fastidious distaste, Segawa watched the proceedings. Wilson wondered, as he had often before, if this grimace was habitual or simply reserved for western medicine. But whichever, he thought, Segawa will not like it when I refuse. As for the woman's husband, a tiny dry little man in painted silk gauze, whose hooded eyes and long thin fingers lend him a spidery appearance. Not once has he indicated the slightest pity for that poor, suffering creature. Quite obviously she is nothing but a body conveniently diseased to challenge the foreign doctor's skill.

And what does Tada Shoh make of all this, seated so neatly there, looking properly humble? Is it an honour for him to be called to the house of a minister of the Tycoon? What does he think of those mauve patterned shojis and the gold screens and those huge Chinese vases? Strike me as vulgar. Still, the way he keeps himself to himself, it is unlikely that I shall ever know if he approves or disapproves, but one thing is certain, those watchful eyes and that quick brain are taking in the whole business. His mind is as eager and open as Segawa's is contemptuous and closed. Tada is too intelligent to have to kow-tow to Segawa, however famous the old bird might be – or to Yasutake, that incompetent reprobate of a son.

Remember to bow respectfully to the revered quack and his ministerial crony. And keep your voice low to spare that dying wife. 'Segawa Sensei, my examination tells me the cancer is far advanced. Surgery would be futile and only increase her misery.'

Shoh translated Wilson's workaday Japanese into formal language. Segawa's grimace slipped momentarily into a smirk but the minister whined waspishly, 'The outsider's examination was too brief. One cannot read a book through its wrapping. How can he decide that cutting away the illness will not be beneficial? I demand that he treat my wife.'

Segawa bowed as easily as a cobra curls. 'Please forgive the barbarian's disgraceful lack of civility. Men of his race do not understand Your Grace's eminence. However, this ignorant Segawa sees that he has employed his most special instrument on your wife.' He gestured greedily towards the bell of hollowed wood resting on a cushion: Wilson's stethoscope which, despite himself, the old man coveted. 'That is an exceptionally sensitive device that sounds the lotus flower of your wife's soul. But I shall inquire further.'

He raised an inquisitive eyebrow at Wilson who replied firmly, 'An operation will not cure. Besides, she is too weak for chloroform. Her pain will be increased.'

'Pain is an illusion. My foolish wife is of ancient samurai stock. She fears only dishonour. It is the English doctor who is afraid, afraid his methods will fail.'

James cut across Shoh's gloss on the minister's rudeness. 'Of course my methods will fail. Only opium will ease her now.'

The minister's whine rose to a vicious buzz. 'I insist the poisonous lump be cut away.'

Segawa decided to take control. 'This gentleman is an important official at the court. Our Enlightened Ruler has expressed the wish that we ignorant people admire the skills of the West. Indeed, Wilson Sensei must be flattered at this opportunity to amaze us with his knowledge.'

Hell and damnation! Resorting to blasphemy may be idle weakness but this situation is blasphemous. Nothing to do with medicine and everything with politics. Well, politics are Sir Radley's country, not mine. Blast the minister and Segawa and the whole race.

'I shall apply an ointment of iodine of potassium and let some blood in the European manner. Perhaps this will ease her.'

Reluctant admiration glittered in Segawa's eyes. This barbarian was not a fool. Draining the life force was a stupid, unnatural practice but it was less violent than the knife. When the wife joined her ancestors as he knew she soon would, neither the barbarian nor Segawa nor the minister would suffer embarrassment.

While Segawa coaxed the minister James glanced back at the screen. The graceful shadow was erect and composed. A brave woman. Perhaps she welcomed death as a

37

release from her husband's spidery presence.

Bleeding agreed to, the husband watched with disgusted glee as the diseased fluid trickled into a crimson pool in a black lacquer bowl. Finally replete, he permitted his wife to return to the women's wing with a draught of laudanum.

After half an hour of formalities and tea the two young doctors were allowed to escape through a succession of rooms to the gatehouse. Pacing gingerly behind them Shoh's servant carried the lacquered medicine box and Wilson's calfskin valise, but once free of the mansion James retrieved his own possession, embarrassed at the idea of a native servant.

He looked back at the high plastered walls and carved double doors. 'At least she will die in luxury. Many have not that. What of our carpenter? Any sign of festering in the stump?'

Shoh did not reply but gazed up and down the silent walled street, efficient hands tucked in the sleeves of his black kimono. Not a man to evade issues, Wilson said patiently, 'That woman was dying.'

'This Tada examined her this morning. Her pulses, tongue, skin, heat, all told this ignorant doctor the final peace is near.'

'Yet you disapprove of my decision. Why?' The answer was very important to him.

Once again Shoh studied the empty street. Slowly, in careful Japanese, he said, 'Segawa Sensei is my teacher. It is the duty of this Tada to obey. Segawa Sensei is not the teacher of Wilson Sensei, and yet I was shocked that you defied a venerable physician of great wisdom.'

'I understand.' And he did understand. 'But what of her life, her suffering?'

'For the people of Nippon, for we of samurai blood especially, suffering and death are not important.'

'Of course suffering and death are important. How can you, a doctor, say such a thing? Do you believe that?' He stared at the strangely curved oriental eyes. Resonant as polished ebony and yet telling him nothing.

'Suffering and pleasure – twin illusions of life. What is death but release?'

38

'And what does a samurai know of it? Drunken brutes.' In his frustration, he equalled Oscar's prejudice.

'You see only the surface. The spirit of the samurai is honourable – disciplined – loyal.'

'Therefore that dying woman must endure the torture of the knife to please her husband?'

'She would wish to. Sensei –' Then, abruptly, Shoh gave up. 'This stupid Tada has not the words.'

The two men stood in the hot sunlight, each deep in his own world. Finally Wilson broke the silence. 'The day is so beautiful now. Shall we take the street along the river?'

Shoh bowed in agreement. 'That would be the most pleasant way to the clinic.' The walk might help both men regain their composure.

As became a fashionable doctor, Segawa's clinic was near the Ryogoku Bridge, just outside the aristocratic inner circle of the city. On the sparkling river laden barges of timber, rice and coal moved slowly in sluggish contrast to the pretty pleasure boats already bright with customers. Although James disapproved of such frivolity during what should be hours of work, these vessels vivid with lanterns and dangling curtains made an undeniably delightful picture. Flycatchers darted greedily through the willows lining the steep bank. Ahead the arc of the Ryogoku Bridge curved across far distant Fuji.

A tall wall masked Segawa's empire from curious eyes. To please his patron, Lord Okubo, the old doctor had accepted Wilson's presence and even observed the Englishman's surgical skills. But although sometimes impressed, Segawa knew the limitations of his prejudices and left it to Shoh to seize upon the westerner's knowledge. Coolly polite, he kept himself and his son at an appropriate distance from the barbarian.

As for Wilson, two years in the blood-stench of Scutari had not inured him to the horror of sawing off a man's living limb but, if it must be done, Segawa's scrubbed light rooms were almost pleasant after the rank filth of the Turkish hospital.

The carpenter lay on a pallet, face pressed against the lowered reed blind. No sweet stink of gangrene corrupted the air and the fluid from the leg stump dripped clear.

'Oi, Grandfather, how are you feeling?' Shoh shouted. The old man was deaf as metal.

The carpenter did not stir.

Quickly Wilson knelt and tugged at his shoulder, rolling him over. Blank eyes. A slow blink. Wilson pressed his stethoscope against the chest, listening to the steady heart. The pulse was sluggish, the forehead cool.

This was the hell of it. Hack off a crushed limb, defeat infection and then watch as they turned their faces to the wall. This was worse than cold or miasma, cholera or flies. More harrowing than sturdy men crying, begging him not to cut. He could cure a body but not a soul that wished for freedom.

'Tada Sensei, tell him that he must fight. The battle is in his hands now.'

'He does not want to die but he is ashamed of his unfilial existence.'

'Ashamed?'

'To lose a foot is a terrible thing for this man. Segawa Sensei has ordered the mutilation of the body his honoured mother brought into the world and that is an insult to his parent's grave. He had to bow to Segawa Sensei's will but he is ashamed because he is a bad son.'

'But Segawa was right. Surely if his mother was alive she would rather her son lose a foot than his life. The man is suffering from melancholy. His whole life has changed. Such a feeling is natural but difficult to treat.'

'Perhaps Japanese medicine for Japanese heart?' Tada said in English.

Wilson nodded and stepped away. 'Why not? There are more things in heaven and earth . . . as our great poet says. The man is beyond my science.'

James watched, first with interest then fascination as Shoh examined every inch of the man's face: the eyes and tongue, the nostrils, ears, lips, teeth and gums. He moved to the hands, stroking and searching calloused palms, worn nails. Then the groin, belly, chest, armpits, neck: pressing and probing. Finally the pulses: wrists, temples, eyes, forearms, thighs, and the sole of his remaining foot, spending minutes over each.

Then in slow Japanese, as if he were speaking to a child,

40

he explained, 'We believe man and universe are one. The two principles yin and yang ebb and flow, increase and decrease for many reasons. But if yin and yang or dark and light, cold and fire, moist and dry are not harmonious, sickness and evil will follow. In this man moist secret darkness quenches the fire of his yang. And because he has lost much blood his life force is low. Therefore I must restore his yang to proper balance and revitalize the life force in his channels.' Shoh rose. 'Will the Sensei accompany me to the pharmacy?'

Wilson's smile was polite. 'Your diagnosis puzzles this humble Christian but your pharmacy always delights me. Shall we go?'

The pharmacy was a small pavilion set in a herb garden adjoining Segawa's living quarters. James loved this garden. Gravel paths wound through beds of flowers and shrubs arranged in an almost English order. Fruit trees rustled against a creeper-covered fence. Many of the plants were comfortingly familiar: foxgloves, mint, chrysanthemum, dandelion, while others were mysteriously Asiatic.

Walking between the neat patterns of foliage in the strong sun-hot scents and insect murmurs, James was overcome with sadness for home and his vanished boyhood. His greatest joy had been excursions to the Sheffield Botanical Gardens with his Grandfather Wilson. Those wide grounds and glittering hot-houses were the old apothecary's passion. Stained fingers stroked leaves as the gruff voice crooned the lost lore of each plant: 'Peony seed must be plucked at night or a man'll go blind. If tha' brews kernel of walnut with onion, salt and honey, tha' has cure for mad dog's bite.' In the damp sweetness of the hot-houses: 'Ginger. Proper bewitchin', lad. Juicy and fresh. But one blast o' winter and he's gone, canna coax nor fret him back. And yet, what he won't do for thee. From palsy to cholera, he soothes and settles.' Gnarled hands fondled glowing red love apples: 'Some say nourishment, some say poison, but beauties they be, eh, lad?'

Wilson had adored that prickly old man, so proudly stubborn. In his shop, a dark den of drawers and green bottles, here and there the dull gleam of copper, shrewd measuring eyes and deft fingers mixed recipes, some fashionably scientific, many more drawn from the old remedies, from cottage gardens in the enfolding Yorkshire hills. But a good Dissenter, a believer in education, the apothecary found the money and the spirit to send his son, Richard, to Glasgow University. He was proud when Richard returned as a modern doctor and a member of the Royal College of Surgeons. Silently he bore with his son's knowledge, endured his contempt. But the old man continued to cure the neighbourhood. And he lived to see his grandson, James, fresh from the Elaboratories and scientists of King's College rush off to fight cholera and Russian cannon.

How the old man would have relished this garden, poking, sniffing, chortling over the unknown. The pavilion too would have pleased him although he would have mistrusted it as tottery, coming as he did from a land of oak and stone. Today the criss-crossing shadow of the latticed windows slid across paper boxes and crocks labelled with ideographs. Bunches of roots and grasses dangled from the beams. Dusty pungent smells mingled with the summer garden to delight James's homesick heart.

Then James shook his head, clearing the sentimental cobwebs he would not allow to clutter his mind. Had he not fled nine thousand miles to practise medicine away from the coldly critical, possessively loving eye of Richard Wilson? Besides, his grandfather, God bless him, was dead now, like the cures in which he had believed.

Absorbed in a large scroll, Shoh was oblivious to everything but the picture and text before him. Curious, James bent over to look but he stepped back hastily, embarrassed by his friend's ignorance. The picture was of the human body, no, barely human; only a fanciful design of tubes and cauldrons, ladders and pumps that could not be dignified by the label of anatomy. Tiny figures in kimono stirred a vast pot that must signify a stomach while a minute pair of samurai stood guard over a gateway that closed the bowel.

Unconscious of Wilson's shocked withdrawal, Shoh

seized a mortar and began measuring an assortment of roots and herbs, choosing, grinding, stirring with hands as deft and loving as Grandfather Wilson's. Finally satisfied, he smiled at James with eyes blind to scientific disapproval: 'A tonic to warm the spleen. And now, most important –' he took up a box of finely grained wood—'the needles. Best applied in the morning, at the Hour of the Dragon, but the warmth of the afternoon is auspicious.'

For the next hour James Wilson passed through a timeless tunnel to a world beyond his grasp. He heard his Unitarian ancestors crying 'Sorcery', his surgeon father snort 'Medieval superstition!', his tutors at King's College accuse 'Quackery!' But when Shoh withdrew the needles from some mysterious points in the carpenter's upper arm and fingers the old man stirred, his eyes flickered with interest and he sat up to accept the cup of brewed herbs.

'And now?' asked James.

'We are doctors. We wait, we watch and then we try again, sunrise after sunrise.'

'So be it. We shall come back tomorrow.'

James's blue eyes met Shoh's opaque brown ones. The two physicians smiled.

Pev felt his eyelids slide down again. Quickly he shook his head and pinched his left hand – hard. From the leafy torpor of the garden the shrill screech of a cicada mocked his weakness. In the chair next to him Oscar was suspiciously still. Was he too drowsing in this sultry morning? Pev forced his concentration on Ito Sensei. Kneeling on the straw cushion, the Japanese teacher's dull gaze rose to his briefly then dropped in mute disdain for his pupils seated above him at the table. After only two mornings of lessons Pev already returned this contempt.

A deep voice cut into Pev's thoughts. 'Sorry to interrupt, but I must have a few words with Fitzpaine. Carry on, Sullivan.'

Oscar jerked and staggered to his feet. He *had* been asleep. 'Very well, Sir Radley,' he spluttered.

Although a hint of sympathetic amusement twinkled in Sir Radley's black eyes he asked sternly, 'What time did you intend to depart for the American Legation?'

'About eleven. Well, that is if it is convenient?' Oscar's reply was now brisk.

'Perfect. Do not let me keep you from your verbs. Come with me, Fitzpaine.' He nodded awkwardly at Ito's respectfully bowed head.

Now fully awake, Pev followed Sir Radley into his room adjoining the dining-room. A table, a bed, a wardrobe: the handiwork of the same bemused carpenter who had made all the Legation furniture. A tantalus, books, a knife of Toledo steel, a Chinese pot and an alpenstock in the corner were the only intimate objects Pev could see. The table was piled with dispatch boxes and papers weighted down with polished stones. As in the dining-room, the outside wall had been removed to catch any breeze.

Pev sat on the edge of his basket chair.

Sir Radley cleared his throat. 'Apologies for delaying this interview but as the *Topaz* was the first contact with the outside world in two months, you will understand there was a lot of business involved. The nearest telegraph station is Ceylon so it is essential that we take advantage of any ship calling in Yedo. So few do. I was sure you would wait for a day or two.' He smiled.

'Of course,' Pev nodded eagerly.

An uneasy silence fell. The two studied each other, Sir Radley openly, Pev covertly. The older man found a youth of average height, dark-complexioned. Regular features. Respectably dressed. An attractive lad, he decided. Intelligent. Young. Very young.

At twenty-two, Pev still expected to be impressed by his superiors. Sir Radley did not disappoint him. His appearance was formidable, his height and burly build accentuated by a thick black mane, side whiskers and bristling eyebrows, all liberally laced with grey. Eyes, also black, deep-set but restless, and the thin lips made the face seem a little hard, a little grim, but his smile, if infrequent, was not unfriendly. The ever informative Oscar had proclaimed him brusque and then added that he was really a good sort made impatient by the difficulties of his position. Pev was not good at judging age but Sir Radley had

had a long career and his hair was turning grey so he *must* be old, at least forty-five. Foxwood at thirty-something would be the closest in age. Without wife or contemporary, perhaps Sir Radley was lonely.

Now the Minister stirred in his chair. 'Ah, cigar? No? Too early. Too hot. Keeps the mosquitoes away though.' He looked pensively at his case. 'Well, Fitzpaine, I trust you have settled down. Foxwood and Sullivan will have filled you in on our routine. Mornings spent at learning the language. Afternoons, more lessons or work on dispatches. Have to report everything, of course, even if the information is dead as mutton by the time it reaches Downing Street. Then we venture out into the city. Ride in the commercial districts. Visit famous temples. Explore the countryside. That sort of thing.'

'Yes. I understand.'

'Not sure you do, Fitzpaine,' Sir Radley said firmly. 'These jaunts are not just for exercise or pleasure. The government provides an escort of samurais for protection but as you saw the other night, there are determined elements in the country that do not want us here. Therefore, it is part of our duty to make our presence – obvious. Commonplace. The Japanese will have to accept foreign faces. We diplomats must be free to travel wherever we choose. The British are here to stay. I hope – we all do – that our continued existence in Japan will be a peaceful one but – should it become necessary, well, there is the Royal Navy in Chinese waters. In any case – have you a pistol?' he asked abruptly.

'No, Sir Radley!' Astonished, Pev patted his jacket pockets as if one might miraculously appear.

'Never mind. Foxwood has one for you. Can you use the things?'

'Yes, quite well.'

'Always carry it.'

'Then one's life is in danger?' Pev gasped but immediately he blushed, afraid that he sounded cowardly. 'I mean, nothing was said in London,' he added hastily.

Sir Radley's smile was bitter. 'London is far away. It is difficult when one is at a desk in Downing Street to imagine what complications might arise in a civilization not yet emerged from the Middle Ages.'

45

'Of course,' Pev murmured, as calmly as he could.

'And, frankly, living on the spot, we do not know much about what goes on. Even the Americans, Jessop and Meylan, who were in Shimoda in the provinces for eighteen months, even they are in the dark. You are to ride over and meet them this morning. Their audience with the Tycoon was a disaster, or so Jessop has indicated. I want more details.'

Ferrier stared thoughtfully at the garden. 'You have read up, naturally. The Dutch reports? The articles in *The Times*? The Tycoon is their king. There is another chap somewhere to the west. The Mikado. We think he is a spiritual ruler. A pope, perhaps. But Yedo is the seat of government and we deal with the Tycoon's councillors.' He glanced at Pev. 'Some of them are fine men, Fitzpaine. As intelligent as you or I. In particular, Lord Ando is an excellent fellow. He understands that the old days are over. Japan cannot remain an isolated feudal state in these days of steamships and telegraphs and trade. He wants the best for his country. All the Legations here appreciate that and respect him – although Jessop does not always give us credit for our sympathies, I fear. Has a bit of a bee in his bonnet about colonies or whatever. Perhaps he is rather naïve, like his nation. But never mind that now.' He leaned forward and frowned at Pev. 'It is the Tycoon's other officials that make the trouble. Bigoted. Conservative. No imagination. They block new negotiations at every turn. Procrastination. Insolence.' His tone was sonorous, impressive. 'It is those men who encourage these ronins. I am positive. These assassins could not continue to escape if powerful men did not covertly favour them.'

'That is terrible,' Pev said.

'It is indeed.' Sir Radley reached for his cigar case. 'Then there is the problem of Yokohama. The original trading port was to be about ten miles down the Tokaido at Kanagawa but the Japanese decided that would put the foreign merchants too close to the Capital. They built a customs house and quays at Yokohama further along the bay and a few miles from the highway. We usually go there by sea although one can reach it by crossing a causeway

46

over the marshes from Kanagawa. But it's safer to keep off the Tokaido. Yokohama is a good port, no doubt about that. The traders have settled there willingly; not a very discriminating crew, it must be said, however. Restricted by the treaties to the settlement and swamps but that may be just as well. Johnstone, our Consul, has moved there from Kanagawa but Jessop refuses to recognize the existence of Yokohama or set foot in the place. The American Consulate is in Kanagawa.'

'In London it was said that Jessop used the threat of our navy to force through the American treaty with the Japanese,' Pev offered.

Sir Radley scowled. 'Things seem easier in London. Jessop had a difficult task. He went about it with all the means at his disposal. Because of his struggles we all have had a much easier time of it.' He pulled a watch from his waistcoat pocket. 'Nearly eleven. I shall let you go in a minute. Have you explored our Tozenji? You are an artist, I am told. What did you make of the Buddha Hall?'

'It was imposing but the idol itself seemed rather – blank. Crude?' Pev ventured.

'Well, of course, their culture is somewhat behindhand. Have not seen a painter to compare with Landseer or Rosa Bonheur although some of their prints have a certain naïve charm. But they don't understand perspective, you know. Holds 'em back. No architecture to speak of either. This temple could hardly touch Saint Paul's.'

They laughed comfortably together, then Sir Radley rose. 'We will discuss this again. Plenty of time. Only the five Legations here. Fifteen, twenty Christian souls altogether. Of course, the Russians – difficult people. And ambitious. Have to watch 'em all the time.'

Pev was not sure if he should shake hands, bow or simply leave the room but in fact Sir Radley swept ahead of him down the corridor to the vestibule where Wilson and Oscar waited.

'Fitzpaine and I have been making acquaintance,' he announced. 'I leave him in your hands now. Remember me to the Americans. We must have another musical evening soon. Jessop is uncommonly agile on that fiddle.' And he vanished back into the cooler shadows of the temple, leaving a startled Pev grinning at James and Oscar.

Oscar looked at him quizzically. 'How did it go?' he asked in a soft voice.

'I don't know,' Pev answered truthfully. 'He was very pleasant. Very informative.'

'He is a lonely man,' James said gently. 'And he worries, for he is patriotic but he fears that he does not advance his country's cause. Not that it is his fault. All of the ministers worry, I believe.'

'I *thought* he might be lonely,' Pev nodded, pleased to have been so astute.

Oscar took Pev's arm. 'Come along. Azabu awaits us.'

A young groom held their horses. Discreetly Pev peered at the tattoos adorning the boy's arm and chest. Revulsion mixed with secret envy for the riot of beasts and landscapes so unashamedly displayed.

'All the grooms do it,' Oscar said. 'Barbaric, isn't it? And that over there is our escort. Hardly an inspiring group.'

Five samurai in shabby jackets and leggings slouched out from the shade of the gateway: wiry, bandy-legged, dwarfish men who moved more like street urchins than soldiers. Pev watched them scramble on to their scrawny ponies. 'My sister is married to an officer in the East Devons. He would not dignify them as cannon fodder.'

'And he would have proved himself most astute.' Oscar urged his dispirited horse towards the avenue.

'Ah, no, Oscar, the class is not entirely without virtue,' Wilson demurred. 'Remember Tada. A most superior character in all ways. And a canny doctor. In the past days I have watched him bid a man who wished for death back to cheerful health. Unscientific. Perhaps witchcraft rather than medicine. But successful. You must come to know him, Fitzpaine.'

'I shall certainly try to make his acquaintance,' Pev answered quickly. He wished to become friends with one Japanese at least, even if a samurai.

But Oscar as always, knew better. 'Each class has its exceptions. One must assume Tada is morally above the conditions of his birth. The chap is a doctor, after all. Consider Ito Sensei if one needs confirmation of my claims. Now, what do you say to him?'

Wilson protested, 'Here, you must credit the man's difficulties. How does one teach a language without alphabet, dictionaries or grammars? Can you envy him his position?'

'Now, you know Ito irritates you too.' Oscar's dark eyes gleamed. 'I think the man is a wooden horse, so to speak. Planted by the government to sabotage our efforts. They wish to keep their fiendish tongue to themselves just as they wish to keep their islands.'

They laughed and rode on together. Once past the cheerful activity of the Tokaido they entered a rural landscape of tiny farmhouses, fruit trees and fields.

'So very different from Devon. No meadows. No cattle or pigs or chickens. Not a barn or a stone wall or a paddock,' Pev exclaimed, 'and yet peasants are the same the world over.'

Three brown labourers straightened from their weeding to watch the outlandish outsiders pass, pushing back their flat hats and wiping their sweating torsos with neck towels.

Pev glanced down regally. 'Odd that they should wear skirts to work in. One would suppose those loose loincloths would be – oh, my God! They are not men at all. They are women! Naked women!' Blushing deep scarlet, he jerked his horse around on the narrow road, causing confusion among the escort. Oscar's ringing laugh increased his discomfort.

'Just like the English peasantry, eh? Do the rustics of Devonshire allow their womenfolk to bare their bosoms to the gentry? I must revisit that county. My first tour was incomplete.'

To Pev's irritation even Wilson was laughing. 'Aye, immodest they may be but cool and unrestrained, withal. I for one am most devilish hot in these tight garments.'

'Heathen!' Pev spluttered, glaring at Oscar's convulsed face.

'Indeed. Indeed. But now I begin to wonder how you will take to Dirk Meylan, he who knows all there is to know of the ladies of Japan. Or perhaps one should say, *les demi-mondaines*.' Oscar leered. 'No doubt, Fitzpaine, you have been curious as to our arrangements for feminine amusement?'

'Oscar –' Wilson warned.

'No. No – We are an intimate group and there can be few secrets. He will soon notice the closed norimon that arrives of an evening.' His tone was lofty. 'Well, hypocrisy is not my way. I shall not shirk from informing him. As you know, Fitzpaine, Sir Radley is a bachelor and Foxwood, although married, is kept by thousands of miles of sea from the connubial comforts. When either desires the company of the softer sex a local brothel most kindly accommodates. Hence the closed norimon. As for myself, I accompany Dirk Meylan on his peregrinations around the tea houses. And Dr Wilson believes in higher things, eh, James?'

When Wilson did not rise to the taunt Oscar pressed harder. 'Tell us of your ideal woman, James.'

'God in His wisdom devised the human character in infinite variations. You enjoy your "peregrinations". I would not,' James replied with North country resolution.

'Really, Sullivan, this conversation becomes embarrassing for James and me,' Pev protested.

Oscar waved a podgy hand. 'Ah, but this is Japan, a land of unbridled sensuality. You will discover it. Wilson has, but his virtue is so great that he can withstand the exotic Yedo air.'

Even Wilson's patience showed strain. 'Naturally I am not blind to an attractive face or pert figure. And the young women of Japan are attractive even with cosmetics and black teeth, but I am not here to dally with native girls,' he finished stolidly.

'Admit it, James. They lack the beauty of a Christian soul,' Oscar teased.

James flushed angrily. 'Nonsense! But I believe a woman's greatest happiness lies in her duty to children and husband. Striving for an atmosphere of harmonious calm in the home, instructing her offspring in piety and usefulness. The companion of her husband's heart. Never do I frown on your *demi-mondaines* – their misfortune is not of their own making. This harsh pagan society holds woman in low esteem, as housekeeper or instrument of pleasure.'

The simmering fury under James's words drew Pev's sympathy but Oscar simply chuckled. 'How stand you,

Fitzpaine? Will you join our peregrinations? With that dark complexion and handsome face the ladies will adore you.'

'James speaks wisely. He describes a perfect wife,' Pev said righteously.

Oscar shrugged. 'Wife, yes. I should hope for such a one myself. But here in Japan conditions force one to temporary liaisons. Mr Jessop, for example. Ahem. But we do not speak of that.'

They were now riding through a quiet street of shops. The few customers were neatly gowned women with attendant servants or men of respectable attitude, although several, Pev noticed, carried the two swords of samurai. As they drew nearer the temple in Azabu, the American Legation, the streets narrowed; the shops were smaller, their gaudy wares thrust at passers-by with encouraging cries. Lanterns, paper charms, candles, Buddhist images were displayed on racks picked over by chattering women with babies strapped to their backs or men in the short jackets or cheap kimono of the labouring class.

'The festival of O-Bon,' Wilson said. 'Buddhism believes the dead return to their former homes so lanterns are lit and food placed on altars for the souls. But really it is a midsummer holiday from the rigours of heat and hard work.'

Manoeuvring their horses through the busy, twisting alleys took full concentration. The crowds grumbled and glared at the jostling riders. Nervously, Pev kept his head down, darting swift glances around him: a score of hard Mongol faces set with opaque brown eyes, all similar and all unfriendly.

Suddenly he felt a sharp blow on his shoulder. The buzzing voices swelled to shouts. Another, fiercer pain across his temple forced him to cry out, to his shame.

'Quickly. They are throwing stones. The temple is just ahead,' Wilson called.

Grasping hands clutched at his horse but Pev slashed out wildly with his whip and kicked the prancing animal through the tall gates of the temple.

Something hot and sticky blinded him. He swept a hand across his face and was amazed to discover red smears on his palm.

'Take my handkerchief, Pev. Are you faint? Buck up,

51

Oscar. You have been stoned before. Hold his bridle while I support him.' Wilson's deep voice echoed in Pev's ears, rising and falling like the sea. Then a brighter chatter joined in and he felt himself propelled up a step and into refreshing gloom.

The bright voice babbled, 'Here, here, boots off, Oscar. We have gone native, you know. We will forgive Mr Whatever-he's-called in the circumstances but not you or James.' The voice slid into incoherent nonsense which Pev, gradually recovering, realized were orders in Japanese. A cool damp cloth caressed his head. His vision cleared.

Pink cheeks, spiky blond hair, brilliant blue eyes smiling into his. A reassuring North European face.

'Peverel Fitzpaine, Esquire? Dirk Meylan at your service. Secretary to Nathaniel Jessop and interpreter to nearly everyone. American by inclination but Dutchman by birth, my dear, and so able to converse with the educated native. Are you better?'

'Oh, yes, thank you. How do you do? I have heard much about you.'

'Naughty Oscar. A little brandy, Pev – may I call you that? It has a rather Dutch ring. And brandy for the rest of us, I think. Mr Jessop is temperance – penance for a riotous youth – but he does not force his convictions.'

'Poor Fitzpaine. This is his second attack,' Wilson said. Oscar had slumped in a chair and loosened his cravat. Freckles stood out against his ashen complexion.

'Alas, what will Pev think of my natives? But they are cross, my dear.' Meylan waved out two houseservants who stood by with a basin and bandages. 'O-Bon is a special festival and they dislike our presence in their temple. Buddhists are peaceful folk. They abhor the eating of meat, for example. But every now and then –'

'They would have eaten us?' Pev cried.

An explosion of laughter greeted this, Pev joining in when he realized his own absurdity.

'Is this merriment I hear? I daresay the attack could not have been too violent.' A tall, bewhiskered man strode into the room, the dignity of his black frock coat somewhat diminished by his stockinged feet and flat New York State vowels.

'Mr Jessop, meet Peverel Fitzpaine. Newly arrived. A student-interpreter.'

Blue eyes perused Pev. He felt very young and inexperienced before this merchant turned diplomat. 'Another student of the lingo! Englishmen eager to learn Japanese seem to grow on trees. Or is it because your Consulates in China are already full to bursting?'

Unaccustomed to Yankee humour, Pev was uncertain whether or not this was intended as a joke. He smiled weakly.

'Now, now, Mr Jessop.' Meylan grinned broadly at Pev. 'You must not mind my Mr Jessop. He detests the British. George the Third's soldiers burnt the Jessop homestead in 1779 and he refuses to forgive the nation.'

Meylan's familiarity startled Pev until he remembered that they had shared eighteen months as the only two Christians for a thousand hostile miles. Meylan must be more a son than a secretary.

'Sir Radley and I understand one another,' Jessop replied austerely. 'Tell me, Sullivan, has he accepted the Tycoon's invitation for an audience?'

'Oh, no, sir. On your advice. As your own reception was so unsatisfactory.'

'Well, I ain't in the business of saving England's face but we cannot let 'em humiliate all of us. The insult tendered the American nation was subtle but deliberate. Only officials below third rank. No court dress. No ceremony. Smiling behind their sleeves. Sir Radley and I see eye to eye on that sort of thing. Too long in the East, both of us.'

Meylan chirruped, 'In we strode. Looked about. Disapproved. Out we strode again. Most melodramatic, my dears.'

'And was your displeasure recognized by the Japanese, sir?' Wilson asked.

The serious eyes embraced the doctor, an Englishman Jessop respected. 'In affairs of national pride the oriental can give lessons to us all. No, our precipitous departure was accepted with unfeigned relief.'

'Disgraceful!' Pev murmured.

The eyes registered this remark, reducing Pev to impertinent schoolboy. 'No, it ain't disgraceful if you see their point of view. We are intruders on their chosen isolation. We have forced them from their feudal age to the lunacy of nineteenth-century diplomacy. We must allow them time to learn to play the "game", more time than Britain and France allowed the mandarins of China, for example.'

Despite himself Pev was impressed by this patience preached with evangelical fervour. And this from the first white man to refuse to kow-tow before the Tycoon!

Jessop frowned sadly. 'Every day in this land I am reminded how much we have to learn about these people. When a white man would weep, a Japanese laughs. He takes pride in performing private acts that we hide behind lace curtains, at least in New York State. I wonder if one day I will say with conviction, "This fellow before me, I know what he will do or say or feel next." Alas, I fear I will never know.'

Oscar laughed bitterly, 'Could it be you mollycoddle them, sir? So Sir Radley would say if he were here and certainly the merchants of Yokohama.'

'Sir Radley don't agree with my views nor would your Lord Palmerston. As for the merchants – Wilson, your young friend comes over pale. Don't you think a norimon suitable for the return journey?'

'No, sir,' Pev grinned. 'Your provocative opinions have spurred my recovery.'

Later they rode back through quiet streets. In the shops and houses exposed to Pev's avid curiosity families bent over their rice bowls. People like those had stoned him. Time, Mr Jessop asked. But was there time enough?

Behind the Englishmen the samurai escot rode in contemptuous silence.

When Meylan returned from seeing them off he found Jessop looking out into the garden.

The Dutchman addressed himself to the sturdy, broad-cloth back. 'Was it wise to bait him so? That boy was upset and inexperienced.'

'And arrogant and humourless and acquisitive. As all Englishmen are. They will have the East if we don't stop them and call it "containing Russian ambition" or "bringing God to the heathen". Bringing textiles from Manchester to new customers is more like it.'

'Myself, I think the Japanese have old Ferrier in a tizzy.' Malice glinted in Meylan's grin. 'Not a patient man for all his fifteen years in China and boasted affection for the wiley celestials.'

Jessop caressed his abundance of whiskers. 'Ferrier is right when he says one must be firm with orientals but he cannot act with resolution towards a government that slips through his fingers like a fish in water. The vacillation of the ministers bewilders him and a bewildered Englishman is a dangerous one.' Jessop dismissed the English nation with a shrug of his broad shoulders. 'Will you dine in?'

'Hm.' Meylan tilted his head slightly. 'Listen, Murasaki is practising her samisen. Such a sad sound. Do you think these lessons increase her proficiency?'

'Who can say with that peculiar cacophony? But she has her little heart set on those lessons. Odd, ain't it?'

Muted, from another part of the temple, the discordant notes faded and swelled.

The two friends' eyes met. Meylan smiled. The older man went to the verandah and stepped down into waiting garden clogs. 'Until dinner –' he murmured.

He followed a narrow path through the greenery towards the music.

The pavilion was small and simple, only six mats. An ink drawing of iris hung in the alcove over a bronze cylinder holding late lilac. The girl, kneeling, head bent over her instrument, wore an iris-patterned kimono under her open robe of mauve gauze.

Jessop slipped off the geta and stepped up behind her but she continued her playing. Delicately, as though her neck were a vase of ancient celadon, he ran one thick finger from beneath the glossy chignon down and around to the deep bosom of her kimono.

In the main hall Meylan listened. The music stopped. He waited.

Silence.

He sighed and turned away from the too bright garden steaming in the sun.

* * *

Afternoon was a quiet time in the Yoshiwara. A sentinel willow dangling feathery boughs over the white highroad from the city stirred in drowsy greeting to the occasional passer-by. Saké vendors and fortune tellers squatted in the dust by their stands. Tea house maids dozed in cool corners behind lowered blinds. One sole stall served bowls of tepid noodles to a few servants from the pleasure houses. At the Great Gate a shampooer, a wiry woman with a face pitted like a ginko nut, scolded her maid bowed under a lacquer chest of lotions. The gatekeeper took Tada Shoh's long sword and waved the kago through into the silent streets. Doctors, unlike samurai and townsmen, were permitted to wear a short sword in the Yoshiwara.

In the dull summer light the two-storey houses with their green-latticed cages made a tatty, even dismal showing: a railing broken here, a paper pane carelessly patched there. Greyish sun faded the banners and lampions. Limp bedding sagged over verandah rails: stained, mute reminders of the Yoshiwara's business.

The girls too, lounging in yukata on the balconies, long pipes drooping from unpainted lips, seemed faded, a little sad. Their chatter was the muffled whir of grasshoppers in hot grass. Few spared Shoh a second look. Doctors in the afternoon were rarely customers.

The Omi-ya was on Sumi-chō. The cage was still empty. No captive butterflies solicited passers-by at this early Hour of the Monkey.

The Oba-san waddled out to greet him. Immensely fat and enormously greedy, the coldness in her narrow eyes belied her fatuous courtesies. A vast toad preying on grasshoppers and butterflies.

'Ah, Sensei. The honourable doctor is always welcome. Could it be Umegawa San you have come to see – again? Such kindness, but the unworthy girl is much better.'

'No doubt, Auntie. However the fever was dangerous and I promised her father I would look after her. Besides, all the Floating World praises the concern that the Omi-ya lavishes on its girls.'

She received the blatant untruth with a shrug. 'Perhaps some honourable saké?' Hard eyes warned him not to expect payment from her. If Umegawa's father wished for a doctor's care, he could produce the zeni.

Shoh declined and slipped off his geta.

'Ara!' Malice sharpened her full, fat cheeks. 'A welcome sight. The sandals of the Tada men again sit in the Omi-ya's vestibule.'

Shoh turned in surprise. 'Was my father known to this house?'

'Tada Sama was honoured in all the Yoshiwara,' Oba-san smirked.

'That is sadly true,' he murmured and escaped into the corridor.

The upstairs of the Omi-ya was simply two huge rooms, encircled by a balcony, divided by shoji and standing screens into a warren of tiny cells where each girl entertained her 'guests'. The smooth cedar austerity of the balcony seemed peaceful and serene in contrast to the riot of colours and patterns in the screens and kimonos of the rooms, all on this warm day open to breezes and the curiosity of doctors.

Umegawa sat on her heels before a battered mirror stand. Beside her the make-up box was open. Brushes and pots and a bronze water jug patterned the spilt powder. Twisting gracefully she mixed white paste in a pottery bowl. Her yukata hung slackly, revealing the smooth tapering of her nape. Shoh stared at her, his mouth dust-dry with desire.

Turning, she carelessly pulled up the yukata and bowed. 'Sensei, good afternoon. It is a pleasure.' In her light voice he could distinguish the sing-song tones of Yoshiwara dialect obliterating the drawl of Odawara. On his first visit he had been surprised – and a little shocked – at how Ayamé the sword-sharpener's daughter had transformed herself into Umegawa, a Yoshiwara courtesan. Now he was accustomed to Umegawa and no longer regretted little Ayamé.

Laughter came from the balcony. A sweet girlish voice exchanged coarse jests with a sweeper on the street. Umegawa frowned slightly into her make-up bowl. Her hair was already elaborately arranged in the Shimada style and her teeth were freshly blackened.

'Umegawa once again unties her sash for customers?'

'Ma, that is so, Sensei. It makes me very tired but the

57

Oba-san –' She shrugged. 'Oharu will bring some saké. I regret I must finish my make-up.' She clapped her hands for the maid.

He knelt next to her. The tatami was old, dried out and prickly to touch. Absently he wondered if her bedding, still folded away in the cupboard, was shabby too, the sure mark of an unimportant courtesan in a second-rank house.

Taking her wrist, he followed the three pulses. After a few minutes he said, 'You are not fully recovered.'

Patiently Umegawa replied, 'The honourable Sensei is most kind but of course I must entertain customers. My food – this room –' she glanced at the tatami. 'Before I was ill my room was a better one. Mokuami, you know, he writes plays for the Nakamura troupe, was one of my danna san.' Pride flashed in her high clear voice but then suddenly she blushed. 'Honourable Sensei, apologies, but as for the problem of payments – The Oba-san refuses. My father cannot give money. Nor can I but – perhaps – early one afternoon – before the time to enter the cage –?' She looked up at him from under her lashes.

She gasped. Shoh hastily released her wrist. Angry red marks sprang out where his grip had tightened. Staring out at the green trees and grey roofs of the pleasure quarter, he thought crossly, 'What sort of doctor am I to be upset by a provocative woman? Does my father's weakness course so strongly in my veins?'

He could think of no answer, either to his own questions or hers. Abruptly he stood. 'You require a tonic to build your strength. Our Odawara remedy is best. I will send the herbs with my servant. Brew them with saké.' He left the room, brushing past the maid who carried a tray laden with a decanter and tiny cups.

Sadly Umegawa watched him go. It would have been pleasant to sip a cup of wine and talk of Odawara. How different he was from his father.

With a sigh she lifted her make-up bowl and stirred the stiffening paste. She must look her best.

On the balcony a cricket in its tiny bamboo cage sat on a half-eaten apricot and sang of trees and long grass hot in the afternoon sun.

*   *   *

58

'Ara, regrets, Sensei. The giant red-haired doctor is in Yokohama. Three of my men escorted him this morning. Bowel flux has struck the barbarians there.' The samurai's satisfaction was all too obvious; the prospect of suffering outsiders had cheered his afternoon watch.

Shoh turned away from the contemptuous triumph in the man's eyes. He felt an unreasonable desire to draw his blade and prove to the smug captain that he, Tada Shoh, was still a swordsman.

On one side of the moss-dark gateway the Tozenji courtyard blazed white in the sun; on the other the cryptomeria avenue stretched dim and inviting. He disliked the Legation when Wilson was absent. They shouted at him in bad Japanese, their voices even louder than usual, always waiting for him to leave. Regretting his futile journey across the hot city, he turned his back on the temple and walked along the carpet of sharp-scented needles under the tall trees. His need to see Wilson was urgent: at the clinic a samurai had just died of summer pestilence, a disease uncommon in Europe, and Wilson would be keen to examine the corpse, but in this weather corpses could not wait. Still, there were many such deaths during the Great Heat. Another chance would come.

An Englishman approached him through the speckled shade. The newest one, Fitzpaine San. About Masayuki's years but lacking his brother's solemnity and attractive for an outsider: brown eyes and hair and a dark, smooth complexion. His smile, dimpled and eager, amused Shoh. He was so like a kitten expecting to be cuddled for its pretty charm. But Shoh preferred this innocent vanity to the cold indifference of Sullivan or Foxwood, who treated him like another piece of their ugly furniture.

In confused Japanese, Fitzpaine greeted Shoh, inquired for his health and remarked on the heat. Under his tight stiff collar and thick jacket he was sweating heavily as did all the outsiders, emitting a rancid, sour smell. If these strangling clothes were such a necessity to their precious civilization Shoh, in cool, loose kimono and bare sandalled feet, wanted none of it. Did they fear the breeze on their splotched, pinky skins?

Under the boy's anxious smile and stumbling courtesies, Shoh sensed friendliness and gradually realized he was being invited to share some tea. Although he had looked forward to a stick of time in the ancient, consoling dimness of the local bathhouse he was touched by the boy's offer and bowed in agreement.

Together they walked through the somnolent afternoon lanes under dusty oaks. Behind a gate, looped with morning glories closed now for another evening, children quarrelled. A bent grandmother enjoying a quiet pipe on a wisteria-shaded verandah glanced up at them, her curiosity dulled by the insect-drowsy heat. But when the white-faced youth stopped a fish vendor plodding by in a cloud of greedily buzzing flies and poked at the odorous wares in his basket, the old man's scowl stifled Fitzpaine's friendly quip before it formed on his lips.

They came to a short street of pleasure houses behind the Tokaido and a proper distance from the fenced decorum of respectable houses. From the barred balconies of the brothels came the piping bird-twitter of girls at ease. Shoh glanced up at their shadowed faces and lurid pongee kimono. A young girl, gaudily painted, peered out at the barbarian. Other faces immediately appeared at the bars.

'Those poor women. It is an evil life for them, né?' Fitzpaine managed to shake his head sorrowfully while still gazing fascinated at the caged whores.

'This is not the quarter for such things,' Shoh muttered. 'The Yoshiwara –' but he broke off, unable to explain the lure of Yoshiwara, a lure he knew he would bow to, once at least.

He hurried Fitzpaine into the quietest tea house, away from the raucous calls of the night-blooming flowers. The bamboo blinds were rolled high. Shoh found an empty corner made private by low standing screens and shaded by a tall mulberry in the garden. The wind bell tinkled merrily in a corner of the verandah roof.

Waitresses crowded around them, peering in rude astonishment at Fitzpaine's face, clothes and shoes. Unperturbed, he flirted gaily and they simpered behind their sleeves, daring each other to touch him, while Shoh wished he were somewhere else.

Tea was brought; the girls scattered to other guests

leaving the two men to find difficult conversation. Fitzpaine struggled manfully with his month's vocabulary and the doctor's English but Shoh's heart rose when the outsider pulled his time machine from one of the little bags tucked inside his jacket. Another foolishness: why bags in tight clothes when loose sleeves and a purse at one's sash could accommodate all a man would need? Shoh glanced at the maniacally ticking disc. Five hours meant the sun was dipping, he had learned.

Fitzpaine waved it proudly. 'Very old. My grandfather's.'

'Ah, Grandfather San gives it to Fitzpaine San? In Japan, grandfather gives sword.'

'Oh.' So ended the conversation. Shoh was visited by a rare and brief curiosity as to what Fitzpaine's grandfather might be like but as he could not even begin to imagine, the curiosity quickly passed.

Fitzpaine insisted on paying the outrageous two bu charged by the waitress.

By the entrance of the short street was a small printseller's stall. The colourful grace of the beauties drawn by popular artists caught Fizpaine's eye and he stopped. Eager for an outsider's silver, the hawker pushed aside the prints on display and whipped out a portfolio to tempt his exotic browser.

Shoh saw the youth glance down and then stare, popeyed. The blood drained from his face. The laughing hawker thrust the picture at him and pointed with a long, unclean fingernail. Recoiling as if from a serpent, the Englishman wheeled and stumbled rapidly down the lane, a clumsy figure in his strange jacket and heavy boots.

Puzzled, Shoh picked up the print. It was the sort commonly sold in the pleasure quarters of the city. A bearded, thick-featured outsider was lustily penetrating a courtesan who looked surprised and suitably appalled. Badly carved and crudely coloured but amusing in its way.

'What happened, Sensei? Shy? Does your honour think so?' The hawker's dirty nail jabbed at the print. 'That's a mighty rod shooting out of that forest of hair! If the Sensei's outsider has a golden staff like that he has nothing to be shy of. Heh? We will have to lock up our women.

Some like a touch of the bizarre.' Chortling he clipped the print to the display frame where all who passed could see it and admire.

Shoh smiled down the empty lane.

The Hour of the Hare. Umegawa stared at the ghostly face quivering at her from the mottled steel of her cheap mirror. When had she ever been so tired?

Yesterday.

She drooped over her make-up box. From the cherry trees a cicada buzzed furiously – just dawn and already so hot. The too-sweet scent of powder and stale sex clung to her sticky skin. Wearily she wiped at the chalky paste streaking her cheeks.

A packet wrapped in the familiar paper of an Odawara herb shop caught her eye. Perhaps the tonic would refresh her. But, no. Not now. To heat the saké and brew the herbs would keep her too long away from her pallet. Tada Sensei's kindness must wait.

At this hour in Odawara pearly light would be creeping through the larches, glowing on weathered walls and shutters. A breeze cool from the mountain forests might hiss through the bamboo groves musical with birdsong. But in the cramped rooms of Zenroku's house no breeze could stir away the suffocating closeness of too many hot bodies. Three little sisters still at home. Were they pretty?

Umegawa remembered the long sad face of her mother, a peasant's daughter who loved the terraced paddies and steep dikes, willows, herons fishing in ditches. Her songs of rice planting, slow, swaying rhythms of mud and sun, praised a better life than starving in the shadow of the castle. Her youngest child strapped to her back, she scratched the crimson soil to grow leeks and radishes. But she never dared grumble. One word against Lord Okubo and Zenroku's hand came down hard. 'The expenses of a daimyo are great,' the sword-sharpener would growl. 'If he must cut the samurai's stipend yet again, so be it. We who serve the bushi understand. What is a day without rice? Peasants have no soul. Like merchants, their hearts are in their bellies.'

It was her mother's task to tell little Ayamé that she had

been sold, but the girl had known for days. Everyone recognized the procurers from the pleasure quarter: brazen dandies in striped pongee with complexions the texture of taro paste; men who clustered in the poorer districts like flies on a suppurating wound. One such had been talking to Zenroku. Playing with her little grey cat, Ayamé felt his eyes stripping open her kimono and she understood the stiff look of tortured pride of her father's face.

Her mother turned dry eyes away. 'Only for seven years. You will fetch and carry for the courtesans and then perhaps, if Ayamé is obedient, there will be samisen and dancing lessons.' Still she would not look into her daughter's face. 'Ayamé has a good karma. Only a pretty daughter may serve her parents this way in hard times.'

'This ignorant person is unworthy of the honour,' she said bravely, but she pressed her little hands together to steady them.

For the last time Ayamé swept the floor, polished the rice cauldron and cleaned the iron stove. She stood in the tiny yard and looked up over the jumbled roofs to the castle. Crows flapped off the tiered curves of tile. She could just make out samurai moving on the walls.

Then Tada Teruhiko strode through the gate into the yard, followed by his son Masayuki. 'Call your father,' the older man barked. 'My sword needs attention,' and Ayamé bowed and scurried off, but her father was already hurrying into his geta.

That night she clutched the grey cat to her chest to hide her shivering while her mother spun flax and her father stared blindly at the brazier. Later she lay wedged between Oasa and Kimi for the last time. Oasa's voice came soft against her ear, 'Elder Sister, our sleeves will be wet with grief tomorrow.' Oasa had seen ten summers, one less than Ayamé. If the samurai did not pay their debts, she would be the next to be sold.

In the morning, before dawn, the procurer arrived fluttering long papers stamped with the seal of the temple where Zenroku was registered. A flat oil-paper-wrapped package of gold ryō slid across the tatami. 'I'll wait outside,' he announced, and the door snapped shut.

Ayamé and her parents knelt in an uneasy triangle.

'Do not disgrace the family.' Her mother spoke gruffly but her lips trembled. 'Remember your people serve the castle. Work well but hold your head high.'

Zenroku passed a rolled slip of paper which she touched to her forehead in obeisance and then tucked into her obi. As she gathered her few belongings tied in Odawara cloth she heard Kimi whisper behind the curtain, 'Oasa, we call you Elder Sister now.'

Outside the procurer waited with two kago. Snivelling hopelessly in one was the fletcher's second daughter, a child of five. One glance at her splotched cheeks steeled Ayamé's spirit. She bowed to her parents and climbed proudly into the sling seat. As the bearers trotted down the alley she caught sight of her grey cat watching quizzically from the roof of the gate and she pressed her rigid face into the greasy curtain of the kago.

White frost glittered on the Tokaido. The sliver of a setting moon slid between tall pines. Her mother's beloved paddies glinted hard as orange glass in the flaming glory of the rising sun.

The journey to Yedo was onerous. The kago tossed like a ship in a typhoon. At the post-stations she timidly eased her cramped, bloodless limbs, trying not to hear the moans of the fletcher's daughter. The first night, in a dark inn stinking of saké and horse dung, she took out her father's note. By the light of the oil lamp she carefully read the characters, working them out one by one as he had taught her on summer evenings.

> Maples turn from
> green to scarlet
> a pause
>> Soon spring
>> returns.

After two days they passed through the Tokaido gate. Never had Ayamé dreamed so many people breathed and walked and laughed. Rows of shops and houses stretched beyond her imaginings. After delivering the fletcher's daughter to a minor house in Fukugawa, the procurer escorted the prettier Ayamé to the Omi-ya, a house of the second rank in the Yoshiwara. Tired as she was, Ayamé's eyes popped with wonder at the lanterns and banners and gaudy creatures strolling the evening streets. The green bars of the cages froze her stomach to a lump of ice but Ayamé forced her gaze past them into busy rooms where bright silk shimmered in the lamplight.

Shrewed eyes appraising, the Oba-san poked her. 'She's old at eleven and skinny of course, but they all are these days. Still, I think the master will agree this little bud promises a pretty flower.'

Ayamé peeped up. Oba-san's fat jowls sagged like two bulging sacks of rice. The slitted eyes above were unfriendly.

The following afternoon she was bathed and brought before Oba-san and a thin pox-faced man who looked up from the finger-polished beads of his abacus. At his brusque commands Ayamé walked, stood, turned, knelt, carried a tray and then submitted to his soft prying fingers. He bent a puckered face close and peered into her eyes, at her teeth and hands and feet.

'Sing!' he ordered.

She whispered one of her mother's country songs then said in a falsely bold voice, 'Please, your worship, this humble Ayamé can read Chinese characters. The abacus, too, I can use one.'

'Hm. Not shy. She will do. She's pretty enough. Mouth too large for my taste but make-up will take care of that. Bright eyes. When you have polished her up a bit she should be quite graceful. Put her as maid to whichever girl needs one. In a few seasons we might make a shinzo out of her.'

'This unworthy woman will work herself to the bone, Kozo Sama,' Oba-San oozed.

'Line her kimono with cotton waste. She can have two and a padded jacket. Cotton waste for her futon too. She is not worth putting any money into yet. Never make the first rank. Too old.' Kozo San turned abruptly to his abacus and Oba-san's neat rolls of prices and fees. 'You feed them too much. Keep the rooms too hot. Comfortable girls are lazy ones.'

Ayamé backed from the room.

So her education began. Cheap green cross-patterned pongee, eyebrows plucked, a mask of white powder. Zenroku's daughter stared unbelieving at the strange little woman-child, slender neck bowed under heavy coils of glossy hair, who stood before the mirror. Her rosebud painted lips parted in a giggle of excited fear.

Kaoru was a courtesan of the second rank. An orphan sold at five by her grandfather, she had spent twelve years at the Omi-ya and remembered no other life. Kaoru's world revolved around whether the russet silk suited the grey underskirt and her silver damask obi or whether the crimson would be smarter. The rules and gossip and scandals of the Floating World were her horizons. No elder sister could be a more practical choice for Ayamé, who was reminded of her little cat when she looked at Kaoru. The pointed face and slanted eyes were feline and so were her moods – one minute aloof in her own world, the next, purringly friendly.

Ayamé made tea, warmed saké, spread Kaoru's bed-clothes, carried hot water, straightened Kaoru's hair, folded her robes, fetched towels and led the danna san to Oba-san's sanctum where he paid for his pleasure. When Kaoru wished to be rid of an exasperating customer, it was Ayamé who twisted a discreet knot in her underskirt, the Yoshiwara charm for driving away poor men or bores. Again, it was Ayamé who stuck needles tied with scarlet silk into the battered walls of the privy to bring on Kaoru's monthly flow when it was late. Rather that than the foul mixture Oba-san would have made her drink!

But most exciting for Ayamé, she minced along in Kaoru's wake when the courtesan promenaded or visited a danna san in a tea house. Ayamé carried the huge green lantern advertising the Omi-ya, swaying on her geta, chin high, ears pricked for compliments.

Kaoru's observations hissed between prim lips formed much of her education: 'See that fat old clerk who sells cloth at Daimaru? He is dressed up like a Boy's Festival doll. Not for me, either. Unfaithful old dog. This Kaoru always knew his love was false as his vigour!' Or, 'Ara! See Hanamurasaki from the Subaki-ya. Her hair is in a double-knot maru-mage style. The cheek of the woman!'

Or, 'What a stupendous kimono Masa is wearing. Ma! She must have wheedled it from a rich danna. Those plovers are embroidered in real silver threads.' Or, 'Listen well, Ayam, never waste love on an actor. Their purses shut as tight as a clam's shell.'

In the tea house Ayamé would curl up prettily, listening to Kaoru's banter, learning when to be coy, when to flirt, the moment to succumb, how to hint for a new hair ornament, when to confuse a dull lad with a torrent of Yoshiwara dialect. As a second-rank courtesan, Kaoru rarely had to sit in the cage, gawked at by any common coolie. Her introductions were conducted discreetly in tea houses, but unlike a first-rank courtesan she could not refuse her favours.

'Né, Elder Sister, perhaps this one will be young and handsome and gentle,' Ayamé would murmur encouragingly as she patted Kaoru's hair into neatness before they set off on their cavalcade.

'Ah, so, perhaps,' she would answer with all the resignation of twelve years' luck.

But life was not unpleasant for Ayamé. Although she attended Kaoru for long hours and was often sleepy or bored, her work was not arduous and Kaoru's moods became easier to anticipate: rain and townsmen with some wit cheered her up; hot days and fat danna depressed her.

One person made Kaoru spit like a cat and that was Tamachiyo.

She arrived during Ayamé's first summer in a flurry of rumour. Tall, slim, a face too long and narrow for beauty but with almond eyes and slender lips that commanded praise, Tamachiyo was samurai and therefore a flower of rare distinction in the Omi-ya. So dazzled was Kozo by his aristocratic acquisition that he paid a packet of ryō for flawless Hachijo silk to be made into an azure over robe for her. Dressed in this magnificence she was drawn by Kunisada and a print of her long, disdainful figure toying with a spray of cherry was all the rage in the streets for a week or so – to Kozo's profit.

'Ma! Just because she strums the koto and writes a fine hand, Oba-san treats her like an Imperial Princess. They say her husband sold her off to redeem a lost sword but I think he tired of that snaky face.' So snapped Kaoru.

Oharu the servant girl, too coarsely plain to attract clients, kept a flapping ear to half-opened shoji. She overheard Kozo tell the Oba-san that Tamachiyo's husband had discovered her with a lover. They were in the act of binding themselves together with her obi on the edge of the precipitous Red Cliff in Shinagawa. Another few minutes and they would have hurled themselves into the void – a love-suicide. Furious, the husband demanded her lover's seppuku and Tamachiyo was ignominiously sold to a second-rank house, the Omi-ya.

Naturally this story increased the courtesan's glamour. During her evening promenades the long sleeves of the girls pressed close against the sombre robes of their customers as all flocked to the balconies to watch the haughty form sway past between two young shinzo. Never had the lanterns of the Omi-ya been carried so high.

At first Ayamé gazed at Tamachiyo, eyes brimming with admiration. Ignoring Kaoru's long tongue, the girl stretched herself tall and twisted her merry face into what she hoped was a copy of the samurai woman's frown of perfect superiority.

But the great lady proved an unbending goddess. Never a smile disturbed her painted lips. Her two shinzo served long and hard with no soft word for comfort. Nor did the generosity of her danna trickle down to the girls as it should.

'Skinny legs, skinny neck. She steps along like a crane with her beak in the air,' Kaoru sneered.

But Ayamé, although her affections had returned swiftly to the jollier Kaoru, still acknowledged Tamachiyo's style. 'Cranes are noble birds, Elder Sister. She is proud, too proud, but, do you know, I will wager that many a dawn she goes to sleep with sleeves wet from tears.'

'Weeping courtesans are the stuff of Kabuki plays. Besides, samurai women never cry,' Kaoru said with ill-gained authority. 'Come and rub my aching back and then we will do something nice.'

For Ayamé's education had recently entered another stage. Now she knelt just outside the folding screens while

Kaoru shared her pillow. Encouraged by the whore, she would peek at the coupling, watching the gyrations with fascination, wondering at Kaoru's agile skill. Kaoru had folders of prints designed to spur on flagging guests and these Ayamé pored over, her curiosity sharpened by the demanding tingle between her thighs. Watching, Kaoru knew it was time and drew the girl into her bedclothes, informing her curious body with experienced fingers. The unexpected star-burst of pleasure thrilled Ayamé and she pestered Kaoru for more until she was pushed away. 'Ara, Ayamé-chan learns too quickly. I am sleepy.'

Kaoru began to initiate Ayamé into all the tricks and instruments of their profession. 'When we fold away your lined kimono, your new unlined one will have the long sleeves of a shinzo's. Oba-san will sell your first night to a rich danna. A virgin is a rarity that brings a good price. But only once. The morning after you must wake up a skilled whore.'

Around Ayamé's third New Year celebration in the Yoshiwara, Kaoru had as a particularly adoring danna the chief of one of the townsmen's leagues, who naturally nurtured his many connections among the merchants of the city. To please Kaoru he provided an opulent kimono for the new young shinzo. Dazzled by the lengths of silk shimmering across the tatami, Ayamé finally chose a deep blue spattered with boughs of early plum blossom to mark the season of her debut. Her underskirt was of rose figured Yuzen silk, girlish enough for her years. An obi of bold green and silver checks was manoeuvred into a huge bow tied in front to show that she was now a citizen of the Floating World. The hairdresser slapped pomade on her water-wrinkled hands and twisted and piled and knotted Ayamé's hair into a complex ginko-leaf style pierced with a long hairpin of false tortoiseshell, a present from Kaoru. 'It is only a cheap trinket but it will do for now. Soon Ayamé-chan will have silver and coral hairpins of her own. May your life be one rich danna after another.'

Kaoru's lover was even more pleased with the result of his gold and negotiations. Kaoru had to scold him for the lusty spice of his compliments.

All the women of the Omi-ya, except Tamachiyo,

flocked to examine Ayamé before she set out on her first promenade as a shinzo. 'Ara! The Shogun himself will want to buy her first night bedclothes, né?' Kaoru prompted and the others twittered in agreement.

As the great bell of Iriya Temple boomed its stern warning over the frozen wastes around the Yoshiwara, Ayamé took her first shivering steps along the frosty street. The night was cloudless and cold. White stars sparkling in an indigo sky mocked the deep blue silk scattered with plum blossom of Ayamé's kimono. The lantern light fell on her heavy head tilted high and her red lips parted eagerly over newly blackened teeth. She stepped delicately through the admiring crowds.

The excited cries brought Tamachiyo's guest to the balcony. Tada Teruhiko peered out at the scene illuminated below. The nervous pride of the fresh young shinzo attracted him and he stood in the sharp spring darkness watching her undulating progress between the green Omi-ya lanterns.

'Has the new girl a patron for her first bedclothes?' he called back into the room.

Tamachiyo chose not to answer. She played with the bamboo pipe in her long fingers and then tossed it impatiently to her shinzo. Her slender hands tore restlessly at the garish bow of her jewel-coloured obi, tied over her belly in continual reminder of her shame. But when Teruhiko, having watched Ayamé disappear among the skeletal cherries on Naka-cho, turned back to the warm brazier, Tamachiyo's face was calm.

'That young novice is from this house. What do you know of her?' His handsome mouth smiled but in the restless eyes an animal glinted.

In cool tones that disdained all taint of Yoshiwara drawl, she replied, 'She has taken no name as yet but she is shinzo to Kaoru.'

'And her first bedclothes?' he pressed.

She waved a languid hand, signifying disinterest. 'Shall I call in a geisha or will my ignorant playing do?'

When he paid his reckoning to Oba-san the next dawn, he inquired about Ayamé.

Oba-san's rice-sack jowls joggled with gold-lust. 'Ma,

70

your worship, a swelling little bud, né? Only the right
touch needed to bring her to flower. A gentleman of Tada
Sama's distinction. Ara, what an honour for our unworthy house.'

Round and round a circuitous path the negotiations
meandered, the samurai's contempt for haggling nearly
confounding Oba-san's passion for the art.

Later Ayamé was called to the fusty room where Oba-
san gloated over her brazier and abacus. 'A samurai
deigns to honour the Omi-ya and Ayamé.' Oba-san surveyed her speculatively, wondering where her hawk's eye
had missed the girl's worth. 'Have you chosen a name and
a motif? The bedclothes must be selected while the
danna's ardour is hot. Then you might get decent silk
ones.'

'A samurai,' Ayamé whispered. For a moment the
sword-sharpener's daughter overwhelmed the apprentice
whore. Then, because she refused to flutter like a drag-
onfly before a greedy toad, she replied firmly, 'This is
the season of plum blossom. Just as the plum marks the
beginning of the year, so this Ayamé begins her new life.
This unworthy shinzo wishes to take Umehana – plum
flower – for my name and the plum blossom as my crest.'

Oba-san pondered this, ready now to spend some
thought on a girl who attracted one of Tamachiyo's
suitors.

'We can do better than that. Umegawa – plum river –
will be your name.'

Ayamé gasped. 'Ara! But the name is a famous one.
Umegawa's story, how she died in the snow for her lover,
is known to all. I am not worthy.'

'Very probably not, but Ayamé is henceforth known as
Umegawa and the plum is her motif.'

Back in Kaoru's room, the whore flapped her sleeves in
amazement. 'So, né. Oba-san must be suffering the woman's disease. Or was she drunk? Umegawa! Ara, they have
plans for you.'

When, a week later, Ayamé raised her eyes to greet the
man Oba-san ushered into the room, her heart caught in
her throat. She almost looked around for the Chrysanthemum blade before she remembered all swords were left

at the Great Gate. The narrow half-moon eyes, once so arrogantly blind to little Ayamé, blazed down at Umegawa.

Tada Teruhiko was pleased with his purchase. The young shaking hands that poured his saké and adjusted the lamp reassured him that the bud was indeed unfurled.

He could not know that the shivering body beneath him feared not the cruel first thrust of his golden spear but trembled with sadness for lost Ayamé, the daughter of Zenroku, servant to the bushi of Odawara.

Later, alone, Umegawa lay on her new bedclothes patterned with plum blossom, Tada San's hoarse cries of pleasure echoing in her ears. Samurai cries were no braver than Kaoru's townsmen or an Osaka fish broker on a spree.

Dawn was shimmering over the broad street when Tada Teruhiko stepped from the Omi-ya. From other houses shadowy figures blurred with fatigue and saké moved through the clean silver light towards the Great Gate and the dark city beyond.

He was approaching the cherry trees of Naka-cho when the agony hit him. Furiously his fingers clawed at the air in a desperate attempt to hold on to this world of illusion. But his karma had come full circle for this life and he toppled face first on to the frozen mud.

Servants carried the limp body to the Great Gate and then, with the Chrysanthemum sword, to the Okubo palace. Five ryō passed from Kozo to the Brothel Association so that the samurai's visit might be forgotten in the record books.

The next evening at the tolling of Iriya Temple bell, Umegawa joined Kaoru and the other courtesans in the lantern-bright streets. Before dawn broke her sash was untied by a bookseller, a fanmaker and a young samurai from Kaga.

But among the cherry trees and willows it was whispered that Tada Teruhiko had spent his last night with a fox-demon disguised as a beautiful maiden.

'Eh, Sensei. Another visit to that unworthy girl? We will begin to wonder if a whore so ill is worth keeping in the house.'

To his irritation Shoh flushed but he acknowledged the warning in Oba-san's words with a curt bow.

Upstairs the shoji of the larger room had been removed to allow breezes from the garden to blow through. All the courtesans sprawled listlessly on the tatami. The Go board was empty, pipes lay cold in the tobacco boxes, only fans waved slowly in the hot afternoon. Even Tamachiyo had abandoned her quarters for the cooler open room. She lolled in a loose yukata, tapered fingers idly stirring the water of a porcelain fish bowl.

Umegawa swept to her feet. 'Welcome. Forgive us, such lazy, ignorant girls. But, ma! The heat!'

Kaoru studiously appraised the doctor but the others accepted him with off-duty indifference.

'Come, let us go to my little room,' Umegawa offered.

He bowed but his attention was drawn to Tamachiyo. Languor vanished, her narrow brown stare roved from his doctor's top-knot to the short sword and dirk thrust through his sash. Lines tensed around her mouth.

'Is this the famous Tamachiyo whose beauty all Yedo praises? Tada Shoh of Odawara is humbled before such charm.' He bowed again but she neither spoke nor acknowledged his words. Even without make-up her face was as white as a silk shroud.

Kaoru relished Shoh's embarrassment. He seemed as unsettled as a leaf in the wind by the presence of Tamachiyo. Perhaps the great lady was more to his taste than little Umegawa. She wondered idly if a doctor would have enough silver for such a courtesan as Tamachiyo and then, loyally, hoped that he would not. If Umegawa liked the Odawara doctor, it was she who should have him.

Umegawa pulled a shoji to enclose her room and arranged a folding screen to provide more privacy. As she poured him cold barley tea, untidy strands from her hair arrangement drooped alluringly around her curved cheeks. Shoh's loins stirred; his days were too empty of women at the time of life when the fluids are raging.

'Your health?' he asked, hoarsely.

'Ara, so much better. The Sensei's tonic was wonderful. A taste of Odawara to ease my heart. Forgive this careless girl, may I take your short sword and dirk? We are so

73

unaccustomed to see weapons in the Yoshiwara. I shall lay them here by the screen.'

The blades put aside, he smiled at her. 'And does Umegawa think often of Odawara? In the season of iris does she remember that castle town?'

'Ah, Sensei, soon, when the maples flame and the geese fly high over the marshes, then I too wish I could fly. Ara, to see the trees in the foothills blaze gold and scarlet in the morning sun! Yedo is never so brilliant and here, in the Yoshiwara, on these swamps – well –' Moved, she stared out over the balcony. 'To some the famous cherries and willows of the pleasure quarter bring happiness. But this Umegawa longs for the crisp larches and maples of the hills.'

'Has Umegawa many more seasons to serve in the Omiya?'

She raised a graceful hand in resignation. 'Alas, this illness has led me deeper into the stream of debt. I fear the Water World will be Umegawa's world until –' Silence fell over the fading blossom of her future. After a moment she roused herself and, touching her forehead to the tatami, she murmured, 'May this humble Umegawa express her gratitude to the Tada family? The kindess of Masayuki San and Shoh Sensei is more than this worthless woman deserves.'

'It is nothing. Zenroku has served my father and brother well as his father served my grandfather.'

'Zenroku and his family have been honoured to care for the Chrysanthemum sword.'

Narrow fingers pressed on the tatami as she bowed. Against the blue patterned yukata her soft skin was translucent as amber.

'Umegawa!'

At the command in his voice she raised her eyes. The chiselled face, a memory of his father's, was twisted in anguish. She smiled gently. 'Do not fear, Sensei. The trusted remedy of Odawara has strengthened me. This Umegawa wishes to bring happiness to the handsome man she loves.'

For an eye's blink the silken lies of the Yoshiwara cooled his blood. But only for an eye's blink.

His gaze met hers, so sweetly mocking.

Footsteps pattered along the balcony on the way to the bathhouse. High voices trilled. But the bustle of evening preparations were lost on Shoh and Umegawa. Nor did they hear the whisper of Umegawa's shoji or see the long slim fingers close on Shoh's discarded short sword.

By the time Shoh missed the sword Tamachiyo was slipping into the Great Void, released at last from the disgrace of the Omi-ya by her own firm samurai hand.

By the Hour of the Rat mosquitoes swarmed through the green bars of the cage, buzzing undaunted over the cold ashes of aromatic herbs, eager for Umegawa's exposed throat and wrists. Beyond the bars shadows danced on the empty lantern-lit street. In this still time, when the samisen were laid aside and the main business of the Yoshiwara was muffled by bedclothes, the sad croaking of the marsh frogs marked the night.

A single drunken samurai lurched past with only an unfocused glance for Umegawa alone in the cage.

'Umegawa attracts more mosquitoes than customers these evenings.' Oba-san's broad shape blocked the door. 'First Tada Sama's death, then Tamachiyo's. News of a bad-luck whore ripples the surface of the Water World.'

Umegawa pulled her collar closer as if it could ward off Oba-san's mosquito stabs.

'When stupid Umegawa chooses to untie her sash – and without payment – she does not even ensure that the doctor's short sword is safely put aside.' Her harsh words drowned the mourning frogs. 'Tamachiyo of the Omi-ya was our only first-rank courtesan. Everyone acknowledged her as such. Kunisada himself drew her! Now she lies rolled in a straw mat in the ward officer's yard.'

'This foolish Umegawa regrets –'

'Kozo San paid many ryō for Tamachiyo. What has he now? A bloodstained room and a useless whore with the reputation of a fox-demon. Ha!'

Shuffling feet announced a replete customer, waiting to pay. Oba-san's snarl twisted to porcelain smiles as her strong fingers clicked the abacus beads. 'Thank you, Kyushiro San, Kaoru's favourite danna, I know. Ah, how generous. Now, hurry back. Mustn't keep poor little Kaoru pining for your manly charms. Good night. Good night. May your journey be a safe one.'

The smile vanished. 'Oi, Umegawa. The Omi-ya has had enough of your bad luck. After sunrise, fold your bedclothes into a bundle with any combs or hairpins or pots that are yours. Leave the silk kimono but take the cotton. Kozo San has sold the rest of your time to a house in Shinagawa. Only the stews in the suburbs are good enough for Umegawa. Umegawa!' The snort shook her lumpy frame. 'A famous name. Too famous a name for a stupid, bad-luck whore.'

Umegawa's letter was carried to the clinic by a Yoshiwara street-boy.

Shoh stared down at the stiff characters painted on grainy paper:

'The Plum River no longer flows blue and sparkling through the Yoshiwara but winds among small pines in Shinagawa. A plum flower floats on a sluggish current. Such is the fate of a sad white blossom.'

Such was the fate of Umegawa. Tada Shoh's sword had brought Zenroku's dignity and his daughter low. The laws of the Water World are strict but so are obligations bred in Odawara.

He crumpled the letter and took up his brush:

'The gentle breeze blows from the hills across the river. The plum blossom seems a fragile flower but when wind tosses the branch, the flower dances in the sun and does not fall before its time.'

He called his servant and gave him the letter and a purse filled with zeni.

'Tell her I will come when I am able.'

The servant nodded and trotted off towards Shinagawa, pleased to escape his duties for an afternoon in that lively suburb.

Yedo sweltered through the dog-days of August. A greasy haze oppressed the city. Tossing on his rancid sweat-soaked sheets, Pev soon learned that if the cicadas began throbbing in the mosquito hum before dawn the coming day would be truly terrible. Clothes were torture: prickly heat raged under his tight collar. His stomach revolted with equal intolerance at Dr Tada's recommended grilled eels and Sir Radley's lascivious memories of the steak and kidney pudding of his club.

The days were passed in boredom and exhaustion. As a teacher, Ito San remained as enervating as the heat. Incomprehensible and uncomprehending, he and his scholars viewed each other with wary contempt. Pev gleaned the rudiments of Japanese language from Oscar, Dirk Meylan and the French interpreter, Abbé Phillippe, a former missionary in the Luchu Islands who had a competent command of the tongue. 'We shall conquer the lingo just to spite that gruesome old ghoul, Ito,' Oscar promised with a wink but Pev despaired, longing for the unobtainable: a grammar book or dictionary.

Without newspapers, church bells or clock chimes, Monday was very like Thursday, Sunday being marked by Ito San's absence and extra prayers in the dining-room. Occasional evenings of whist or music with the Americans or French only left him more aware of the tedium of their lives. Conversations centred on the heat, the Japanese and the dribble of news from China or Europe. Fresh from his school and university, accustomed to the society of men, Pev did not miss feminine chatter as much as the others but one afternoon, wiping the mildew from his sketching pad, he reflected that a cotillion or a picnic, a pair of flirtatious blue eyes, would seem a dispensation from the Gods.

At least afternoon rides through the sultry city were peaceful as heat drained even the samurai. But after dark, stifled by his mosquito net despite the shutters and shoji open to the night, Pev often heard drunken shouts from the high road beyond the banks thick with trees. Once or twice a man's shriek or the agonized howl of a dog warned that some unwary victim had strayed across the path of a sword-carrying brute.

Pev looked forward to visiting Yokohama, eager to walk among Christians with various coloured hair and eyes after the monotony of the Legation. Sir Radley's determined belief in the superiority of all things English; Foxwood's vacuous snobbery; James's abstraction, lost in the affairs of his clinic; Oscar's omniscience: these minor peccadilloes could blossom into major irritations on a hot evening. Yet he respected Sir Radley's lonely dedication and genuinely enjoyed the company of Oscar and James. If in twenty years' time they were to meet by chance in Piccadilly, they might find themselves talking in the stilted courtesies of strangers. But now, comradeship was easy. Still, Pev longed for a change of epigram and opinion.

As usual, Oscar was his guide. They walked through the insect-filled woods of pine and maple to the fishing village at Takanawa where the Legation kept a small craft. An old fisherman, too crippled by rheumatism to brave the rigours of the mackerel fleet, was on a retainer to pilot the Englishmen to Yokohama. Accustomed by now to the long noses, the women glanced up briefly from the fish they were gutting for the drying racks. The children hardly paused in their games.

The journey took an hour or so. Once Oscar pointed out a cluster of roofs huddled under red cliffs: 'Shinagawa. The government claims ronins plot in the inns there. It is a rather sordid place on the Tokaido just outside the city gates. Tea houses, brothels. You know the sort of thing.'

Pev did not, but he nodded.

At Yokohama, Oscar stood on the stone quay and waved his hand. 'Behold. The riff-raff of the Asian ports. Men of every hue and race and persuasion and all with one god – gold. But the shops are fascinating. Veritable caves of Ali Baba.'

Pev beheld. A ramshackle collection of shops and godowns. A square stone customs house. A characterless marketplace crossed by muddy streets and fetid canals beyond which a causeway stretched out to disappear in a sweltering swamp – the way to Kanagawa and thence the Tokaido and Yedo.

They started down the wide main street. On one side sprawled the disorder of the native town, on the other were open shops lined with a breathtaking array of treasures to tempt the foreigner with money to spend.

Pev stopped to admire some lacquer boxes on shelves set right on the street.

78

'New in Yokohama?' The gruff American voice broke into his contemplation. A leather-hard face pushed closer. 'You off the *Mary Eliza* from Canton?'

'No. Not the *Mary Eliza*. I have been in Japan a month or so. In Yedo.'

Suspicion fired the small eyes. 'Yedo? How d'ye go about managing that? No one's allowed in Yedo. Britisher, ain't you?'

Oscar joined in briskly. 'My friend, we are interpreters at the British Legation. Have you heard of that?'

'Diplomats! Accursed diplomats. Standing between a Christian trader and his deserved profit!'

'Oh, I say –' Pev began feebly.

'Toadying to those heathen killers. You and your regulations. Ruined us gold traders, you have. You nosy bastards.'

Oscar pulled himself up. 'And you and your ilk would kill the goose that lays the golden egg. Spare a thought for this poor race working itself to death to fill the ravening maw of Yokohama.'

'Ha!' An evil yellow stream of spit just missed Oscar's boot.

'Are you aware, sir, that the average Japanese must now pay two or three times more for his rice, not to mention his tea, because of your lust to sell his food and drink in Boston and San Francisco?'

Another ruddy-faced man appeared behind the first. 'I thought I heard you, Sullivan, spouting sympathy for the native.'

'Pev, meet Mr Donalds, dealer in curios and gew-gaws.'

'Antiquities,' Donalds corrected sourly. 'Only your precious natives are not much help to me. They do not wish to make or sell. Lazy –' he shrugged off the insult. 'Why, I could ship out twice the number of cases of combs or little lacquer trinkets but all I get is: "Vellee sollee. Lacquer takee manee dayee. Ancient skill." Balderdash!' He picked up a superb box fingered to lustre. 'Cheap goods sell as well as this quality stuff. Who knows the difference?'

'The Japanese,' Oscar replied.

'D'you hear?' Donalds ignored him and turned to the

American who was nodding sympathetically. 'Some Jap official told me the other day that we'd ruin 'em. Take away all their tea and silk. Destroy the skill of their craftsmen. "Relax" I said, "Look. Look what you gain. English textiles, American wheat, telegraph, railways. It will work out. Adam Smith says so." But that stupid native just could not understand. Could not grasp the principles of *laissez-faire*.'

'One must admit that a comprehension of political economy is lacking but one must see their side,' Oscar said.

'Jap-lover,' the American snarled. 'Fry in hell, you will, if there's Christian justice,' and he stalked away.

'Well!' Pev exclaimed.

'They are all like that,' Oscar said briskly.

Donalds glared at him with ill-concealed contempt. 'You think you are above commerce, Sullivan, but you are not. Without us, there would be no purpose for you here.' And he followed the American.

'The flower of the English community. Pillar of Yokohama society. Pride of the civic committee and stalwart of the Yokohama Club, from which, incidentally, we, as Yedo "diplomats", are banned. Come, let's go to the Consulate. Johnstone has to welcome us.'

The Consul, William Johnstone, a worried man with the sere complexion of a malaria sufferer, poured them a large tot of whisky and held forth for two hours, frequently refilling their glasses and his, on the impossibilities of his position. In his eyes poaching the Tycoon's game constituted a far greater problem than the robberies and brawls that enlived Yokohama's back alleys.

'How do I stop 'em? The marshes are teeming with fowl. Well, you must have seen for yourself as you sailed along the coast today. Supposing a Japanese policeman catches one of these bastards at it? Capital crime, you know, for a native. Consular Court cannot just fine a fellow and set him free. I have told 'em all that – Donalds, Morrison, all of them – but they just laugh and go after deer. Pity that they are allowed over the causeway. Coop 'em up here. Safer for everybody. That's what I say.'

'You have had trouble with samurais again, have you not?' Oscar asked, tired of poaching as a topic.

Johnstone waved away the samurai. 'Cut up a Dutchman. Oh, they ask for it. Drunken brutes.'

'Samurais or Dutchmen, sir?' Pev felt his tongue numbed by whisky.

'Dutchmen! Cool killers, those samurais. Hate 'em but respect 'em.' He laughed bitterly. 'Help keep the riff-raff in order, you might say.' At the students' shocked expressions, he added, 'Of course, I don't mean that. And as for the native traders – sawdust in the tea, waste in the silk bales. Cheat their grandmothers for a string of cash.'

By the time Pev and Oscar wove their way back to the quay, both were in agreement that Yokohama was a hell-hole but William Johnstone was a damn fine chap.

A merciful rainstorm blew up as they reached Takanawa to clear their heads before they reported to Sir Radley.

The other summer distraction was an audience with the Tycoon. Once Sir Radley had determined that Her Majesty's Legation would receive the proper respect due the chief power of Europe, preparations advanced for the presentation. Pev had anticipated the occasion as a lark until he saw how seriously the others took it. Swallow-tail coats sponged and brushed, linen starched, boots polished, the Legation assembled nervously in the courtyard. Sir Radley coughed uneasily as he inspected his juniors.

'I do not have to remind you that the utmost decorum is required. Step with care. Bow low, but not too low. Not a hint of a kow-tow. We are not Dutchmen but Englishmen.'

Escorted by fifty samurai, they rode through cleared streets to the inner city of daimyo palaces. But here bridges and trees and roofs were all Pev glimpsed. Plaster walls pierced by grilled windows or heavy gates formed a hot tunnel through which their unshod horses clomped.

The citadel itself was everything Pev could have hoped for – the vast palace of an oriental potentate. Delicate bridges, green vistas and exquisite pavilions lent an appealing air of fragility to the medieval fortress. Samurai, many in steel corselets and wonderfully outrageous helmets – 'Like Vikings!' he whispered to Oscar – stood as scowling reminders of the violence beneath the filigree surface.

Once inside the palace they passed along from room to spacious room through sliding doors sumptuously decorated with flowers and animals beautifully painted on gold leaf with a vigour that entranced Pev, the amateur artist. Walls of fine-grained wood, ceilings inlaid with flowers and insects of gold, subtly shaded shoji colouring the ever-changing light made the palace seem a masterpiece of cool, airy magnificence.

At last, in the Audience Hall, acre upon acre of noblemen knelt in attendance. So tiny and immaculate, so cool and composed despite their voluminous robes, these courtiers made Pev feel clumsy and gross as though he carried an excess of bones and flesh. Sweat trickled down his neck. He longed to mop his face and scratch his prickly heat.

However, his misery vanished when they finally approached the Tycoon. Seated on a silk cushion on a low dais, the ruler was richly gowned in bold patterns of gold thread on heavy satin robes. The face beneath the lacquered headdress did not match the majesty of those robes: coarsely featured with the dull eyes of either a half-wit or an invalid, the youth – for he was not even Pev's age – barely responded to Lord Ando's tedious presentation. But for Pev disappointment succumbed to awe, for in this atmosphere of glorious reverence he bowed for the first time to a ruler of men.

His patriotism too was appeased. Sir Radley stepped forward, an upright figure in manly black, a proud sight among the too-delicate orientals. And even to Pev's still inexperienced ear the minister acquitted himself tolerably well in the complicated courtesies of the Japanese tongue. At least no courtier laughed or drew his dagger in fury.

Restrained obeisance offered, the Queen's presents displayed, the Tycoon's presents received, the Englishmen prepared to withdraw.

Step by solemn step they backed through the forest of kneeling courtiers. One room, two rooms. Golden doors slid shut on the immobile Tycoon.

Suddenly there was a stifled gasp followed by a screech of tearing silk. Pev's heart stopped. Sir Radley had caught his foot in the spreading gown of a courtier. The Englishman froze briefly and then shuffled on. Silence oppressive with contempt engulfed their retreat. Pev swallowed a desperate giggle. After what seemed hours he felt the warmth of sunlight and then they were out in a courtyard. Another interminable ceremony finally freed them from Lord Ando and the foreign ministers.

Sir Radley pronounced himself pleased. Pity about the robe but proper respect had been shown Her Majesty's servants. The palace he dismissed as plain and the screens as vulgar. All agreed the Tycoon looked a poor sort.

Back at the Tozenji, Sir Radley provided a cold collation for celebration. Oscar relieved his nerves with champagne, but wine could not refresh Pev and after a short while he slipped away for a bath. In his room he tore off his woollen clothes and reached for one of the cotton native robes worn to the bathhouse. Suddenly he caught sight of himself in his shaving mirror: tallow-coloured skin splotched with a rosy rash and a sprinkling of brown hairs. He remembered the sea-captain in the print and shivered.

Another robe hung from a peg in the anteroom of the bathhouse. The same desire for a bath had struck James Wilson and he was already soaking in the deep tub.

'Room for two, Pev. Come along.'

'Yes, I will, if you do not object. I feel very – sticky.'

'And big! Two of those chaps would make up one of me.' His face split in a friendly grin.

Hunkering on the slatted boards Pev rubbed himself with the bran-bag. The warm comforting water he tipped over his shoulders hit the gravelled soil with a gurgle.

'Do they not sweat and suffer in the heat as we do?'

'Aye, must do. But they just do not seem to show it.'

They soaked in companionable silence. Beyond the dim room pleasant murmurs of a summer night soothed: frogs, insects and the rustling of small busy creatures.

James laughed suddenly. 'Would not folk in Sheffield be 'mazed to see their lad in a bath like this? And the third this week!'

Pev laughed too. 'I suppose we have gone native.' After a moment he asked, curious about this serious young man whose full life set him so apart from the others in the

Legation, 'Do you miss Sheffield? Your family and all?'

'Oh, aye. Often at Segawa's clinic I wish my father were there to consult. Or my grandfather. He was an apothecary with more in common with Segawa than he would credit. Did not reckon foreigners much. Nor does Segawa.'

'Will you return to Sheffield when your Japanese adventure finishes?'

James did not answer. Fearing that he had been unduly inquisitive, Pev squirmed unhappily.

Then James said, 'I'm not certain I want my "Japanese adventure" to finish.

'As for Sheffield, do you know of Grinder's Disease?' His voice in the dusk sounded suddenly old, tired.

'No, I am afraid not.'

'A form of asthma, common in the Sheffield cutlery mills. The lungs of the cutlery polishers are ravaged by the fine dust made by steel against the grinders' wheel. A cutlery polisher is a sick man at thirty, dead at forty-five. Consider that.'

'It is appalling.'

'Each year my father petitions the mill owners to provide some protection for the men and women, if only a mask. Each year the employers argue that asthma is a common ailment among the workers. Damp houses, bad food. True, of course, but not all the story. My father experiments with cures – inhalation of ether or decoction of seneca. For those far gone, gin and water is the solution. He is obsessed with the ailment. As he should be. Such suffering is not necessary.' Again he paused. Pev waited in the warm dark silence. 'But if I return to Sheffield, his fight must become mine. I will never be Dr James Wilson but Richard Wilson's son. Not to involve myself entirely in his crusade, for it is a crusade, would be the most terrible, unthinkable disloyalty. But there is so much else that interests me. Beri-beri. Cholera. Now *there* is a contagion! Summer pestilence. The action of tumours.' He laughed, a rich warm sound, and suddenly he was a young man again. 'Does that seem selfish? Aye, it does. I know it.'

His tone was casual but through the intimacy of darkness Pev sensed unspoken emotion: guilt, perhaps even defiance.

He remembered the evening he told his parents of his intention to join the Far Eastern Service. Late summer sun had dappled the pattern of lace curtains over mahogany and maroon plush in the drawing-room. Such an overwhelming room, exuberant with pictures and flowers and bowls and lamps and mirrors and gilt and tables and chairs and stools and shelves and books. His lace-capped mother, intent on her cards; his father, leaning against the carved garlands of the mantelpiece and yearning for the quiet of his library and brandy bottle; his stolid brother; his silly sister-in-law; each spared half-attention as he described his ambition, his ache to see the East. And then: 'Very well, Peverel. If your tutor is in agreement. The prospects seem reasonable although I am sure your mother would prefer that you remained here in Exeter,' his father said. His mother smiled up from the cards in her jewelled hands, love vague in her eyes: 'Well, of course you will not settle there. A year or two, perhaps.' He was her handsome son, an MA of Oxford University, the envy of her 'circle'. This choice would most certainly enhance his glamour. Although it might be as well to describe his appointment as 'something in the Foreign Office'. The Consular Service was rather – But of course this Far Eastern affair must be different. Peverel had said so.

Now in the dark camphor-scented bath Pev found himself grateful that never had he needed to feel guilt or defiance – but he was also just a little sad. Had James known something he had missed?

3
Masayuki

In the time of the Great Heat, Lord Okubo finished his
year's service at the Shogun's court. A train of mounted
samurai, foot soldiers and porters plodded down the
Tokaido over pine-cooled hills, across marshes and
through emerald rice paddies to Odawara. The procession
toiled up the steep angled ramps between stone walls greasy
in the sun. A spreading cedar as old as the castle itself cast its
spiky shadow over the glittering gravel of the great courtyard. Sweating bearers gently lowered the norimon. Geta
were arranged under its sliding panel. The daimyo stepped
out. He travelled alone; his wife and children remained
as permanent hostages in his Yedo palace according to
Tokugawa custom.

His impassive gaze swept over the bowed heads of his
retainers, kneeling rank after rank to the corners of the vast
courtyard. Words of greeting murmured through the men,
welcoming their lord to his castle where he would spend the
next twelve months. With a grunt of acceptance he turned
and walked stiffly towards the keep where his Odawara
household awaited him in prostrate rows. Behind him the
samurai still knelt on the hot gravel.

As soon as a command dismissed the castle samurai
Masayuki looked anxiously around. Ohno Tatsuya was
nowhere to be seen. Yet he must be there. He could not
simply ignore the daimyo's yearly arrival. Through the
shifting confusion of brown or black kami-shiro he sought
out the Ohno crest, but when he found it the curled rice
shaft was not on his friend but on the broad back of Ohno's
father stepping into the privileged company of the keep,
but hesitantly, as though not sure of his welcome. An
official of importance, the head of the Ohno family had
aged suddenly in the last months. White streaked his top-
knot, his yellowing face was wrinkled like a golden plum

86

abandoned in the sun. It was whispered that his youngest child, Tatsuya, believed to be seduced by the xenophobes of the Jōi party, caused him not just much sorrow but fear for his family's position with the daimyo.

Fretting over his friend's absence, Masayuki walked slowly past a group of castle bureaucrats chatting under the shade of the cedar. One, Iruka, Ohno's older brother, reached out to stop him. Plump and soft, a samurai of the writing brush not the sword, Iruka studied Masayuki coldly. 'It has been said that Tada Masayuki too frequents the Zen temple by the Mountain Gate. Is that true?'

'I have visited that temple, Ohno San.'

'Yet you show your face at the castle. Before the daimyo. Why have you not fled to Shinagawa with my brother? Why have you not joined the Jōi rebels who plot against the Bafuku and kill the barbarians?'

'Has Tatsuya done this? Has it gone this far?'

'So I believe. He praises their patriotism and speaks against our daimyo.'

'Will he now become a ronin? Is it definite?' But he knew his question was foolish. Today, the most important of the year at the castle, Ohno Tatsuya was absent.

'So I suppose. To his father's shame.' He added sourly, 'Wise is Tada Masayuki that he deafens himself to the serpent hissings of Mito and Satsuma.'

But Masayuki, turning away, did not feel wise. He felt bewildered and betrayed – and afraid. Ohno had moved beyond his grasp into a new world and had not bid Masayuki join him in dedicating his sword, his very life, to the Imperial Will. Ohno now walked by the side of men such as Kojima, the Mito ronin with the fire of action in his eyes. And Masayuki had been left behind.

And yet was this not Masayuki's own fault? After the first meeting at the Zen temple he had given in to doubts and fears. Service to the daimyo of Odawara was the root of his life; from this root reached out vines to bind him to the Emperor, to his family and to the laws of bushido.

Ohno had replied truthfully to his fears: 'Loyalty to the Emperor is the highest loyalty. "To know and act are one and the same." You *know* the Emperor's will. It is no mystery. He has spoken against the presence of the barbarians.

Now Masayuki must act on the knowledge as I do. There is no choice. Abandon Odawara.'

The enormity of such an act terrified Masayuki. If he were not a man of Odawara, who was he?

Desperately, he pleaded, 'You are the third son. If I leave the daimyo's service, what will be the fate of my family?'

'Have you not a brother? Lord Okubo's chosen scholar of medicine? Will his stipend not fill the bellies of the Tada if Tada bellies crave rice over loyalty?'

Masayuki had murmured, 'I do not think my mother will accept rice from Shoh.'

Ohno snapped, 'Do you think Akiko Sama, daughter and wife and mother of samurai, wishes her son to serve a daimyo who refuses to obey the Emperor's will?'

'It is a terrible circle, Ohno,' he had cried. 'I cannot know my mother's karma. If she starves, it will be on my hands.'

Suddenly Ohno softened. 'Yes, your decision is hard, harder than mine was. But, Masayuki, the correct path is the only path.'

His head whirling, Masayuki had turned away. But now, in the hot sun of the courtyard, he knew that Ohno had understood that it was not just for Akiko that Masayuki feared, but for himself. And so Ohno abandoned him to that fear and stepped out on the path alone.

In the last sultry days of summer he stalked the castle, attacking his duties like a tiger seizes its prey. At night he hurried through the larch woods to the Zen temple but found only monks in those gloomy halls.

Akiko watched Masayuki train Shohtaro in swordsmanship, pushing the child to his limit as though fearing – or hoping – time was short. But the relentless confusion in her son's manner worried her. Each afternoon she went to pray for his spirit, begging the gods to steel his soul. One son, Shoh, was lost to her, a despised medicine man, an ally of Nippon's enemies. May the gods guide Masayuki along the path of the samurai, a path he must choose himself.

The season of storms arrived. Winds tugged the leaves on the trees, blew down fences, freshened the stifling air. Flame and gold streaked the dark foothills. Hanae laid away the mosquito nets and swept the storage sheds. Ohisa scrubbed the pickle barrels. Another autumn and still her womb was empty but Akiko no longer mocked her. It was almost as though she had ceased to exist for her mother-in-law.

One cool clear evening a messenger from Yedo rushed into Lord Okubo's audience chamber. Three days later Masayuki was among a company of thirty samurai ordered to appear in formal kami-shiro at the castle. He found the horses groomed, their wooden saddles polished. A forest of banners tilted and rustled, awaiting a cause. He chose a mount and climbed into the saddle.

'What is this all about?' he asked Kamada, a samurai his own age, but before an answer came orders were shouted and the procession of unshod horses shuffled down the ramps and through empty streets to the Tokaido.

The highway was deserted. All the tea houses and inns were shuttered, hidden from travellers by high screens of thick cotton painted with the Okubo crest stretching along both sides of the road. As they rode between these quivering walls towards the river Kamada whispered, 'We go to meet a party of barbarians. Officials travelling from Yedo to Fuji San will spend the night at the daimyo's guest house. Incredible, is it not? I cannot wait to see what they look like.'

'This cannot be true. Outsiders on the road to Miyako! Outsiders to climb Fuji San!'

'Certainly they will not be permitted to climb the Sacred Peak? Just to worship there. Eh?'

'This government of old women will let the barbarians walk over them with their boots on,' Masayuki protested.

'Steady, Tada,' Kamada cautioned. 'Speak not like Ohno Tatsuya. You know full well where our lord's loyalty lies.'

Masayuki glared at him but said no more.

On the river bank an enclosure had been encircled with vast lengths of silk cloth marked with the Okubo crest. Commanded into two lines, the samurai waited. Down here on the low-lying river bank the air was hot and heavy. Late mosquitoes swirled over the still water. Chevrons of geese flapped overhead on their way to winter feeding grounds. Further down river Masayuki could see a crane making stately progress through the reeds. All familiar. Soon to be contaminated by what? Masayuki had just remembered Shoh. Would he be with these foreign devils?

A messenger darted out from the pine-shadowed road on the opposite bank and waved his arms. The barbarians were in sight. Another messenger ran off towards the castle to summon the lord.

The expedition was ridiculously large. Over a hundred men and fifty horses straggled up to the ford. Masayuki snorted. They travelled like daimyo. Crossing the river took hours. The porters made trip after trip bearing officials and servants and finally the long-nosed devils themselves across the stretch of shallow water as the sun glowed, a gold disc over the purple foothills.

Lord Okubo's norimon arrived. Resplendent in court robes, he slid out to greet the leader.

'From what country are they?' Masayuki asked Kamada, who was always versed in castle gossip.

'England, I heard.'

England! Was that not the nation Shoh served? Masayuki could not remember but now the enemy was before him and he narrowed his eyes the better to study them. Huge, pink-faced, grossly covered with thick hair, they were every bit as repulsive as he had hoped. The leader, bristling with evil black eyebrows and whiskers, peered down from his unnatural height, dwarfing Lord Okubo. His manner was condescending, clumsy. With ill grace he entered the screened enclosure followed by his compatriots; one, even taller than himself; a second, who had a head covered with hair curled like a dog's, glared nervously around him at all times. He is frightened, Masayuki thought with pleasure.

The rituals of welcome would take a stick of time at least. Tea, saké, presents, courtesies all given their proper importance. Masayuki now had time to scan the crowds of attendants for Shoh, half-dreading, half-hoping to find him. But he was not there. Akiko would be relieved. Or would she? Masayuki was not sure. If Shoh had been in the party it would be gratifying to show contempt for the treasonous Tada.

Abruptly the barbarians emerged from the enclosure and

strode to their horses. A grumble of amazement went through the samurai. The welcoming rituals could have hardly begun. Lord Okubo appeared looking bemused and rather put out.

With much shouting and jostling the Englishmen mounted. The leader paced his horse up and down, growling with impatience as the daimyo's procession arranged itself slowly as befitted the dignity of a great man.

Masayuki rode back into Odawara, to all appearances one of thirty Odawara samurai escorting his lord's guests to the official inn. But in his heart Masayuki recognized that Ohno had been wise, far-seeing. Motionless on his horse, a well-built figure in his kami-shiro marked with the Okubo crest, he watched the daimyo lead the barbarians through the gates of the guest house. When the thirty samurai were dismissed, he walked back to the Tada home determined that he must serve the Emperor alone.

A hulking form stepped from the shadow of the cherry tree by the Tada gate.

'Oi, Tada Masayuki. Have you seen enough? Are you ready to decide?'

'Ohno! Where have you come from?'

'That does not matter. It is where I am going that matters. Will you come with me?'

'Do we strike now at the barbarians before they further defile our sacred places?'

'No. You are not yet ready for that. Come with me now to Shinagawa. Then make your final decision.'

Masayuki glanced through the gate at the Tada house but Ohno touched his arm.

'Akiko Sama is samurai. She understands perhaps better than Masayuki does. Come. Talk to Kojima. He will help you.'

The causeway baked in the sun, a white streak across the marshes. Stone block houses, oven-hot, dotted its length from Kanagawa to Yokohama. In the far distance the bay glittered.

'By day,' Ohno said, 'it is impossible without papers to pass the guards. The Bafuku seek to protect the corruption they inflict on Nippon. But, after dark, by boat along the

91

coast to the beach, it is possible, even easy, to enter the town.'

Masayuki strained his eyes but could see only reeds and willows. Water fowl chuntered in thick clumps of swamp grass. But in his mind the raw new port gaped like an open sore on the coast of Nippon.

Ohno touched his sleeve. 'Come, let us hurry on to Shinagawa. The sun dips and we must be at the tea house by dusk.'

One more look at the causeway and then Masayuki tipped down his wide hat and turned towards Kanagawa.

A massive figure came crashing down the path toward them. Suddenly the sweet day was tainted by a peculiarly sour odour.

Masayuki glimpsed coarse features and a hooked nose in a blotched red face darkened by a wiry growth of beard. The man's frame was large but he was soft, no soldier, although a pistol protruded from his belt and a long-barrelled gun rested on his shoulder. Slung over the other shoulder were two limp ducks.

At the sight of the samurai the outsider stopped dead, grabbing at the butt of his pistol. Masayuki jerked his sword half from his scabbard before Ohno's hissed 'No!' stopped him.

'He has killed. Within the Shogun's domain to kill is a crime. For us or for an outsider. He who shoots the Shogun's game dies!'

'No. Put back the sword!' Ohno's tone of command so startled Masayuki that he obeyed immediately.

Tensed, the three men waited, watching obliquely like tom cats poised for a signal to attack or withdraw. After minutes, the outsider, hand on pistol, edged around to circle the samurai, who held their ground. Finally free, he strode rapidly to the causeway.

'Why?' Masayuki demanded.

'Do not be a fool. The samurai in the guardhouse would seize you. See. Two stand by watching now. Besides, he had a pistol.'

'My sword would have had his hand off before he could fire.'

'Be not so sure.'

'Ha!'

'Tada, this is not the killing we want. Any dead outsider is a victory but this death would not be in accordance with bushido. Whatever loyalty may be written on your heart, you still wear Lord Okubo's crest on your haori. To kill in sunlight or moonlight one must be a ronin. What samurai would deliberately embarrass his lord, whatever the lord's error might be?'

'Ohno speaks truly.' But suddenly Masayuki wheeled back to the causeway. The barbarian could still be seen, ducks bumping against his back. 'Ohno! The samurai on guard. Why did they not seize the man for his crime? He still has the ducks.'

'One piece of silver buys the soul of Nippon in Yokohama. Come. To the Tokaido.'

The great highroad curved around the edge of the bay to Shinagawa, last post-station before the gates of Yedo. This disorderly suburb beyond the grasp of the city's constables was made up of narrow lanes packed with brothels and tea houses, all overlooked by rich temples nestling in the wooded hills.

Ohno and Masayuki passed through the barrier before the Hour of the Dog and negotiated streets lively with food vendors and musicians touting their skills in any opening in the thronging crowds. Purposefully Ohno threaded his way to a curtained booth where the hoarse voice of a story-teller chanted a rousing tale of Miyamoto Musashi. Ohno did not part the curtains to enter the crowded booth but darted instead into a twisting alley winding down towards the bay. A salt, fishy sea smell freshened the city air.

On the edge of the beach were two buildings: one was hidden by a high fence but over the narrow gateway a discreet sign declared the Komatsu-ya, the House of the Small Pine. The other, a tea house called The Dragon's Pearl, stood apart in a fan-shaped spread of gardens.

Masayuki followed Ohno into the tea house where a proprietress greeted them. Ohno ignored her purred compliments and strode around the verandah past noisy open rooms to a flight of stairs masked by wisteria. Upstairs an outside corridor ran along a series of rooms discreetly

93

screened for privacy. Ohno knelt by a half-opened shoji and Masayuki did the same.

'Humble greetings. Ohno Tatsuya of Odawara accompanied by Tada Masayuki.'

'Welcome, Ohno Tatsuya and Tada Masayuki. Enter, sit. We shall watch the sun set on the sea. Then we shall talk.'

A ronin with a top-knot as silver as a badger's back sat by the low balustrade gazing out at the wind-bent pines and the glowing bay. A tray with saké decanter and cups waited beside him. No maid was in attendance.

Masayuki settled on his heels and composed himself for the sunset. Sea birds cried, greedily wheeling from beach to fishing boats. The scent of pines in the sea air was stronger than the mountain pines of Odawara. The colours of the water shifted from gold to pearly white to grey to black.

Finally the silver-haired ronin turned to survey his companions. Masayuki recognized Kojima, the Mito man who had sat apart at Odawara, the man who had killed the Russian.

'Pine scents. Late summer
One last seagull is floating,
the bay now turns dark.
Sun sets over Yamato,
truly island of the gods.'

Silently the two younger men bowed in praise of the poem.

'Has the news reached Odawara? Old Lord Mito is dead. Of summer pestilence or Bafuku poison. The truth is unknown.'

Ohno said, 'My heart weeps.'

Kojima's lined handsome face remained a mask but Masayuki sensed the pain behind the mask.

'Although circumstances forced me to become a ronin, in my heart old Lord Mito always remained my lord.' He pointed out towards the shadowy island forts in Yedo harbour. 'Those guns made from the bronze of Mito temple bells are his memorial. Copies of the outsiders' own cannon. He had them cast by the swordsmiths of Nippon to fire on the outsiders. If only the Bafuku were not too weak to use them.'

94

'A fine memorial, Kojima San.'

'A fine memorial only when their fire destroys barbarian ships.' He poured saké. 'Ohno has made his preparations? He too is now a ronin, ready to serve his Emperor until death?'

Masayuki looked at Ohno's round white face, so calm, so sure. Gone for ever was his shambling playmate of the practice yard and lesson room, replaced by this man dedicated to a cause in which he believed.

Ohno answered solemnly, 'This Ohno Tatsuya is ready to die rather than exist in a Nippon polluted by barbarians. My filial duty to my parents is complete. I am the third son.'

'Yes, and your wife?'

'I have divorced her. She, and my child, will however remain in my family home.'

'Well done. A man cannot act surely unless his family duties are accomplished. Welcome to the Brotherhood of the White Cherry.'

Kojima now turned to Masayuki. 'And this young samurai? Have I seen him before?'

Ohno replied, 'In Odawara. But since then he has seen the barbarians approach Fuji San and he has learned that the danger of defilement is real. He wishes to serve the Emperor but I believe his heart is not yet certain. And he has a mother whose future he fears for if he leaves home. This Ohno brought him to Kojima San who can convince the quicksand to stand firm.'

Kojima laughed, a startling sound in the dimming room quiet but for the wind in the pines and muffled merriment from downstairs. 'How great is Ohno's faith. Would all our movement shared it! Then we could move as surely as a tiger to victory. As for Tada Masayuki, trust only in your own reverence for the Imperial Throne and its will.' Stern eyes bent on Masayuki. The boy forced himself to meet the stare. 'Go back to Odawara. Filial obligations must come first or the Nippon for which we die is a sham. When your mother's peaceful future is assured, return. There is work for Tada Masayuki in Shinagawa and the Brotherhood of the White Cherry will welcome him.'

*　　*　　*

Masayuki's absence went unmentioned in the Tada household. The women bent to their tasks, eyes averted from Akiko's indomitable presence. Ohisa was berated for salting two kegs of aubergine rather than cabbage although the vegetable seller brought aubergine and not cabbage. In her confusion the girl split some precious salt and had to endure Akiko's fury as she swept it into the dirt floor of the kitchen.

On the verandah Hanae took apart and relined winter kimono. As her fingers picked and sewed her mind ran over the charcoal and oil, vegetables and salt to be bought when Masayuki's rice stipend was granted. But if he did not return . . .

Avoiding the tense women, Hideko skulked around the kitchen yard dodging even her brother, who practised his sword exercises with passionate determination.

Nor was the visit of the barbarians discussed. The vegetable seller's gossip was hushed by Ohisa's frown. If Kimi, the little maid, chattered on such matters to shopkeepers or in the public baths, she knew to still her tongue in a house of samurai women.

On the sixth day Masayuki returned. Ohisa heated the bath and removed grimy sweat-stiff clothes. Bathed, dressed in hakama and black kimono with the maple leaf crest of the Tadas, he retired to the tea pavilion to await Akiko.

Neatly boxed between the wall bright with the last morning glories and a small screen of willows, the four-and-a-half-mat thatched hut exuded calm. Delicately latticed shoji opened on to a tiny pond clogged with water reeds. The main house could be neither seen nor heard.

He took the tea utensils from a cupboard. The rough earthenware between his hands soothed him. Methodically he arranged them, clearing his mind of all but the ritual to be performed.

Akiko arrived and knelt formally opposite him, her back to the alcove framed by two smooth columns of twisted red pine.

Silently, with great ceremony, Masayuki made the tea and passed the coarse bowl of black Raku ware to his mother. She gazed at the treasure, feeling the warmth of the tea on her palms. Then she drank, turned the bowl and, bowing, gave it to Masayuki.

'This Masayuki has returned with unresolved problems he humbly asks his honoured parent to receive.' The measured old-fashioned cadence of his language emphasized his fatigue.

' "To know and to act are one and the same!" So says the great scholar.'

'That is true.'

'Right knowledge is duty.'

'This Masayuki believes he has right knowledge. To serve the Emperor. To drive away the barbarians who contaminate Nippon. But the execution of knowledge proves difficult.'

'The correct path is often the steepest where thorns grow thick.' Unflinching, Akiko stared at him.

'This Masayuki must embrace the life of a ronin. Lord Okubo cannot be held responsible for my actions.'

'The decision is truly a serious one. But my younger son has the iron resolution of samurai just as the Chrysanthemum sword is forged on an iron core.' Pride flared in the sinuous Buddha eyes. 'Masayuki is a true son of a samurai family, the Iwa family of Suruga.'

Even through the numbness of his exhaustion, Akiko's implication shocked him. Never had she made so clear her contempt for his father and Shoh.

Coolly she continued, 'Ohisa must be divorced.'

'Yes. But it is for my mother that my heart cries out. This house may be lost to her. And what of her daily rice?'

'Samurai women do not fear hunger. Only the shame of failed duty. Masayuki is now my sole son, Shohtaro my sole grandchild. We will go to Suruga. The Iwa family will be proud to receive the mother and the nephew of one who serves the Emperor.'

Masayuki felt a dizzying surge of release. His feet were set on the path. Then the emotion ebbed and his head drooped in exhaustion. But he tensed his muscles and drew himself up again.

Akiko smiled.

He would not turn back now.

4
The House of the Small Pine

Dirk Meylan smiled up at Pev. Sprawled in one of the Tozenji's basket chairs, blond hair in stiff spikes, red cheeks bright from a brisk ride, he looked like an irredeemably naughty elf.

'So, my poor dear Pev has been abandoned? A sad orphan toddling through the empty rooms of the Legation.'

'Well, almost. James, Oscar and Sir Radley may be standing on Fujiyama's summit this very moment but Basil Foxwood is still here, in charge.'

'Ah.'

'Quite. He bleats at me over dinner,' Pev complained. 'I am his captive; the recipient of far more information about his ancestral home in Sussex than any but a Foxwood heir would wish to learn.'

'So even Oscar Sullivan has undertaken this momentous expedition to Fujiyama? Venturing outside the treaty lands straight into the teeth of the Tycoon's killers?'

'Against his own wishes. But Sir Radley was definite. I should have adored to go but Oscar has the greater command of Japanese – although my sketches would have made a useful record. Just think – the first Englishmen in four hundred years to travel in the interior. I am sure Oscar is chewing on his handkerchief in terror.' Pev slapped crossly at a fly.

'Poor old Sullivan.'

'Nonsense.'

Dirk looked quizzically at Pev. 'Oscar lacks the John Bull spirit, does he? The playing fields of Eton and all that?'

'You sound rather like Mr Jessop.'

'Mr Jessop is an American and I am Dutch. Allow us our little prejudices.'

'Were it not for the Royal Navy cruising Chinese waters

none of us would be here!' Pev retorted. 'Your precious Mr Jessop snatched his treaty from the smoking barrel of our cannon in Canton!'

For a second the elfin face hardened, then Meylan shrugged and leapt to his feet. 'Let us not quarrel. What shall we do? Shall we explore the seamy haunts of bandits and ruffians? Storm the Tycoon's palace?'

Pev laughed nervously, never entirely convinced that Dirk would not explore a seamy haunt. A polite cough from the doorway saved him from the embarrassment of rejecting these preposterously dangerous ideas. 'Aha! Tada Shoh,' he cried gratefully.

The doctor bowed and returned Meylan's greeting in Japanese.

Pev said, 'I asked Tada Sensei to join us for dinner. Basil and I were dull and required a change of company. And naturally the doctor's conversation improves my Japanese.' He frowned. 'But in the surprise of your visit, Dirk, I quite forgot about Tada Sensei.'

'I have a capital idea,' Dirk declared. Pev regarded the Dutchman with hope, Shoh with interest. 'Shall we three bachelors leave Foxwood to the stringy fowl and no doubt lumpy puddings of your Legation cook and betake ourselves to a tea-house? I feel a compelling desire for feminine companionship.' To Shoh he added in Japanese, 'A lively, playful place. Somewhere the doctor patronizes himself.'

The Dutchman's request was an awesome one and at first Shoh was puzzled. Few tea houses would welcome these strange creatures. But in Shinagawa, where silver opened doors and closed mouths, a few hours' pleasure might be purchased. On his visits to Umegawa he found her not too low at heart; the plum was indeed a tenacious flower but she sadly missed her friend Kaoru and the promenades and excitements of the Yoshiwara. In Shinagawa, that town of loose laws, scandals were rare as purple plum blossom. Two barbarians would enliven her day and coax up her little chin.

Horses and an escort were called for. Pev chattered gaily about this first visit to the notorious suburb while Meylan probed gently for details of the British excursion to Fuji. Although he liked Pev, his visit today was not wholly innocent. Mr Jessop wished to be kept informed of Perfidious Albion's ambitions.

As for Shoh, the welcome signs of autumn were everywhere: a city washed to sparkling by the typhoon rains. Piled high in baskets were crunchy green soya beans. Scarlet persimmons glowed like fox-fires on stray trays. Shaggy-headed chrysanthemums stood prim in cerulean pots, tamed cousins of the wild maroon flowers sprouting in profusion in any neglected corner.

At the Tokaido gate they joined the wide ribbon of road unrolling through hills emblazoned with vermilion, orange and saffron. Only the dark conifers kept their sombre dignity. At Shinagawa the road cut between the bay and the cliffs. Narrow streets wound away between tall walls and mysteriously shuttered houses: closed, evil streets that sent a shiver down Pev's spine as had the filthy back stews of Exeter that he and a friend once nervously prowled on a dare.

Shoh turned blithely down such an alley. Peeping through the greasy curtains half-masking the shanties' interiors, Pev glimpsed men, many vigorously tattooed, lounging on tatami-covered benches or grouped around dice games.

'Perhaps this was not so wise,' Dirk murmured. 'It quite slipped my mind that Shinagawa is frequented by the lowest scoundrels.'

'I have noticed several with swords,' Pev agreed unhappily. 'Two swords.'

'This district is a haunt of samurai, I fear. Maybe we should turn back.'

But then the alley twisted and widened and before them the sea sparkled through a copse of pines.

'Aha! Now this is what I had imagined.' Samurai forgotten, Dirk slid from his horse and breathed in the sharp air.

'You think it is all right then?' Pev asked worriedly but already he was falling under the spell of the lonely autumn beach, the gnarled pines and the mewing sea birds. 'Well, it looks peaceful enough here.'

On their left was another of the blank uninviting houses

like those they had passed. A few scarlet trees rose above the tall bamboo fence. The gate was narrow with posts fashioned from two rough pine trunks. The other establishment, on their right, was larger, a more graceful structure with verandahs and balconies, set among gardens running down to the beach.

'The "Abode of the Dragon's Pearl",' Dirk read the characters painted on a slab of wood. 'Pretty name. Pretty gardens.' He glanced over at the closed house. 'Let us hope pretty maidens.'

Shoh was negotiating with a middle-aged woman who screwed her painted face into a grimace of distrust. Unhappily she surveyed the two over-sized barbarians with their heavy boots. Finally, at Shoh's urging (and when Dirk and Pev had removed the offending boots), she led them to a large pleasant room opening out on to a sheltered garden. With an incomprehensible burst of Japanese she firmly slid the shoji shut, enclosing them in a small private den.

Shoh explained, 'The Oba-san worries over white men. Many samurai come here. But early now. No other guests.'

Dirk turned from contemplating the garden. He pulled off his gloves. 'And young ladies?' he asked in Japanese.

'They will come from the Komatsu-ya across the way. A house of night-blooming flowers. Not the finest in Shinagawa but a good house. No obligations. Meylan San understands?'

'Very well,' Dirk laughed. 'You have chosen the perfect place. Have you a favourite or a girl you would recommend? I am feeling uncommonly in need of affection.'

'Three will come. Only one of these I know and Meylan San is welcome to her.'

'Never mind. All three will be charming. This will do the youngster some good. And not just his grasp of Japanese although any language is enriched by pillow talk, eh, Tada Sensei?'

Shoh nodded, somewhat surprised by Meylan's concern for the puppy, Peverel Fitzpaine.

Pev had been exploring. 'Is it not pretty? Those chrysanthemums in the alcove. It is all so charmingly fragile,

101

one is almost afraid to step. And the garden is lovely, although I suspect one has a view of the sea from the other side. I wish we had such places in England.' He did not see Dirk's amused glance at Shoh. 'Ah, someone is coming.'

The shoji slid back. Pev stared at the tiny bowed form kneeling in the entrance. His first impression was of a child in a garish kimono topped by glossy rolls of hair. The child murmured to Shoh and slipped gracefully into the room, eyes modestly down.

'Other women will follow but this lovely blossom is Umegawa whose home city is the same as mine. She bids you welcome to The Dragon's Pearl,' Shoh said.

'Greetings, Umegawa Sama,' Pev whispered.

Slowly she raised her heavy head. He looked down at the loveliest girl he had ever seen: a gently arched nose, sweetly rounded cheeks curving down to red lips, a firm chin and a tender throat. Her eyes were gently slanting, soft brown, shy and curious, and from somewhere, in the unplumbed depths, a merry smile twinkled up at him.

For the first time in his twenty-two years, Peverel Fitzpaine lost his heart.

The garden was melting into darkening shadows when Dirk returned to the little room followed by a giggling girl, Rika. He smiled at the litter of cups and bowls on the lacquered table. A plump moon-faced woman dressed in an orange-patterned kimono was pouring saké for a rather bored Shoh Sitting by a half-opened window, Pev bent his face, flushed with eagerness, toward Umegawa, whose deft fingers folded coloured paper into birds and animals for his rapt amusement.

'A convivial scene. Pity, my dear, but see how the light fails. We must depart, you know. The Tokaido gate closes at dusk and we dare not be stranded in Shinagawa with samurai about. Good gracious! Listen to that noise in the next room. The Dragon's Pearl comes to life in the evening and we must flee.'

Pev tore his gaze from Umegawa. 'Have you been away? I thought I missed you.'

'Ahem, Rika San has been showing me the neighbourhood.' The girl smirked behind a raised sleeve. She had a pleasant face with a mouth as wide as a frog's. 'She is a friendly lass. Reminds me of a Dutch housewife. But jollier. Come, Pev. We really must be through the gate by dusk. Shinagawa is not the place for us after dark. Tada Sensei, will you leave or stay?' He shot a pertinent glance at the girl in the orange kimono.

Shoh turned his cup upside down. Two hours of saké and Takao's aimless chatter had given him a headache. For a second he was tempted to stay behind and engage Umegawa for the evening but a glimpse of her absorbed face warned him that she would be a dutiful rather than passionate bedmate. Besides, Takao was the senior whore at the Komatsu-ya. It would not do to reject her company for a younger girl.

Pev gazed sadly into Umegawa's little face, oblivious to the thick coating of white powder and blackened teeth. 'This humble person must leave but this humble person has enjoyed the distinguished company of honourable Umegawa Sama and will endeavour to return soon to The Dragon's Pearl if honourable Umegawa will be generous enough to meet him again.'

This elevation of a whore to the rank of samurai's wife caused much merriment from Takao and Rika. Shoh noticed a naughty gleam in Umegawa's eye as well as she bowed. Lithe as a shrine dancer, conscious that every movement was fascinating to her admirer, she rose and handed Pev his hat and gloves. Shyly yet skilfully she brushed his fingers with hers, peeping up from under her elaborate hair arrangement.

The arrival of the Oba-san with the reckoning dispelled this tender picture. Firmly ushering the white men down a closed corridor, she took no chances with her dangerous clientele. Umegawa and Rika fluttered along behind, bowing and giggling and sighing at the sad separation to come. Takao followed in stately solitude as befitted a senior whore.

Just as they approached the vestibule a ronin came through the outer gate. One glance at the proud figure told the Oba-san that she was in trouble. Before Pev or Meylan could gasp she had whisked open a sliding door and pushed them into a room among a party of surprised farmers enjoying a forbidden evening with some geisha and courtesans. Shoh had seen the two swords and had observed the arrogant bearing. Quickly he took command of the confusion in the room while the Oba-san sailed out to greet her guest and speed him as graciously as possible to the more expensive – and isolated – upstairs rooms where ronin often gathered.

Muttering a steady flow of courtesies Shoh led Pev and Dirk through the bewildered farmers and their ladies, slid open the outside shoji and shoved the two men on to the verandah.

'Go to the horses. Ride back to Yedo. Now. Né, Meylan San, understand?'

'Very much so, my dear. We are off like the wind. Farewell.' And off they went, towering over their giggling escort of Komatsu-ya whores. The garden was empty and so was the open area before the tea house. Waved off by Umegawa and Rika, they departed as quickly as their disorganized samurai guard would permit.

The Oba-san returned to find Shoh alone. In words of extreme courtesy and tones as steely cold as an heirloom sword she made it clear that never again was an outsider to set boot in the vestibule of The Dragon's Pearl.

Nathaniel Jessop looked up from his book as his secretary slid open the shoji. Lamps shed circles of light on the few pieces of heavy furniture – a desk, a table, chairs, planted stolidly on the tatami – a room neither Japanese nor western. Even the American stove, shipped four thousand miles to warm their icy eastern winters, seemed oddly temporary against wooden walls and fragile bric-à-brac picked up during Dirk's perusals of Yedo's back streets.

Jessop listened carefully as Dirk reported on his visit to the British Legation. His fierce blue eyes narrowed as he learned that Sir Radley Ferrier had extracted Lord Ando's permission for the excursion to Fuji.

'Not easily, of course. Apparently the government tried everything: wrong season, sacred mountain, unrest in the countryside, probably rampaging dragons. But you know Sir Radley.' At Jessop's frown, Dirk added, 'Well, you also know the Japanese. They have saddled him with dozens of officials – all, no doubt, spies – and dozens of coolies. Fitzpaine said the cavalcade was quite absurd.'

'But damned if Ando don't play the naïve fool sometimes. If he buckles in to the British on this he will wake up one morning to discover a portrait of Queen Victoria in the alcove and British customs officials running Yedo.'

Meylan smiled in affectionate amusement at his minister's irritation. He had heard this all so often. To lighten the mood he said, 'I wonder if in every town they pass through all the houses and shops will be swathed in cotton cloth – just like huge parcels – as they were when we came up from Shimoda. Remember that journey?'

But Jessop would not be distracted. 'How can Ando ensure there will be no violence against them? The peasants may be calm, the harvest was a good one, but what of the samurai? And on Fujiyama, too. A holy place. Ain't that just asking for trouble?' He peered up at Meylan.

Dirk shrugged. 'I am for bed. Spent the evening in Shinagawa. On your behalf. Pleasant chap, that Fitzpaine, but so – young. Really, he had no inkling of the profession of the woman in the tea house. Quite endearing. Wonder what they do for amusement in Oxford.'

Jessop closed his book and blew out the lamp. 'No point losing sleep over the mysteries of the Japanese official mind.' He rose and not looking at Meylan said, 'I am aware that you like Fitzpaine. So do I now, by the way. It was not quite fair to ask you to pump the boy for information about his fellows. Don't think I am not grateful. Disagreeable world we live in sometimes.'

Meylan grinned. 'You are the walking embodiment of Yankee virtue. Straight as a die. Whatever tempted you into the treacherous shallows of diplomacy?'

'Hrrumph. Good night, Meylan. And I perceive you mix your metaphors. Being Dutch, perhaps. Not born to our tongue.'

Chuckling, the two men separated, each to his own business.

A few moments later, in his room, Dirk extinguished his candle and stood gazing out into the night. Far across the compound dull lights moved in the Buddha Hall and he heard the drone of monks punctuated by the hollow click of a prayer drum. Familiar sounds now, once so exotic, marking the end of each day in Japan.

Nearer, partly obscured by snaky branches shifted by the autumn night wind, lambent squares of shoji glowed gently. Straining his eyes he could just distinguish the blurred figure of a woman dressed in loose house kimono. The sharp edge of the window sill bit into his gripping fingers but, in his concentration, he felt no pain. He waited and watched. Then, as though a black velvet curtain had been drawn, the soft orange light vanished.

Still he kept watch.

Somewhere, close by, a door slid quietly shut. Firm footsteps crunched on a gravelled path, diminishing to silence.

A harsh sigh tore at Dirk's lungs. His head ached. He tried not to imagine what might be taking place in that darkened room across the garden.

Umegawa yawned, stretched, and wriggled from her plum-spattered quilt. Stepping over two other snuffling humps of stirring bedclothes, she pushed back the window. A high sun gilded the bay. Beyond the fringe of creaking pines a few peasant women splashed their sturdy brown legs through crisp wavelets in search of shellfish.

'What a beautiful day!' Fresh salt air blew the fug of stale powder and sleeping women from her head and a sea breeze ruffled her elaborate hair arrangement. Reluctantly she turned from the pleasant beach scene to the ten-mat room. Dusty sunlight filtered over the racks of kimono, their dingy patterns dull against plastered walls. Sprawled among battered mirror stands and make-up chests were the ten pallets of the ten girls of the Komatsu-ya.

How she loathed this low dark cavern, fetid with yesterday's sweat, pickled vegetables, tears. An animal den, seldom swept or aired. Her new home. In her memory the tiny cell in the Omi-ya had blossomed into a spacious pavilion since her banishment behind the high fence of the Komatsu-ya.

But the clients were admiring. There was the bay and the beach and, in Rika, one sympathetic soul at least. She nudged the yawning girl with a bare toe. 'Né, Rika, come and look at the sea. On a day like this Shinagawa is not such a bad place. In the Yoshiwara such a sun never sparkled on the river flats.'

Rika grunted, 'Sleepy.'

'Rika-chan sleeps too much. No wonder old Auntie beats you. Lazy cat.'

'Never enough sleep. Never enough rice.'

Shige, thin-nosed and petulant, peered up from the wooden pillow next to Rika. 'It's cold. If Umegawa is not too important to close that window, might she not do it? Our quilts in Shinagawa are cotton waste, not the warm swansdown of the Yoshiwara.'

Her lips a tight line, Umegawa scooped up a towel and hopped over the row of heaving pallets to the door, which she banged shut behind her on a chorus of angry squeals.

The sea wind snapped through the open window.

'At least tell that stupid servant to bring the noodles!' Shige bellowed furiously at the closed door.

'Waaa! Always with her nose in the air. Proud as a crane just because she first had her sash untied in the Yoshiwara.'

'I like her stories of the Yoshiwara,' Rika mused. 'Imagine a new kimono – silk – made especially for you and then a promenade through the streets just because it's to be your first night. Ara, at the Hour of the Dragon my father snatched Auntie's gold and ran back to his dice games. By the Hour of the Dog the old she-louse was shoving me into the arms of the highest bidder. No samisen lessons or dance steps for Rika. Just a bath, a splash of powder and a cup of saké afterwards. Can't even remember whether he was old or young.'

'Old. They always are. Scrawny and wet-lipped. But Princess Umegawa spends as much time on her back as the rest of us. Who applauds her dance steps now?'

'Né, Shige, that is not all of it, you know. She has a style about her. Customers feel it. It is not just that she has that way of talking or that she paints her face in a new fashion or that Auntie allows her better robes. Her conversation is – smarter – and the customers know she has belonged to a better house. And they spend more silver.'

'Well, I grant that Auntie never hits her. And Takao is afraid of her.' Shige's voice dropped to a whisper; she gestured at Takao, rolled in her quilt in a corner behind a kimono rack. 'What troubles her? She has not spoken since last night and then she threw her powder box at the wall.'

Rika hissed back, 'She is chewing her sleeve because Umegawa's doctor preferred saké to Takao. He wanted Umegawa but he had to give her up so he dipped his nose in his wine cup. Takao kept step with him, decanter by decanter.'

'Each day creases deepen Takao's brow. Soon Auntie will make Umegawa senior whore.'

Rika nodded. 'If Auntie has her way, when we change back to unlined kimono, Takao will be a lone leaf adrift.'

'So, né, such is the life of a woman in the Floating World.' Shige pulled her quilt up to her chin. Her eyes were dark hollows in a pale face, wan beyond her years.

Umegawa slipped back into the room followed by an aged servant who tottered under a tray laden with bowls of noodles.

'At last!' Rika sat up and shivered. She sent a pleading look to Umegawa, 'Né, please?'

Umegawa glanced at the gaping window and then at Rika's quivering shoulders. For a second she wavered and then, chin high, she slid the paper panes across her view.

Ignoring Shige's victorious smirk she settled down next to Rika, already slurping up her food. 'Noodles. Always noodles,' Umegawa muttered.

' "If a girl is clever, she prises open her danna's purse and never suffers from a begging belly".' Between mouthfuls, Rika skilfully mimicked Auntie's dictum.

'Pooh, Shinagawa cook-house rice is gritty and the broiled fish hard as a stone.'

Greed glazed Rika's eyes. 'Describe the dumplings and rice cakes in the Yoshiwara. Console my emptiness with mouth-watering words.'

'Another time. *You* tell *me* about the barbarian last night. What was he like? Were his ivory rod and golden jewels the same as our men's? Né, tell me.'

A whoop came from Shige, 'Ara! Rika clam-mouth!

You had a *barbarian* last night?' Then she looked puzzled. 'Did Rika alone play with the barbarian? Umegawa and Takao were with Rika last night. Né. Here is news.'

Several other girls gathered around an embarrassed Umegawa.

Rika put down her bowl. 'Two barbarians and the Yedo doctor came. One of the barbarians was so heart-struck with Umegawa that his trembling fingers could not untie her sash. Mine was not so shy.' She leered.

'Did he have cloven feet? They say that is why they wear leather sacks on them instead of sandals.'

'Was he hairy as a badger?'

'Ugh, I have heard they have pointed teeth, sharp as daggers and they chew their women.'

'And they smell like the rotting animals they eat.'

'His feet were very big but like ours. He did smell,' Rika admitted. 'And he was covered in yellow hair. His eyes were blue as shallow water. So clear I thought I might peer through them into the workings of his head but, no – weird, those eyes. And his nose was long.'

'And his man-part? Forget his nose. Tell us the interesting things.'

'So, né, Rika, tell us of his loving,' Umegawa pleaded.

'Hm. Well, it was the usual things. Yes, if it were not for the smell, I might have quite enjoyed it.'

One of the girls tugged at her sleeve. 'Did silver pieces slide through his fingers? Some of my danna say the barbarians have chests of gold so heavy a sumo wrestler can hardly lift them.'

Shige agreed. 'The farmers and merchants who sell to Yokohama always have money to spend on a girl. I have heard that one of the white-faces keeps a country courtesan in his quarters and dresses her in silk.'

Umegawa stared at her. 'Shige speaks the truth. This I too have heard. That woman was spoken of in the Yoshiwara. Murasaki San of Shimoda. Many spoke with long tongues of her disgrace but if the barbarians buy our silk and tea, why not our women?' Remembering the young outsider's eager deer-like eyes and shaking hands, she smiled softly. Despite his smell and outlandish conversation, he was oddly attractive to her. After parting from him, later in the evening as she played all too familiar games, her thoughts had wandered back to the barbarian, bringing a shiver of curiosity and, yes, anticipation, that startled her. When mounted high on her third customer of the evening she found herself imagining his shoving golden shaft was that of the barbarian. Afterwards, the panting danna had praised her vigour and promised her an ebony sash toggle she had slyly mentioned as desirable. 'Né, why not our women?' she repeated dreamily.

'Why not our women? Let this Takao tell you why not our women.' The senior courtesan's tense whine shattered Umegawa's thigh-moistening speculations. Shuffling out from her corner, putty-skinned from too little sleep and too much saké, Takao surveyed her juniors petulantly. 'If you were called to play with ronin as I am, you would know the way they talk against the outsider devils. Before they are far gone in wine they boast of how they will cleanse Nippon of this contamination. Do you think they will allow a woman to live who is so little a patriot she permits her flesh to be corrupted? It is a foolish woman who risks their anger.'

'Who speaks of anger? I will not have arguments in my house.'

The Oba-san of the Komatsu-ya bustled into the room. The girls bowed, gliding out of her path, for she was free with slaps and pinches.

Thin as the Omi-ya's Oba-san had been fat, Auntie was a sharp-boned, sharp-minded proprietress wrapped in second quality silk. Uninterrupted by chin, her long face slid down into a skinny neck. Hers were not the solid rice-sack jowls of the Yoshiwara. The vagaries of sub-urban vice kept her quick as a whip-lash.

Her father's only child, Auntie had taken over the Komatsu-ya on his death. She had married and survived the fourth son of the owner of The Dragon's Pearl, a charmer who lavished his short span of days on saké and girls, avoiding his adoring wife except to pleasure her – once each season – with casual efficiency. And yet, now, she kept the flowers fresh before his memorial tablet even when the blooms honouring her ancestors wilted. At least once a day the ping of her little brass altar bell called

110

her husband's spirit for the friendly chat he would not spare her when alive.

Now she coldly surveyed her charges. 'Only those who are too well fed argue. Men pay for sweet women. If jealousy curdles any natures in my house, it is the one with the soured heart who leaves.' Her narrow serpent's eyes flickered over Takao's mottled complexion. 'Especially if that heart is soured by saké.'

Takao's wince chilled Umegawa's blood.

But before too many days passed, Takao's warnings were proved true.

A party of ronin drinking at The Dragon's Pearl called for the Komatsu-ya's finest. Dressed in good figured satin instead of the usual crêpe, Takao, Umegawa and Rika minced across the road led by the doorkeeper's lantern. Between games and dances and trips to the discreet siderooms, Umegawa listened gravely to the growled bravado of her hosts.

In the blackest hour before dawn, the Hour of the Tiger, Umegawa and Rika trudged back. Between them, unravelled by saké, Takao relished her triumph. 'Drive 'em out!' She waved at the dark bay. 'Drive 'em into the sea. Umegawa knows now. Didn't b'lieve Takao. Did you hear me ask about t'Merican whore? Kill 'er. They said that. Kill everybody. White faces. Whores. Everybody.'

Rika caught her as she slumped.

'Ara.' Umegawa took the other shoulder. 'Né, we should wake her up. Auntie –'

Rika yawned. 'May Auntie boil in the same hell as the barbarians; Takao too. I'm sleepy and she's heavy.'

Umegawa grasped Takao's hair-knot and yanked up the lolling head. She slapped the senior whore twice across the face.

'Enjoy that?' Rika asked coolly.

'No!' Umegawa snapped. 'We must not let Auntie see her like this.'

'Why do you care? It will all be to the good for you if Auntie does see her. Anyway, what can we do about it? Auntie will hear. Him, for example. His mouth flows like the Sumida.' The doorkeeper watched them with the bored distaste of a man who knows too much about women.

'Let's drag her. Rika, did you hear what they were saying, those samurai?'

'Yes. Barbarians on Fuji San. Barbarians at Yedo. Our people in America. Kill the lot. Né, Umegawa-chan, their faces were crimson with drink. Those were saké words. True bushi do not wallow in the pleasure quarters.'

Umegawa thought of her father's pride in the samurai of Odawara. Rika was right, of course. Saké boasts spoken by low-class bushi. Shinagawa ronin.

Nothing to worry about.

Together they propelled limp Takao through the narrow pine gate of the Komatsu-ya.

Sir Radley's party returned from Fuji haloed in a rosy glow of triumph. No untoward incident had marred the Englishmen's passage through bucolic Japanese countryside. In Odawara, they reported, they had been welcomed by the daimyo himself, such was their recognized importance.

An evangelical gleam in his eye, James was most impressed by the peasants' cleanliness and rude health. Miss Nightingale's passion for hot water and fresh air seemed vindicated by the native specimens.

Oscar waxed quite astonishingly eloquent describing Fujiyama: 'I stood on the rim of the crater and peered down into that murk and do you know, Pev, I felt as though I were gazing into the soul of the earth. And when one looks out over miles of forest sloping away through drifting clouds, one feels almost a pilgrim at a shrine in this ancient land.' This admission was made with unexpected emotion, surprising Pev, accustomed as he was to Oscar's continual mockery.

His nerve refreshed by the uneventful excursion, Oscar suggested, one fine crisp day, a visit to Asakusa Temple, a great sight of Yedo. But as so often, they found themselves a larger attraction than the famed red Thunder Gate. After a few minutes of the gawping, poking crowds, they fled back to their horses.

'I suppose we should have persevered. The main hall must be full of Buddhist treasure,' Pev called as they urged their mounts through the teeming pilgrims thronged

112

around the stalls selling heathen artifacts.

'Ah, but in this uncharted city one is freed from the Tyranny of the Guide Book. Asakusa is not an Italian cathedral, well documented. As we do not know what we have missed, it cannot matter that we have missed it.'

They passed from the swarming temple district into a broad street lined with theatres and eating houses. Here vividly coloured posters of snarling or simpering actors rivalled their white faces for attention.

The theatre-goers were discreetly dressed, almost entirely men although a few women passed in kago. Before one tall banner-festooned building an exquisite creature in subtly coloured brocades was just stepping from a lowered norimon. This pretty apparition bowed to a gathering crowd and tripped daintily through the heavy door curtains, followed by admiring sighs.

'That, if I am not mistaken, was a man,' Oscar said knowingly. 'Those actors who play women dress and talk like 'em, you know. Even visit the women's side of the public baths.'

'Oh, I say! What a very peculiar race they are!' Pev paused to stare with sharpened appreciation at a poster of two lovers, she melting shyly against his manly bosom as he glared at the world through fiercely crossed eyes. 'Oh, I say!'

The street opened on to the river bank, busy as always with all manner of folk, from the mountainous sumo wrestler to a frail fortune teller with his trained birds, or a black-robed monk holding out his begging bowl. Pev sniffed in the mingling odours of fish and perfume and smoke and freshly cut wood that seemed the very essence of Yedo.

Oscar pointed at a cluster of tiled roofs huddled among dull bronze cherries and sere willows. 'The Yoshiwara. Like the theatres, forbidden to us, more's the pity.'

'Is *that* the Yoshiwara? It seems a rather flat uninteresting spot. I had imagined –'

'So had we all, but like Yokohama it is simply a settlement on the marshes. The Japanese seem to banish all their embarrassments to swamps.'

'Perhaps you are wrong. Those buildings down river are far more impressive.'

'Granaries. So much for glamour.'

'Do the – women – ever leave it?'

'I believe the important ones do. Such as that woman in the kimono with the silver dragons we just passed. You saw her. Teetering along on absurdly high geta with her sash tied in a big bow in front. That is the sure sign of a prostitute. The girl supporting her must have been an apprentice. It is a very organized profession, or so one hears. All the girls have ranks. Very Japanese.'

'Life must be terrible for them. Yet they should not flaunt themselves so, should they?'

Oscar raised a Londoner's eyebrow. 'Do they not flaunt themselves in Exeter and Oxford?'

'Not in silver satin! Or with an apprentice. Like a – a – milliner.' His innocence blazed like a beacon. 'A sensitive Englishwoman would be most compromised here. It is well there is none.'

'Until the missionaries bring black-clothed decency to the heathen.'

'Hm.' Pev was thinking about Umegawa.

'And then, dear Pev, our fun will be over. Mr Jessop will send his "lady" back to Shimoda. No longer will closed norimon slip up to Sir Radley's verandah. Or Foxwood's. And we young bachelors will find ourselves sipping tea with pallid, crinolined daughters of said missionaries. My God, how gruesome. Let us pray the sensible Japanese have understood the horrors wrought in China by Bible-bearing gentlemen and preserve their paganism.'

Pev laughed. 'No more naked coolies or fine ladies passing water in a ditch. Bathhouse windows would be firmly closed against prying eyes.'

'No more Yoshiwara. One wife and one wife only for every man. The likes of Tada Shoh, who has a family in Odawara, by the way, would no longer be the intimate of the Shinagawa women.' Oscar had heard all about The Dragon's Pearl and Umegawa.

'He was very well acquainted with Umegawa,' Pev said in a small voice.

'There you are,' Oscar's tone held a familiar edge of malice. 'One must be a man of the world. Yedo is a city of pleasure. A brothel quarter as large as Chelsea. Have you

114

never wondered about those cosy little alcoves in the tea-houses?'

Pev flushed an angry scarlet. Oscar's meaning was unmistakable. 'Not Umegawa. She is just a maid. A charming waitress. She is not – she could not – such sweetness – such purity.'

'Oh, she is Tada's mistress. No doubt about it. Anyone's mistress for a few string of cash. Yours, even.' He laughed rather cruelly.

A group of half-naked carpenters carrying the saws and chisels of their trade trudged past them. Oscar stared at the bandy little men with ropy muscles and flat incurious faces. 'Just like monkeys,' he said.

One of the labourers poked his companion and, gesturing at the white men, growled a few words. A shout of sudden laughter blasted Pev's ears. He blushed and sank miserably in the saddle.

Sir Radley picked at his stewed apples without enthusiasm. 'Jessop is an odd bird. He fulminates against western ambition, terrifies Lord Ando with exaggerated tales of European expansion in China and then allows his interpreter to service each delegation of evil Europeans that set avaricious foot on Japanese soil. Now Meylan is carrying on negotiations for the Prussians. I don't wonder it will be the Russians themselves next.'

'Oh, I say, steady on. Not the Russians!' Foxwood exclaimed.

Sir Radley regarded his secretary with the same distaste he had allotted the apples, 'I was being facetious.'

'I cannot imagine Prussians will bring much gaiety to our international society,' Oscar complained.

Sir Radley pushed away the offending apples. 'Why is all Japanese fruit so tasteless? Eh? It is a puzzle.' He rose. 'Come, Foxwood, I fear we must spend the evening pondering this affair of Morrison.' He glanced at his interested student-interpreters. 'You must be kept up to date. Wilson here brought a dispatch from the Yokohama Consulate this afternoon. The inevitable has happened. A fool of a merchant – one Matthew Morrison – shot himself a fat goose and then shot and wounded the native policeman who unwisely attempted to apprehend him.'

Oscar paled. 'My God, what will happen? Will he suffer Japanese justice?'

'Of course, according to the treaty his case must be tried by a Consulate Court. But I fear the policeman's injury will complicate the affair.'

'That man was doing his duty,' James Wilson said angrily. 'Morrison claims the gun – cocked, mind you – went off by accident, but the Japanese police reckon that he shot at them in cold blood. Either way, the policeman has a shattered shoulder. The devil of the matter is that his family refuse to let a foreigner – me – examine the wound.'

'If Morrison were a native –' Pev murmured.

'Quite,' Sir Radley grimaced. 'Crucifixion is the penalty for shooting the Tycoon's game, not to mention his officials. Morrison must not suffer that hideous punishment. But this is a test for both sides. The government must ensure that Morrison is heard by Johnstone at the Consulate and Johnstone must ensure that justice is done.'

'If he is sober.'

Oscar's liberty drew a frown from Sir Radley but the frown was one of worry. 'There will be complete sympathy with Morrison in the settlement. All the merchants poach game. If only Morrison had not been caught with the damned goose –'

'Those marshes are teeming with wild fowl.' Foxwood cast a reproachful look at the remains of a bream and the unavoidable stewed chicken left on the dinner table as he followed Sir Radley out.

Pev hoped to escape to the star-lit gardens and his own thoughts but before he could go out Oscar caught his arm.

'Listen, Pev, I must apologize for this afternoon. I do not know what comes over me sometimes. When I catch a glimmer of weakness in a chap, I have to pounce. Then, of course, afterwards, I feel beastly.'

Pev nodded quickly, 'Let's speak no more about it.' He dodged Oscar's sorrowing eyes.

'Thanks, old man. And look, when we next have a free

day, we'll enlist Dirk and make an excursion to your tea house. Is that a jolly idea?'

'That will be capital, Oscar,' Pev replied, but without conviction, not sure that he wanted Oscar's cynical appraisal of Umegawa's virtue.

But Oscar gainsaid him, 'Look, do keep an open mind. Even if she is a – you know – remember, she is Japanese. Not a Christian girl. No morals to speak of. You must not judge her too harshly.'

'No, Oscar, I shall keep an open mind.' And he fled to the frosty garden.

The colourful folk of Shinagawa bustled around the three friends. Riding between Oscar and Pev, Dirk was holding forth, ignoring curious or belligerent stares. 'Well, my dears, they really look too Prussian for belief. Stiff collars up to their noses; backs straight as pokers. I shouldn't be at all surprised if they wear gloves in the bath.'

'But you must help them in their negotiations?' Pev asked.

'God help me, yes. Who else can speak Dutch, German and Japanese? Oh, the boredom of it all. Gallons, simply gallons of tea and then the little green cakes. Ugh! Bowing until one fears one will snap in half, my dear. And then, then, when the Japanese just seem to understand and agree to a point, an official commits suicide or the moon is in the wrong quarter or the Tycoon sneezes, and everybody bows and says, "So very sorry. Misunderstanding. No. No. Impossible." Months of that. Every single point.' He ran an impatient hand over his spiky head. 'Damn Mr Jessop.'

'Dirk!'

'Oh, no. Not really. Perhaps a miracle will happen and the government will become more amenable. Things have been quieter since Lord Mito died. Fewer dire warnings.'

Pev was in no mood for politics; excitement bubbled up in him. 'Oscar wished to meet Umegawa San. I've told him about her.'

Oscar met Dirk's quizzical glance with a shrug.

'A charming young lady,' Dirk murmured.

'Dirk, if I ask you – a rather difficult question – about

117

Mr Jessop – would you give me an answer?'

The Dutchman studied the earnest, eager young face. Had he ever been that innocent? Even as a youth, his first day off the ship in New York, blue eyes round with amazement, pacing the raw, alien streets of the New World, had he been that young? 'You can but ask, my dear,' he replied gently.

'Tell me about Mr Jessop's – wife.'

'Now? In Shinagawa? When I must concentrate on our destination? Which one of these alleys is ours?'

'Please, Dirk.'

He had not the heart to rebuff such an agonized plea. 'Here. Yes. By the story-teller's booth.' He turned his horse into the lane down to the sea.

'Please, now.'

Dirk sighed. 'She was a courtesan from the best house in Shimoda. The daughter of a farmer. Poor land. A drought. Heavy taxes. Daimyos need silver too. The farmer sold Murasaki to meet the taxes. It is the oldest story in the East. Because she was pretty and gifted, she soon made a name for herself – in Shimoda. Singing a little, dancing a little. Country dances. Hardly the stuff of the Yoshiwara, one gathers.' He shrugged, 'Not that one knows. When we arrived, I remember, the girls used to peep between the bamboo slats to catch a glimpse of the terrible barbarians. We could hear them giggling,' he smiled. 'They were shy but friendly, and so curious. Well, wishing to honour Mr Jessop, the town officials gave him Murasaki as a present.'

Pev gasped and then blushed at Meylan's annoyed look. 'Yes, a present. Different lands, different customs. Mr Jessop was appalled, of course. Despite his intemperate youth, he is a god-fearing Yankee and women are not given as presents in upper New York State. Or so I assume. He tried to "return" her but we – he – soon realized that would be impossible. Loss of face for the officials. Loss of face for Murasaki. So. She stayed with us at our temple. In separate quarters.'

The round pink face was bland but his eyes were as hard as blue glass.

'In separate quarters,' Pev repeated. 'Then she is not a – um – what we thought.'

118

'Here we are at The Dragon's Pearl.' Dirk slid off his horse. He smiled an unyielding smile at Pev. 'You asked me about Mr Jessop's "wife". I have related her history but it is neither for you nor me to speculate on what passes between them. Now, shall we go in?' The brittleness in his voice matched his eyes.

But the pretty rooms of The Dragon's Pearl were not for them. The Oba-san proved resolutely unwelcoming. Bowing, smiling, fluttering a fan before her painted lips, she blocked their entrance as perfectly as a brick wall.

Disconcerted, they returned to their horses. One of the giggling escort took pity and pointed to the narrow pine-flanked gate opposite: 'Women.'

Dirk ignored this licentious announcement with great dignity. 'Well, gentlemen, do we retreat with our tails between our legs or do we track the lovelies to their lair?' Clearly, he was keen for adventure.

Pev held back. 'What kind of establishment do you imagine that is? It looks – closed.'

'Do you wish or do you not wish to visit Umegawa?' Oscar asked. 'We have had a long ride, you know. At least there should be saké.'

'But do you think Umegawa is – in there?'

'I rather think she is, my dear,' Dirk said gently.

All the confusions of the last weeks swarmed through Pev as he watched his companions stride up to the gate and pull the bell-rope. Too weak to resist, he followed.

Tattoos rippled over the burly bare chest of the amazed doorman. When Dirk addressed him in Japanese his mouth fell slack, leaving him with a foolish rather than ferocious mien, and hastily he pulled his loose jacket closer as if his vivid chest embarrassed him before strangers. When Auntie hastened out he stood aside, square head, square body, poised to charge these tall but inferior interlopers.

Auntie was in a dilemma. On one hand, she fancied the notoriety that barbarian custom might bring; on the other hand, what would the Brothel Association say? And what sort of activities did outsiders get up to in the bedclothes? Would the wooden frame of the Komatsu-ya bear their great weight? Would her girls bear their great weight?

For a moment she contemplated retiring to her husband's memorial tablet to consult his shade on the best course of action but then she remembered that three girls had been called to The Dragon's Pearl to service outsiders. No doubt these very outsiders. Leaving the doorkeeper to glower, she dashed up to the whores' room. Reassured by Rika that silver was silver and men were men, she returned to the gate and ushered her new clients into an eight-mat room where she poured out saké herself.

Pev studied Auntie covertly. But apart from her own obvious curiosity and eyes as unfriendly as pebbles set in a chinless face, she gave no clue to the sort of establishment they had fallen into. Her discreetly painted kimono was a sombre grey and the room itself was surprisingly barren, seeming dispirited as if it were seldom admired. On a set of shelves irregularly set on the plaster wall were various trinkets, pairs of figurines in rather tortuous poses. A vase in the alcove held one perfect chrysanthemum but the scroll above . . . Pev flushed and looked quickly away. Watching, Dirk was relieved that the boy could not yet read the salacious poem that elaborated on the sensuous drawing.

Upstairs, Umegawa was no less nervous. Scrabbling among her brushes, she quizzed the old maid, 'A darkish one, a pink-faced one and a greenish one with hair like a cabbage leaf? Né, what use are you? Do my hair, not Rika's.'

Takao sat in her corner, plumply stubborn. 'Oba-san can beat me until I faint. Any woman who beds a barbarian will die at the hands of a patriot. Did you not understand the ronin the other night at The Dragon's Pearl? They promised death to the barbarians and all who serve them.' She shivered.

'Bah!' Umegawa replied with a confidence she did not feel. 'Who will know they are here?'

'Ara, did they drop from heaven? All Shinagawa will have seen them.'

Umegawa's hand faltered, smearing her lip rouge. 'Oh, Takao screeches louder than a cicada. All will be well, né, Rika?'

'So, né. Let Shige go down instead. With that long-nosed face of hers they will feel at home.'

Umegawa's reflection swam in the steel mirror. She examined herself closely for she wished to appear as the perfect courtesan. Ginko-leaf hair style; blackened teeth; powder; false eyebrows painted on; red lips. Would he be pleased? Why wouldn't sour, chinless old Auntie give her a better kimono? This one stank of old cosmetics and stale flesh. She arranged her collar lower at the back. Her nape was one of her best points.

But the preparations were all in vain. Her long sleeves shimmering, giggling merrily with Rika, she swept into the room to find it empty except for a bewildered Auntie.

'They fled.' She shrugged her scrawny shoulders. 'One rushed out and the others followed. They are mad as well as ugly.'

Umegawa stared at the scattered saké cups and then around the room for a hint. On the tatami, splayed across a folder of Atami paper, were several prints, the usual ones used to excite anticipation in clients. Auntie followed her gaze. 'Those were the problem. I thought to amuse them but whoosh, out like an east wind; first one, then the others. Those are good prints by Kuniyoshi, bought by my husband who knew a thing or two about artists.' She held her hand out, her lips spread in greedy satisfaction. 'But look, one left with me a whole silver ryō. I hope they come again.'

Dizzy with disappointment, Umegawa kicked back her heavy hem and swung stiffly about to return upstairs, ignoring Rika's cheerful giggles.

Wind rattled the window, sneaking around the frame to ruffle the pages of Pev's book. Wet leaves blown by the wind slapped against the paper panes, a desolate counterpoint to the staccato drumming of rain on the tiles.

Pev pushed away *Adam Bede*. English countryside could not contend with his mood. He slid open the window to gaze out at the dripping garden. Stripped branches spread waving patterns against mysterious evergreens. Rain pitted the surface of the lake.

This was no good. He went in search of company.

James Wilson was at the table in the dining-room, hunched over a pile of papers.

'Filthy day,' Pev offered.

'Hm. Call a servant for a lamp. There's a good chap.'

Pev did not move. 'Are you busy?'

'What? Oh, aye. Aye, I am busy.'

'Oh. May I ask your opinion before I call for a light?'

With a sigh, Wilson rocked back in his chair. 'Carry on.'

'Do you believe woman to be inferior to man – morally, I mean. Is she made of weaker fibre?'

The doctor glanced longingly at his papers. 'Women require guidance and protection but I do not believe their souls are inferior. No.'

'Oh.'

'Not often have they the experience to form proper judgements – perhaps. Pev, I must read Gregory's monograph on beri-beri. I have been awaiting it for months.'

'Oh, yes. Of course. Forgive me.' He backed away.

'Pev, that lamp. Please.'

Not for the first time James reflected that if all men received a practical education founded on the principles of modern science, there would be much less time wasted in this world.

Pev had left the window open. Rain spattered the tatami. A spread V of geese flapped over the hollow toward Fujiyama, their honking cries sorrowful in the dusk.

He started to slide the window shut when something caught his attention. Four grunting bearers carrying a norimon trotted around the end of the building. The green reed blinds were rolled down. Not just against the rain. Pev watched as the chair was lowered by Sir Radley's verandah.

A tiny but voluminous figure in shimmering yellow silk stepped daintily on to the verandah, her exotic head proud under a wealth of black hair stuck like a glittering hedgehog with hairpins. In his mind he almost caught her fragrance, roses and sensuous eastern perfumes without name. He could just make out a pattern of leaves on her wide obi, the long sash flowing down the front of her kimono. That bow, tied in front, distinguished her from

122

respectable women. She was a prostitute. Oscar had told him.

Umegawa's obi was tied in front.

He closed the window with a snap. Tomorrow, the next day at the latest, he would go to Shinagawa alone. To talk to her. This evil life was not her choice. He knew that. In all conscience, he must, as an Englishman and a Christian, help her.

The tattooed doorkeeper glowered at Pev who hovered nervously by the gate. One hand held modestly over her blackened mouth, Auntie tried to decide whether this was the same outsider who had been so free with his silver, but only a mother could tell one white face from another. After deciphering from his appalling language that he wished Umegawa, she put on a suitably tragic expression.

'Ah, Umegawa-chan? She has been called to a tea house by a very rich man. Rich rice merchant who gives her silk dresses and coral hairpins. Regrets, Outsider San, but come into my humble house. Here I have many other fine girls all from good homes. Samurai daughters! Né, come in and see. No? Ara, then come again, for Umegawa will wet her sleeves with tears when she learns she has missed you.'

'Né, is the clink of their coins so musical to Auntie's honourable ears?' growled the doorkeeper as Pev slouched miserably to his horse.

A shrewed light gleamed in the pebble eyes. 'Many barbarians will arrive in Yedo. And they will have gold. They will spread zeni like millet seed. Why should not some of this wealth come to an honest seller of women, eh?'

'But the Brothel Association?'

'I'll tell you why your ancestors were doorkeepers and why mine owned the doors that yours guarded. These barbarians are curiosities. People want to see them. Eating, walking, playing. Customers will flock to the Komatsu-ya.'

'But the Brothel Association?'

'Hora! The government will never permit them into the Yoshiwara but in Shinagawa, anything goes.'

'But Shinagawa is as full of ronin as a dung heap is full of flies. Ronin do not like barbarians.'

'You wait. Barbarians will be the fashion soon and the Komtasu-ya will be the name in the wind.'

Not until long after dusk did the lanterns of the Komatsu-ya guide Umegawa and her companions home, their high voices ringing in the frosty air. All chatter was of the delegation of samurai who, that afternoon, they had watched disembark from an American ship in Shinagawa port. The balconies of the tea house opened on to the quay and Umegawa had nearly tumbled over the railing into the street in her eagerness to see these men of Nippon who had travelled to an unimaginable land. Nor was she disappointed. Tears streamed down their sunburnt cheeks as the bushi set foot once again on the soil of their homeland. Their emotion-wrought faces were aged by what wonderful and terrible experiences?

Once Takao had nudged Umegawa with her fan and murmured, 'There, under that camphor tree – those ronin from The Dragon's Pearl. Né, remember?'

She remembered. A small cluster of scowling men watching the travellers with hatred-twisted faces. Umegawa caught her breath. She wanted to scream a warning but the ronin only spat and turned away.

An ebullient Auntie met her in the vestibule. 'It was only you he wanted. Umegawa has made an important conquest, for herself and for the Komatsu-ya.' She leant close, 'Be nice to the white-face, né. Now, you have a customer waiting at The Lotus. Shige, too. Hurry.'

Umegawa proved a distracted companion at The Lotus. If Auntie ordered her to receive the young barbarian she must do so. But Zenroku's daughter still hesitated. And yet, in her world of a thousand lovers, one or another was only flotsam in the tides. Would Umegawa be less a daughter of Nippon if she were kind for a brief flicker in the eons of time?

The next morning when the rain shutters were pushed back Umegawa woke to find Takao, crimson-eyed, bent over her. Her words hissed through her blackened teeth like wind from a deep cavern. 'Ara, now Umegawa is the senior whore of the Komatsu-ya. Today, Umegawa moves to the quietest place in the corner. Rika will carry the plum blossom bedclothes and this unworthy Takao will bring her the morning noodles.'

Umegawa caught her arm. 'This was not my doing. Please forgive me.'

In the hard winter light Takao's face seemed pitted with shadows. Stale powder deepened the crinkles around her eyes into snow-filled ravines. 'I know. The seasons pass too quickly for Takao now. But they will pass for Umegawa too. As dew dries in the morning sun, so dries beauty. Too late we understand what an illusion a pretty face is.' She rose stiffly. 'But beware the barbarian's love, Elder Sister. Unless, of course, it is in Elder Sister's karma to die in the full blossom of her life.'

5
Season of White Frost

Masayuki set about the preparations for his departure with a determined heart. Ohisa's fate he left to Akiko. He noticed his wife's resignation as little as he had noticed her prettiness, her loneliness, her barrenness. A swordmaster was found for Shotaro, although Akiko assured him the boy would soon accompany her to Suruga. Neither acknowledged that Shohtaro's future was not theirs to dispose of. As Hanae never asked questions – a dutiful daughter-in-law – she was simply acquainted with Akiko's intentions and ordered not to write to her husband.

One evening Akiko called Masayuki to her room. Solemnly she lifted the Chrysanthemum sword from its carved rack and held it out. Masayuki accepted the blade, raising it to his brow as a sign of respect. No words were needed.

The letter to Lord Okubo declaring Masayuki a ronin was sent to the castle by messenger. The daimyo did not deign to reply. He had only lost two men. Other lords had lost enough samurai to make up the day's duty roll.

Masayuki paid one last visit to his father's grave and to the temple and shrine where the Tadas were registered. And then with a brief farewell to Akiko and Shohtaro, he passed through the gate and down the lane.

It took him two days to walk the Tokaido from Odawara to Shinagawa. At every village barrier he waited while the guards checked his papers, but each time a bored hand waved him through. Just another shabby ronin without master or home.

When the sun was high he stopped at a tea house near Fujisawa post-station. Sprawled on the tatami benches were kago bearers and grooms. In a corner a troupe of pale men talked loudly, making extravagant gestures and

126

poses about a performance the previous evening at the local shrine. Covertly, Masayuki studied them. He had never seen actors at ease before, strange creatures on the fringes of life.

But no one even noticed Masayuki. He found himself examining his hands, assuring himself that those square, familiar extremities belonged to the Tada Masayuki he thought himself to be. Even the smooth scabbard of the Chrysanthemum sword felt changed, alien. For the first time in his life he was alone: no longer Lord Okubo's retainer; the younger son of Tada Teruhiko; Ohisa's husband. He belonged to no one. His place in the scheme of life was less than one of those gesticulating actors.

When, next dawn, he left his cheap inn, snipe were calling through mists rising off the marshes. The air was chill, yearning for the sun's warmth. By midday he was drawing into the enfolding hills near his destination. Tired and hungry, he stopped to eat his last rice balls, made by Akiko herself. Nearby a small shrine huddled under a sakaki tree. Before it were two stone statues, rounded with age and draped in red cloth. Wild chrysanthemums and aubergine lay as offerings. The torii was clean and in good repair.

In all directions around him spread the drained paddies of autumn. A short way off, in the next fields, some peasants shuffled across the dried mud, slicing at stalks heavy with precious rice. Warmth surged through him, love for those bent shapes, grunting at each flash of the sickle. These were his people. He belonged to them. It would be Masayuki who would shield them from the barbarians' evil so that autumn after autumn farmers would cut rice crops as had their fathers and their fathers' fathers back to the golden age of Jimmu, the first Emperor. He would lay down his life for these sullen peasants who spared not a glance for their dusty saviour.

Refreshed, he rinsed his mouth at the stone bowl by the shaded sanctuary and laid his last rice ball before the two gods of the road.

Over Shinagawa sombre clouds swirled. A steady cold drizzle penetrated the canopy of pine boughs. By the time he turned from the highway he was drenched.

This time he did not seek the alley to The Dragon's Pearl. But despite Ohno Tatsuya's directions he could not find his way easily through the tangled darkening streets to the lodging of the Brotherhood. As every dripping building had the same brown, blank look through a curtain of rain it took him some time to locate the dark lane behind the money lenders' street. The house was unmarked but he knew it stood between a sandal maker's and a row of shacks inhabited by itinerant shampooers and street hawkers. Fine neighbours for the Emperor's samurai!

He barely recognized the hulking man who opened the gate to him. A barber had not set blade to Ohno's head or chin for days and the bean-bun face was much thinner.

Ohno's greeting was solemn, without surprise. 'Welcome. Follow me. You must speak with Kojima San.'

'Forgive me, but I am very wet, I left Odawara in sun but tonight winter has closed on the plain.'

'It does not matter. As you see, we have no silk hangings or Kano screens to splash.'

Indeed the house was shabby in its austerity. They walked through an eight-mat room where several men sat cross-legged cleaning their swords. Two others, marked by their crests as from Choshu, played Go at a wooden board.

Masayuki immediately recognized the silvered head bent over a low writing table in the four-mat room beyond. His proffered loyal service was accepted with grave formality by Kojima and he was made welcome with hastily warmed saké.

Sitting in the dim room, wind and rain battering at the shutters, Masayuki again felt totally alone. Neither Kojima nor Ohno suggested that he retire to remove his wet clothes. They talked in low voices while he shivered miserably. Finally Kojima looked at him. 'Has Tada Masayuki any questions?'

'Many, Kojima Sama.'

'I shall answer what I can with Ohno's help.' Ohno was obviously the leader's chosen lieutenant, for the others kept to the eight-mat room.

'How many men are there in the Brotherhood?'

'Here, in this House of the White Cherry, we have ten ronin. But of the Jōi party, several hundred are gathered in Shinagawa. Many from Satsuma, Tosa, Kaga, Bizen and the Home Provinces as well as Mito. Only you two from Odawara.'

'And what do we do?'

'Wait. And talk. And argue. And wait.' He smiled as Masayuki's face crumbled. 'We must have patience. There are many questions: would it be wisest to mount an attack on Yokohama? Or on the Legations in Yedo? Or to concentrate on those in the Bafuku who betray the Emperor's will? We cannot yet accomplish all three aims for we have not the men.'

'Oh, I see.'

'And there is the question of who leads us. Lord Mito is dead. Many, especially those from Kyushu, wish Shimazu, Lord of Satsuma, to take up the cause. But others, myself, believe the Shimazu family have ambitions for themselves alone. Would it be the Emperor they served or Satsuma? Lord Tosa is another possibility, but he is an irascible, intemperate man.'

'Yes, I see.' Masayuki's black and white certainty of the last weeks was becoming smudged like a spoiled ink drawing.

The room was silent except for the wind.

'Ohno Kun trusts Tada Masayuki,' Kojima continued at last.

Masayuki bowed in gratitude.

'Therefore I will tell you that we in this house, the White Cherry Brotherhood, intend to take action on our own. Spies in the Legations assure us that there is one barbarian, a particularly necessary man, that we would do well to eliminate. Without him the outsiders cannot negotiate with the Bafuku. We will ensure that his death will strike terror in the hearts of the survivors.' Kojima's face was grim.

Masayuki held out the Chrysanthemum sword. 'I am with you to the death. Not to act would be a terrible betrayal of my honoured mother.'

'And His Sacred Highness, the Emperor,' Kojima reminded him gently.

*   *   *

129

One dull dawn his servant roused Shoh with a message commanding the doctor to Lord Okubo's compound where several samurai were ill. Reluctantly, for cold crept from the corners of the room, he slipped off his warm padded robe to don a black crested kimono and black striped hakama.

The sandalled feet of the kago bearers slipped on the icy stones leading to the inner ring of daimyo residences. Samurai and townspeople alike hunched in cloaks on the frosty bridges.

The white plastered wall of the Okubo compound loomed coldly forbidding under a pewter sky. Two guards admitted Shoh, a third led him among the cluster of fortified long-houses that served to protect the compound and house the samurai.

An avenue of almond trees led away from the grim gatehouse across the careful landscape of the palace gardens. Set on a gentle slope, the pink-tiled roofs of the Okubo mansion skimmed gracefully over the trees. A bronze lily, symbol of the family, could just be glimpsed on the ridge-pole of the audience hall; not a year ago, kneeling beneath the gilded beams of that exquisite room, Shoh learned he was to work with the barbarians.

But this bleak morning was out of joint. Something bad was coming.

Groaning and green-skinned as under-sunned fruit, the three sick samurai admitted to an over-indulgence in oysters. Shoh brewed a potion to soothe their tortured bellies and spent the rest of the morning examining his other patients and distributing powders for ague and sprained limbs. A grey sun hung high in a grey sky when he strode back to the gatehouse.

'Oi, Tada Kun. What a long time it has been!' He wheeled to meet Kuwana grinning at him. A companion at the castle school, Kuwana had become an official in Lord Okubo's household. One of the few to praise Shoh's appointment to the Dutch School, he and Shoh rarely met but their memories were warm.

'I am glad to see that Tada Shoh still attends Lord Okubo's men. I suppose doctors are a law to themselves, né?' But his jollity faded before Shoh's bewildered stare.

'What are these words? Since when do the Tada family not serve the daimyo?' His blood was as chill as the damp air, dreading the answer.

'Forgive me, I –'

'Kuwana Kun's words must have some meaning. Is there news from Odawara?'

'Forgive me, but after Ohno Tatsuya's disappearance this stupid samurai assumed Tada Masayuki too – They were both rumoured to be among those young hot-bloods. I had heard Masayuki Kun had forsaken the castle.'

Shoh stared without seeing Kuwana. Abruptly, he bowed. 'My greeting to your family,' he said formally, without thinking. And then, turning to his servant, he continued urgently, 'Hurry. We are required in Odawara.'

Two days later Shoh was sitting in his mother's room in the Tada House.

'Shoh San, welcome. Welcome.' Hanae touched her forehead to the tatami. 'Forgive us. Once again we are unprepared for your arrival.

'What is happening in this house? Why is the alcove bare? Where is the Chrysanthemum sword? The sword rack?'

'Please rest after your journey. I will fetch saké. Kimi must heat the bath.'

'Stay! Where is my honourable mother? My brother? I have heard strange rumours in Yedo.'

'Akiko Sama visits the Hachiman Shrine near the castle. Shohtaro accompanies her. The saké.' She escaped.

Impatiently he glared around the room. Shadowed branches played across the papered panes patterning the smooth cedar. His father's memorial tablet gleamed on the open altar, no longer sealed from the gaze of the godless son, who should be in Yedo. But the room was wrong. The charcoal in a big iron brazier was unlit, unwelcoming. A bronze vase replaced the lacquered sword rest and the wall behind was blank. At this season a scroll of water fowl painted in the style of the Tosa school should hang on that staring wall. The entrance court too had been wrong. Debris huddled against the stained plaster street wall. The stepping stones were unswept and weeds straggled over their smoothness.

Hanae came back with a tray. Although she had removed her smock and head covering, she still seemed drab.

'This Hanae must apologize. The stove was low. Kimi is neglectful.' She glanced anxiously at the unlit brazier.

'Where is Ohisa?'

The hands Hanae twisted on her lap were thinner, rougher than Shoh remembered. Her face too was thinner and the fine skin stretched over her cheekbones like cream silk on a frame.

'Our circumstances are changing, Shoh San.'

He growled at her downcast head, 'I am head of the Tada family, am I not? My father was the eldest son. I am the eldest son. This is the main branch of the Tada, is it not? Why have I not been informed of these changing circumstances?'

'Forgive me –' Hanae began but the dry rattle of the main door heralded Akiko's return and a moment later the shoji slid back.

Bands of grey dulled the gloss of his mother's chignon. Mauve shadows bruised filigree skin around the Buddha eyes. She had faded to an old woman but her disdain was still vigorous, chilling his greeting as frost kills a blossom.

Behind her Shohtaro too bowed. His cheeks no longer swelled in baby plumpness and his shoulders were thickening. He watched his father from curved, quiet eyes. Surprised, Shoh realized that his son would resemble him.

'What brings the Doctor to Odawara?' Akiko asked but her tone was indifferent. 'It is not yet the Festival of New Year. Nor the anniversary of his father's death. Has the Doctor, so busy in Yedo, forgotten this?'

'Rumours of disquiet in the Tada family bring me here.' Determination not to let her overpower him lent his words a spurious echo of authority.

Hanae moved toward the shoji but, uncertain, paused. Hideko could be heard chattering to Kimi in the garden. Shoh nodded to his wife to leave and then included Shohtaro.

Akiko's continued silence drained the room, sucking

him into a vacuum. If he did not speak now . . .

'Honourable Mother, our family affairs are discussed in Yedo.'

No curiosity. No regret. Smooth, passionless, the face of an ivory bauble.

'It is said that Masayuki intends to break his allegiance to Lord Okubo and then join this Jōi party against the Bafuku's negotiations with the outsiders.'

'Masayuki is no longer a retainer of the Okubo clan.'

'But this is an important act. It should be discussed among ourselves and with the uncles and members of the cadet branch. Masayuki cannot decide alone what to do.'

'Samurai make the decisions of samurai. Doctors make the decisions of doctors.'

'Have my uncles been consulted?'

'Of the five loyalties Confucius laid down, loyalty to the Emperor is paramount, far above loyalty to the family. However, the uncles have been informed.'

'But not Tada Shoh, the head of the family.'

Akiko lowered her eyes. To Shoh she seemed as lifeless as a figurine wrapped in layers of grey silk.

'Tada Shoh should not concern himself with the actions of bushi. The Doctor has turned from the teachings of his youth. He no longer walks the path of correct knowledge, the knowledge for which a samurai joyfully gives up his life. Tada Shoh accepts only the false world of illusions, a world that he must taste or touch or smell to understand. In this he has become one with the barbarians to whom he so traitorously submits.'

The Buddha eyes raised to his, probing out his doubts. But those eyes did not deign to understand.

'Why, Hanae, did you not write to me?' Shoh asked later, when they were alone together. 'A wife has a duty to her husband just as a widow owes obedience to her eldest son.' He did not strive to conceal his bitterness.

'Akiko Sama forbade my writing. I knew not what to do.'

Her hands twisted in her lap. Surprised by pity, he found himself saddened by the suffering of this woman caught between husband and mother-in-law. Always so

133

controlled, so proud of her own samurai breeding, she was reduced to this nervous wraith by an impossible clash of obligation. He could not despise her if Akiko, the stronger, had triumphed.

Gently he took Hanae's hand in his. With a moan of release, tears rushed down her cheeks and spilled on to their clasped fingers. A sense of completion, of peace, filled him. A deep moment of harmony.

But the problem could not so easily be dispelled. Those things Akiko would not tell him, Hanae must.

'Ohisa? What is her fate?'

Hanae took paper from her bosom and wiped away the tears, looking straight at her husband for the first time since his arrival. 'Ohisa is divorced. Another marriage has been arranged. With a farmer near Mishima. Her family was angry but as she is no longer their daughter, Akiko could act as she chose. Ohisa left for her new home on the first day of the eleventh month, the first auspicious date.' These practical details seemed to calm Hanae and she became almost as he remembered her. 'As the divorce was honourable and her family respectable, this new marriage is quite a good one. Samurai girls sometimes marry into farming families. The children – no – Hideko-chan misses her very much.'

'This affair accomplished too, without the permission of the head of the family! My mother's determination is very great. And what of the Chrysanthemum sword? The sword rack? The Tosa scroll? All these possessions of my father and his father and his father's father since Ieyasu's time? Where are they?' But he knew the answer.

'The sword has gone to Masayuki. Akiko gave it to him. The rest and some of the tea ceremony utensils have been taken to the street of the money lenders.'

Now very angry, he said, 'The sword's fate I had expected. As the eldest son it should pass to me but I have known since spring Masayuki would have it. However, the heirlooms of the Tada family should not be sold without my approval. Without consulting me.'

'A samurai does not care for worldly possession. So Akiko Sama says. And she speaks the truth. The material world is only an illusion.'

'But the Tada family is not an illusion and I should have been consulted. Is money more important than the honour of the family? Is food so scarce? I still serve the daimyo and receive a stipend. And this house. Is this not sufficient for my unworldly samurai mother?'

Hanae did not answer, but once again misery emanated from her curved shoulders.

'Hanae, tell me.'

'Akiko Sama will not eat the Doctor's rice. Nor will she allow Shohtaro to do so.'

'My son!'

'Akiko Sama has written to her brother, the head of the Iwa main house in Suruga. She has asked him to accept Shohtaro. She plans to take Shohtaro to Suruga to be raised as samurai. Until then she buys her own rice and she has purchased a fine sword for Shohtaro with the money lender's silver.'

'This cannot be. She is mad.'

'Shohtaro is no longer a baby, my husband. Sometimes he seems as old as Masayuki. It is with Masayuki and Akiko Sama that his heart lies. He will go willingly to Suruga.'

'And my mother? When she entered the Tada household she became a dead child to the Iwa. What of her?'

Hanae looked up at her husband, her eyes hardening slightly. 'Akiko Sama will never eat the Doctor's rice. So she has said and so it will be. She is samurai.'

Odawara held Shoh only a day longer. His mother's indifference, his son's incurious courtesy made the house unbearable. But as he strode out to the freedom of the Tokaido, Hanae's pleading eyes seemed to follow. 'Masayuki will do what he will do,' he murmured to her in the darkness before cock-crow. 'Whatever Akiko's fate, I will protect you and the children.'

'If Shohtaro goes with Akiko Sama?' No longer could either parent add the affectionately childish 'chan' to their son's name.

'He is bushi. To live with women at his age is wrong. I will place him in the castle school as Lord Okubo would expect and as I, his father, wish.'

135

'My husband is wise as always. Shohtaro must learn the ways of samurai.' But her brave words seemed sadly hollow.

It was the season of bright cold, pleasant for travelling, yet Shoh could not enjoy the dry stacks of rice in the fields outlined with an engraver's precision against the porcelain sky. As he neared Yokohama, the white man's town, he slowed his steps.

Whether driven by curiosity or shame or something unknown, he sent his servant on to Yedo and set off alone across the frosty marshes, silent but for the lonely call of wintering geese. His papers passed him through the block-houses and then, for the first time, he gazed at the arrogant stone box of the customs house, looming by the solid quay like a huge, ugly storehouse with windows. Loitering on the steps were several 'scroffs', greasy pigtailed Chinese brought to Yokohama for their skill in assaying gold coin. Their stained silk gowns and onyx-hard eyes confirmed Shoh's prejudice of a dirty race, fit only to handle money for merchants.

Coarse-featured outsiders dressed in unkempt clothes stalked the wooden sidewalks, shouting in their harsh abrupt tongue. Few passed Shoh without a wary glance at his swords. All gave him a wide berth.

From the customs house ran two streets, one along the sea front and the other, which he chose, led into the town: a paved way lined with shops. Some were discreetly closed to public gaze but most were open, their shelves crammed with the porcelain and bronzes, dolls and lacquers, fans and scrolls of Nippon. Most were of shocking quality but the age and fine workmanship of several pieces surprised Shoh. Would the ancient sword rest and the Tosa scroll of the Tadas find their way to Yokohama?

Bored shopkeepers eyed him without interest, nor were the people darting about the streets impressive. No one was above a second-rank merchant but these down to the scrawniest coolie showed scant respect for his position. The women, too, whether dusting racks of pottery or buying vegetables, had a boldness of manner that was displeasing. Even a baby peeped from out of his nest of his mother's back with what seemed like round-eyed insolence.

On impulse he turned on to an unsteady bridge spanning one of the many canals criss-crossing the swamp city. Now he was in the 'native town'. The street was narrow, lined with rickety houses packed side by side. No gardens, no trees, only an occasional potted shrub on a sunless balcony. The only spot of colour was a checkered quilt airing on a roof drying-rack. Through an open door he looked through to the still, brown canal. The houses must stand on the mud banks. Three women gossiping with an oil seller stared curiously at him. He glared back and was satisfied when they dropped their eyes in shame. All wore kimono of good quality cotton fashionably patterned in indigo. Plump children playing in a wavering patch of sunlight had firm rosy cheeks. Silver must be plentiful in Yokohama even if respect was lacking.

There was an odour over the district that Shoh did not like – sweetish, a sickly smell sharpened by acrid woods-moke.

From a winding cross-street a black-robed priest of the Nicheren sect suddenly appeared. He bowed sedately to Shoh. 'Ah, Sensei. If the Doctor has come to minister to the earthly bodies of my folk, this unworthy priest fears the Doctor comes too late. They pass from the suffering world of illusion to the peace of the Great Void so quickly.'

'Forgive me, but I am a stranger, here by chance.'

The priest's eyebrow flicked, a cat's tail of impatience. 'It is the Chinese sickness. Did the Doctor not know? The pyres burn brightly through the night,' he added sharply, lest his efficiency be doubted.

Behind the priest two men in white mourning staggered out of a doorway carrying between them a sealed white tub. 'Another passes along the chain of existence. Forgive us, but the street is narrow. This coffin must go to the temple.'

Muttering apologies Shoh retreated, hurrying along the dark canyon, his sleeve protecting his face from the fetid stench of burning flesh. The squawk of a bean-curd seller's bugle came from somewhere in the warren of alleys – a homely sound that brought Shoh sudden comfort, but still he longed for the busy street of shops, swept clean by salt air.

'Tada Sensei! Imagine you here! God has brought you!'

Wilson's voice was as familiar as the bean-curd seller's melancholy horn, but the slouching, ginger-grizzled man who clutched his arm must be one of those wine-sodden seamen. Instinctively, Shoh turned away from the man's stink of death.

'Tada! Oh, dear Lord help me. Have you not heard? Why are you here? Never mind. Come. I need you.' The man tugged at Shoh's clean sleeve.

'Wilson Sensei? Is it the English doctor?'

James rubbed at his weary unshaven face. 'No wonder. Aye, it is Wilson. Then you do not know? About the cholera?'

'Chinese sickness. Just now, a priest told me.'

'Then you have been in the native town?' James changed to Japanese. 'Well, I am relieved. They have need of help. I was going in later today when I finished at the Consulate. If you are working with your own people, I will not keep you, né. I understand.'

Shoh scowled. 'There is nothing for me in there. If it is a man's karma to die, he dies. The Chinese sickness is not serious for my island people. Those whose body and soul are not in harmony with nature will die.' He dismissed the native town with a wave. 'But for the outsiders – they die like spring flies until the disease blows away. I will help Wilson Sensei.'

Too exhausted for courtesy, James gripped Tada's arm. 'No, no. This time it is different. This time *your* people in the native town die. Twenty, thirty already. Of the outsiders, only six deaths and a handful of sick in the Consulate.' Crimson-lined eyes glared at Shoh. 'More will die. But this is just as I suspected. The miasma from these filthy canals is killing your people. Here, where there is a fresh sea breeze, space, clean privies, here the disease has not taken hold.' He sucked in the cool air. 'I came out to breathe again. It is a foul business, cholera. Now, if you will excuse me, I shall return.'

Puzzled, Shoh followed him. 'My duty is with Wilson Sensei.'

'Well, I cannot see that. Don't know how many native doctors there are but an extra hand must be welcome. Still, I can use you in the Consulate. I am giving them calomel

138

with opium and brandy and water. It is a matter of chance. Karma, as you say.'

'We use warm salt water. Sometimes that works.'

James stopped. 'Warm salt water? Now, common sense tells me that's no better than Wray's essence of ginger and yet – There were rumours in the Crimea. The Russians were supposed to give warm salt water.'

'One must be quick. Bowls and bowls of salt water immediately. At the first sign – before they shrivel up and turn black. Rub their limbs and bellies. Massage. Chinese sickness. Chinese cure.'

James burst into a run, calling over his shoulder, 'Then come on. Quickly.'

The 'Chinese cure' was too late for three American sailors and an English trader but three seamen survived plus a Japanese merchant whose family dared to chance the barbarian's makeshift hospital in the stable behind a hedge of crêpe myrtle in the large Consulate grounds.

Suspicious, the Englishmen gagged over the sickening mixture forced down their throats by the gallon. A clerk from the Consulate who had appeared mid-afternoon, cramped and shivering, pushed the beaker away from his blue lips. 'Don't want that filthy native brew,' he groaned. 'In my sea trunk, a copy of *Dr Hogg's Surgical Guide*. My mother packed it. At least give me Christian medicine.'

Exasperated, James shoved the cup against the man's chattering teeth, 'Dr Hogg's "remedies" have claimed more victims than cholera. Drink this and then drink more unless you wish to shrivel up like a prune.'

The clerk drank and drank again and again. By cock-crow his cramps eased and James believed the salt water had saved him.

At dawn he sent a message with the recipe to the French Consulate doctor who also had several cases; then he collapsed on a spare pallet. But his sleep was wracked with guilty dreams of men curled in the filth of Scutari's corridors, calling out for Russian doctors. Awake but unrested, he stared at the rice cauldrons warming on braziers and knew little could have been accomplished in the Turkish hospital. Too many sick men; pure water too scarce; too few nurses. The organization would have been a task beyond even Miss Nightingale. No, laudanum and calomel were the best remedies in that cold damp place. Miasma rose through the fouled privies and the drains just as it rose from those canals in the native quarter. Damp and filth. Those were his enemies. And perhaps impure water, as some held.

He rubbed his eyes, scratchy sore.

His travelling kimono grimy and his face blurred with fatigue, Shoh shuffled in. 'A girl from the Gankiro tea house. Too late, I think. Forgive me, but this unworthy doctor has commanded the pallets burned on the pyre with the bodies.'

'Hm. A wise precaution. Fire cleanses.'

'A servant brought this for Wilson Sensei.' Shoh leant against the rough wall to watch him read the note.

'Capital! Two dead at the French Consulate but no new patients for twenty-four hours. The Consul believes an American ship from Canton brought the contagion but the vessel has quarantined itself outside the bay. Our first cases were American sailors.' He scratched his stubbly beard. 'Thank God it is not summer. This dry cold has been our ally.' He stood up. 'Now, you rest, Tada Sensei. Then, if we have no new patients, you and I will set off to the native town. God Himself only knows what the situation is there.'

Shoh shook his head. 'No. Forgive me, but you and I have no obligation to those people. They will have their own doctors.'

Three days with little rest had obliterated James Wilson's patience. 'But this salt water cure needs many hands. Of course we can help.'

'It is not our obligation, Sensei. Doctors and priests of the quarter will look after the sick. If no new cases arrive here, I am obliged to return to Segawa Sensei's clinic in Yedo where I belong.'

'Are you mad? Return to Yedo now? Sick are sick. All sick are our "obligation".'

'No, Sensei.' Shoh heard his own voice rise. 'The Sensei does not understand. We should not intrude. It would not be correct.'

'People are dying. Does that mean nothing?' The

140

Japanese language could no longer contain his passion. He cried out in English, 'You are a nation of heathens. Other nations have morals but the Japanese have rituals. I am expected to cut into a dying woman to please her important husband. A policeman lies between life and death because his family fear for his soul if I touch him. And now I must desert a stricken town because it would not be "correct" to help.' He jumped up, his huge frame blocking the cool winter light from the stable door. 'Well, these irresponsible conventions do not bind an English doctor. After I have looked at my patients and I have washed and shaved, I'll go to the Japanese quarter alone.'

He shoved past Shoh and began his rounds, trying to drown his fury in familiar actions.

The tea house girl would die. He could not force laudanum through her clenched teeth. Under his hands her flesh was horribly clammy. She was young, young as the boys in Scutari. Once, yesterday, she had been pretty. A round-faced country girl perhaps. Now she was withered and blackened. A prostitute dying among strangers of *Cholera morbus*. He looked at the other pallets – Consulate clerks, seamen, traders. Perhaps she was not among strangers. Perhaps a day or so ago one of these men had fondled her, laughed with her.

He turned away. God help him, he was becoming morbid.

He hung up a peeling mirror on one of the thick stable posts and began to scrape away at his ginger bristles. Suddenly he found himself staring into his own eyes. Richard Wilson's son. Aye, there was a look of his father now. A tense line from cheek to jaw aged his young face.

As a child his father's near apoplectic attacks on the immovable righteousness of the mill owners and city fathers had terrified James. He would hide behind the curtains, wracked with guilt over smug indifference that was not his but others'. That small house had rattled under his father's frustrated fury while James and his mother clutched hands and prayed that – this time – someone would do something; someone would meet at least one of Richard Wilson's demands. But each year the powers-that-be just smiled and nodded and ignored. And finally James had fled to London, to the Crimea, to Japan.

Now, hands trembling with fatigue, he entered Richard Wilson's rage. Men died while their masters considered. Well, he, James Wilson, would not tread softly where his duty was clear.

Cut off by the Englishman's anger, Shoh watched James make his preparations. His own calm restored, he regretted the squabble, a natural result of their fatigue. And yet, the Englishman's insensitivity repelled him. He was coming to suspect that Europeans lacked any code for proper behaviour themselves and this was the reason they could not appreciate the intricacies – and superiorities – of life in Nippon. How could Wilson even imagine blundering into the native town where he could only offend the doctors and affront the already suffering families of the sick? One cannot disrupt the order of the cosmos just to delay a few spirits on the wheel of life.

And then, among the confused pictures in his own aching head, Shoh saw again those dark streets of Yokohama and their cold-eyed inhabitants. He had never walked such streets in Odawara or Yedo.

Perhaps, after all, Masayuki was right. Perhaps he had found the correct path. Perhaps the corruption seeped from Yokohama throughout Nippon. Oh, Lord Amida, he was tired.

Wilson picked up his valise of instruments. 'Tada Sensei will not then do this unworthy doctor the honour of accompanying him?'

'Sensei, please forgive this Tada but what you intend to do is – not wise. Impolite. Against the ways of my people.'

James listened to Shoh grasping for words. The native doctor's face was ashen, his cheekbones sharpened by lack of sleep. He was like a Buddha, one of those disturbing idols that stared out from the heavy scented gloom of a temple, serenely indifferent to pain and hunger, to the needs of man.

'I will go alone then.'

Four hours later he returned, bearing a woman in his arms. Shoh asked no questions. Wilson offered no explanations. In fact, all doors had been barred against him, for it was well known that the Chinese sickness was brought by the outsiders to Yokohama. He found a coolie dying in the cold mud for whom he could do nothing; a child showing first signs of the disease who summoned his failing strength to flee, screaming with terror, from the giant long-nosed devil; and, finally, a woman in spasms doubled over the railing of the brothel from which she had been driven out. It was she he lifted and carried gently to the Consulate, oblivious to the hostile stares of white and yellow alike.

She died before dawn.

That night a violent storm blew up over the bay, sweeping great gusts of rain over the port for twelve hours. The canals were flushed clean. The miasma vanished with the storm.

The Chinese disease disappeared.

6
Coming of Age

Rosily warm from the bathhouse, Umegawa dabbed languidly at her damp neck. Soon the other girls would chatter in and the noisy dressing rituals of evening would begin. But now the room was silent as a snow-muffled dawn. She usually tried to leave the bath first in order to have these few quiet minutes alone.

The clatter of the sliding door demolished her peace.

'Hora! Umegawa Elder Sister's outsider is here again.' Rika plumped down beside her, the wide frog's mouth split in a grin. 'He wants to see you. Auntie says dress and come down. Mine, the yellow-haired one, did not come again,' she added crossly.

Umegawa's languor fled and her heart pounded like a festival drum. Trying to conceal this excitement, she reached for the powder box but it dropped from her shaking fingers.

'Oi, Elder Sister, look at this mess. Here, use mine.'

'What should I do, Rika? Should I see him? Né, Takao is right. I should send him away, shouldn't I?'

Rika enjoyed this fuss over the outsider. Anything that coloured her monochrome life was welcome. Now she said slyly, 'Well, that Murasaki of Shimoda must have a soft time with the American. But if Elder Sister thinks she should put off the barbarian, why not go down as you are? No paint, no blackened teeth, no silk. He will be so horrified by your naked face that he will run away again, I bet.' She brought up her sleeve to hide a giggle. Umegawa might fool herself but she could not fool Rika.

'Ara, I do not know. If Auntie says – I cannot be rude.'

'If you go down in that kimono with only a loose sash, he will think you mean to accommodate him. Since you do not wish to –' here the sleeve hid another smile – 'better to put on a proper obi, at least.'

'Oh, and the plum-splashed crêpe. This is too plain. Help me, Rika, please. And just a few pins to keep my hair firm.' Avoiding Rika's smirk in the steel disc of the mirror, her nervous fingers plunged Kaoru's present, the false tortoise-shell pin, into the thick roll of hair. It was only a cheap trinket but it was her favourite and she knew Kaoru would wish her well.

'Enjoy yourself,' Rika carolled after Umegawa as she tottered down the stairs.

She knelt in the corridor, pushed open the door and slipped into the room. Boldly lifting her naked face to his, she waited for the shocked gasp. But his cry was one of delight: 'How beautiful you are! Oh, you are even lovelier than I ever dreamed without all that paint.'

Recoiling, she raised her hand in protest against his happiness. But she had forgotten how large and soft his eyes were; his odour, peculiar, not pleasant and yet exciting.

'Umegawa San,' he clasped her waiting hand in his.

'Né, forgive this Umegawa but it is better that the Outsider San should go away. At least, in a minute, after some saké, perhaps.'

And then, how could her intentions go so far astray? He seized her by the shoulders and kissed her on the mouth. Ara! A kiss. On the mouth of all places! The most intimate of all caresses. And they were not even in the bedclothes. Yet his lips were smooth and strong and the hands clutching at her were clumsily insistent. His words were harsh sounds of anger and desire - and sweetness.

Warnings, rules, negotiations spun dizzily in her head. Somehow she found herself at the cupboard pulling at the quilts and spreading them across the tatami.

He watched her fingers move deftly at the obi's fastening. Suddenly, with a snarl almost of pain, he grabbed the bow and yanked it viciously. Torn, the sash slithered away, lost. The loosened outer kimono parted, its weight tugging her under-robes free.

He pulled her down on the pallet. The rough wool of his jacket and trousers rasped against her breasts. She struggled under him, trying to seize back the mastery of the situation but he was too strong, too heavy. And then, abruptly, with no warning, he was inside her, thrusting hard, before he collapsed with a groan. A hot, prickly weight smothering her scratched disappointed flesh.

Warm salt tears trickled on her neck. The outsider was crying, sobbing against her hair. Partly to preserve her ginko-leaf hairstyle intact but more in an attempt to understand this peculiar human being, she gently shoved him off on to his back and then wrapped her arms around the coarse woollen bulk. Staring into his swollen flushed face she felt again the mysterious pull to this alien creature who now seemed little more than a child.

She found her roll of mopping paper to wipe away the tears and then stroked his hot sticky cheek until he was calm.

The kiss had been very pleasant. Maybe that would please him again. She brushed her lips against his. For a moment his body tightened, became unfriendly, then slowly he relaxed and his arms slid around her.

That was better.

She was determined to have no more of this rough and tumble mating. Were he to become her lover, things must progress in a manner acceptable to the Floating World. If Rika's barbarian could perform with style, so could this one. With a little help.

Gently, she removed his horrible clothes. So many knobs and fastenings and straps but, oddly, no loin cloth. As his pale body emerged from its woollen cocoon she explored with light curious fingers. Everything seemed to be in a familiar place. When he did not reciprocate she picked up one of his hands and guided it to her breast. Clumsy but willing he was soon eagerly fondling.

Thanks to the resilience and vigour of youth, affairs were eventually brought to an agreeable – if not entirely perfect – conclusion.

Later, after Umegawa left him to the tender avarice of Auntie, she climbed the stairs slowly, her pretty face suffused with a soft glow and a warmth in her heart.

Pev grinned happily all the way from Shinagawa to the Tozenji. His escort even noticed him and speculated on what might have taken place behind the walls of the

Komatsu-ya. But their guffaws, ribald in any language, could not pierce his cloud of joy.

Sir Radley, however, could. He had barely slid from his horse before a thunderbolt flashed from the Minister's room. Within seconds, nervous as a schoolboy, Pev found himself facing the furious whiskers.

'Forbear to enlighten me on how you have been occupied all afternoon, Fitzpaine. Just listen. You have work to do in Yokohama. That fool, Johnstone, has accepted Morrison's lie that he shot the policeman by accident and has seen fit to punish the poacher with a thousand pound fine and deportation. Not even does he demand compensation for the wounded policeman. He excuses this flagrant breach of justice on the grounds that public sympathy in Yokohama is with Morrison. A more severe penalty would disrupt the settlement. Disrupt!'

Pev stepped back from the bellow. 'Why, that seems outrageous, sir. If a consular court is to be respected –'

'It is not just a matter of the court, although that is now nothing but a jest. How am I to explain this farce to the Foreign Ministers? A thousand pound fine for a crime they deem worthy of public execution! And calling their policeman a liar in the bargain.' Sir Radley slumped down in his chair. 'Tomorrow you carry this document to Johnstone. In it I use my authority to overturn his judgement and instruct him that before Morrison is deported he must be imprisoned for three months in the Governor's prison as well as fined.'

'A Japanese prison, sir?'

He nodded. 'Your task will not be a pleasant one. The combined wrath of the Yokohama riff-raff is a daunting prospect. But remember that most *are* riff-raff and it is essential that they as well as the Japanese see justice done. If the Japanese do not, how can we expect them to honour the treaties? I fear our whole future in Japan may rest on this case.' The bushy eyebrows arched together in concentration. 'This is a lot to put on your shoulders. Really, Foxwood should go but –' He cleared his throat hoarsely. 'While you are in Yokohama I shall be dealing with Lord Ando and his fellow ministers. Naturally I shall require Oscar Sullivan. That will not be a pleasant task either,' he finished grimly.

The next morning was a brilliantly dry, sunny one such as

147

Pev had learned to expect of the Japanese winter. The silver cone of Fujiyama stood out crisply against a cloudless sky. As the little boat skimmed over the sapphire bay, Pev felt exhilarated and ready for battle. But his spirits dropped as he climbed on to the quay at Yokohama. Walking past stony, unwelcoming white faces, he reached the equally unwelcoming portals of the Consulate.

Johnstone had already calmed his nerves with several whiskies. 'I suppose that this was to be expected.' He laid the document on the desk and gazed morosely at Pev. 'Why you? Why did he not come himself? This is no job for a tadpole.'

'Someone had to explain to Lord Ando,' Pev answered stiffly.

'Oh, yes. Keep in with the Japs. That is all you think of in Yedo. Well, you will find things different here.' He sighed. 'Come on. We shall require at least a dozen of the Governor's samurai to "escort" Morrison to prison.'

Matthew Morrison lived in one of several houses clustered along the river under the overhanging bluff that lurched up out of Yokohama's marshes. He was exactly as Pev had expected he would be: square in face and in body and very belligerent.

'Hell and damnation. No interfering diplomat is going to lock up Matthew Morrison. Bleeding injustice. I'll pay my fine but I'll not go back to that prison! It was an accident. Bleeding interfering policeman. If they hadn't jumped me the gun would not have gone off.'

If he had been reasonable, scared or remorseful, Pev might have wavered. But the angry red face and starting eyes were those of a bully and Pev was too young to find sympathy with a bully.

'The gun was cocked, Mr Morrison. You have admitted that. If you hadn't cocked the gun, the "accident" would not have occurred. But as the gun *was* cocked, you must have intended to use it.' Pev knew his brief by heart.

'Damnation, boy! Fire at their feet. Scare 'em. That's all. Bleeding unfair of 'em to pounce on me like that anyway. Everybody shoots wild fowl.' He glared at Johnstone who was attempting to remain unnoticed in the background. '*He* is the best bleeding shot in Yokohama. Bag a brace of duck before breakfast, he can. Put him in a Jap prison, why don't you?'

Johnstone dodged the anger in those popping eyes. 'Come along, be a good fellow. Don't make us have to tie you up. Eh?'

'Tie me up! Not bleeding likely!' He grabbed Johnstone's arm and shook the Consul fiercely. 'Make damned sure nothing happens to the goods in my go-down and make damned sure every Englishman – aye, and every American – knows what the bleeding Yedo diplomats have done to me.'

At the prison Pev's resolve nearly failed. A squat, dark lock-up set behind an earthen embankment topped by bamboo spears, it seemed barely Christian to enclose an Englishman in those damp, urine-streaked walls. Morrison too flinched at the barred gate. 'I'll see Ferrier dismissed for this. There's courts in Hong Kong, you know. They'll do me justice. Tell the bastard that,' were his last words as the surly prison guard bound his hands.

News travelled quickly in Yokohama. Two merchants were waiting in the Consulate; one was Donalds, the 'antiquities' dealer.

The leader was a well-dressed Englishman in his late forties, his strong-featured face lined with years of eastern seas and sun. 'Mr Fitzpaine, my name is Tilly. Primarily, I am in silk and tea. Donalds here deals in curios. Now, I am sure you and Sir Radley are reasonable men and can understand our concern about this business. Even if we forget – momentarily – that Morrison pleaded an accident, quite frankly, the idea of an Englishman, even a guilty one, in a native prison is repellent. Impossible. We do not have to tell you what barbarians these people are. Morrison, a Christian merchant, faces torture and the good Lord knows what in their hands.'

Sir Radley had prepared Pev for this: 'Naturally the Minister is requiring a guarantee from the government that Morrison will be treated with the utmost care.' He frowned, hoping that his manner and words would impress these seasoned eastern hands.

'These heathen bastards cannot be trusted,' Donalds, unimpressed, shouted.

'Donalds's point may be crudely presented but it is valid, none the less.'

'Mr Tilly, I am not sure you understand the case. Matthew Morrison knowingly broke one of the Tycoon's laws. The proof is a dead goose. He compounded his crime by wounding the officer who arrested him.'

'An accident!' Donalds yelped.

Pev blinked and marched on. 'He is protected from the severity of the Japanese penal code by the extra-territorial clause of the treaty but if the Japanese are led to believe that English justice is so markedly inferior to theirs or that we do not sufficiently punish our own malefactors, how can we win their respect?'

'Is the respect of heathens so very important that we must sacrifice a Christian soul?' Tilly was a formidable opponent.

'Are you not threatened by ronins in Yokohama? If we cannot control our own criminals, can we demand that they control theirs? The sword threatens Christian souls, too, you know.'

Pev and Tilly surveyed each other with respect, then Tilly nodded at the truth in Pev's words but added, 'One could wish for a detachment of Her Majesty's marines, but in the circumstances –'

Donalds exclaimed, 'Morrison is no criminal but a red-blooded Englishman exercising his liberties! God in Heaven! All the man did was to shoot a goose and wound a native. Has Ferrier lost his senses?'

'There you hear, Fitzpaine, the sentiment in Yokohama. And to sound the depth of that sentiment, this wallet contains half the fine, five hundred pounds, raised by local citizens. And also a petition requesting, no, demanding, Morrison's immediate release. Come along, Donalds, shouting will accomplish nothing more.'

As Pev watched the London-tailored frock coat swish from the room, he told himself that he had won the battle, if not the war.

'A very competent performance. You should make an excellent diplomat.' Johnstone was clearly impressed. Pev wished he could be flattered, but the Consul's own deficiencies were too apparent as he reached a puffy hand for the whisky. 'No, not a tadpole at all,' he murmured as he lifted the amber comfort to his lips.

Pev dreamed that he was back at school. Something was wrong. He had transgressed a serious rule although he did not know which one, and a master, new and unfamiliar, stood before him screaming abuse. Somewhere, in the corridor perhaps, boys were shouting. Tolling over all this noise was the solemn boom of cathedral bells.

He opened his eyes. No, this was not Exeter but Yokohama. There was no church and certainly no cathedral, no schoolboys, but a bell boomed and there was shouting.

A strange orange haze lit the small room. The air was dry, choking.

He leapt out of bed and hurled back the window. Flames shot into the night sky. Stars that should be sparkling diamonds were only dull topaz through a veil of smoke. Dark figures ran along the Bund. The fire-bells of Yokohama summoned the settlement to action.

Hastily dressed, he met Johnstone moving blurrily toward the gate. 'Go-downs. Must save the merchandise,' he mumbled. 'Sea wind blowing the fire inland.'

Men in nightshirts and overcoats staggered along the road carrying crates and boxes. Already black heaps of goods were piled along the sea front away from the hungry flames.

'Come on, you. Quick.' A man grabbed his arm and dragged him toward an alley running parallel to the Bund; here stood the go-downs of the merchants. A large crate was thrust into Pev's arms. 'Take this and come back for more,' the man ordered.

Pev did as he was told. Out to the sea-fresh Bund and back into the acrid smoke stench of the alley. Tears ran from his eyes until they burned dry, scratching and itching beyond belief. Flames leapt from winter-dry wooden house to plaster go-down to thatched roof, illuminating the rushing, struggling, coughing men. Somewhere animals screamed in terrible gut-wrenching fear. He remembered Poultry Row, the street where Japanese sold pets to sailors: monkeys, birds, dogs, cats, trapped in their bamboo cages beyond the walls of burning houses.

Back to the waterfront, still a cool haven. As he dumped another crate a furtive figure darting among the piles caught his eye. Against the tumult of the fire the sudden crack of a pistol startled him. A shriek followed. Pev saw a long pigtail snake out against the flame-bright night in a limp arc. A man, soot-smeared and red-eyed, stepped around a pile of bales and looked down on the silk robes twitching at Pev's feet.

'Damned Chinese scroffs. Steal their grandmother's teeth.' Tilly kicked the body. 'Finished. Blasted celestials. So superior. You, get back to the go-downs. Those under the Bluff, now.'

Another armful and another. Pev's body ached. His nose and mouth and eyes were scorched sirocco dry. Cracked, bleeding.

In the cinnamon dawn sullen circles of smoke drifted up from the ruins of Yokohama. The houses along the Bund, a bungalow here, a go-down there, the stone customs house were all that remained. The rest was ashes. But the fire was out.

Pev collapsed against the Consulate gate. A ragged, blackened creature dragged towards him with exhausted steps.

'You. Fitzpaine, isn't it? You saved my goods. My curios. I owe you a lot.' Donalds peered into Pev's empty, blood-shot eyes. 'D'you hear me? You are a damned Yedo diplomat but thanks anyway.'

Pev slumped on the ash-covered road and began to laugh until pain from his bleeding lips turned the laughter to sobs. He sank his filthy face in his blistered hands.

Later in the day a Japanese official from the Yokohama Governor's office arrived at the crowded Consulate. In the confusion of the fire, he reported, no one knew quite how, Matthew Morrison had escaped from the prison, vanishing with the other prisoners into the smoky night.

The prison guard's seppuku would take place at sunset.

* * *

152

Several days later, with no regrets, Pev abandoned Yokohama to its rebuilding. Scores of roofers and carpenters scurried along the causeway, attracted from Yedo and Shinagawa to make their fortune. The early birds found rich pickings in the foreign settlement; late arrivals had to haggle with their parsimonious countrymen in the native town. Even as he walked down the stone quay towards his boat raw skeletons of new buildings pierced the blue winter sunshine.

The Peverel Fitzpaine who trudged up to the Tozenji Legation in Yedo from the fishy bustle of Takanawa port felt many years away from the love-happy youth of days before. His memories were more disturbing than just singed eyebrows and an aching throat.

At dusk after the fire was extinguished an official from the Governor's office had appeared unbidden at the Consulate. Behind him a servant carried a large box wrapped in white cloth. The official knelt in the hall among the carved tables and umbrella stands and crates from the go-downs, relentlessly exotic in his voluminous robes and odd hat in such very commercial surroundings.

Johnstone surveyed the official with distaste and said, matter-of-factly, 'He has brought the head for us to view. So that we will be certain the prison guard cut his belly.'

Pev stared from Englishman to Japanese in speechless horror.

Johnstone barked at the official, 'Off you go. Can you not see the English diplomat wants none of your barbarian rituals.'

But the Governor's man continued to kneel. His orders were to display the head and it would cost him his own life if he failed. Pev looked into the cold arrogant face and knew he must look at the head. And he knew he must not be sick if his country were not to be disgraced.

In fact his ordeal was brief although the official unveiled and opened the box with the slow solemnity of a man preparing a sacrament. In one quick jerk of his head Pev managed to take in the grisly, grinning object and turn away.

Disgusted by the barbarian's lack of respect for an important ceremony, the official swept out without a glance at the boxes and bales that converted the Consulate into a go-down.

At the Tozenji, Pev found Sir Radley waiting at his desk. Johnstone's letter of commendation hardly balanced against the guard's futile death. If Pev had acquitted himself well, did not Morrison's escape and the useless seppuku cancel out his achievement?

However, Sir Radley was pleased and said so. After all, Morrison was a pest, but it had been from a Japanese prison he escaped. *English* justice had been done and that was all that mattered. Pity about the guard but these people had their own strict standards, however brutal.

After a few days in the Legation, Pev lost his feeling of dislocation. Life returned to its pattern. His colleagues' admiration soon wore off and he found himself eager for the Komatsu-ya. Relying on his current high standing and convincing himself that he deserved a reward, he managed to slip away one afternoon a week later.

Yokohama's blaze had coloured the night sky as far as Shinagawa so Pev's singed hair was made much of by Umegawa. As she fluttered about him, her long scented sleeves brushing his cheeks, he felt a peace he had not known at the Tozenji.

When after an agony of giggling and saké pouring, gentle approaches and demure withdrawals, Umegawa finally curled into his arms, he wondered that such an insubstantial wood-sprite could rouse such excitement in him. She was so tiny, a golden toy. Her clear bell-like voice in his ear set his bones vibrating. She manoeuvred him to her own liking, using her skill to control his movements. As her polite moans turned to excited gasps, Pev struggled against his own release, appalled yet aroused by her abandon, urged on by her tiny hands clawing his flesh.

Later, in the calm, he suddenly asked, 'How old are you?'

'This Umegawa has seen fifteen winters.'

He pulled away to stare at her. 'What! How long have – This life? This place?' When she looked puzzled he said, 'When did you leave home?'

'In my eleventh autumn. What troubles Pebu San?'

'Eleven! A mere child sent into – It is terrible. Have you no parents?'

154

'Why, yes. It was my honour to serve them in their need. My father received fifteen ryō from the Omi-ya in the Yoshiwara,' she said proudly.

'Did he feel no shame? Do you feel no shame? Think what your parents sold you into.'

'So, né,' she said sadly. 'To be sold to Shinagawa, that is a disgrace. My shame would be unbearable if my father found out. I can never return home now.'

'But to sell a child of eleven to the Yoshiwara where she can only fall into evil –'

'Evil?' Then she understood. 'Ara, Pebu San only knows Shinagawa, a second-class world. He is forbidden the glories of the Yoshiwara. Ma, there my life was good. Rice, not noodles. Kimono of patterned silk, not cheap crêpe. Fine hairdressers. If Pebu San could see the promenades! The lanterns on the cherry trees. A parade of famous courtesans. Why, Kunisada himself drew Tama-chiyo of the Omi-ya.' She lowered her voice. 'All the girls here envy me although only Rika-chan will admit it.'

Pev pulled a little further away from her warm, proud body. 'Evil is not less if the girl wears silk,' he said firmly. 'To sell one's daughter to –' No Japanese word he knew was suitable so he finished in English – 'a life of sin. Sin.'

'And what do the daughters of poor fathers do in England? Is it not their filial duty to help their parents? Ara, truly the English *are* barbarians if a child does not serve her parents.' She frowned at such primitive behaviour.

'Terrible things happen, of course. But. But –' He did not wish to hurt her yet he knew he must explain that she was, through no fault of her own, debased. An English prostitute could be considered a victim of misfortune or her own nature but to be sold by one's own parents – Yet he could not find the words and she, soon bored with serious conversation, found ways to distract him.

But later, riding through the evening streets, he re-lived his afternoon and was again slightly repelled by his experiences. And should Umegawa take such voracious enjoyment in love making? Could there be Englishwomen who abandoned themselves to passion so totally? Harriet, his proper sister, or his silly goose of a sister-in-law, Marion?

His mother? Then his own shameful thoughts sickened him. Disgusted with himself he rode down the avenue to the Tozenji where he would be with his own people who understood sin and debasement and, for all their faults, disapproved.

For several weeks after the cholera incident relations between Tada Shoh and James Wilson were marked by circumspect courtesy. Both were uncomfortably aware that fatigue – or misunderstanding – had brought them near raw truths that once voiced could not be withdrawn.

One afternoon when Yedo glittered in December brilliance Shoh invited Wilson on an excursion. 'The Doctor has seen so little of the city. Even here near the Tozenji there is another very famous temple that pilgrims come from all over Nippon to visit.'

Therefore James was surprised when after a short walk down the Tokaido they turned into a lane and passed through a rather ill-kept gateway that in Sheffield would be considered in sore need of paint. But soon the sloping path became neater; straggly shrubs gave way to pleasant vistas of rock, fine trees and lawns. They approached a bell tower and an impressive Buddha Hall under sweeping canopies of roofs. Shoh paused only briefly. 'Sengakuji Temple, but this is our way over here. I will tell you a story of Nippon.'

The path now was wide, winding between rhododendrons and camellias. Ginko trees, magnificent in their winter simplicity, dotted the pleasantly rolling compound.

Tada began in simple Japanese. 'In the fourteenth year of Higashi-yama era, a disgraceful event took place in the Shogun's palace. Two daimyo on duty to the Shogun quarrelled. Lord Asano was taunted by Lord Kira and called a rustic lout stupid in the ways of court procedure. Insulted, he struck Lord Kira with his short sword – such a terrible thing to do in the palace that only Lord Asano's death could atone. So, although Lord Kira was known by all to be an avaricious, unpleasant man deserving of Lord Asano's blow, Lord Asano willingly paid for his crime by committing seppuku. His lands were confiscated, his

156

family disinherited and his retainers became ronin: samurai without a lord.

'But forty-seven of these retainers were so imbued with bushido – the way of the warrior – that they could see no choice but to avenge their lord's unjust death.'

'Such occurrences are not unknown in the West,' James said dryly.

Unyielding, Shoh replied, 'But this is a story of Nippon. A secret oath was sworn and the men dispersed around the country taking up the lowly occupations open to ronin: swordmaster, carpenter, umbrella maker. Kuranosuke, the leader, left his family and apparently abandoned himself to a life of dissipation. Often he was found drunk in the street and when this was reported back to Lord Kira the daimyo smiled to himself, for he believed he was safe. To kill in vengeance is against Bafuku law. Death is the punishment so Lord Kira believed that Lord Asano's retainers were too cowardly to risk their lives in revenge. Many samurai in Yedo were disgusted by Kuranosuke's apparent weakness. Since all accepted that Lord Asano had been a brave man who was driven by wanton insult to a cruel death, these proud samurai believed, according to bushido, that this death should be avenged by Lord Asano's retainers, whatever the cost. Such is the spirit of samurai. Kuranosuke and the forty-six ronin were spat upon and despised.'

'Although they were only acting in accordance with the law?' asked James, puzzled.

'So, né. After two years, however, when Lord Kira had completely relaxed, on a snowy winter night Kuranosuke led the forty-six ronin in a carefully planned surprise attack on Lord Kira's mansion. The daimyo hid himself in a woodshed but Kuranosuke found him and offered him the chance of an honourable death. Seppuku. Lord Kira had not the spirit for so noble a samurai act. Kuranosuke beheaded him.'

' "Vengeance is mine," saith the Lord,' James muttered. 'But not among heathens.'

They had stopped by a low well. A small bundle of incense sputtered in a sandfilled brazier on stones worn smooth by reverent hands.

'Here Kira's head was washed before Kuranosuke placed it on Lord Asano's tomb. Come.'

The cemetery was large, the mossy graves shaded by solemn cryptomeria, but James did not need the row of low columns pointed out. Nor did he need to count to know there were forty-seven buried in that row. One stone was slightly larger than the others. Before it a samurai stood, head bent to Kuranosuke.

'At the Shogun's expected command all forty-seven committed seppuku, but by the Shogun's permission they were buried with great dignity. These graves are a shrine to bushido. Beyond is the grave of Lord Asano.'

'What did these deaths accomplish? Was Lord Asano's family reinstated? His lands returned? His name cleared?'

'Lord Asano was avenged by forty-seven retainers who placed loyalty above all else. This is the spirit of Nippon.'

'Yes, but think a minute, Tada Sensei. If these men had lived, perhaps they could have helped devise a more equitable code. As I see it, their deaths just embellished an injustice.' Genuinely perplexed, James looked from the revered graves to Tada's stern face. 'Do you, Tada, admire these forty-seven men?'

Shoh looked down the peaceful row of tombstones. Offerings of rice or saké lay nearby, homage to forty-seven men who had seen the right path and followed it to its inevitable conclusion, just as somewhere Masayuki pursued the right path.

'Do you admire these men? Are they heroes to you?' Wilson asked again.

Shoh replied slowly, 'These ronin recognized their place in the scheme of existence and acted correctly. They are heroes to my people.'

'Tada Sensei has not answered my question.'

I cannot, Shoh thought, and walked away.

James followed him, respecting Shoh's silence. The huge scarlet ball of winter sun blazed low in the sky. 'It will be a superb sunset but a cold night,' James said. 'Tada Sensei, forgive me, but what does being samurai mean to you?'

Shoh turned angrily. 'Samurai are not just the drunken killers you believe them to be. Their code is one of honour.

158

Self-knowledge. Loyalty. Duty. Men with such beliefs make Nippon strong.'

They walked in silence through the landscape washed in rose and gold. Finally James spoke. 'We do not know enough of each other. Be it Tada and Wilson or your people and mine. There is a gulf of ignorance.'

'That is true. I feel it strongly. That is why I brought you here.'

'Aye, but I have failed. Now I offer a challenge in return. Soon, it should be possible for some of your people to travel to England. If you are willing, I will ask that you be among the first. It will be arranged for you to work in a hospital in London. There you will study under great doctors. Men of science.'

Shoh could not help grinning at the enormity of the idea. 'London. Ara. My eyes would pop from my head at the strange sights.'

'You will think it over, though, will you not?'

How tempting it would be! Whole oceans of salt water between him and Odawara. Only Shoh alone. Would he not be like a fish flapping helplessly on dry land? Yet, the wisdom of western healing was a teasing lure.

'Forgive me but there is much to consider. My family. Lord Okubo.'

'Of course. And Segawa Sensei.' James was determined to show that he understood the tangled skeins of Japanese life. But as so often in this topsy-turvy land things were not as they appeared, for Shoh brushed away Segawa, saying that as the physician had a son, Shoh's future was not really at the clinic.

They parted at the avenue to the Tozenji. 'You will have a long time to think about it, Tada Sensei. Affairs move slowly where your government and mine are concerned.' They both smiled at the foolishness of officials, never men of science. 'And thank you for taking me to the temple. I shall ponder upon your heroes.'

Suddenly, for the first time, Shoh thrust his hand towards James in imitation of the greeting he had noticed among outsiders.

James took the hand and pressed it firmly.

* * *

In the sitting room of the Tozenji, Dirk Meylan sprawled, fresh-faced and fair-haired while Pev glowered over the chess board, setting out the pieces and then pushing them angrily about.

'Well, James, my dear,' Dirk said, as Wilson came in, 'we are relieved to see you safely gathered in. No terrifying tales of rampaging ronin?'

'The only ronin I saw were dead and buried. Forty-seven of them. What is this about rampaging ones?' He sank into a basket chair finding himself surprisingly exhausted by the afternoon's excursion and, as always, puzzled and wearied by the complexities of this mysterious country he had fallen into.

Pev shot him a truculent glance before returning to his manic chess game. 'Shinagawa is *supposed* to be teeming with samurais thirsting for foreign blood. Dirk and I were on our way there when a lackey arrived full of portentous pomp from the Foreign Ministry with dire warnings. Our day has been ruined,' he added in disgust.

James studied Pev briefly. Always so involved in his own world of disease and healing, he rarely thought about his companions in the Legation. The boy was changing. Were they all? Of course they were, but James Wilson did not notice such things. And he should. He should notice more than fevers and bowel flux.

The door slid back. A servant knelt in the corridor. 'Will the Doctor have the kindness to come to the courtyard?'

With a sigh James lurched to his feet.

Abbé Phillippe, the French interpreter, met him at the outer door.

'Hulloa, Abbé, are you poorly? I say, you are rather pale.'

'*Non, non, ce n'est pas moi. Vite.*' The priest caught his arm and pulled him to the courtyard. A norimon squatted on the gravel surrounded by four bemused sweating bearers, stamping their feet against the evening chill. '*Voilà.* Be careful.'

As the Abbé slid back the panelled door a slashed, bleeding body slumped out against the chair's frame. 'Giovanni, servant of M. de Treilles,' announced the priest.

'Good God!' James shouted to the hovering servants for help and gathered the limp form in his arms. 'He has been cut to ribbons. Quickly, to my bed.'

Pev appeared, attracted by the commotion. At the sight of Wilson's bundle his face blanched.

'Make these blasted servants move! Hot water, bandages. Linen. Lots of it.'

Half an hour later, after Sir Radley had revived the fainting priest with brandy, the Abbé recounted the events as he understood them to the assembled Legation. As a mere servant, Giovanni did not merit a samurai escort but being a man of nervous disposition ('and an Italian' Sir Radley muttered), he always carried an ostentatious collection of pistols and daggers. That afternoon he had stepped out for a stroll accompanied by his pet dog. At the very gateway of the French Legation, guarded by the Tycoon's men, two samurai accosted him. Eager for a quarrel, one kicked the little dog, and when Giovanni protested both assailants whipped out their swords and struck viciously at the servant, who just managed to jerk out one of his many pistols and fire it although the bullet ploughed harmlessly into a wall of the Legation gateway.

'And what of the samurai guards?' Sir Radley demanded. 'What action did they take?'

'*Rien.*' The Abbé shook his head. 'Giovanni, he says they made no protection. No sword. No chase. No assistance.'

'Did no one help him back to the Legation?' Pev asked, horrified.

'No, he walked, crawled from the gateway, crying for help. I heard him and sent for a norimon to bring him to Doctor Wilson.'

James came into the room, drying his hands. 'He is not as badly off as he looks. But of course he has lost pints of blood. He is weak, but he'll live.'

Sir Radley bristled with rage. 'He need only be strong enough to describe his version of this disgraceful business to the proper officials. De Treilles will require my support – and Jessop's –' he glanced at Dirk Meylan. 'Come, Abbé, you must interpret for us at the Foreign Ministry. These people must be made to understand that the powers

161

of the West will not tolerate their citizens being cut down like cattle. If the government will not protect us, we will take steps to protect ourselves. Marines from the China Fleet if necessary. Meylan, advise Mr Jessop that we are on our way to the Ministry. Perhaps if he came to the French Legation. We must make a united party –'

The Abbé staggered to his feet. 'This is my blame. I have been warned.'

'Eh?' Sir Radley wheeled from the door. They all stared at the white-faced priest.

'Last week. In Ueno. I visited the big temple there. A samurai stop me and say me – all foreigners will be killed. It is order of Mikado. I think nothing. What is this Mikado? But now – It was the warning.'

Dirk and Pev exchanged looks. 'Shinagawa,' Dirk murmured. 'A gathering of ronins in Shinagawa. Is this the beginning of the end?'

Suddenly, Pev felt very, very cold, as though the chill steel blade of a sword had touched his throat.

7
Dirk Meylan

'Now I propose a toast to our guests, intrepid as they are charming. To Sir Alastair who has met the dreaded samurai and faced him down, and to Lady Elliot whose beauty brings cheer to our stale masculine society and whose ingenuity guided Cook to new gastronomic delights for this Christmas feast. Gentlemen, raise your glasses to Sir Alastair and Lady Elliot of Hong Kong.'

'Hear! Hear! To Sir Alastair and Lady Elliot.'

Chairs and boots scraped across the tatami as the assembled members of the Legations rose – somewhat unsteadily – to the tribute. Crystal glittered and lacquer gleamed under the candles. Lady Elliot's diamonds flashed against her creamy *décolletage*, a target for all eyes. Swags of greenery drooped from the old beams and in a corner stood a proud little conifer, a Christmas tree decorated after the German custom introduced by the Prince Consort.

'Fine figure of a woman. Lovely shoulders,' Oscar said appreciatively into his glass. 'Superb complexion.'

'Ah, my dear, how starved we are for women of our own kind.' Dirk sparkled down the table to Lady Elliot who sparkled back. At thirty-four, no longer young but still vivacious, the first European woman to visit Yedo, she was thoroughly enjoying being the centrepiece of this Christmas celebration.

'I demand a perfect complexion in a woman. What d'you say, Pev?' Oscar reeled slightly.

'Fine figure of a woman. A bit – buxom and rather pale, perhaps. But, as you say –' Pev raised his glass cheerily – 'a fine figure of a woman.'

Oscar slapped the table firmly. 'One does admire the bravado with which old Sir Alastair drove off that drunken samurai who accosted him. A true Briton. Told that Japanese to go to hell and the villain slunk away like a dog. Then Sir Alastair rode on to look at Asakusa, cool as you please.' He raised his refilled glass in admiration. 'Wonderful!'

Dirk broke in quickly, for Tada Shoh, on Oscar's left, was listening in puzzled silence. 'Now, my dear, this is not the time for such talk. For here we are and it is truly "Peace on earth, goodwill to men." Look at us – Prussians in epaulettes next to republicans in broadcloth next to Japanese in silk. Our Catholic Abbé lies down with the heathen native. Is it not a merry evening?'

'So it is,' Pev agreed. 'But for myself, there are things one misses. The great peal of cathedral bells. A blazing fireplace.'

'No goose – except in Yokohama where no doubt the poachers dine gloriously,' Wilson grinned.

'Let us drink to poachers!' cried Oscar.

'Rot! You've had more than enough,' Pev said prissily. 'Has he not, James?'

'Aye, so have we all, young Pev. Look at Tada's scarlet phizog. Foxwood's eyes are revolving and Dirk is more like a gremlin than ever.'

'My dears, I think I might just hop down to the grown-ups' end of the table and amuse Lady Elliot for a while. Sir Radley has monopolized her pretty smile and white bosom for too long.'

'Alas, alack. Too late.' Pev giggled. 'Presents now. Off we go. Grown-ups by the warm stove; children by the brazier.'

The party lurched and mingled in three languages. Lady Elliot received more Christmas kisses than would have been dreamt possible in Stirling. Presents were exchanged with great good spirit: English books, Nara bronzes, French cognac and Bizen pots. Pev, known to be developing a taste for local wood-cuts, received two prints of Fujiyama and one – from Oscar – of a warm-eyed courtesan stroking a camellia. With great enjoyment he handed out his own choices, carefully thought out treasures. Then as the festivities slowed Ito San, the Japanese teacher, and Tada Shoh were singled out to receive pocket watches ordered from Hong Kong by the Legation staff.

Oscar insisted on tucking the watch into Shoh's sleeve and draping the chain across the sash of his kami-shiro, much to the general amusement of the Europeans and Japanese discomfort.

Dirk smiled wryly at the shenanigans. 'Poor Tada. Does not know whether to be flattered or offended. One man's jape, another man's insult.'

Pev looked at him, surprised. 'Why, Tada can take a joke if any Japanese can. Now, old Ito with his bulging eyes, that's another matter.'

'Would you like a kitten?' Dirk asked abruptly. 'Sweet little black thing. No tail. I found it abandoned at the temple. They do that, you know. Against Buddha's teaching to take life so they bring their unwanted animals – and babies – to the temples. If the kitten's – or baby's – karma is to survive, it survives. If not, it dies. Very Japanese. No one has to assume responsibility.'

'You seem very morose suddenly.'

'Attribute it to the Prussians and those blasted ronins.'

'Not homesickness?' Pev was surprised at how strong the sentiment had proved all evening in himself. Pictures of family celebrations, the groaning board, a candlelit church, had rushed in unbidden time and again to darken the corners of this festive occasion.

'Homesick? And where for, my dear? The Holland I fled as a youth or the New York I hardly had time to know? My mother is an independent widowed lady of Amsterdam. She wished me into the wide world and so I went. Yedo is my home as much as anywhere.' He glanced around the noisy room. 'Oscar is very merry, is he not?'

'These rumours of massacre terrify him. He drowns his apprehensions in wine.'

'Oscar has a very proper regard for his own mortality. He knows that he will die some day and it seems to him perfectly possible that that death may come soon, and violently, at the hands of wild-eyed ronins.' Dirk grinned. 'Now you, my dear, and I as well, we are too vain. We don't really believe we are going to die at all and certainly not murdered by foreigners. How would the world go on without us?'

Pev thought for a few seconds, struggling through the

165

wine fumes. 'Do you know, Dirk,' he said seriously, 'I do believe you are right.'

'Of course I am, my dear. Ah, it is time for music. I have my flute and Mr Jessop brought his fiddle and I am sure Lady Elliot has a sweet voice. How would you like that kitten?'

'Very much. I'll name it after you.'

'Bracing, this Yedo December. Reminds me of Christmas in New York State.'

'Rather colder than we are used to in Surrey but, as you say, bracing indeed.'

Two cigars glowed red points in the starless night.

'Ain't you off for Hong Kong soon? A few months' leave? I envy you. I ain't been away from here in nearly four years.'

'I had hoped to return with the Elliots but these rumours of massacre force me to stay on a bit, much to my regret.'

'They don't realize at home just how – exhausting – this posting is, do they?' For a few moments the two diplomats stood in common sympathy puffing their cigars under the lowering Yedo sky, many thousand miles from home and family on this Christmas night. Finally Mr Jessop said, 'Your friend Lady Elliot is a fine figure of a woman, ain't she? One misses the company of one's own womankind, don't one?'

'Indeed, indeed,' Sir Radley replied absently.

'I hear Sir Alastair met one of our samurai friends in a state of inebriation. No harm done?'

'No harm done. And de Treilles' servant will live, although the sword cut has crippled his left arm and the man is reduced to a gibbering idiot at the very sight of a Japanese. Did you know two Dutchmen – sailors – were murdered in Nagasaki? And an attack on a Russian in Yokohama failed only because a party of his shipmates happened along. All within a month.'

Again the red points glowed. 'Still,' Jessop said at last, 'not the massacre we were promised.'

'Not yet. You heard about our Legation fire, I suppose. Last week?'

'Deliberate?'

'Possibly. Probably. However, the servants fell to splendidly. Furthermore, the carpenter from Takanawa was measuring and sawing before sun-up. No matter how infuriating the upper classes one cannot help but like the common people.'

Jessop digested this observation in silence. After a minute Sir Radley said thoughtfully, 'You know, the case of Giovanni, de Treilles' servant, worries me the most. Not one samurai of the French Legation lifted a finger to help the man.'

'Hm,' Jessop sighed. 'Excitable sort of chap, of course. Italian. The government claims he provoked the attackers, taunted them with his pistol.'

'Do you really believe that?'

'No. The attackers have been identified as Satsuma men, by the way.'

'Hm. Satsuma behind the Nagasaki affair as well. Ancient clan, isn't it? One of the largest?'

'Major landowners in the southern island. Rich. Powerful. And hungry for more power, or so Lord Ando says.'

Lord Ando never says such things to me, Sir Radley thought irritably, but to Jessop he said, 'Yet the government does nothing about them. Positively medieval.'

'What would you have them do? Set one clan against another and you would have a certain receipt for civil war. The Government cannot keep its own house in order. There have been several more "sudden deaths" among ministers, I understand.'

Sir Radley ground his cigar under his heel. 'Look here, Jessop, you know as well as I do this ronin business is out of hand. De Treilles' servant proves no one is safe. Not one murderous ruffian has been caught. The government allows these people to slash us to pieces while the ministers wring their hands and suggest we return home.'

'What is your solution?' Jessop spoke sharply. 'Land some marines and burn the Tycoon's palace? That is what you and de Treilles really want, ain't it?'

'You may sneer at our China campaign but that country is quiet now. Trade advances. I admit that Summer Palace affair did not sit too well with me, but a stand has to be made and Lord Elgin was probably right to burn it. Show them we mean business. Consider Hong Kong. Pirates routed. British customs officers. Honest weights and measures. No more dust mixed in the tea. Thriving place. Yokohama could be the same.'

An eloquent silence followed.

'I heard an interesting Japanese tale the other day. May I tell it to you?'

'If you must, Sir Radley.'

'A century or so ago, the Prince of Owari was a powerful man in Yedo. His retainers were arrogant and undisciplined, roaming the streets rather like today's ronins. One day a samurai of Lord Misou had the misfortune to brush into eight of Owari's men in Shinagawa, then as now a lawless suburb. Ignoring the man's apologies the eight fell on him with their swords and left him for dead. But he managed to crawl to his lord's mansion where he told his tale before he died.'

'As it happens, I am well acquainted with this story.'

'I will finish it just the same. Lord Misou rushed to Owari Palace to demand the execution of the eight. When the prince refused, Misou began to prepare to disembowel himself. There and then. His honour being at stake, don't you know. The prince agreed the eight would die if Misou would leave but Misou refused to leave without seeing the deed done. So the killers were brought to his presence, beheaded and the lord went home. Honour preserved.'

'Are you suggesting we should encourage de Treilles to disembowel himself in the Tycoon's best parlour?'

'Really, Jessop, you might take this seriously. A show of strength is essential.'

'And?'

'When the frigate picks up Sir Alastair and Lady Elliot I shall request a company of marines be put ashore. De Treilles will do the same when the French navy is next in Yedo Bay. The honour of the western powers must be maintained, by forceful retribution if necessary!'

Jessop said slowly, 'In the East, a man without honour don't exist.'

Sir Radley snorted with relief. 'You will do the same? Request a detachment of American marines?'

'No.'

'My God, Jessop!'

'We are uninvited here. Tolerated by sufferance only.
The opening of this nation to trade may be – is – inevitable but we need not use force to make a tragedy of it.'

'Damn it, man, I could not agree more. Do not assume
that your nation has a monopoly of sentiment for these
peoples' turmoil. But what of our own safety?'

'Forbear a little longer.'

'The English will not tolerate another situation such as
India in Fifty-seven. I cannot answer for my government
if there is a massacre here.'

'Come now, the circumstances don't bear comparison.'

'I do not want Japanese civil strife on my conscience
any more than you do, but we must take steps to protect
ourselves, for the sake of the Japanese as well as ourselves.'

'I do not wish to see Japanese against Japanese; I do not
wish to see Japanese against European; but most of all I
do not wish to see the Union Flag atop Yedo Castle. Good
night.' And Mr Jessop turned on his heel and vanished
into the Christmas blackness.

The ancient cedar beams of the temple groaned. Wind
nosed through cracks in the shutters, snuffling under
windows.

The midnight chill of two centuries penetrated Dirk
Meylan's bones, a chill that all the burnished efficiency of
an American stove could not comfort.

Why are old buildings so much colder than new ones?
Why do I not just stub out this cigar – my third or fourth
too many anyway – and go to my bed? Why do I sit here in
the frigid dark of this Christmas night – waiting? The
Legation is long silent. Jessop, clerks, servants, monks, all
snuggled in their quilts.

And Murasaki? Does she sleep now? Is her tiny frame
cuddled beside the breadth of Nathaniel Jessop? Or perhaps she sleeps alone, wrapped in padded warmth?

No. On Christmas night she will be with him. This is a
night of celebration, for merry-making, even between a
teetotal Yankee and a godless prostitute.

If this were Amsterdam or New York, I would not be sitting listening to my blood freeze in heathen silence. Church bells. Songs. Laughter.

Such melancholy. I *am* homesick. No doubt the drink tells. Far too much claret. Dirk, my dear, go to bed. You are waiting in vain for a forbidden pleasure that now breathes in gentle slumber. Faithful slumber.

Dare I stroll the grounds or would one of those cursed samurai slash me to pieces? No. Not me. I like these people.

Is that a rustling against the boards of the corridor? A greedy mouse or a silk robe?

Be not a fool, Dirk. It is a mouse lusting after our crumbs just as I lust after the crumbs dropped unnoticed by poor Mr Jessop.

A touch on his shoulder.

Beside him a small shadow quivered against the purple gloom. He tossed his cigar into the cooling stove. And then, before sly guilt could smother him, he clasped her in his arms. That silken softness against him drove away all thought of his betrayal.

Pev blew impatiently on his cold fingers. Once one moved more than a foot from the warmth of the stove, the January cold numbed the very marrow of one's bones.

'Checkmate! Once again. I say, old chap, you are makin' this damned easy for me. Don't usually beat you so handily, you know.' Foxwood squinted at Pev's flushed angry face. 'Feelin' under the weather? Here, Wilson –'

'Oh, never mind. I am just not in the mood for chess. We play too much of the blasted game. Take on Oscar or James. They will give you a keener challenge.' Pev shoved back his chair and stalked to the carved blackwood table.

Sir Radley frowned, watching the boy sift irritably through piles of months-old journals recently arrived on the frigate that carried the Elliots back to Hong Kong. This restlessness had been on him for days. At table he picked rapidly over the dishes, barely concealing his impatience at James's slow methodical progress through the courses or Foxwood's repetitious chit-chat.

Damnation, Sir Radley thought, if only that blasted Admiral Penworthy had seen fit to leave us a company of marines! With those infernal Japanese ministers scaremongering about ronins and massacres and with not one reliable protector on the spot, this temple is a prison. Shinagawa and half Yedo out of bounds. Nothing to life but work and chess and short rides through the city. No wonder the youngster is tetchy. Sullivan as well. At their age, at home or in India, they would have a round of parties or balls; pretty girls their own sort, too. A fellow has to sow a few wild oats. But no, for these two, for all of us, every day, the same faces, the same frustrations, the same fears. No doubt about it, we are all so many caged tigers with tempers to match.

Blast that admiral! Too eager by half to see the sights, promise the Foreign Ministers an English frigate some day (my God!) and then sail back to Hong Kong. Could have spared us a few armed men we could trust. Not even Sir Alastair could convince the arrogant old fool. Would a samurai had jumped out at *him*, sword raised! That would have made him promise us a regiment!

A scuffling in the corridor caught his attention. Ah, brandy. The diplomat's release.

But the servant was not carrying a tray. Behind him hovered a groom with unfamiliar tattoos, wringing his hands anxiously.

'Please, honourable gentlemen, Wilson Sensei is requested at the American Legation.'

But the groom pushed the servant aside and gabbled incoherently at the startled men. Pev, struggling for the sense of his words, could afterwards only recollect the guttering of the candles in a blast of freezing air from the corridor. He had thought, incongruously, that the courtyard door had been stupidly left open to the wind and had felt a sudden sense of panic.

Oscar cried out, 'He is talking about Meylan! He says, come quickly to Azabu.' He turned a ghastly face to the others. 'I think Dirk has been hurt. Oh God, not Dirk!'

Wilson rushed from the room. Pev clutched at Sir Radley, 'Let me go too. Please, I beg you. Dirk is my friend. Please.'

171

'Yes. Go on. Quickly. James may require assistance.' Sir Radley stood, bewildered, among the confusion. 'If it has come to this –' He turned to Foxwood, 'Arrange an escort. Ten, fifteen men. This may be an ambush of some kind.'

All his life Pev remembered that terrible ride across the fields and through the black streets of Azabu. The jerking lanterns, horses whickering in panic, the shouts of the escort against a night so cold it tore the breath from his lungs. In the daytime the shops and stalls of Azabu bustled with pilgrims and townspeople but now the low expanse of shutters and walls turned the district into a maze of blind alleys and anonymous lanes. Finally the lanterns of the Azabu Temple glowed at the end of a darkened street. In the flickering torchlight of the compound men moved furtively along the shadows.

Jessop met them in the vestibule. His brilliant eyes glittered in a gaunt face. 'Quickly. Pray God you are not too late.'

Meylan lay in a small side chamber illuminated by a brace of candles. Pev gazed down at his friend. The scarlet cheeks had sunk to dark hollows in a grey face. But it was not this awful death mask that made Pev pull back, sour vomit in his throat. Blood soaked the pallet, the tatami, the covers. Dirk himself was smeared with his own gore. Stinking fresh, the smell clogged Pev's nostrils and churned his stomach.

A weak echo of Dirk's merriment came from the white lips. 'Ah, my dears, here I am, laid out already to save your labours.'

'Be still,' Wilson murmured. He knelt and gently pulled away the covering; his broad back hid the wounds from Pev who was greatly relieved not to see the hacked body.

James sat back on his heels. His eyes met Jessop's.

Dirk said softly, 'Not much time, is there, James? Well, never mind. Enough for my story. But, please, when you write to my mother of this, do not tell her how I died. Spare her the horror.'

Jessop sank to his knees beside the pallet. His voice was as hoarsely loud as Dirk's was weak. 'Don't talk nonsense. Wilson here will fix you up in no time. Ain't that true, Wilson?' he pleaded.

'Yes, Dirk. Look how James patched up de Treilles' servant. He was a terrible mess. Was he not, James?' Pev's hopeless eyes begged Wilson's agreement.

'Alas, my dears, James and I know better. Now, listen.' He swallowed, a spasm of pain contorted his face and then, strength gathered, he began. 'Left the Prussians after dinner. Quite dark, of course. No moon. One samurai preceded me with a lantern, the other three followed. Prussians' temple in a lonely spot. Bamboo groves along the river bank, thick-growing and whistling and rattling in the wind. Unearthly noise in the blackness. I was, I confess, a bit nervous after the alarms of the last weeks. But only owls seemed to notice us. The streets were deserted. A few lanterns, a few bright tea houses. Samisens – a strange plinky sound. When we turned into the familiar lane to the Legation, my fears seemed so foolish. I was quite embarrassed –' His voice trailed.

Mr Jessop said, 'Perhaps some brandy?'

'No.' James shook his head firmly.

The voice strengthened. 'A shriek. The most terrible sound. A banshee. A devil's scream. I can hear it now. Six, perhaps seven rushed out from – a garden, an alley. I know not. The lantern bearer vanished and so did those behind me. I saw and heard them go. Whatever excuses are offered, they ran and left me to defend myself against half-a-dozen. I spurred my horse and laid about me with my whip.'

Jessop groaned, a deep, barely human sound.

'You have guessed. No pistol. Despite your commands I would always forget the blasted thing. Yet, now such is my experience, I can tell you a pistol is of little use. No time to draw and cock it. So be consoled. And prepared.

'I fell from my horse. They disappeared, believing me dead, I think. I felt no pain. Perhaps I fainted.

'My groom came to me. And then the brave warriors of the Tycoon returned, surprised no doubt that I still lived. They carried me here.'

Gently Wilson bathed the clay-white face, wiping back spiky hair stiffened brown with blood.

'I saw one of them. Handsome, of middle years. Silvery hair. A gentleman, even with a snarl of hate on his face. Oh, the hate.'

He lay breathing thickly for a moment, then smiled at Pev. 'Farewell, my dear. I wish you had not seen this. Do not let my sordid end tarnish your bright dream of Japan. Such a child you are.'

'And James. Bless you for a good man. I wish you had come gallivanting with us sometimes.'

His eyes moved to Jessop. 'Nearly four years. What an old married couple we are. Grouchy – but fond. So fond. That silly little doll's temple in Shimoda. Those long, long days when we thought we were the only two white men left in the world.'

Grey lids slid down. Then he opened his eyes, so brightly blue. 'Forgive me.'

He spoke a few words more but in Dutch. Wracked with sobs, Pev did not know the final moment, only that Jessop brushed by him as he hurried from the room.

Unable to face the streets, Pev and James Wilson sat up the rest of the short night in hard chairs. At dawn Nathaniel Jessop came to bid them farewell. His eyes were red-rimmed and bloodshot. Through the night, mourning his secretary, he had aged a decade.

On the way home Pev asked only one question: 'If help had come sooner, would he have lived?'

'No,' Wilson replied shortly. 'They gutted him like a fish.'

Slim fingers struggled with a tiny iron camellia that concealed the lock of the secret drawer. The fragile cosmetic box shivered under the fierce assault before the drawer snapped open.

Murasaki drew out a small box of patterned Atami paper. Inside, nestled in silk waste, was a man's gold ring. She touched it gently. Hidden away in the little drawer, seldom to gleam in the sunlight, the ring seemed an apt symbol for their love.

And now he was of the Great Void, his life cut short by her own people.

A slow heavy step on the verandah warned her. She pushed the little Atami box back and closed the drawer on it. The camellia lock clicked firm.

When Jessop stepped into the room her face was a pow-dered mask.

Sir Radley glanced around the table. The last occasion when these five met at the Tozenji had been a celebration. A Christmas festivity. Today's gathering was an altogether grimmer business.

Jessop spoke slowly in his accurate but atrociously accented French. 'Do not believe I am indifferent to your sympathy. Without the help of the Legations we could not have buried Dirk Meylan with the honours he deserved and for that I and my government shall be eternally grateful. The affair is not concluded. I have protested on behalf of President Buchanan. A demand for compensation for his widowed mother has been made.'

De Treilles broke in impatiently. 'A protest! Compensa-tion! But M. Jessop, the man was your secretary. The Japa-nese have done nothing, *nothing*, in response to his murder. They even tried to prevent his funeral. A protest! Does his death mean so little to you and your government?'

Jessop turned a haggard face to de Treilles. 'He was a son to me,' he said harshly. 'But that does not mean he was not often foolhardy. He should not have been out alone so late.' He glanced at Von Strappenhausen. The Prussian lowered his eyes in brief regret. Jessop continued. 'Meylan invited attack. He was aware of the menace but he was – rash.' His shoulders sagged slightly. Only stubborn deter-mination to fight the European challenge kept him going.

Sir Radley fought down pity for the man. He said firmly, 'Whether Meylan courted danger or not, his death is an insult, a crime against the western powers. And it is a crime the Japanese government is allowing to go unpunished. This iniquity cannot be tolerated. We must express our con-tempt forcibly.'

Jessop rose and looked down on his colleagues: British, French, Dutch, Prussian. 'Dirk Meylan's murder will not be used as an excuse to start another eastern war or to appropriate chunks of another eastern nation. We will have no British or French gunboats firing on Yedo in his name. Is that understood?'

De Treilles sighed wearily. 'Do sit down, M. Jessop. As

175

smallpox rages in the English ships and the admirals – French and English – apparently do not regard our position as dangerous, they are unlikely to bombard the Japanese coast without orders from Europe. It is a pity, but there we are.'

Van der Hooten, the Dutch minister, spoke. 'In the circumstances, Sir Radley's solution seems the best. We all retire to Yokohama until the Japanese government shows proper remorse. When we are invited back to Yedo with full honours and a guarantee of protection, we shall know the government is sincere in its desire for contact with the West.'

Von Strappenhausen said, 'In such a small town as Yokohama my soldiers from the frigate could defend us against attack. So I believe. The Japanese are not impressive as fighters. Brigands, merely. I agree with Sir Radley that we cannot continue in this manner in Yedo.'

Jessop looked around the table. 'What of the Russians? They are not present today, as usual. Will you abandon Yedo to their ambitions?'

It was Sir Radley's turn to be impatient. 'Their interest is in the northern islands. We can watch them as well from Yokohama. Do not decoy us with the Russians, Jessop.'

'I – decoy you! Is it not Lord Palmerston who cries the Russian threat to cover his own nation's aspirations, just as he punishes the impudence of the mandarins to establish British hegemony in China?' Jessop rose. 'Good day, gentlemen. Do as you think fit but the American Legation will remain at Azabu Temple as long as I am Minister.' He began gathering his papers.

'Just a moment, Jessop,' Sir Radley rose too. He said in English, 'It is imperative that we act in concert. We must not let the Japanese sense division in our ranks.'

'I see no purpose in this wholesale removal to Yokohama. Indeed, you hand victory to the government. Ain't they succeeding in driving you from Yedo as they hoped?'

'They will ask us back,' Ferrier replied firmly.

'It is my hope that they do. You will be sorely missed. We shall be dull in Yedo without you. Good day, gentlemen.'

* * *

Foxwood strode into the sitting-room rubbing his hands together briskly. His narrow face was pink from the cold of the courtyard. 'Well, chaps, they have all departed. And in high dudgeon! Never trusted Americans, meself. No gentlemen. Just fur trappers and tradesmen.'

Pev was playing disconsolately with his black kitten, Dirk. 'What is the news?'

'We are off to Yokohama in a week or two. When we get our affairs in order. Staying at the Consulate. Be damned crowded.' Foxwood scowled.

Pev stared at him in horror. 'Yokohama! Oh, no!'

'I say, old chap. Steady on. Yokohama's a bit of a rat hole admittedly, but the shootin's fine. Besides, we will be among our own kind. Well, perhaps not the sort one would choose for a shootin' party but white faces at least.'

'And Prussian soldiers!' Oscar appeared in the doorway looking quite cheered for the first time since Dirk's death. 'Twenty of them are a match for a regiment of Japanese.'

Pev said desperately, 'But we will be trapped there. On that swamp. No trips to Shinagawa – or anywhere. For how long? For how long?'

Sir Radley came into the room; he glanced sternly at Pev and said, 'Until the Japanese see sense and invite us back. I do not relish Yokohama any more than you do, Fitzpaine, but despite Jessop's eccentric determination to remain in Yedo the other nations will demonstrate their displeasure with the government. Damn Jessop,' he added furiously under his breath.

'Mr Jessop is not going?' Pev asked. 'Will he be safe here?'

'Who can say,' Ferrier replied. 'His conversations with Lord Ando have been more intimate than mine or de Treilles' but Lord Ando cannot protect him from ronins.'

'He certainly did not protect Dirk,' Pev said bitterly.

James Wilson had been sitting quietly by the stove. Now he rose. 'If you will excuse me, I must find an escort and ride to the clinic. This removal is a blow. My work with Tada Shoh and with the patients – my patients – will be suspended.' He looked hopefully at Sir Radley, 'This change will cause grave difficulties. I do not suppose I could stay there while you are in Yokohama? Live at the clinic? No, I thought as much.' He turned dejectedly.

Pev watched the distracted doctor leave the room, bowing his chestnut head under the low lintel of the door. He was too filled with pity for himself to sympathize. Disease would be here when James returned to Yedo, but would Umegawa forget Pev? Japan without Dirk or Umegawa was a prospect so bleak he could not envisage it. James's distress was real enough to Sir Radley, however. But in Yokohama, James would find sick to cure. He would not cool his heels in frustrating inactivity like the rest of them. Not for the first time Sir Radley found himself envying James Wilson.

8
Akiko's Triumph

When the dying moon of the old year burned saffron, Shoh joined the throngs of homeward travellers on the Tokaido. Odawara gaped at his journey's end, a baited trap, yet he knew that to have the family's future unresolved when the sliver of the new year's moon rose would bring misfortune to them all.

No snow lay on the coast but at evening as he crossed the marshes to Hirasuka fat flakes drifted down from the mauve sky, sparkling, freshly white over the dull drifts of last week's fall.

The inn was already stirring when his servant roused him before dawn. 'Come, master, let us be on our way. Everyone will be hurrying to cross the mountains before the passes close. Already people are pressed sleeve to sleeve at the barrier.' And indeed the guards at the Hirasuka barrier growled their cold morning disgust at samurai and commoner alike.

In the quick-gathering dusk the Tada house had a shabby look. One camellia glowed, a pink pearl in the dark straggling hedge. The paths were unswept; the lantern unlit; the shutters were pulled tight against the cold.

Tears filled Hanae's eyes as she greeted him. She seemed as winter-grey as the evening, with the tired face and tallow complexion of a woman whose sleep is haunted by ghosts.

'This unworthy Hanae must welcome Shoh San to a house of sadness.'

His heart went cold. 'Is it Akiko?'

'Your honourable mother has vanished with Shohtaro. This stupid Hanae believes they have gone to the Iwa house, her family in Suruga. I sent a message to you in Yedo by the courier three days ago. You must have passed on the Tokaido.'

179

Shoh sat cross-legged on the tatami, his face in his hands, overwhelmed by this half-feared news after the fatigue of the journey.

'Has my uncle in Suruga welcomed her back into the Iwa family? He is a hard man, not a reed to bend in the wind, and when she came to the Tada house she died to the Iwa. Surely she has not gone so far for nothing?'

'I fear that she would risk the winter journey and her brother's wrath rather than accept rice from Shoh San's hand. But it is Shohtaro of whom she thinks. His is the breath that keeps her alive.'

'But has she silver? She must hire kago at the relay stations. Food. Inns.'

'As for silver, Akiko Sama's kimono trays are empty. All her robes are gone even – her white silk, the one she put aside after mourning for her husband.'

'Certainly to be sold,' he said sharply. 'The silk was fine. It would bring a good price.'

Kimi brought warmed saké. From around the door little Hideko's bright eyes peeped at her father. He held out his arms and the round child flopped in a respectful bow and then scuttled shyly to his lap.

'Well, my little apricot bud. Elder Brother has gone off on an adventure with Honourable Grandmother. A secret adventure, né?'

'That is so, Father,' she whispered.

'Did Elder Brother share his secret with Hide-chan?'

'Oh, no, Father! Shohtaro is too busy for sisters. He learns the way of the samurai in Suruga. He will blossom and fall like the cherry flower.'

Shoh looked over her daughter's glossy head to his wife weeping quietly behind her sleeve. 'Are the passes over the mountains clear? I will leave for Suruga tomorrow.'

The Tokaido climbed and plunged, twisting its narrow way across the Hakone peaks. Shoh stumbled over the hard ruts and crawled up ice-bound steps carved in sharp rock. At dusk he stopped at inns built where steam from the hot springs puffed up through the snow. Here he soothed his cold, aching body in sulphur baths. Life in Yedo had made him soft as a lap dog and he lacked

Akiko's iron will to carry him over the heights in a few gigantic strides like a long-nosed mountain demon. How else could an old woman and a boy manage such a journey? Even the Kago bearers refused fat purses when the ice was slippery in the passes.

After three days he descended into the province of Suruga. Glittering fearlessly in the sun, Fuji taunted the tiny figures struggling through melting snow towards the small castle town where the Iwa served.

Shoh paused at an inn to bathe and dress in black silk haori and hakama while his servant carried a scarlet name card to his uncle's house.

Iwa replied that he would receive his nephew at once.

The mansion was an ancient sprawling affair near the castle. The iron-panelled gate was barred with emblems of mourning. Shoh was led through courtyards and along polished corridors to a reception room of simple but elegant proportion. Against the aged pine of the alcove a spray of early plum spread bony branches sprinkled with a few flowers chaste as death. Seated on a cushion his uncle waited, a small spare man with the same smooth carved features, the same air of humourless disdain that Akiko had passed to her second son.

After the obeisances and courtesies had been offered and received, Shoh said, 'Forgive me, Uncle, but this Shoh has come at an unpropitious time for I did not know your house was in mourning.'

Iwa raised an eyebrow. 'Then, Nephew, were you not aware of your mother's intention? Left she no letters at the Tada house?'

His fears were confirmed yet his lips could not form the questions. Unperturbed, his uncle continued in his brittle voice, 'It is my proud task to inform you that Akiko, my younger sister, committed seppuku three days past. I myself witnessed her death. She passed into the Great Void with the true resolution of her samurai breeding.'

Unable to bear his uncle's cool white stare, Shoh dropped his eyes.

'You will want to honour her and the graves of your maternal ancestors at the Kannon Temple. My sister's ashes await you there. They must be removed to the Tada burial ground where she belongs.'

'My son?' Shoh's question rang too loud in the austere stillness of the room.

'Naturally, he will remain here. Although Akiko was of the Tada house, we, the Iwa, must honour her dying wish to educate Shohtaro as bushido dictates.'

'He is my son.'

'He will be adopted into the Iwa family after he lays aside his mourning clothes. To go against Akiko's final desire would be unfilial, as Tada Shoh must realize.'

Tada Shoh did realize. Through her death Akiko had achieved complete victory.

Her brother folded his fan and replaced it in his sash. The audience was over. Affairs between the Iwa and the Tada were closed.

A servant brought Shohtaro to his father, but Shoh could not meet the grave eyes of the child before him.

'Your grandmother made her wishes known to you before her death?'

'Yes, Honoured Father.' He drew a familiar cloisonné-handled dagger from the sash of his white hakama. 'Here is her wedding dagger, the blade she used. Now it belongs to this Shohtaro and I have cleaned it very carefully as Grandmother commanded.'

'You were there?' Shoh stared horrified at the Buddha-calm face.

'Ara, yes. Grandmother's death was fine. She needed no assistance from my Uncle Iwa. The cut was deep and true. She departed this world of sorrow in peace.' A priest could not have been more detached.

Shoh turned away from this terrifying child who would soon cease to be his son. Without regret he abandoned Shohtaro to the stale, airless world of the Iwa, Masayuki and Akiko. Empty of all sorrow, he pushed back the shoji and left this house of ordered elegance.

Kneeling in the centre of the room Shohtaro touched his forehead to the tatami in polite farewell to his father.

The setting winter sun bathed the ancient weather-worn cedar of the Kannon Temple in strange terracotta light. A priest glanced incuriously at Shoh, standing with empty hands and empty heart before the shadowed altar. The dying sun just caught the white brocade funeral wrapping, staining it a dull blood-red. Inside the wrapping was a pawlonia box with Akiko's ashes.

Shoh attempted to say the right words for his mother's soul, but after a few moments he turned from the altar railing.

The ritual was as meaningless as the ashes in the pawlonia box.

Shoh reached Odawara on the second day of the New Year. Pine branches and bamboo, mikan and rice cakes decorated the gates he hurried past. Sacred ropes of straw looped from the eaves of houses and swathed the Inari Shrine. Bustling worshippers in new kimono stared at the tired dirty man and darted through the torii in case this peculiar creature who travelled at this time when no one travelled should bring misfortune for the New Year.

As though in anticipation of Shoh's tidings, Hanae had ritually swept the room but no boughs of pine or bamboo graced the gates of the Tada house. The salt of death lay on the doorstep.

Defiled by his mother's seppuku, Shoh could not take comfort in Hanae's body, although he longed for a few moments of oblivion. He lay beside her in the house prepared for mourning, listening to the rain on the verandah. Sleep would not come to obliterate his thoughts. Finally he took the lamp and slipped into the corridor. The old boards groaned as though they too longed for rest but Hanae and Hideko slept on in the dreamless peace of exhaustion.

The flickering lamplight darted into the shadows of Akiko's room. Even now, he thought of it as Akiko's room although all his life this had been the place where rice was eaten, ancestors honoured, lessons learned. Here he and Masayuki had played as babies, quarrelled as youths. And now, how barren the room was, the Chrysanthemum sword vanished from the alcove and the family treasures sold for silver.

Yet the room was not empty. From the silence of the

family shrine, from under the eaves, swirling from the corners, ghosts gathered. Limbless wraiths watched him with cobwebbed eyes – and mocked the physician who was not strong enough to live by bushido.

Akiko's ashes were buried by the Tada monument in the cemetery. The proper prayers were said in the temple. Shoh accepted phrases of sympathy from his uncles in the Tada family, but their sleeves and his remained dry. Akiko was not a woman over whom one wept.

As soon as he could without showing disrespect for his mother's spirit, Shoh prepared to return to the clinic in Yedo. With surprising firmness Hanae declined to accompany him.

'The Tada house is the home of Shoh San and of Shohtaro. Should your son return to his own family, it is here he will come.'

Shoh replied, 'He will not leave Suruga. I am sure of it.' He remembered the cool, grave face of his child.

'But if he should, I must be in this house. Waiting. The Tada house is the Tada house. This Hanae belongs here.'

He did not touch her but said gently, 'This Shoh would welcome Hanae and Hideko in Yedo.'

'It is my duty to keep this house ready for Shoh – and Shohtaro.'

And so, when Shoh set off once again for Yedo, Hanae was alone with Hideko and Kimi in the cold shadowed rooms.

On the day of Akiko's seppuku Masayuki strode across the scarlet sweep of the Sanjo Bridge in Miyako, the city of the Emperor. As his mother's blood was dyeing the death silk to crimson he bowed his head in reverence before the icicle-fringed walls of the Imperial Enclosure. Although cold, fatigued, still dressed in muddy leggings spattered with brown stains from Dirk Meylan's fatal wounds, his spirit soared, for he had come to lay his deed before the Descendant of the Sun Goddess.

Secluded inside those crumbling walls the object of Masayuki's devotion, Emperor Komei, sat on worn cushions shivering in his layers of ancient, threadbare brocade.

Chinese screens blocked whispering draughts but no brazier even of the finest Arita porcelain could defeat the bone-numbing river valley chill or the steady plink of melting snow dripping through the broken tiles of the Imperial roofs.

Around him his courtiers murmured: plump, painted men cloistered in a dead city mewing their contempt for the rich vulgar world beyond the bridges of the Capital. Intelligent, bored, his mind festering under the subtle poisons of rumour and flattery, Emperor Komei turned his frustration against the Tokugawa Shogun in Yedo who usurped his powers and the long-nosed intruders from over the seas who trampled, unbidden, across his precious islands. And to his Capital came many men eager to serve the Emperor in his blind hatred.

Reverence paid, Masayuki turned his back on the cloistered Presence he had walked the frozen Tokaido to adore and made his way towards the Gion Shrine. On Kojima's instructions he was to seek out one Sometani, formerly of Mito. 'A fine man,' Kojima had promised. 'In his veins runs the blood of the Tokugawa – his mother was my lord's half-sister – but his loyalty to the Emperor is as pure as new snow. He works for the Jōi cause among the dissatisfied warriors gathering in the Capital. Only a man of his birth could be accepted by the courtiers and the samurai.' To Sometani, he was to carry news of the interpreter's murder and to learn how the cause progressed in the Capital.

Sometani lodged in the Inn of the Peach Moon – 'somewhere on the outskirts of the Gion pleasure quarter' – but once away from the wide straight boulevards and with the shrine behind him Masayuki was soon lost in a serpent's coil of hilly streets. He stopped a ronin to ask the way but the man merely shrugged, muttering something in a dense Shikoku dialect. A jovial townsman bent on enjoyment was no more informative and Masayuki was beginning to despair among the confusion of lanterns and door curtains painted with every name but Peach Moon. He entered a cook shop warm with the fragrance of noodles and to his relief the proprietor looked up from his iron pot of bubbling soup, wiped his brow with a grimy headband and gave directions in his soft, sibilant Capital drawl. As Masayuki returned to the street he heard the cook hiss at a customer, 'City's full of strangers nowadays. Too many brawny lads with swords for my taste. You'd think he would buy a bowl of noodles in gratitude. I'm a businessman not a barrier guard with nothing better to do than hand out city guides.' Masayuki let the door curtain drop. He was learning quickly how very out of place a brisk-speaking eastern samurai was among the scented venomous shades of an Imperial glory long past. Little charmed him in the venal arrogance of these folk languishing in the Emperor's shadow.

At a small shrine among brooding evergreen oaks he turned into a lane. Koto music, odd melodies unfamiliar in Yedo, drifted into the afternoon from a few clustered tea houses. A straggly bamboo copse edged a canal of still, black water and blighted reeds.

The road turned around a wooded slope. Masayuki stopped, struck stone-still with astonishment. Ahead, listing drunkenly in the frozen ruts of the mud street was an ox-carriage! Servants in silk hakama and high-pointed hats moved restlessly around the lacquered wickerwork cart, looking about the bleak surroundings with ill-concealed nervousness. Only the ox himself, stupidly patient, seemed unaware how startling this aristocratic vehicle appeared in such a desolate district. Just off the road stood a two-storey thatched building with broken window bars and blistered walls. Black characters on an orange lantern proclaimed the Inn of the Peach Moon.

Masayuki hunkered down by a thicket of scrub to wait and watch, shivering in the cold fetid mist off the canal. Suddenly the greasy door curtain swung back. Several servants strode out and then a tiny plump apparition in swansdown-padded brocade fluttered majestically from the inn to the carriage. A tall, spare ronin followed and fell to his knees in the hard mud. Another man, obviously the innkeeper, crawled out in obeisance to the noble, his belly as low as a man's could go.

In a flurry of activity the noble was packed into the lurching carriage and with much shouting and pushing and urging the servants persuaded the ox to plod down the street past Masayuki. The ronin and the landlord remained in the mud.

Masayuki waited until the street returned to empty silence and then made his way to the inn, rather nervous at approaching a place, however humble, where a court noble had stopped.

At his hesitant call the landlord slipped out from an inner room. Excitement over his Imperial visitor still glittered in his crossed eyes and vibrated from his scrawny frame. He bowed and, with the same soft insolence as the noodle cook, directed Masayuki along a dim corridor to a sour garden that had never been sweet. Lingering in the acid air the last subtle scents of court robes lent a disturbing luxury to the damp walls and cracked shoji.

At the door of the second verandah room he knelt and called out his name, family and mission. A low, firm voice bade him enter.

When Masayuki lifted his eyes, he found himself in a small immaculate room furnished only with a kotatsu and a letter box of superb Yedo gold lacquer. Studying him from narrow obsidian eyes was the spare man who had escorted the noble to his ox cart. Although Masayuki had seen few portraits of the Shogun or his ancestors something in the slack line of the throat and the heavy jaw spoke of Tokugawa lineage. Despite the shabby surroundings he found himself acutely aware not just of his stained leggings but that he was the second son of a low-ranking samurai in service to a minor daimyo.

Precisely he intoned his tale of the Dutchman's murder and affairs as they stood with the White Cherry Brotherhood, always conscious of that appraising stare. Sometani asked several questions. Masayuki explained that as the Brotherhood's numbers were small, it had not been possible to follow the interpreter's death with further attacks. Sometani nodded. Masayuki hoped he had not guessed that Meylan was his first killing.

'Your news pleases me, Tada Masayuki, and your presence in the Capital is most appropriate at this time. After refreshment I will explain how you can serve your cause, here, in the next few days.'

A servant, shabby but respectful in manner, brought

saké and a few simple dishes from a cook shop, but Masayuki was too much in awe of his host to relish anything. Despite his hunger, the rice and vegetables were no more than dust in his mouth.

Presently Sometani spoke. 'This afternoon this humble samurai had the honour to receive an important guest: Fujioaka no Kami, who you may know is the Chancellor of the Imperial Library.'

Masayuki knew little of the Court but the position would have impressed him even without the reverence reverberating in Sometani's voice and the same glitter of excitement in the obsidian eyes Masayuki had sensed in the landlord.

'The message he carried is a serious one for the Jōi movement.' A shadow weakened the hard stare for a moment.'Fujioaka no Kami honoured this humble bushi by showing me a letter he received from Shimazu, Lord of Satsuma, the man nearly all are agreed should lead our movement. In this letter Shimazu reveals how ronin have approached him to take command of the Jōi party. In great detail he relates the terrible violence these ronin promise to inflict on the barbarians and those of our people who serve these intruders. Massacres. Total annihilation by sword and flame.'

He peered closely at Masayuki as though looking for signs of slaughter in his eyes. Masayuki returned the stare, but blandly, for some instinct warned him to empty all hatred from his mind.

Sometani nodded, apparently satisfied. 'Naturally, deaths such as the interpreter's are necessary, but these cries for massacre do our cause no good if they repel the courtiers and His Sacred Highness.' The soft voice dropped a tone lower. 'No one but Shimazu himself knows what motives move the great Lord of Satsuma. Those who have left his service to become ronin claim he covets rich overseas trade for his southern ports and therefore he does not truly revile the barbarians but wishes to use their ships to bring wealth to Satsuma. Does he wish to obey the Divine Will or simply to accrue greater power for his clan, so long neglected by the Yedo samurai? His distrust of the Tokugawa is certainly for the authority held by the

Bafuku. But of one thing I am certain: Shimazu will act only with the approval of the Imperial Court and now these threats of violence have upset the courtiers who have most influence on His Majesty. His Majesty has called for the expulsion of the outsiders, but what if his mind should be changed by timid aristocrats who live in a world apart? Without the Mandate of Heaven, what purpose have we?'

Masayuki had no need to answer, but he wondered why he was being taken into Sometani's confidence. How could all this concern a lowly member of the White Cherry Brotherhood?

As Sometani waved to his servant to pour more saké, Masayuki saw that the Mito ronin's hands were as soft as his voice, smooth, without callouses, uncoarsened by the sharkskin hilt of a sword, and he felt a brief, disrespectful moment of contempt.

'Your arrival in the Capital at this moment is an act of the Gods. A secret meeting has been arranged between this Sometani and Shimazu himself at an inn on the Nara road.' The hard eyes fell on Masayuki. 'To cut out the tongue of the barbarians was wise; killing the interpreter was the restrained act of true bushi. Your story may well help convince Shimazu that the Jōi party deserves his illustrious participation. Does Tada understand?'

Masayuki was not sure that he did understand, but he hid his confusion in a low bow. It was his duty to obey the orders of Kojima's colleague.

'Good. When the last moon of the year wanes, we shall meet with the Lord of Satsuma. Then we shall reveal the sincerity of our hearts.'

'Oi, listen to me, Sometani. I tell you this meeting is a waste of time. Why do you think so many once loyal men of Satsuma have abandoned their lord? If Shimazu really wished to drive out the barbarians we should not now be ronin but at home, in Satsuma, sharpening our swords in preparation.'

The Satsuma ronin urged his horse hard against Sometani's, thrusting his arguments again and again at the impassive Mito back.

Another southern voice rose from the knot of horsemen.

'Iwaki speaks the truth. It is only plots against the Tokugawa Bafuku that stir our former lord's ambition. Let us turn back to the Capital and choose another to lead an attack on Yokohama and Nagasaki. That is our concern as warriors. Leave politics to the Court and daimyo.'

'If this meeting is so pointless, why do you Satsuma men accompany us, prattling disaster like so many Kyushu crows?' growled another ronin, voicing Masayuki's unspoken thoughts.

'Lord Shimazu only pretends to despise the barbarians in order to please the Emperor,' Iwaki snapped. 'Already he has ordered the harbour deepened at Kagoshima to receive western trading ships. Or so it is said.'

Thus they had quarrelled ever since setting out from the Inn of the Peach Moon: ronin from Satsuma, Tosa, Mito and one, Masayuki, from Odawara. Picking their way through the dusk-shadowed streets, over ruined walls, past the rubble of the Rashomon Gate to the Nara road, the dispute had circled as completely as the Wheel of Fate. Masayuki, following Sometani's example, kept himself aloof but he marvelled that men swimming in such a wide river of hatred could be so divided by the flowing currents. One praised him for the Dutchman's murder, another sneered at the White Cherry Brotherhood's single paltry death while barbarians poured into the treaty ports, a third wished to slaughter Lord Ando, a fourth to die fighting the barbarians in the streets of Nagasaki.

Dank chill discouraged all but necessary travellers. Ragged layers of heavy blue-black clouds gathered in sluggish masses, sullen witness to the bickering ronin, but as they approached the burnt-out castle of Fushimi an orange moon slid through to illuminate briefly the snow-covered spiky ruins of wars fought long ago. An owl, startled by the horses, called crossly from a clump of conifers to her mate circling the low dark hills.

The meeting place was a large inn with several wings. Grooms walked a number of horses snorting silver breath into the night. The Satsuma party had already arrived.

Flustered by so many armed men under his roof, the innkeeper hurried Sometani's group to a two-storey wing at the end of the long outside corridor, away from the glowing shoji of the main building. The flare of lanterns dangling from the deep eaves dazzled Masayuki after his dark ride.

The door slid back. A tall samurai rose to greet Sometani. Masayuki's impression was one of sombre dignity: a dark, lined face, deep eyes under thick brows, a formal kimono marked with the black encircled cross of Satsuma.

'Greetings, Sometani San. This person is Narage, retainer of Lord Shimazu. My lord has been detained but requests that this unworthy Narage serve as his deputy.'

The voice too was dark, sombre, and sent a thrill of unease through Masayuki's bones.

Sometani bowed, his irritation ill-concealed yet with no choice but to accept the surrogate.

By the light of several standing iron-framed lanterns Masayuki saw a semi-circle of samurai also wearing the Satsuma crest. Gaily kimonoed maids scurried about with trays. The scene should have been a cheery one but it did not cheer Masayuki.

Narage introduced the other Satsuma men and then in his smooth dark tones suggested, almost commanded, that as Sometani had brought so many men only his chosen lieutenants should remain, the others not immediately necessary adjourning to the upstairs room. As the lower chamber was indeed far too crowded Sometani waved half a score men to the ladder.

Surprised to be among the dismissed, Masayuki was the last to leave. Just before he stepped up into the dim upper room, his hand on the top rung, he looked down. In the light of the standing lanterns the shaved foreheads of the Satsuma samurai shone in gleaming contrast to the ronins' bristling hair as the two groups settled themselves on the rectangular pattern of mats.

Grumbling at their exclusion, the Jōi men upstairs applied themselves to the saké so generously poured by pretty maid-servants. At first Masayuki held back for he was temperate by nature and discipline. He knelt, the Chrysanthemum sword lying at his side, slightly apart from the others. Eventually a slim lass with a face shaped like a melon seed approached him with a decanter and, beguiled by her gentle smile, he lifted his cup. Gracefully she slid from man to man pouring wine. Another girl brought trays of delicacies, insubstantial slivers of burdock and dried river fish that only teased Masayuki's hunger. Moving quickly around the room a third girl gathered up the swords and placed them out of temptation's way.

Soon Masayuki found himself comfortably numb, at ease with his amusing companions. His eyes throbbed in a head that no longer seemed connected to his suddenly clumsy body. The unease that had dogged him from the Inn of the Peach Moon faded to a distant unimportance.

From somewhere, in that distance, came a crash and then another. The fragile pavilion shuddered. An earthquake, perhaps.

Iwaki, the Satsuma man, lurched toward him, gesticulating wildly with his empty sword hand. Some men could not take wine at all. It was as well all the swords had been removed to safety. Masayuki smiled with blurred tolerance into the angrily distorted face until Iwaki gave up and stamped furiously off into the shadows creeping up the ladder.

When Masayuki awoke he was lying sprawled on the tatami, legs entangled with his neighbour's. Slowly he became aware of one discomfort after another – his bladder full, his throat rough as sand, his limbs cramped, a pounding in his head like festival drums. He shifted, winced, opened his eyes, closed them again, but the demands of his bladder forced him back to consciousness. Thick grey light filled the room. Here and there a body twitched or snorted but the maids had vanished. As Masayuki struggled to his feet hot acid vomit surged up his aching throat but he managed to control himself. Dull dawn light turned the shoji to unpolished slabs of pewter but beyond must be fresh air at least. He pushed one sliding door back and stepped out on to a balcony slick under rain. First things first. He sighed with a release almost painfully pleasurable as his urine shot in a silvery arc over the railing. Then he threw back his head to let the needles of rain refresh his eyes and mouth, cooling his tongue, seeping through his hair down his throbbing cheeks into the sticky heat of his haori.

Now fully awake, he began to take in his surroundings.

The inn was dark, all the bright lanterns of the night extinguished like black apples hanging in the streaming dawn. Somewhere horses snuffled and stamped. Below him he heard the dull murmur of a man's voice.

Sometani. The others downstairs. Were they too numbed by wine so freely poured?

He crossed the room to the trap door where the ladder should rest, but nothing, no wooden rungs, led down into the dimness. Without thinking he lowered himself into the hole, swinging a moment in dark space, his hand clutching at the frame of the opening, before he let himself drop. He fell on to something lumpy, stiffening and cold that made him gasp in shivery horror.

The shutters had not been closed. A man stood in silhouette against rain-silvered light crawling across the rectangles of colourless tatami, across men sprawled, but men who neither stirred nor groaned but lay like rigid staring puppets. Black patches stained the mats, blobs of ink shaken from a giant brush on to the abandoned puppets.

From the silhouetted figure came a sombre voice, smooth as a death plaque: 'So. The first of the revellers appears. Stand still, ronin, and listen to what this Narage has to say.'

As Masayuki's hand clawed at the empty sash where the Chrysanthemum sword should be the voice continued, coolly sardonic. 'Your swords have been appropriated, ronin, while you lay in drunken stupidity. They will be returned. We of Satsuma do not wish to deny you your honour.'

A harsh cry of rage and disgust tore from Masayuki's throat as he sank down beside a slashed corpse. Those pretty maids, smiling, obliging: one poured saké, one brought food, one gathered up the swords. But his dagger was still his. He drew it and stumbled to his feet toward Narage. First this Satsuma killer must be dispatched to the Void then he, Masayuki, must follow to atone for his disgrace.

A strong hand caught his wrist and shook the dagger free. 'Not now. Listen to Narage!' commanded another Satsuma voice at his side.

Grey light from the window filtered across Narage's face, washing away his dark features, but Masayuki knew he would never mistake that sombre voice.

'Hear me, ronin. I serve Lord Shimazu and I have killed at his bidding. Satsuma has no quarrel with the barbarians or with you. We wish only to contain the power of the Bafuku and see His Sacred Highness restored to his proper authority over the land. The Jōi path is a treacherous path, one that may bring war and desolation to Nippon. Therefore, although Lord Shimazu appreciates the sincerity of Sometani San and his followers, he cannot be associated with such reckless plans. Last night, while you and the others caroused, we explained Lord Shimazu's position to Sometani San but we soon realized he, like his party, was bent on the barbarians' destruction. He had chosen his way. We have chosen ours. We did not murder wantonly but to show the Imperial Court that Satsuma does not wish to be distracted by the question of the outsiders' presence in Nippon.'

'Sometani San was armed?' Masayuki demanded.

'Of course. All the Jōi men were. Three of my best samurai lie dead there slashed by Jōi swords.' He pointed to three bodies, rolled in mats. 'We took the weapons of the ronin in the room above. A necessary precaution.'

Masayuki stood, confused and angry. The rattle of rain sounded in the empty room. Upstairs men moved, shaking the building. Like an earthquake. Slowly, as though through a river mist, Masayuki recalled Iwaki's desperate face. Pleading. Vanishing. Now he gazed at the surprising limbs angular on the blood-blackened tatami. Iwaki's eyes no longer pleaded but glared up at him, contempt and justification across their glassy surface.

Masayuki looked from the corpse to question Narage. 'This man was upstairs.'

'He fell. We removed the ladder. Another precaution. The lanterns had been doused. I deeply regret Iwaki's death. His father and my mother are cousins. But he chose one path, I the other. I acted at my lord's command. Iwaki will have understood that.'

'So does this ronin.' Masayuki nodded. 'But so many deaths –'

194

Narage swept a grey arm around the room. 'All these men died in the service of the Emperor. Satsuma. Mito. Tosa. It matters not their clan or birthplace. All that matters is loyalty to His Divine Highness.'

'And this disgraced ronin? And the others, upstairs?'

'We have no quarrel with you or the others. That is why we have waited to explain our actions. Your swords are with the innkeeper. Take them and return to the Capital. No disgrace lies upon you. Sometani died fighting. Honourably.' The voice rose, taking on the hard edge of command as he barked orders to his men.

The Satsuma samurai bustled around him. Masayuki blinked with bare recognition when Sometani's awkward body was dragged past him. Soft, uncalloused by a sword, the hands of the Mito ronin had stiffened into useless claws. Now the samurai pushed past him, bearing their own dead to horses gathered in the courtyard.

Grey morning lit the signs of last night's battle. Smashed shoji, lanterns torn. The ladder lay broken against a blood-spattered wall. The scent of death filled his nostrils, his mouth, his soul, following him along the rainswept corridor, under the darkened lanterns swinging from dripping eaves, as he made his escape from that terrible room.

The innkeeper returned the Chrysanthemum sword but without meeting Masayuki's eyes, just as he avoided looking at the party of horsemen jostling around the gate. As they passed out to the Nara road Masayuki saw that three horses carried not living samurai but large rolled bundles the size of a man. Trailing the group were a string of extra mounts roped together and led by a groom in Satsuma livery. Among those he recognized the scrawny bay that had carried him from the Inn of the Peach Moon last night. Obviously Narage was taking another necessary precaution. The freshness of the rested Satsuma horses would easily outdistance any ronin with a heart for revenge if that ronin must travel on foot.

The innkeeper shuffled away, leaving Masayuki alone on the verandah. Confused shouts came from the direction of the pavilion, but the fury of the Jōi men meant nothing now to Masayuki. From the inn behind him he heard the scrape of rain shutters pushed quickly across the windows and doors. The innkeeper too was taking necessary precaution against angry, betrayed ronin.

A feeling of isolation and stupidity was still upon him. Even Sometani was a stranger; the corpse lying in the courtyard unmindful of the rain was not Masayuki's concern. Why should son of Nippon kill son of Nippon when in the streets of Yokohama and Nagasaki barbarians waited to die?

He wrapped his swords in oil-paper and, thrusting them under his cloak, started down the Nara road, plodding in the muddy wake of the Satsuma horsemen bound for the Imperial Capital.

The rain stopped as he reached the straggling suburbs. The snowy peak of Mount Hiei, pagodas and tall trees, the straight streets, the wood and tiled expanses of the hundreds of temples stood out under a washed dun sky. Masayuki stopped and shifted his burden. He could smell snow in the air. The wind moaning through the pines felt sharp, unwelcoming.

Where should he go! The Inn of the Peach Moon? The forbidding walls of the Imperial Enclosure? No. He wished to escape this city where patriot killed patriot.

Around him citizens scurried about their tasks, eager to be home before the first flakes fell. Many carried boughs of pine or parcels wrapped with New Year's paper. The fence and gate of a shrine floated in the cold grey light, one crimson brightness before the snowfall blotted out all colour. The priest, plump in his padded robes, shouted useless orders to puffing acolytes who struggled to loop a thick twisted rope around the eaves of the sanctuary. Ceremonial barrels of saké, cheerfully painted with their donators' names, stood under the sakaki trees. From the dark branches fluttered white paper prayers, hopeful in the damp wind.

The Festival of the New Year. He had forgotten all about it.

A doctor with unshaven head and two swords pushed past him into a fan shop, hissing sibilant complaints at the shabby ronin blocking his path. It was the time to pay debts. To give presents.

196

To pray for the future.

To be at home.

At the next crossroads he turned north-east toward the Sanjo bridge. The tall cryptomeria on the Tokaido marched away into the hills toward Odawara and on to Yedo, a simpler, purer world on the eastern plain.

The first moon of the New Year was waning when he reached the Tada house. Hanae's white mourning kimono glimmering in the dim vestibule as she bowed in welcome explained his mother's absence more completely than any words.

That night he lay on his pallet staring into desolate darkness, utterly alone. For the first time since Ohisa's wedding palanquin had been carried over the threshold he wished for his wife's presence, longed for the still, gently breathing warmth beside him. But Ohisa was divorced. Akiko was dead. For Masayuki, his home was empty now but for ghosts and death plaques on the family altar.

The next morning he walked as a visitor through the familiar streets, carrying a basket of persimmons for Akiko's grave behind the temple. Busy with other tasks, the monks devoted little time to their cemetery and Masayuki had to push aside heavy boughs dangling over the overgrown path to the Tada monument. A nervous movement in a thicket of dry vines caught his eye: he turned just in time to see a deer bolt over the broken wall and vanish into the larches climbing the foothills.

The Tada monument had been recently cleared by Shoh; the plinth looked surprised and naked without the covering of moss and lichen that obscured other families' memorials.

Masayuki had last come here the day before he left Odawara for Shinagawa. Then it was at his father's grave that he bowed his head. Now, on another stone marker on the disturbed earth, he read the raw, newly chiselled characters of his mother's name.

From the woods the deer called. A fresh wind bent the larches, rattling the bare graceful branches of a ginko by the cemetery gateway. Mournful sounds, yet for Masayuki, staring down at Akiko's grave, grief was tempered by pride at his mother's samurai spirit. Who else remembered in this lonely place had died so magnificently? Renewed ferocity of purpose, Akiko's purpose, surged through him. Banishing the confusions of the Capital from his mind, he strode from the cemetery toward the Tokaido. He would best serve Akiko's spirit not by weeping over her ashes but by working in Shinagawa.

He had left Shinagawa in barren winter but tight white flowers sparkled among the red buds on the plum branches when Masayuki returned, eager to be once again in the house of the Brotherhood. Suddenly a succession of booms, deep as thunder but with the regularity of a drum, reverberated through the hills, shaking the inns and tea houses that hid the bay from the highway.

'Oi! It's nowhere near dusk,' muttered a farmer next to Masayuki. 'Is that the bell at the Tokaji Temple?'

'That's not a bell. An earthquake perhaps,' Masayuki replied.

Another boom followed, clattering the doors and windows but not with the determination of an earthquake. At the cross street a wooden fire tower shivered in the noise. Masayuki shouted up at the watchman who clutched the railing and peered out over the town.

'Oi! Grandfather. What is all the commotion? Can you see?'

The watchman called down to the curious crowd gathering: 'Ara, ma! An amazing sight! The black ships of the barbarians are sailing up the coast from Yokohama. Puffing big clouds of smoke, they are, like so many volcanoes! What a thing to tell my grandchildren!'

'The barbarians? I do not understand. Is that noise from their ships?' Masayuki asked the farmer, who merely shrugged and hoisted his pannier of leeks on to his shoulder. Barbarians did not interest him.

Masayuki asked again, 'What is that row? It sounds like the gods' fireworks.'

A familiar voice spoke out behind him. 'Do you not understand, Tada Masayuki? But, then, you have been long away. To the Capital and back again. Many things can happen in the changing of two moons.'

198

He wheeled and gasped in pleasure at Ohno's white round bean-bun face so close to his own. He clasped his shoulder, overjoyed at the familiar presence, all that remained of his vanished youth.

'Ohno Kun! I was on my way to the House of the White Cherry. Ara, I am so glad to see you. The Capital was terrible.'

Another boom drowned Ohno's reply but Masayuki recognized bitterness in the dark eyes.

'What is all this about the barbarians?'

'Do you hear that devilish sound?' Ohno waved towards the invisible bay beyond the suburb. 'It is Lord Mito's cannon that you hear. The batteries on the islands in the bay. The guns he ordered cast from the temple bells of Mito. The Bafuku fire them not to kill the outsiders but to salute them. Today the diplomats return to Yedo from Yokohama.'

'Ha! This cannot be true. Ara, Lord Mito's cannon are aimed against their ships. Surely!'

'No. Today the barbarians return to Yedo at the Bafuku's invitation. Lord Mito's cannon welcome them to the mouth of the Sumida.' A brief smile lit Ohno's face, eliminating for a second the tired lines around his mouth and eyes. 'But, come. Kojima Elder Brother will be glad you have returned.'

9
Questions of Loyalty

Pev laid down his pen. The creamy paper was smooth as Umegawa's remembered flesh under his fingers. Before Yedo he had never appreciated paper, never imagined the colours and textures and strengths that a craftsman might create.

Writing letters home had become almost an impossible chore. What had he said so far? Their triumphant return to the temple; Mr Jessop's contempt unrelieved; the boredom of life in Yokohama – but then his parents would not understand how he could be bored among his own people. His father would protest at what he had written, he knew; throw the letter down on the table in puzzled disgust. However vulgarly commercial the merchants in Yokohama might be, they were at least white-complexioned and Christian. What had his son come to, preferring the native to his own kind? The East had been the ruin of many of a good man, it was said. Never mind. Pev had not bothered to conceal his relief at being free of the settlement. He had never been despised before and had found it difficult work. Not that he minded being banned from the Yokohama Club but then, remembering the day a clipper straight from Hong Kong brought news that Matthew Morrison, poacher and marksman, had turned up in the Colony and convinced the Consular Court there to overthrow Sir Radley's judgement, Pev shuddered even now. The smirks and taunts had been infuriating. How did one reply to such treatment? Or how did one explain to one's parents that one was a pariah? Even Donalds, the curio dealer, who had sheepishly handed Pev a superb box of gold lacquer as thanks for his help in the fire ('Go on, take it. You'll not see anything so fine again. I swear it!'), even Donalds had jeered when next they met on the muddy boardwalk. Poor Johnstone had been drunk for three days to everyone's embarrassment.

The black kitten yowled at the door for freedom. Although Pev worried about the stray dogs that roamed the temple grounds, he released the cat and watched its long-legged bounce down the verandah towards the kitchen quarters.

Dirk Meylan was dead, buried in the frozen earth of a Japanese cemetery by a brown river. Soon Sir Radley would take his much desired leave in China – a prospect somewhat soured now by Matthew Morrison's victory in Hong Kong. And then Mr Jessop too would quit Yedo, but not on leave. The new American President, Mr Lincoln, was a Republican and Mr Jessop was of the Democratic party, President James Buchanan's man. Because of an election fought over slavery thousands of miles away from Yedo, Mr Jessop would sever his ties with this land he so loved. Absurd.

Pev closed the window and went back to his table. Really, he must get on. Besides, the afternoon was too wet for a stroll before dinner and he had already read *Blackwood's* and *All the Year Round*.

He struggled to envision Exeter and the solid red-stone house behind its thick yew hedge. Eyes closed, he tried to recapture the giddy excitement of an Easter ball: bare shoulders warmed to ivory by hundreds of candles; laughing, rosy-cheeked girls; blonde curls, white teeth. Could he really have been so gauche that the dry dead scent of lavender once roused his ardour?

He opened his eyes, profoundly relieved that many miles lay between him and Exeter; many days of sea voyage which might be spent polishing a veneer of 'young Pev' that his family could welcome. Intent upon a surface, dazzled by exotic tales and presents, they might remain blind to the awakened stranger they embraced. Or would one glance into his eyes warn them that he had tasted delights they could not imagine?

Is this suffering? he wondered idly, enjoying the idea that it might be. To be kept from the woman I love, the light of my life, is this the pain that gnaws my heart?

He pushed back the chair. Oh, do not be ridiculous. Yet, my God, I must see Umegawa soon!

* * *

Early one March morning, viewed by what seemed to Pev to be a myriad silk-bundled officials of the Tycoon, Sir Radley embarked from the bamboo quay in a little boat which would meet the frigate waiting in the bay to carry him to China and a few months of civilized peace. Cold spring mists swirled through the reeds, soon obscuring the black broadclothed figure as the dinghy slid down the tawny Sumida towards the sea.

The afternoon following Sir Radley's departure a surprise fall of spring snow brought Pev his first chance for Shinagawa since the New Year. Foxwood and Oscar were occupied, James zealously pursued beri-beri, but Pev was unencumbered by tasks or responsibilities. He had *not* been ordered *not* to venture to Shinagawa, so, quickly, lest such an order be thought of, he wrapped himself in a warm straw cloak, pulled on a deep-brimmed hat – both souvenirs of the Tokaido – and after a satisfied glance in Oscar's pier glass he slipped out of an unshuttered door. He trusted to the storm for protection, hoping his leather boots thrusting from the straw cloak would not give him away.

The courtyard and stone gateway were unmanned. Not even a groom of their much promised guardians was in sight. Giggling with excitement and success Pev marched along the avenue, plunging through the banks of light wet snow already sloping against the cryptomeria.

Once on the Tokaido he felt an odd companionship with the other becloaked travellers, heads lowered against the swishing snow. Only those who must plodded the muffled city, dark shapes against white-washed streets, locked in solitary yet sympathetic combat with wind and wet and cold. At the war barriers shivering guards paid little heed, heads tucked in their collars, hands clutching earthenware warmers in their sleeves.

The Komatsu-ya was dark when Pev banged at the gate but the tattooed gatekeeper greeted him in sullen surprise. After issuing him into the downstairs room Auntie sent a maid running for a brazier to set under the frame of the kotatsu and poured out warmed saké with her own hand.

Pev drank impatiently, struggling over the banalities of Auntie's conversation while Umegawa prepared herself.

The warmth of the kotatsu numbed his cold wet feet and legs while icy draughts fingered his shoulders and back. Late plum blossom in the alcove filled the damp room with a heavy fragrance.

Finally Umegawa appeared, a trailing sleeve raised against her happy blushes. With a silky 'Take your honourable time. Enjoy yourself,' Auntie retired.

Soon the bedclothes were spread and Umegawa's lessons in love resumed.

Later he murmured, 'Forgive me for this long absence but Shinagawa was forbidden to us while the ronin were troublesome. Such a cruel sadness.'

'Ma, but we were closed to guests. You could not visit the Komatsu-ya, not while the sickness of the moth-egg-rash was upon us.'

He peered bewildered into her smooth face, only lightly painted in his honour.

'Did Pebu San not know? Several houses suffered. The sickness that covers the skin with bumps like moths' eggs came to the Komatsu-ya. Terrible fire seizes the body, burning up all dark moisture. The bumps fester and ooze poison. Poor Takao's face and breast was pitted like a peach stone so Auntie turned her out.' Umegawa trembled in his arms. The picture of a weeping Takao clutching her few possessions clinging desperately, pleading, at the gatepost was still too strong for Umegawa. 'I fear only a very low-ranking house will take her now. Poor Takao-chan. Her karma has always been one of sorrow.' She sighed for Takao, a sad victim of the entangling weeds lying under the smooth surface of the Water World.

'Smallpox! Oh, my God. How terrible for you. Thank God you were not touched.'

'But it has passed now. Since the New Year the sickness has vanished. I ached with longing for Pebu San though.'

'We could not visit Shinagawa because of the ronin,' he repeated. 'Dirk Meylan was killed. By ronin. It was terrible. He was my friend and I miss him very much.' He shuddered at the memory of that terrible January night.

'Ma, what a tragedy,' but Umegawa's thoughts were still with Takao. Her body withdrew from Pev's. Taking this as sadness for Dirk, or sweeter still, fear for his own

203

safety, Pev caressed her, but instead of her usual warm response she seemed distracted. Finally she murmured, 'Would it not be happiness if Pebu San and Umegawa could always be together, in a little house somewhere, away from those who threaten our love?'

'Who threatens our love? Ronin! Nonsense, Umegawa. They have disappeared, I think. And anyway, a little house would be no more secure, unless it were in the Tozenji gardens.' He laughed at the picture of a love nest among the azalea bushes.

'Pebu San does not want to spend his days with silly, ugly Umegawa?'

'Oh, I do. To have you to touch, to hold, to kiss all day long.' His eyes glazed at the mere imagining of her body always within reach.

'Né, would it not be wonderful? I could scrub your back and even cook your rice. Although,' she added practically, 'food from a cook house might be tastier.'

'We must have a kotatsu, né? Wonderful things.'

'And a tiny garden with a plum tree and a pond for water lilies.'

'A fence to hide us from peering eyes, né, Umegawa.' He caught her up in his arms, laughing at the idea of their dream house.

'Umegawa will spend all day just with Pebu San. No other danna. Only Pebu San.'

'Would you really like that? Just me? No other men?' Touched by her silly pronunciation of his name, gratified by her loyalty, he gazed at her with eyes of love.

Umegawa purred in his arms. 'Ara, so much I would like it, to be alone with the man I love. Will you make the arrangements or shall I? But it is difficult for me here in the Komatsu-ya to find a house so it must be Pebu San. But soon? Before the plum blows from the branches.' She was unable to control her urgency, her desire for escape from the Floating World.

He released her quickly. 'But it is impossible. Only a dream.' Frowning, he stared at the ceiling, ignoring the still body next to him.

'Né, forgive me, but it is possible. All Yedo knows of

the woman who lives with the American in Azabu. Just a country courtesan, it is said, but the American clothes her in Hachijo silk. Her hairpins are filigree gold butterflies with pearls and corals in the wings. And she eats rice three times a day. And sweetfish in the spring and mountain mushrooms when the leaves fall.' These gastronomic luxuries had been envisioned by Rika of the ever-hungry belly so those details might be exaggerated but Umegawa threw them in for good measure.

Pev stared at her in amazement. 'How is this known? Have we outsiders no privacy? But anyway, the American is a –' he groped for the most impressive Japanese rank he knew –'he is a councillor to his Tycoon. An important man. But I – the lowest rank – I cannot bring a woman to the Legation.'

'Ma, that is regrettable, but just a little house then. Near the Tozenji.'

'Ah, Umegawa,' he said sadly.

'A step from the gate. Only two rooms and perhaps a tiny garden with a plum tree. No pond or bathhouse, even. I should so like to spend my days making Pebu San happy.' Practised fingers travelled his body.

He groaned. 'Umegawa, I would like to spend my days with you. Oh, how I would like it, but it just cannot be. I have not the power, the silver.'

The fingers pressed and stroked. 'Né, Pebu San, just the littlest house. I will be a respectable woman. No silk. Only cotton. No rice. Millet is fine. Please. I do not wish to die at the Komatsu-ya.'

The fierce desperation in her voice terrified him. 'No, no. Impossible.'

Silence lay between them like a cold stone.

Finally, with the formality of a new customer, he threw aside the quilt and began to dress. Umegawa chose not to help but picked restlessly at the tatami.

He pulled his clothes on quickly, eager to be quit of the room that was now like a trap. The suffocating sweetness of the plum in the alcove was giving him a headache and he longed to escape into snow-freshened air.

But escape, like a little house in the Tozenji garden, proved impossible. Angrily forbidding, the doorkeeper gestured out into blackness lightened only by twisting spirals of silver flakes.

Too late. The Tokaido gate was long ago closed. He was trapped at the Komatsu-ya until dawn.

Auntie clucked cheerfully and relieved him of the rest of his silver and his gold collar pin, a present from his mother when he entered Oxford. A new maid, pop-eyed at serving an outsider, set up a little table laden with bowls of dumplings and vegetables 'to build up the honourable outsider for the night', Auntie encouraged.

Umegawa's charming care soon relaxed him and saké helped him forget that he was absent overnight from the Legation without either permission or escort. But Umegawa's skill could not completely obliterate what had passed between them and it was with some relief that he turned from her to sleep. Yet sleep would not come. Lying in the warm quilts he understood too well that he had become her chosen avenue of escape from her present life. His own pious disapproval of her 'occupation', his determination to rescue her, now mocked him. If she had come to realize the degradation of her sordid existence, would it not be sweetness itself to free her, to make her his own? Indeed, was it not his duty? And yet, he could see no way towards it. Sir Radley's undoubted objection apart, he knew just enough of life in Yedo to suspect that two hundred pounds a year would not comfortably support an establishment for a woman who dreamed in silk and gold filigree hairpins. Two hundred pounds a year would certainly not be enough even in Exeter, not to keep a wife in comfort.

A wife. That posed another, deeper question. For Pev now peered into the vast gulf between a paid female visited on occasions of need and a woman whose very livelihood was in his hands. Even though she was Japanese and a heathen, the idea of a long-lasting liaison without blessing of clergy shocked him profoundly. For once in his short life, he felt his immortal soul endangered.

Then again, how did one release such a woman from the Komatsu-ya? Certainly she could not just wave Oba-san farewell and walk out through the gate. Money must be involved; it always was in this world.

Through the long night he tossed on the plum-spattered quilts, his head throbbing from the unrelenting wooden pillow and the creeping, smothering perfume of the blossom in the alcove. Sometimes he hated Umegawa; other times a warm rustle would remind him of her nearness and he longed for a little house, a refuge somewhere for their love. Then again he railed against himself, caught in this predicament of his own making. It was only when the soft stirrings of the house betokened dawn that he realized that he had just accomplished his dearest dream of the last months – a whole night spent alone with his loved one. But he had enjoyed barely a second of it.

Although release must come soon, the thick-smelling room suddenly became more than he could bear. He groped at the wooden shutters until he found a latch and pushed them back. The garden, pines, the verandah, even the graceful skeleton of a little potted maple lay under an unblemished covering of snow tinted to the warmest rose-gold by the rising sun. Caught in the corner of the verandah like an exquisite collar of rubies and diamonds, a frozen cobweb sparkled in crimson winter light, lacy perfection lying in wait for a victim.

Hurriedly washed and dressed again in his straw coat, he prepared to leave. His head still ached, now as much from hunger as from sleeplessness. Dislike himself as he might for it, he could not help being repelled by Umegawa's unfocused morning mood and the greying blotched make-up on her still professional face. From beneath the lurid kimono he caught glimpses of skin that last night by lantern light had glowed like Devon honey but that now seemed dingy.

They parted with courtesy, like strangers.

Outside the gate the air was cold as a knife. His spirits soared and he threw his head up to clear his mind of the stifling plum-scented pleasure house. Across the glistening expanse of white, where the straggling chain of low houses marked the lane to the Tokaido, a fox stood, poised, one paw held clear of the snow. The animal watched Pev for a second, blinked and then picked its way delicately towards a fenced yard. Somewhere a cock crowed in joy or warning.

On the Tokaido he dug out a few zeni unaccountably missed by Auntie's purse-penetrating eyes and bought himself a sweet potato seared by the hawker's charcoal. His teeth tore into the steaming orange flesh. Rarely had he breakfasted on anything so delicious.

By the time he entered Yedo the town was stirring; shutters pushed back, a few well-wrapped merchants setting out their wares. Cooking-oil sellers and broom pedlars stalked the streets.

Wearily Pev plodded through the deep drifts along the avenue to the Tozenji. A dark figure waited by the gateway but as he came closer he saw to his relief that it was not a samurai but the tall form of James Wilson.

'Halloa. You are out early. Marvellous morning, eh?'

Wilson stonily ignored his bright greeting. 'Where have you been all night?'

For the last mile Pev had been preparing for this. 'All night? In bed. But I woke early and I came out for a walk. I love snow, don't you? We don't have much in Exeter.'

'Rubbish.'

Pev blinked at this uncharacteristic curtness, but a glance at James's stern face warned him against further prevarication.

'I went to Shinagawa. Last evening. But the snow held me there overnight.'

'Without an escort? Without a word to Foxwood? He is responsible, you know, if anything should happen to you.'

'Very well, I am sorry. It was rash of me. But what could happen at this hour?' Guiltily he avoided James's glare.

'When you did not come to dinner and Oscar found your room empty, we assumed you had stupidly set out on your own. Why we should, I do not know, but we have concealed your absence from Foxwood who would most certainly – and rightly – report it to London. He believes you are under the weather. You might sniff and cough a bit this morning.'

Stung by James's unforgiving mien and a belated recognition of his own impetuosity, Pev struck back. 'Well, you see that I am safe enough. It was only a lark. Really,

James, sometimes your puritan disapproval becomes most unbearable. I wish Dirk were alive. He would relish it as amusing.'

James looked at him coldly. 'If, on one of your "larks", a samurai sword fillets you as it did Dirk, I hope it will be another doctor and not myself who is forced to attend your deathbed.'

'Oh, Lord, I am sorry. I was foolish, I suppose. God, what a frightful night it has been!'

This outburst caught James by surprise and he looked again at the red-eyed haggard youth. The envy of Pev's adventure that had lurked so disconcertingly beneath his anger evaporated. He allowed himself to soften. 'Aye, it was only a lark. But a dangerous one, you know. I was not disapproving but worried. Come, get out of those absurd clothes before Foxwood is about.'

Gratefully Pev trotted after James into the familiar vestibule, following after the doctor like a spaniel at his master's heels.

Snow kept customers away from the tea houses and therefore the brothels too were quiet. Usually Umegawa would rejoice at a day or more spent mending tabi, gossiping and sleeping but now the long hours allowed too much time to think of Pebu San. Outsiders were no different from her own men; their love too dried up like dew in the morning sun. With sadness she remembered him as he was when she came down to bid him welcome: tucked in the kotatsu, red-cheeked from the cold, eyes bright with adventure and love; then, his parting: silent, eyes averted, his formality a knife thrust in her heart.

Ara, life was a circle. Love like beauty and wealth was an illusion.

But, just in case, she decided to try a charm for luring a false lover, remembered from her Yoshiwara days. However, when she came to write the Chinese characters for his name on the back of a paper frog, as the charm demanded, she realized her folly. Pebu. How could one write that outlandish word? Crossly she threw down her brush and tore up the frog. Charms that really worked were rare as square eggs anyway.

She forced herself to think of Itaemon San, the wall-eyed but rich pawnbroker who always spent lavishly. His house had many rooms. His first wife was dead and no man could enjoy too many concubines. She tried to shift her dreams of freedom upon Itaemon's askew shoulders, pushing away sweet memories of Pebu San's young body.

Takao's forlorn retreat from the barred gate of the Komatsu-ya was always with Umegawa, a spectre that would not rest. No matter how often Rika chided her, reminding her that Takao drank and had eyebrows too close together (a sure sign of bad karma), Umegawa could not forget. She dreaded to venture abroad, fearing the kago might pass those women who lounge under the cherry trees, a rolled straw mat under their arm. Most of all she dreaded despairing eyes peering out from a face so corrugated by the pox that only darkness could conceal the horror.

To make amends for his illicit adventure Pev applied himself to his Japanese lessons, practising calligraphy and conning vocabulary with an energy that bewildered Ito San. Much of the language he had learned on Umegawa's pillow was not suitable for a young diplomat but all experience is valuable. As so many have before him, Pev discovered that love talk deepens a language, lending a past, memories, and opening up enticing possibilities for the future. If Ito often closed his eyes in shocked contempt, Oscar was forced to be impressed.

'I do believe you've picked up more tea house lingo than even Dirk. If you go on working like a coolie you may actually beat this impossible tongue.'

'Not with Ito as a teacher. Could you – be honest, now – could you make head or tail of what he was muttering about this morning?'

'No! God, what I would not give for a grammar or a dictionary. Or even a working knowledge of Dutch.'

Pev pushed his notebook away and shot Oscar a quizzical glance. 'Look, I have not been to Shinagawa for three weeks. That is penance enough. What do you say to an afternoon? A holiday?' He was not certain that he really wanted to go to Shinagawa but guilt and lust nagged him.

Still, if Oscar said no, well, that would be that. Therefore it would not be his fault if he could not see Umegawa.

'Hm. Do you think it is safe? Perhaps Takanawa would be wiser.' Oscar had lost most of his hardearned courage since Dirk's death. Seldom did he wander far into the city.

'There has not been a hint of trouble. And we are not always welcome in Takanawa. I know Rika looks like a frog, well, a bit like one, but she is a friendly lass. Dirk liked her. I say, how about it? With Foxwood's approval, of course.'

Basil Foxwood stroked down his few remaining strands of ginger hair. 'Shinagawa, eh? Well, why not? Those damned ronin johnnies seem to have gone to earth. Sir Radley wanted us to ride out as much as possible. Why not Shinagawa? Enjoy yourselves, chaps.'

So, off they went.

Surprised and delighted by his visit, Umegawa spared no coquetry, no sweetness to please him. Pev rode home feeling fully satisfied with himself. All had gone well. Nothing awkward had been touched upon. Umegawa was pretty and pert and willing. If his heart did not sing as it had once, well, he was not the child he had been a few months ago. He had not chosen to see the sorrow in her almond eyes as he plunged his watch in his pocket and marched out to join Oscar, leaving Umegawa feeling tired and plain and rather old.

Tucked into the deep sleeves of her kimono was a little silk bag. She reached in and fingered the shape of a hairpin, a silver plum blossom with a coral centre, a present from Pev handed to her with great ceremony and cold-eyed satisfaction that did not really deceive her. Without being told she knew that he had paused at the first cheap silversmith in Shinagawa and hurriedly purchased the trinket. She tried to be touched; she wanted to be touched, but as she withdrew her hand the sharp end of the pin stabbed her finger, making it bleed. Slowly she lifted the wound to her full lips and sucked. Kaoru had always promised she would receive silver hairpins.

The two lotharios returned to the Tozenji after dinner to find Foxwood eager for a chess game and James leafing through a well-read copy of *Blackwood's Magazine*. The

211

young doctor watched his two contemporaries chattering over their tea, his broad face pensive. Finally, he said abruptly, 'Made my fortnightly call to Yokohama today.'

'Ah, yes,' replied Oscar brightly. 'How is the Slough of Despond?'

'Bustling as always. Nearly two hundred foreigners there now. Johnstone at the Consulate has a touch of malaria. He was in India, you know.'

'Isn't whisky good for malaria?' Pev giggled at Oscar. They, the new generation, so easily saw the foibles of the older one – and momentarily James disliked them for making him feel too serious for his twenty-five years. He went on coldly: 'While I was at the Consulate a coolie came from the Gankiro tea house. They had heard I was in the settlement and, of course, no native doctor will bother with the Gankiro. They will flock to the courtesans in the Yoshiwara but the common stews are beneath 'em.'

'No doubt they are an irresponsible, unfeelin' race,' Foxwood remarked. 'If it were not for you doin' your Christian duty those girls would be left to the itinerant medicine men and their pickled snakes.' His freckled nose wrinkled fastidiously.

James's solemnity broke for an instant. 'As it happens, a lot of the women prefer the medicine men to me. But, no, this was a confinement. A difficult one. A young girl, too young, had been in labour a day and night. So the proprietress – whatever you call her, you all would know – called for me. Seems her screams were bad for business.'

The three laymen winced at this intrusion of gynaecology among the tea cups.

'The result was a happy one, I trust?' asked Pev.

'No. I could do nothing for the girl. She died. But I saved the child, which was a pity. For, you see, it was a white man's child. Mixed blood. And of course they won't tolerate that. While I was easing the mother's last moments an old midwife whisked the infant away. By the time I realized it was too late. She had – disposed of it.'

'Good God.'

James looked at them, his usually generous mouth tight with distaste. 'This is the second baby I have brought into the world only to have it helped out again because its blood was impure. The first one: I did not guess, I could not imagine. It was in February, while we were skulking in Yokohama. One of the first times I was called to the Gankiro. When I went back to see the mother the following day there was no baby. She was not at all distressed when she told me of its fate. But I thought that was exceptional. Now I realize infanticide is the common practice in such circumstances.'

James sat on stolidly, his presence heavy with accusation. Finally he rose, nodded to the three men and left the room, abandoning them to their thoughts.

Again Pev hurled himself into his studies but the harder he tried, the greater grew his frustration with Ito's limp convoluted non-teaching. With Dirk gone only Abbé Phillippe offered any enlightenment. While serving as a missionary in the Luchu Islands the priest had learned the language, although the simple life on those tropical isles was poor preparation for the linguistic and social complexities of the sophisticated and subtle mainland culture. The Abbé *knew* that there were dozens of ranks in Japanese society but what these ranks actually were and the myriad different forms of address required were no clearer than beech trees in a snowy forest obscured by thick fog.

The Abbé suggested that Pev and Oscar might ride to Kanagawa to sit at the feet of one Doctor Holloway, an American medical missionary who was making phenomenal progress with the language. In fact, the impressed if disapproving Abbé said, a translation of the Bible into Japanese was under consideration.

At James Wilson's request Tada Shoh accompanied Oscar and Pev. Holloway was always eager to meet Japanese physicians and James hoped that Shoh would find the good doctor's Christian manner appealing. Besides, since his return from Odawara, Shoh had thrown himself so completely into the work at Segawa's clinic that James, as a doctor, recommended a holiday.

The day was fine with scudding clouds and a ruffling breeze which helped disperse the stench of manure rising from the fields and from the tubs standing by the road-side, an invitation to travellers to contribute to the richness of the crops. By contrast to this unavoidable earthiness, the cherry trees were in full, ethereal bloom, as fragile as life itself.

Because daimyo and their retinues were arriving daily along the Tokaido to spend their months of duty in Yedo, the samurai escort demanded the foreigners use a round-about route to Kanagawa. Within a mile of the Tozenji they were lost. The escort, made up of Hitachi men new to the city, remained unconcerned as they wound between hedges glistening with spring green or clopped past low wooden houses. Strips of kimono drying on poles flapped like gay pennants in the breeze. Smooth bowls, iron pots, bolts of cloth, piles of leeks spilled out of the shops to tempt passers-by.

Suddenly they came out on to a bleak open plain. Cedars and clusters of Japanese oaks replaced the bright street life.

Ahead loomed a dark ring of conifers. Croaking angrily a crow flapped up out of the grim circle. One of the escort giggled.

'My God, Pev, do you see that?' Oscar cried out hoarsely, pointing at the clearing fringed by lowering evergreens.

Pev saw. A long wooden rack. On it, displayed like five grisly apples set out to dry in the sun, were five heads, teeth bared in a last cry, blind eyes staring, all fear or regret erased by death. Far worse, however, were the two double crosses standing behind the rack of heads. Hanging like torn rag dolls spilling out their stuffing were a man and woman. Crows perched on the crossbars, evil stage villains hunched in black cloaks. The neatly swept earth of this awful place reeked with sour suffering that brought a metallic taste into Pev's mouth.

He pulled his handkerchief over his face. Behind him the samurai's disturbing giggle came again, like an imbecile child's.

Oscar muttered, 'I had heard – Dirk told me – but my God, it is barbaric.'

Understanding Pev's green face, Shoh caught the boy's

214

reins and spurred his own horse, leading Pev past the execution ground, much to the amusement of the samurai.

'Tada San, why the man and a woman? What did they do?'

'The woman was unfaithful to her husband. She and her lover died as the law says.'

'But like that! Skewered! And left for all to see.'

Shoh looked at Pev in amazement. 'But of course. Now other wives are warned by her shame. Those beheaded were thieves or killers. People must see their punishment and learn from it. That is what the law is for. Is it not the same in England? Do thieves and murderers and unfaithful women walk the streets proudly?'

Pev shook his head. 'Thieves and murderers suffer for their crimes. But their punishment is not quite so violent or so public.'

Oscar said softly, 'Maybe it is. Our bootboy always goes to Newgate. Waits for hours to get a clear view if the condemned is famous. He used to treat me to the details. How bravely the man or woman faced death. How many kicks into empty air before the end.'

Subdued by their unpleasant detour, the Englishmen approached the Shinagawa suburb with barely another word spoken. Their road to Kanagawa wound over low hills cloaked with delicate clouds of pink blossom. Parties of picnickers drifted under the effervescent cherries, the women pretty in fresh spring colours, tittering over their male companions' already scarlet, saké-stained cheeks. Discreet tea houses nestled among the trees, the sort of places Umegawa must go to, Pev thought. Laughter sparkling from the balconies left him wondering at these carefree people savouring the brief perfection of the cherries while their unfortunate countrymen gazed into oblivion from the executioner's rack.

He rode slightly ahead of Shoh and Oscar. The execution ground had so disturbed his thoughts and turned the lovely day to disorder that perhaps he was hardly surprised when the man sprang out. Suddenly his way was blocked by a clumsy loose-limbed figure dressed in faded striped hakama. Startled, the nervous Japanese pony reared, hurling Pev into the dust. He had only an instant to wonder why this was happening to him before a strong hand grasped his jacket and jerked him to his feet.

He stared into the man's face, studying with detachment the round white cheeks distorted into a scowling mask.

Released, he staggered back, watching as though frozen in unending time as the man yanked his sword arm free and, with a twist, tied up the floppy sleeve of his jacket. His hand dropped to the hilt and slowly, with dreamlike grace, he drew his sword into a magnificent crescent above Pev's head.

A shot rang out. The ronin, his eyes fixed on Pev's, stepped forward. An actor in his own murder, Pev waited, accepting, entranced by the ronin's slow advance. Another shot. The man staggered. The sword plummeted down, a gleaming spike in the earth.

Astonishment smoothed the scowl from the young face. Pev stared into the bewildered eyes of a youth his own age. The ronin crumpled into a heap.

Oscar's shouts and hands pushing at Pev woke him up abruptly. He grabbed the reins of his dancing horse and clambered into the saddle, wheeling the animal through the excited jumble of horses and samurai crowding the road.

Oscar shouted from somewhere near by, 'That blasted Tada! He is helping the killer.'

But a belated appreciation of his danger had struck Pev. Blood seemed to drain away from his head and heart, leaving only ringing emptiness. He slumped over his saddle and did not regain his wits until, led by a muttering angry Oscar, he found himself riding through the Tokaido gate into familiar streets.

'Leave me. Return to your barbarians. Do not touch this son of Nippon with defiled hands.'

'Idiot! Lie still.'

A sigh of agony hissed through Ohno's clenched teeth as Shoh gently probed his mangled, gushing arm. 'The bullet must come out but the bone –' He probed again despite Ohno's groan. 'This blood flow must be stopped first.' Using the torn jacket he tied a tight bandage to slow Ohno's life fluids.

Curious samurai from the Legation escort shuffled

around the pair, discussing the wound among themselves. When the leader barked an order the men mounted, doctor and patient abandoned, neither the responsibility of Lord Hitachi.

Shoh ignored their departure, knowing too well they would not give help. 'Are you alone, Ohno Kun? I need another man.'

'Leave me, traitor!' But he could not resist Shoh's arm around his waist and allowed himself to be supported. The crowd that had gathered to relish a ronin's discomfort drew back to let them stumble to a tea house set in a grove of cherries.

The proprietor, a solid wall of a man, blocked the steps to the verandah. The brown and white stripes of his kimono swerved crazily before Ohno's eyes.

'Forgive me but the Sensei cannot bring that man in here. A wounded ronin will give my respectable place a bad name.'

Shoh pulled out the purse that dangled at his sash. 'I have zeni for shelter and hot water. I must help this man for he is known to my family.'

'Ara, but he is not known to mine, nor is the Sensei. His karma decides if he lives or dies, not the owner of the Sakura-ya.' The man turned away.

'Leave me, Tada Shoh. Ohno Tatsuya releases you from all obligation and as I am no longer a samurai of Odawara, you owe me nothing.' His words faded.

Back in the crease of the hills a small shrine stood, but the weak popping of Ohno's heart pulse and his hectic colouring warned Shoh that the life force was waning. He dared not sully the Gods' precinct with a dying man. Then he saw a hut, a storage shed for the tea house, behind a cluster of maples. It would do.

'Ohno! Elder Brother! What has happened?'

Masayuki stood before him. Thinner, harder, older. No longer a smooth-muscled young castle samurai.

'Help me to that shed beyond the trees,' Shoh commanded.

Without a word Masayuki lifted the fainting Ohno as easily as a bundle of reeds. Shoh hurried ahead. Pushing aside straw-wrapped saké barrels and crocks of

217

fermenting soy, he cleared a spot on the board floor.

'Fetch hot water from the kitchen but avoid the landlord. There is no time to find safflower juice. We will have to use urine to clean the wound. Is the rhythm of your body in harmony with the season and the stars?'

'So I believe.'

'Good. Give me your haori to tear for bandages. Now go to the kitchen.'

The setting sun tinged the cherry blossom to warm flesh tints before Shoh finally sank back on his heels. Ohno lay, mercifully unconscious, between the brothers.

'Well?' Masayuki demanded softly. His grey face was a testament to his friend's suffering.

Wearily Shoh began wiping his utensils and replacing them neatly in the small lacquer case he always carried. 'He attacked two Englishmen from the Legation. One of them shot him. I have never treated a bullet wound but the bone is obviously shattered. The English doctor must examine it but I think he will say that the arm should be cut away to save Ohno's life. Anyway he will never use the limb again.'

'His sword arm,' murmured Masayuki, rolling the bloody bullet in his fingers.

'It was not his karma to be a swordsman. You always said he was clumsy.' Shoh loosened his tied-up sleeves and tucked the instrument case into one.

Masayuki held up the bullet. 'He has been defiled by this thing. He will not wish to live.'

For the first time Shoh noticed Masayuki's blood-spattered kimono; the bleached hemp was coarse but new.

'You wear white for Akiko San?'

'Yes, as do you.' Masayuki brushed his hand over his face as if to brush away this added sorrow. 'When she – I was in Miyako and did not know until I stopped at Odawara. Hanae told me.'

Masayuki's obvious grief made Shoh regret his harshness. Softly he offered his brother acceptable words of comfort. 'Our mother died well. Her ancestors will have received her with rejoicing.'

'The purity of her act fills my spirit with pride. I have given up prayers for her. I hoped to visit her grave on the seventieth day but now –' He looked down at Ohno's clay-white face.

'He must rest, but not here. Find a kago and we will take him to Segawa's clinic.'

'No! The Doctor's work is finished. He will return to our lodging house.'

'You are as great a fool as he! What do doctors in Shinagawa know of bullet wounds? If you will not bring him to the clinic then we will go together to your lodging house. These dressings should be wrapped again. He needs medicine. Feel his head. Go. Find a kago.'

'Neither Ohno nor I wish to be under your obligation.'

'There is no choice.'

Masayuki led the kago to a back street dark as a lair. On one side of the small fenced house a sandal maker sat cross-legged on his rickety verandah, bent over a clog. The smell of fresh wood rose from the piles of shavings around him. From the low shacks on the other side came a sad song of love on a samisen wearily played but suiting Shoh's own fatigue.

Thatched eaves hunched over the latticed windows of the house. No light showed behind coarse paper panes. Stench from the open ditch in the lane mocked the spring night.

The warped door jammed in its track until struck an experienced blow by Masayuki. Inside the rough tatami was swept but a cold depressing odour of mildew hung in the empty rooms.

'Buy a new pallet tomorrow. Have you zeni?' What Masayuki used to pay for his lodging or rice, Shoh could not imagine. Perhaps some of the vanished Tada heirlooms smoothed his way. In any case, Masayuki did not answer the question.

'Brew a handful of these herbs in a shō of clean water until half has boiled away. Give him a bowl of it before his morning rice. Our urine smelt pure but if a green, ill-smelling fluid seeps from the wound you must apply poultices soaked in forsythia extract.' Shoh knew that the wound would fester as certainly as the sun would rise but he could not destroy Masayuki's hopes. 'My servant will bring a mixture of forsythia and honeysuckle. That is the best.'

'No,' Masayuki said quickly. 'No. The herb-seller near

the shrine will have what we need or you bring it yourself. No strangers must come here.'

Shoh glanced around the eight-mat room. A weapon rack against the damp splotched wall would hold five or six swords and halberds. He had noticed several rolls of bedding in the cupboard when Masayuki had pulled out Ohno's. Poems, recently brushed on fresh paper, hung in the alcove and nearby a solid Go board stood ready for a game. The room spoke of men – samurai – bound in austere union.

'So be it. Go now to the herb-seller for I cannot be sure to come tomorrow. Segawa Sensei is ageing and I must see to his patients. Oh, and buy a cake of poppy. Give him some to eat when his pain is great.' Shoh added sharply, '*Do* give it to him. Pain will not temper his samurai spirit but weaken him, perhaps to death.'

'I understand.'

'Do you? Then you will allow the English doctor here?'

'No!' Masayuki almost screamed.

Shoh looked down at Ohno, moaning even through the blackness that protected him. 'Prepare yourself and Ohno to accept that the arm may be poisoned. For such wounds the barbarians' medicine is best.'

'Is it not enough that his body has been contaminated by a barbarian's bullet? Do you ask corruption of his soul as well?'

Shoh looked into his brother's half-moon eyes and read death in them. Vanished for ever was the merry admiring playmate of his youth. Had death always lurked in those eyes, unseen by Shoh but watched and nourished by Akiko?

'Naturally no decision can be reached until James Wilson has been consulted. After all, he does know the chap a damned sight better than we do.' Basil Foxwood looked down at his thin long-fingered hands lying on the carved ebony table, the table made in China for Sir Radley. But Sir Radley was now thousands of miles away in Hong Kong and Basil Foxwood was the senior officer in Yedo. In these hands lay the safety of the British Legation.

A brandy-induced flush stained Oscar's pallid cheeks.

His podgier hands were less controlled than Foxwood's. 'If we only knew if the attack were planned.'

'Why?' Pev asked in surprise. 'How could it be planned? No one knew that we were riding to Kanagawa. No one but – Oh! Oh! I see.' He frowned at Oscar.

Determined to be the commandant as was his right, Foxwood said testily, 'Damned if I see. What are you chaps gettin' at?'

Oscar knew his reply must be patient, befitting his contempt for Foxwood. Gentry the man might be, intelligent he was not. Normally, as a Legation secretary, Foxwood was harmless but now, with Sir Radley on leave – Well, thank God for Pev's quick mind and Wilson's stability.

'Don't quite take Fitzpaine's point,' Foxwood was complaining.

'Only members of the Legation knew we planned to ride to Kanagawa today. And Tada Shoh. Suppose he is in sympathy with the anti-foreign party and sent them word about our intentions. That ronin might have been waiting for us.'

'By Jove, never thought of that! But see here, d'you really think that Jap doctor is such a bounder?'

'No,' Pev said firmly. 'No. I do not. Anyway, suppose we chose to go by boat or the Tokaido? Eh, Oscar?'

'Did you see any sign of a daimyo's entourage on the Tokaido when we joined it? Neither did I. As for a boat, if we had suggested it, he might have claimed sea-sickness or something. And how do you explain the way he rushed to the aid of that wounded man?' Oscar demanded.

'Oh, I don't know. Hippocratic oath or whatever they have.'

'No good. You know how Wilson is always railing about their callous attitude to anyone but their own patients.'

'But this was an emergency. You damned near shot the scoundrel's arm off.'

'Good shot, was it? Jolly clever,' Foxwood said.

Pev pushed his chair back. 'There must be an explanation. We know so little about Tada. His background. His family.'

'We do know he is a samurai,' Oscar reminded him wearily.

221

'But what are samurais? Are they a class? Gentry? Or are they soldiers? Officers? Bandits?'

Foxwood shook his head. 'Now, I know I do not speak the lingo like you chaps. Don't take much interest in that sort of thing. But someone, somewhere, told me samurais are gentlemen. After all, all the government johnnies are samurais, don't you know. Rather think it was Jessop who told me. Chap may be a Yankee but he knows his Japs.'

'Well, it appears we will have to wait for James. Where is he?' Oscar asked.

'Fellow sick in the French Legation. Wilson might have to spend the night, he said. Cannot think why they don't bring in a doctor of their own.' Foxwood rose. 'Time to change for dinner. Know you have had a shock but don't overdo that brandy, Sullivan.'

Slowly, with a barely trembling hand, Oscar poured himself another small drink, rejecting the hint of kindness in Foxwood's voice. 'It is not every day I shoot a man.' He slid the bottle toward Pev. 'Have one?'

The secretary frowned at the Londoner and then left the room.

Pev shook his head. 'Nothing could erase that man's face. And the sword. You know, Oscar, he was only about our age.'

When Oscar made no sharp rejoinder Pev looked up. The last hours had changed his friend. The dull ginger curls were the same, flopping around a white freckled face. But his eyes held something Pev had not seen before.

'Not only have I never shot at a man, I have never shot at anything as a matter of fact. Or killed a creature. At school, when the others went ratting or fishing, I begged off. Perhaps it is different for you in the provinces.' There was none of the usual taunt in the words. 'I guess country ways are bound to be violent.'

Pev could not help laughing. 'It is not the custom to shoot people down in the streets of Exeter but of course I have gone after pigeon and rabbits and such. Never felt much about it one way or the other. But I say, Oscar, that shot of yours today saved my life, you know. I shall always, eternally, be grateful. If it were not for you, I would be cat's meat now.'

Oscar nodded in acceptance. They sat in embarrassed silence, then he asked, 'What do you think about, Pev? When you wake up in the morning? Or last thing at night? What kind of thoughts are in your mind?'

'All different notions. Is it a fine day? How tired I am. Even sometimes, if you can credit this, Japanese verbs. Or Umegawa. I am an empty sort of chap, Oscar.'

'Do you never wake wondering if there is a ronin leaning over you with a knife at your throat?' The question was almost a sob of pain.

'No. Oh, well, perhaps when we expected trouble from Shinagawa. Or when Dirk died. Why do you worry so much about such things?'

'I can think of nothing else. All through the day and at night the same fears come to haunt my dreams. I hate violence. Blood. These repulsive people. First the execution ground and then that man. Oh, God, what a frightful day.'

'Yes, frightful.' Pev gave the plump white fist on the table a clumsy pat.

'It was a love of languages that brought me here, you know, Pev. Always fascinated by languages and I wanted to learn one that was different. As a boy, I fancied an Indian tongue – my uncle is in the tea trade – but then the Mutiny – those terrible tales of Delhi and Cawnpore – Well, I could not face those brutes. Obviously Russia was out. China was in turmoil. Japan seemed the answer. But the first time I rode into Takanawa, two samurai, drunk as lords, hacked a stray cur to pieces. No reason for it but that they wished to test the edge of their swords. Made a – a contest – of it. Poor howling devil. It was terrible and I have hated 'em from that moment on. And feared them.'

Pev sat miserably, wishing Oscar would not lay bare his feelings like this and yet groping for some words of comfort.

Tears glistened in Oscar's sad eyes. 'D'you think I am a coward? Naturally, you do. No sort of man at all. Blubbing like a baby.' He poured another drink.

'Oh, Oscar, don't go on like this. Look, it is the brandy. Put it aside.'

'You think I am a coward, don't you? After all you're not blubbing and it was you he went for. I was safe on my horse.'

'But you shot him. If you were afraid you could have galloped off. But instead you saved my life. Now, where is the cowardice in that?'

'That is true. Bolting never occurred to me. Therefore I cannot be a complete weakling, can I?'

'No, certainly not!'

Oscar thought a moment. 'I say, was he – the chap – was he scared? Could you tell?'

Pev closed his eyes. The young round face swam before him. 'No. He was not scared. I keep thinking of what Dirk said about one of his attackers – a gentleman, even with a snarl of hate on his face. As to this man being a gentleman, I cannot say, but I felt he was, despite the hatred in his eyes.'

He looked at Oscar and said, in surprise, 'Do you know, I – respected him.'

'And I hope and pray he will not die. Could it be we have been here too long?'

As Shoh had foreseen there was much to occupy him at the clinic for the next few days. The Spring Festivals always enticed Segawa's son, Yasutake, away from his patients to the delights of the Green Houses and age had gently sapped the old doctor's vigour. This year when the cherries bloomed Segawa ignored the official day when lined robes were changed for unlined ones, preferring the warmth of winter kimono until the rains came. Each day he spent a little longer strumming his samisen, singing ItchJū ballads, plaintive melodies that had been popular in the Yoshiwara during the Bunsei era, the time of his youth. Tended by his newest concubine, a plump, uncomprehending girl, he dreamt of the past, easily forgiving the hours and silver Yasutake spent in the pleasure quarters and assuring himself that, with Tada's skills to draw upon, all would be well until Yasutake tired of Yoshiwara life. And if all was not well, there was always the barbarian doctor who could be blamed.

When Shoh finally found a few hours free he decided to

stop first at the Tozenji to consult Wilson.

In just these few days spring had settled in. Fuji, so vivid in winter, vanished into mists. Green shimmered on maples and pawlonia branches; flycatchers sang in the golden red leaves of the plum boughs. Peasants from the hills went from gate to gate selling the first young bamboo shoots.

However, as soon as Shoh's kago touched the raked gravel of the Tozenji courtyard, his joy in the day evaporated. Before him the bulk of the Legation hunched like a tense cat, crouching, poised to leap on its victim. The outer door gaped like a mouth latticed with spiky teeth.

The Englishmen were at their lessons, sprawled in chairs, disconsolately glaring over the dining-room table at Ito San, bland and obdurate, perched on a silk cushion on the tatami. Shoh bowed, apologizing for the disturbance but smiling, for he knew they always welcomed any interruption. This time, however, the two men only stared at him, nervously, shyly, as though he were a stranger. Oscar would not meet his eyes at all and shuffled through the piles of paper on the table, but Fitzpaine San continued to study him, his brown, handsome face clouded with distrust. Again Shoh bowed and apologized, bewildered and confused by this singular silence.

At Wilson's familiar step in the corridor he wheeled in relief.

The doctor did not smile either. His eyes, usually frank and blue as a winter sky, shifted from the white faces to Shoh's and away again.

'We did not expect to see you again, Tada Sensei, but I am relieved you have come.' He glanced again at Sullivan's stony expression. 'This way. We shall talk in Radley Sama's empty room.'

Gentle sunlight through the paper panes warmed the chamber yet Shoh shivered. 'What brings you back to the Tozenji? Why have you come?' Wilson asked.

'This uneducated doctor must beg advice from the Englishman. I have to treat a wound that is beyond my experience.'

James Wilson asked coldly, 'Could the wound be from

a bullet? Shot by Sullivan San into the arm of a young ronin?'

Shoh bowed. 'The honourable Doctor understands the situation already. His years in the war hospital have brought him great knowledge for one so young. May Wilson Sensei lighten Tada's dark ignorance.'

Wilson, in turn, was nonplussed by Shoh's guileless honesty. He had dismissed Foxwood's suspicion and Oscar's shrill accusations as so much panic. He knew and trusted Tada Shoh. But the problem would not just disappear. Why had the doctor hurried to the aid of Pev's attacker? The explanation must lie somewhere in the confusions of Japanese loyalties and James Wilson had to find the answer if he were to continue with Shoh as a colleague.

'That man tried to kill Fitzpaine. And yet you helped him and now you ask my assistance for him! I am at a loss, Tada San.'

'The ronin is a man of Odawara. His family is known to me, to my parents and to my parents' parents. I have an obligation. Naturally, I went to him.'

'I see. Perhaps it is as well for us in the Legation to realize that your first loyalty lies with your own people. Of course. How could it be otherwise?' Wilson struggled to reconcile his deep hurt. 'This occurrence has been unfortunate but illuminating. Forgive me, but the complexities of your race are beyond me.'

In Wilson's pain Shoh began to see how the affair must look to the outsider and the dilemma that now presented itself to him. Ohno's attack on Fitzpaine had split open a chasm at Shoh's feet as surely as an earthquake would split open the earth. But he could not hover on the edge of the chasm. He must leap over or step back.

He tried to explain, to choose the right words. 'Fitzpaine San was unhurt. If Ohno's sword had cut him – this Tada would not have gone to Ohno but would have drawn his own sword.'

'Would you? I wonder.'

Shoh cried out, 'Sensei, I do not know. At the moment, I saw that Sullivan San had saved Fitzpaine San and that the ronin was Ohno Tatsuya of Odawara in need of my service.'

226

'Do you share this Ohno's beliefs? His hatreds? Again, forgive me but I must ask.'

'Ohno's way is not mine. The world in which he – and my brother – believe is for me an airless room: no door, no windows, no sliding walls. They do not wish, perhaps they fear, to investigate beyond that room, a room that they say the outsider with his new and different ways must despoil if he enters it.'

Wilson was tensed, incredulous. 'Your brother? Do you say your own brother is one with this Ohno? With these killers?'

'Unhappily, that is true, Sensei. My brother is a member of this party sworn to expel the outsider. He has become a ronin. Do you understand? No longer does he bow his will and his judgement and his sword to our daimyo, Lord Okubo. Masayuki and I are now brothers in blood only. We travel separate paths.'

Wilson paced the tatami, back and forth through squares of sunlight cast by the shoji.

'If only you were an Englishman. If only I could ask for your word on it as a gentleman. If I could go to Foxwood and say, "Look here, Tada has given me his word that he can be trusted, so there we are. This matter of Pev's attacker can be put aside, forgotten." But this is the insidious evil of our lives here. Do we mean the same thing by such words as honour or loyalty or truth? Perhaps so. Perhaps not. But –' He stopped in front of Shoh. 'This much I can do. I will come with you and examine this Ohno. In good faith. No swords. No guns. My word as a Christian and an Englishman. A Yorkshireman. I will come armed only with a medicine box.'

'No. No. Wilson Sensei cannot go. It is not possible.'

'Is it dangerous? I am not afraid of danger.'

'No. Impossible. To reach out and touch the sun would be easier.'

'Aye. You are right. They would have no choice but to kill me. Nothing would be gained. Then tell me about the wound. Is it clean? What of the bones and tissues?'

'I cleaned it with urine. The bullet has been removed. But the bone is shattered and splinters like shivered ice have torn muscle and blood channels.'

'The arm should be amputated before gangrene develops.'

Shoh shook his head sadly. 'That too is not possible, I fear.'

'No. This Ohno is a samurai, is he not? His life is in his sword arm.' He stared down at his own broad palms. 'Would I think myself a doctor, a man, without my hands? At times I believe my very soul lies here, in these.' To Shoh he said, 'There is very little I can do, but take a vial of chloroform and a saw in case he will permit amputation. If the wound is poisoned he will die unless your medicines can disperse the poison, and perhaps they can. I have come to respect the efficacy of many of your brews. If this fails, have you morphia?'

'Yes.'

The tall Englishman in dark broadcloth looked down at the Japanese. No longer was the striped gown and rolled top-knot of hair womanishly odd, nor the fine olive-skinned face mysterious. In those first months working together Tada's smallness, his smooth neatness had been slightly repulsive to James; too doll-like for a man. Now Wilson respected the skill in the precise hands and he desperately wanted to understand the spirit behind the strangely beautiful curved eyes. Just as he was beginning to be able to look on a statue of their Buddha and feel serenity, so those eyes of Shoh's had become the eyes of a man, different from himself but a man none the less for that.

He said reluctantly, for it must be said, 'The others – well, Foxwood certainly – do not want Tada Sensei here at the Legation for the time being. But do not worry. I trust you and I will convince them but give me some time. In any case the final decision must lie with Radley Sama.'

'Will the honourable Radley Sama return to Yedo?'

'Aye, in a month or two. He intends to travel by land from Nagasaki to Yedo. Let us pray for all our sakes that his journey is a quiet one.' He smiled.

This time it was James Wilson who held out his hand in friendship. Tada Shoh gripped it warmly. The two doctors parted: James to talk to Foxwood, Shoh to the damp house in the dark back lane.

* * *

In Shinagawa the cherries were beginning to fade. Battered blossoms torn by the breeze piled under hedges and verandahs like drifts of fragile snow.

Spring had not touched Masayuki's lane. No hint of green softened the black skeleton of a persimmon tree. Songless birds pecked at sour refuse scattered around the rickety line of shacks.

The sickening sweetness of corrupting flesh met Shoh as he slid back the latticed door. A burly ronin, young as Masayuki, greeted him solemnly, ushering him into the eight-mat room. Several other men rose from their tasks, bowed curtly, took up their swords and dismissed themselves, leaving Shoh alone with Ohno and Masayuki.

Too far gone with fever to recognize him, Ohno screamed like an animal when Shoh lifted the pus-stiffened dressing.

Deep lines of fatigue and guilt etched Masayuki's sharpened features. 'He has raved like a madman since yesterday sunrise. I soaked the wound with safflower and honeysuckle at each stick of time. The herb-seller came with more opium. He applied different dressings.' Masayuki handed him a twist of paper. Shoh sniffed dried magnolia bud.

'The herb-seller was wise. This draws out corruption but the poison had spread too quickly. Surprisingly quickly for one so young and strong.'

'He will die?'

'There is one chance to save him. I have medicine to make him sleep like a dead man. He will feel nothing when I cut away the destroyed bone and poisoned channels. If this is done now, immediately, he may recover.'

'Never will I permit such a mutilation. To live like a three-legged dog is not to be alive at all.'

'Masayuki decides this for Ohno? Once again, Masayuki alone finds the right way?' But at his brother's desolate look Shoh wished he had not spoken. This was no time to draw family-honed knives.

Masayuki said, 'In his waking hours we talked it over, Ohno, Kojima San and myself. The barbarian's bullet was his karma but it will not be his death.'

'Masayuki, the poison is in his blood channels. It sours

his life force. Alas, we have no medicine, nor have the barbarians, that can save him now.'

'The doctor no longer understands the way of samurai. Ohno will die, now, in his prime. His life is a cherry blossom, fragile yet clinging stubbornly to the branch despite the tugging of the wind. But just as the blossom must finally fall and be blown away, so Ohno will die. But he will not die of the barbarian bullet. That defilement will be spared him.' Masayuki rose and walked to the tall sword rack. One blade, a familiar one, lay there. 'With the Chrysanthemum sword I shall cut the blossom free from the branch. A clean death purified by a blade of Nippon. He is prepared. As you can see, he faces west, towards his Emperor.'

'You will take Ohno's life?' Again Shoh felt the same deadening, airless horror he had felt in Shohtaro's presence.

'It is my duty. I have waited only to be sure your medicine could not save him.'

'But as I told you, it may be that he can be saved. If you will let me cut off the arm, he may live.'

Masayuki turned away but Shoh caught the contempt in his brother's eyes. Masayuki said, 'When you were a boy, you had a favourite story from the Classics that you often told me. A Chinese general, wounded in battle, rode to his physician, a famous surgeon. While the warrior manfully played a game of Go, the doctor cut out the poisoned arrowhead, applied the proper ointments and stitched up the wound. The general finished his game, mounted his steed and led his soldiers to victory against the enemy. I had hoped you could do the same for Ohno but if you cannot –'

Shoh walked over to the window and pushed it open. A damp smell of earth filled his nostrils. Somewhere azaleas burgeoned and birds sang in their nests but not in this dank garden.

'So many are dead now,' he murmured. 'Our father, Akiko San, soon Ohno.'

'Death is part of life. All but our father died to purify Nippon. The price of purity is high. It cannot be bargained for at a street stall. Only dedicated blood will buy purity.'

Masayuki leaned towards him, his voice now low, insistent. 'We of the White Cherry Brotherhood will save Nippon. Elder Brother can help us. You *must* help us, for your soul is the soul of Nippon just as is mine, Ohno's, every tree's, every rock's, every insect's.'

Shoh wanted to escape but he could not. Masayuki's voice held him in a net of silk and steel.

'A handful of herbs in their rice. All the Englishmen will die and the other barbarians will take fright and flee; with them will go their evil medicine, their jealous god, and their foul greed.'

'No.' Shoh shook his head firmly, freeing himself. 'They will send their ships and cannon to destroy Yedo. Nagasaki. Even the Capital.'

'What do these cities matter? Wood and paper. The dens of merchants and courtesans. But the sacred islands will protect their own. We shall go to the mountains where barbarian cannon cannot follow. There, with His Imperial Majesty to inspire us, we shall rediscover the old ways of Yamato; the old gods of Yamato. So, purified and strengthened, we shall come forth with our swords to cut out the corruption.'

Masayuki's hard confidence impressed Shoh but still he asked, 'Do you never wonder about the world beyond these islands? Do you never wonder about other peoples, their minds, their hearts, their beliefs?'

Masayuki laughed. 'Always Elder Brother questions. Always he wonders. Is not faith in the Divine Presence enough for you? I have been to the Capital. I have stood at the walls of the Imperial Enclosure. Oh, yes, there is confusion in that city. There is quarrelling among those who gather to serve the Emperor. But that is not important. His Sacred Highness himself has cried out for our help. He commands us to kill the cancer eating at our land. No true patriot could live in a Nippon where the Emperor's command is not obeyed. We have moved too far away from the Divine Presence. The secret of Nippon's future lies in her past. Be a part of this future, Elder Brother, I implore you.'

Shoh pleaded desperately, 'The barbarians bring a future too; a future like a mountain path hidden by morning mist. Only when the mists have dispersed can we see our way clearly.'

Masayuki shook his head but Shoh went on. 'By taking careful steps, peering about us in the mist, we may discover the landscape. So, if we approach the barbarians cautiously, questioning and wondering, we may discover those accomplishments that can be valuable, useful, to Nippon.'

'Ha!'

Across the room Ohno moaned, a hollow, rattling protest against pain.

Shoh said wearily, 'Fetch him some water. Opium will ease his way to the next world.'

'No.' A silver-haired ronin stood in the doorway, an austere figure in stiff blue cotton hakama.

Kojima ignored Shoh's bow. 'The medicines of Tada Shoh are not required. The Brotherhood of the White Cherry looks after its own sick. Farewell, Doctor.'

He stepped away from the door, leaving Shoh no choice but to pass him. Softly, he spoke to Shoh, 'Beware paths shrouded by mountain mists, Tada Shoh. Many dangers lie along such a way.'

Shoh did not reply but turned once more to Masayuki. His brother was lifting the Chrysanthemum sword from the rack. His face, when Shoh glimpsed it, was pale and set.

10
The Storm

The swallow must have a nest tucked in the eaves of the farmhouse. Playfully she swooped and curled over Pev, her wings glossy in the sun before she darted into the cool gloom of the overhanging thatch. Something homely about her busy grace made Pev think for a second he was back in England. Heavy thatch, firewood piled in a lean-to, a whining child. This might be a Devon farm. Down by the river thickets of young trees in fresh leaf bristled like alders mixed with hawthorn. He almost expected the merry yellow of daffodils. Then a woman in jacket and leggings with a plump child strapped to her back shot open the latticed door and stepped down into a pair of clogs waiting in the dust. Curiosity, hostility and suspicion mingled in the narrow black eyes set in a flat brown face. When Pev's samurai companion growled a warning at the staring woman, she instantly fell into a cringing bow. The picture of home evaporated into a poor farm set in rice fields edged with bamboo and mulberry trees.

Golden brown under the sun, the river wound around to the cedars and towering ginko that marked the temple graveyard. Banks of tall grass sweet with iris and honeysuckle protectively enclosed the dirt road that he remembered as cold and exposed in January. Although bruised clouds, fat with rain, moved over the hills, here, on the road, warmed by the sun and cheered by the lovely song of warblers nesting in the green underbrush, Pev almost banished from his mind that bitter winter journey with Dirk's coffin.

Someone stood by the grave: a sombre shape in black broadcloth.

Pev hesitated but, sensing a presence, the man looked up, revealing a deeply seamed face and grizzled whiskers. Yet the eyes still blazed a brilliant, uncompromising blue.

'Mr Jessop. Forgive me. I shall come another time.'

'No, no, young man. Fitzpaine, ain't it? Don't see much of you British nowadays. No, Dirk and I have said our farewells. I take my final leave of these shores within the week. The *China Queen* is now in Yokohama; when she sails to Yedo I'll join her.' He added with some satisfaction, 'And that way I shall leave without ever having set foot in Yokohama. A small victory but one I cherish!'

A sprinkling of tender grass covered the low hummock of earth. Clumps of wild flowers, yellow as Dirk's hair, waved gaily in the sunshine. 'Pretty little things, ain't they?'

'Very pretty. I've not seen them before but their brightness is most appealing.'

'So it is.'

Silence followed. Uncertain whether he should leave or stay or what words or forms were appropriate in such circumstances, Pev shifted uneasily and gazed out over the neutral river, sparkling along its rocky bed.

'Have I heard rightly that you and Sullivan had a spot of bother?' Jessop asked abruptly.

'Oh, yes, sir,' Pev replied eagerly and, giving a summary of the whole business, he finished: 'But James Wilson has been assured of Tada Shoh's loyalty and so, at his insistence, they remain colleagues.'

Jessop studied him with uncomfortably shrewd eyes. 'Sensible man, Wilson. But how about the rest of you? How do you feel about a murderer's acquaintance in your midst? Basil Foxwood's in charge, ain't he?'

Pev avoided the penetrating gaze. 'Well, sir, yes, Foxwood's responsible until Sir Radley comes back. Well, he – um – is – perhaps not – quite convinced of Tada's – reliability – but, well – Wilson – and after all, Tada does not live at the Legation.'

'Quite so. What was the ronin's fate?'

'He died of his wounds, I am afraid. Oscar Sullivan is rather upset. He only meant to scare him off.'

'Sullivan strikes me as a man of nervous disposition. Yedo ain't the best spot for him. Or Foxwood. But then I'm being presumptuous. What is young Fitzpaine's feeling on all this?'

'I am only a language student, sir.'

234

'Come, come. You have opinions. Dirk was fond of you. Thought you the liveliest of the English lot. You have a healthy curiosity, he said.' Jessop smiled down at the grave, remembering Meylan's amusement over the boy's innocence. That had gone by the boards according to the efficient cat's cradle of Legation gossip. 'What judgement do you make of this Tada's character?'

For an instant Pev wondered if the American Minister was mocking his youth but he found only alert interest in the stern face. Besides, they shared affection for Dirk. Both had chosen to visit his grave and here, standing above it – Daring to be flattered, he answered boldly, 'Tada Shoh seems to me a respectable man and a conscientious doctor. I trust him.'

'Ah, but what knowledge d'you have of him?'

'He is samurai. Born in Odawara, a castle town on the Tokaido where Sir Radley's Fuji expedition was welcomed most graciously by the daimyo himself.'

'Well, now usually we are told it is Satsuma men or Mito men who make these wild attacks but I heard this was an Odawara man who attacked you. Odd, ain't it?'

Pev's confidence crumbled. 'Oh, Mr Jessop, does nothing in this topsy-turvy country make sense? Please tell me. No one has your experience.'

'Ha! You don't talk like an Englishman!' Then Jessop held up his hand. 'No, no. That was a cheap jibe. As for my experience –' He walked away from the grave towards the river. Islands of grey cloud now threatened the bright day and blotted the gold from the water.

'Four years and what do I know of this ancient land? Very little. That Mikado in the west for example. We don't properly comprehend him and that may be an important piece in the puzzle.'

'He is a sort of High Priest, is he not? What else could he be?' Pev frowned. He had not thought much about the Mikado.

'Very well then, but what do I know about the samurais who challenge our days and make anxious our nights? Never have I set foot in a samurai house. Not one word have I exchanged with a samurai woman. Are they disciplined military men or an indolent class of unearned privilege? Is their loyalty to the Tycoon or Mikado or both?' He paused and stared unseeing at a swallow swooping over the river bank. Finally he glanced back at Pev. 'As Japan has existed in isolation for two hundred years without a war, what need is there of a warrior class? Ain't that perhaps the samurais' tragedy? Men without a purpose. Don't this explain their enthusiastic antagonism to the foreigner? At last, a real enemy to fight! But then we must recollect that the government officials we have regular intercourse with come from that same samurai class. Rulers or ruffians. A topsy-turvy land, as you say.'

'Tada has told James much about their code of behaviour,' Pev offered. 'It seems loyalty to one's lord is the paramount virtue.'

'Ah, yes. Bushido. That is the key that unlocks their hearts. Their Ten Commandments as it were. No doubt there is much to be gleaned from it.' His seamed face softened with a rare smile. 'Perhaps that will be young Fitzpaine's task. How d'you progress with the language?'

'Slowly. We were on our way to your Doctor Holloway when the man attacked.'

'Once the lingo is conquered life will be easier. But consider. We are not permitted to attend their theatres, to enter their homes or indeed most of their establishments of relaxation. Oh, we peer into an open door. We see them naked as babes in the lit bathhouse. In fact, we are encouraged to see them die on the execution ground. But rarely do we see them live. You know, Fitzpaine, that delegation of Japanese youngsters we sent last year saw more of American life in six months than I have seen of Japan in four years. Reflect on that!'

'Will one ever make friends among them? What do you think, sir? I often wonder.'

'Friends? Intimate friends? Alas, it is too late for me, but for you it may be that friendship will be possible with someone who does not despise your white face.'

Pev thought of Umegawa and Mr Jessop's woman. Shame, a feeling increasingly familiar in the last weeks, flushed his cheeks.

Jessop was watching him, but thoughtfully, without censure.

'You know, for a young fellow like you, life in Yedo ain't altogether a good thing.'

'I love Yedo. I know there are difficulties but the bustle in the streets; the liveliness of it all.'

'Yes, there is that side, of course. But as a foreign diplomat or whatever, this is an empty existence. Passive. We drift on the tides of Japanese whim. Oh, Sir Radley tries to fight the current to accomplish something, anything.' He reflected briefly. 'And in a different way, I take the same struggle. But when you come right down to it, we are all like chips of driftwood bobbing in the ocean. We bob here, we bob there, we're washed upon the beach or out to sea, but it ain't our choice, if you see what I mean.' He smiled and the sharp blue eyes softened briefly.

'I have enjoyed our conversation, Fitzpaine. But now I must take myself back. There is much to do before the *China Queen* sails.' A splat of rain fell on his nose. 'Too late to avoid a soaking. Both of us.'

'Will you return to Japan? If I may ask.'

Jessop sighed. 'I doubt it. After four years of treading delicately to avoid a civil war here, it seems I shall walk straight into one at home. That bears thinking about. We come nine thousand miles to interfere in the fragile affairs of a nation as though we were gods of perfection. And we ain't! In the year of our Lord, 1861, America prepares to tear herself to pieces over black slavery. It sickens me.'

A samurai, obviously Jessop's escort, appeared and glared impatiently.

'Farewell, Fitzpaine. Take care and have patience with 'em. Learn patience and you may just prove to be the Englishman Japan can respect.'

As he walked away across the bright grass, head bent against the drizzle, his broad black form dwarfed his wiry escort.

Suddenly struck by sadness, Pev felt he had lost a friend.

Rough sand tickled Umegawa's toes. Ma; it was hot. She paused in her climb from the beach to glance over her shoulder at the hazy blue sky dissolving into a milky sea. Sails of fishing boats dotted the water with crimson

237

splashes like a pattern of Kanoko silk. The breeze tugging at her hat and sifting the layers of cotton cooled her skin. She closed her eyes, relishing the sensuous flutter against her flesh, the warm dry smell of sand in the sun. For a moment, she was completely happy. Then Rika coughed and the moment vanished as such moments always do.

Adjusting her broad hat she continued up the path behind Rika, who trudged on bearing a basket of sea-shells. As they drew near the band of pines a fragrance of hot resin refreshed her. Once in the shade she stopped to put on her geta for the walk across the dusty-brown needles to the Komatsu-ya.

'Oi, who is that? Is a new girl joining us?' hissed Rika.

A woman stood by the gate, her face hidden by a tilted parasol. Her kimono was rinzu satin of pale violet figured in purple. The wide obi too was good, pale green satin embroidered with iris in purple and gold thread. But the unseasonably heavy clothes overpowered the slim woman; drooping, her shoulders seemed weighed with sorrow as she turned away from the Komatsu-ya.

Tattoos writhing in the sun, the doorkeeper blocked the gateway. 'Go on with you. You heard what the Oba-san said. Go ply your trade on the night ferries. River scum is all you are good for now.'

'There is no need to be so rude,' Rika snapped as she clattered up, measuring the sad woman as she passed.

Umegawa peered under the parasol at a pretty but wan face. 'Are you all right? You seem faint.'

'Thank you. If I could find a place to rest.'

A rustic pavilion stood in the pine grove overlooking the beach. Ignoring the doorkeeper's glower, Umegawa led her to it. She sank gratefully in the scented shade and drew a fan from her sleeve. Covered with gold leaf, decorated with purple iris, it was a fine expensive piece.

But the purple iris told Umegawa everything. Very conscious of her own commonplace striped cotton kimono, nevertheless she asked timidly, 'Forgive me but I could not help hearing the doorkeeper, a vulgar rude man. Has not this humble person the honour of speaking to Murasaki San?'

A wry smile twisted her full lips. 'Ara, has my shame

spread so quickly? Yes, this is Murasaki, formerly of Shimoda.'

'This humble person is Umegawa, once of the Yoshiwara's Omi-ya.'

'So, né, Umegawa San's name is known to me. You too have a barbarian for a danna sama.' Bitterness hardened the gentle lines of her face. 'Yet the Komatsu-ya keeps you on and will not take me.'

Umegawa hung her head. 'He comes very seldom now. His love melted just as the spring snows on Fuji. But why does Murasaki San wish to enter the Komatsu-ya? It is a poor house and Shinagawa is not the Yoshiwara.'

'This Murasaki is now a poor woman. My danna sama has returned to America. My ornaments are gone. I have but two kimono left unsold and this obi. Soon I shall have no zeni to buy rice.'

Umegawa took a discreet peep at her companion. Murasaki's ginko-leaf hairstyle was still black but no longer held the rich shine of a pampered woman. Her shoulders hunched in a thin ridge under the heavy satin and powder only emphasized a cobweb tracery of fine lines around her eyes and mouth.

'Did the barbarian not give you a farewell present?'

'Oh, yes, he was generous but, foolishly, I borrowed money from my shampooer to buy a Hachijo kimono. Barbarians do not always understand that a woman must look her position and although he gave me many clothes they were not always quite what such an important man's mistress should wear. Do you understand?'

Umegawa nodded. Pebu San had rarely taken in the tremendous importance of Umegawa's rank in the Komatsu-ya.

'Ah, you do understand. They are so uncivilized in so many ways, these white-faces,' Murasaki continued. 'When Jessopu San left and I had no protection, the evil old shampooer demanded her ryō. With no danna or family or house to put her off – here I am.'

'But Murasaki San is a famous courtesan. The best houses in the Yoshiwara would be eager for her.'

'Ara, no. I am a country whore, given to the barbarian before I learned the skills of my trade. Jessopu San allowed me a teacher for the samisen and that I can play a little but who wants a barbarian's cast-off with a country tongue and clumsy ways? Ma, not even the Komatsu-ya. I had thought because of Umegawa San – But no, it will be an unrolled mat under the cherry trees for Murasaki.'

Umegawa pulled a pin from her hair; Pebu's silver and coral plum blossom which in her longing for him she had taken to wearing always, although plum was no longer appropriate to the season. She pressed it into Murasaki's hand. 'Please take this. There is no bond of family or clan between us but the women of the Floating World are as flotsam adrift on the sea. The shifting waters are our bond.'

Murasaki stared at the hairpin, then at Umegawa. 'Your barbarian's passion has cooled? He comes no more?'

'Rarely.'

'Do you love him?'

'So, né,' Umegawa whispered.

'Is this from him?'

'No,' she lied. 'From Itaemon San of Shinagawa. He is old and rich and promises to redeem my debts if he does not die first. Take it. It means nothing. I have others.' Her eyes raked Pebu's hairpin, hungrily fixing its cheap prettiness in her heart before it disappeared.

Murasaki's small hand closed firmly over the pin. 'If it is not from him, I will accept it with gratitude. My barbarian – A barbarian gave me a ring of gold. He is dead now and his ring is the last treasure I could part with. My life first.'

Smoothing down her kimono with a thin hand, she knelt on the pine needles carpeting the floor of the pavilion. 'Accept this Murasaki's thanks. For ever I am in Umegawa's obligation.'

Tears choked Umegawa's reply. Quickly she fled to the safety of the Komatsu-ya.

Auntie always took a stick of time from the afternoon to spend before the family altar in conversation with her husband. During his days on earth he had retired after the noon rice with a saké jug and the prettiest of the

Komatsu-ya girls but now, with a ting of her bronze bell, his widow could summon his wayward spirit to harangue with the problems and triumphs he would have ignored in life.

Umegawa called out 'excuse me' but knelt waiting just inside Auntie's door. The room was as austere as her kimono. Not a zeni's extravagance was wasted on tatami or clothes chest or alcove. Fresh white peonies to honour her husband were the only bright note in the dim room. But despite her cool dislike for the proprietress, Umegawa found herself moved by this spare woman, chinless as a chicken, rapturously intent on communication with the shade of a husband whose absentminded, wine-fuddled caresses had brought her occasional bliss.

But when Oba-san turned to regard her waiting property, the cold eyes and animal-snare lips drove away any sentiment in Umegawa.

'Well?'

'This humble person has come to beg a great favour. Might not Murasaki San of Shimoda be brought into the Komatsu-ya as one of us?'

'No, she might not. Umegawa is foolish to bother with that provincial harlot. What loyal son of Nippon would waste his manhood on a barbarian's leavings?' The bright black eyes glittered. 'Futhermore, barbarians are no longer welcome at the Komatsu-ya. The Brothel Association has so decreed at the command of the bushi in Shinagawa. It is a pity, for outsiders' gold flowed easily through their fingers, but what must be must be. Fortunately, Umegawa's liaison was not too well known among the customers or you would follow Murasaki to the night ferry. Now,' she waved a bony hand to the kimono trays in the corner, 'take the apricot patterned pongee. Itaemon San has commanded your presence at the House of Perfect Joy.'

Her face as smoothly, coolly controlled as a Noh mask, Umegawa lifted the pongee. Apricot suited her, made her look younger. Itaemon San liked them young, which was just as well, for tonight would cost him more than three bu for her company. A lot more. She fancied a new lined over-robe for cold weather. In pale satin with perhaps a blue river swirling up from padded hem to shoulder. And plum blossom scattered about like Murasaki's iris. A motif suitable for a courtesan named Plum River.

One of Auntie's many economies was in laundry. Why pay good zeni to a maid to wash kimono that could be scrubbed by the girls during their free mornings? At first Umegawa, accustomed to the Omi-ya's laundresses, rebelled, but to her surprise the task proved enjoyable on a summer's day. Splashing in the camphor tub was cooling and long-tongued gossip enlivened the chore of unstitching and stitching the clothes.

Now, sleeves tied up and a cloth over her hair, she surveyed strips of gay cloth flapping on bamboo poles with the same complacency as any housewife.

'Come, Elder Sister, help me wring this one out. Ara, it is heavy,' Rika called, up to her elbows in a tub of rice water.

The two women lifted and twisted the length of cotton, giggling as cool starchy water splashed over their faces and yukata.

A commotion at the front gate stopped them. On the verandah the other girls, busy with their needles, looked up. The kitchen boy stayed his cleaver over a board of vegetables.

'Oi! No! Forbidden. Halt!' bellowed the doorkeeper.

Flushed and harried, Pebu San appeared by the kitchen wicket. Umegawa gasped and started forward but, remembering, looked back at Auntie's small room. The reed blinds were rolled up for the breeze and so that Auntie could supervise her girls. Swift as a striking snake she turned from her abacus to glare at the banned outsider.

'Excuse me. I heard women laughing. Just a moment, a few minutes. That is all I ask,' Pev cried, bowing clumsily.

Auntie's narrow black eyes hardened to onyx. 'The Komatsu-ya no longer welcomes barbarians. My regrets.'

'But Oba-san, I only wish to speak to Umegawa San for a moment.'

Thin lips tightened over the sloping chin. Pev took a purse from his jacket pocket. Auntie weighed the purse with her eyes and found it heavy.

'A few minutes only. Not inside. In the garden beyond. Go, Umegawa.'

Abundant foliage swathed the little garden Pev remembered in barren spring snow. Morning glories twined over the shrubs and fence in a tumbling net of gorgeous flower. Insects droned through the hot air and, beyond, the long-needled pines of Shinagawa beach rustled in a slight wind off the bay.

The room, their little room, was masked against the sun steaming off the garden. The blinds creaked as they slowly swayed. That sound and the scents of hot cedar and pine resin, the sea and bush clover stayed in Pev's memory for years, always bringing an unbidden, uncomfortable flush of shame.

Stealthily Umegawa slipped off the headcloth and smoothed her hair. Nothing could be done about her naked face or the damp yukata.

'It has been a long time, Pebu San.'

'Yes. Forgive me, Umegawa. Much has happened.' His eyes flickered nervously over the morning glories, the dusty leaves, the concealing blinds, anywhere but her face.

'Please forgive Oba-san's unfriendliness but the Brothel Association has decided that outsiders are no longer to play in Shinagawa. This is a sadness. Umegawa's sleeves are wet with tears.' But she spoke with a pouting formality that exaggerated the ritual sorrow, the only sorrow she chose to reveal.

'Ah, forbidden? Oh, I see.' Pebu's relief nearly made her gasp. His sudden smile wounded her as no cruel words could ever have done. 'Then I will not embarrass you or Oba-san any longer. Here. I owe you this.'

He thrust out a flat packet wrapped in a silk cloth marked with the crest of a Yokohama moneychanger.

Umegawa's pout deepened into a frown. 'I do not understand.'

'But it is the custom in your country. When a woman is kind to a man – At the parting.' He jerked the packet at her, pleading, 'Tada Shoh told me. I asked him.'

She stared at the pinky-white hand lightly covered with soft brown hairs. A strange hand, an unnatural colour.

243

The hairs made her shiver, half in disgust, half in memory.

'No,' she began. 'Pebu San is poor. He cannot afford gifts to women. He told me himself. Do you remember, the night of the spring snow?' And then she paused. The almond shaped eyes, so softly brown, hardened into onyx glinting black as Auntie's. 'But this unworthy girl accepts Pebu San's generosity. Thank you.'

'Goodbye, Umegawa. Farewell. Farewell.'

The clumsy youth in his scratchy, graceless wool coat darted through the gate to freedom.

Umegawa judged the weight of the packet in her hand. Fifteen ryō at least. He had been generous.

Ara. And why not? The pleasures of the Floating World do not come cheap.

'You should not have come here, Tada Shoh. Ohno is dead. The Brotherhood of the White Cherry does not welcome those who lick dust from the boots of his murderers.'

Masayuki blocked the doorway. Unsteady lamplight threw a wavering latticework of shadow across his defiant face. Someone in the back of the house was playing a warrior's lament on the flute.

'Ohno's death is a sadness but I wish to talk about family matters.'

'This Masayuki has no family but the Brotherhood.' Feral eyes glittered in the dimness.

'Masayuki. Young Brother –'

The flute ceased. A door hissed. Behind Masayuki appeared the bulky shape of a man, his silver hair haloed by the light. Although shadows concealed his face, Shoh sensed Kojima's fierce presence.

'Go.' The command was soft but absolute.

'I have family affairs to discuss with my brother.'

'Go.' A drawn sword glimmered.

'So be it.'

The door rattled under Shoh's anger. From behind it came a nervous mocking laugh.

Masayuki.

Shoh stood in the still lane. Unsettled. Danger seeped from the darkened house of the Brotherhood. He turned and started off swiftly into the dusk. He must reach the Tokaido gate before it was closed for the night.

Sir Radley lifted the decanter and waved it at John Nicholson, the Consul from Nagasaki. 'More brandy? No? Cannot think why not. It is no worse than your Nagasaki poison. Foxwood? Good. Keep me company. You too, Fitzpaine. But not for you, James. No, naturally not. Clear head, steady eye. And Sullivan too declines.' He dropped into a basket chair and lit a cigar. 'Just this last one to celebrate our safe return to Yedo and then bed for me. Too damned old for a month living in the saddle. Eh? Or do I speak for myself alone, Nicholson?'

Balding, podgy-soft, John Nicholson looked a man for whom an hour in the saddle would be daunting. But, illuminated by brandy and excitement, the Consul was prepared to sit up all night to regale the stay-at-homes with accounts of the epic journey to Yedo from Nagasaki.

'All in all, I am most encouraged,' Sir Radley continued. 'British clocks on sale in Nagasaki and Lancashire textiles in Osaka. Never dared hope for such progress a year ago. Good show, I say.'

Nicholson broke in enthusiastically. 'Osaka, now there is a charming city. Crisscrossed by canals. Venice of Japan. Pity the government wish to delay setting up a consulate there. I would jump at it.'

'Yes, now it was in Osaka that we were taken to the Kabuki theatre. Deuced proud of it they were, but it is extraordinary stuff and nonsense. Yet, affecting in its way. And of course by taking us they put aside another absurd prohibition on our movements. We shall hope the Yedo theatres cease to be forbidden territory.'

Nicholson launched into a description of the wild acting and lavish costumes but brandy buzzed the words around in Pev's head. Definitely, this must be his last one. Trying to unfuddle his mind, he concentrated on the circle of men. Oscar sat by the verandah, silent, immobile but for the occasional quick slap at a mosquito. Perversely, Pev found himself missing the teasing Oscar of old. This subdued observer with the maturity of middle years was too staid a replacement for the sardonic trifler who had irritated Pev so many times over the past year.

Next to Oscar, jacket and cravat exquisite despite the sultry evening, was Foxwood, his usually pale face quite shiny pink from brandy and with relief that today his months of responsibility ended without a major disaster. Nicholson, a sloppy cherub, bounced eagerly in his chair, arms flailing in an exhibition of Japanese acting. Beside him the rawboned bulk of James Wilson overflowed his chair. James was not listening but dreaming, his pleasant face creased by an empty smile. Beri-beri or summer pestilence? Seduced by Asian contagion, he would never return to the common or garden ailments of Sheffield. Or would he?

Japan had streaked Sir Radley's fierce whiskers with grey but five months of leave had brought bold confidence back to his eyes. In Hong Kong, despite the unavoidable embarrassment of the Morrison affair, Sir Radley had found the Consular Service triumphant, proof positive of British supremacy in woollen cloth, mechanical necessities and colonial administration. Refreshed, he was ready to take on the ambiguities of the Japanese government.

And Peverel Fitzpaine? What of himself? A glance in the looking glass would reassure him that he was still a handsome young man; his smile friendly, although perhaps more guarded than that of the boy who climbed down into the small boat in Yedo harbour a year ago. But would a second, longer look into the glass reveal more? In twelve months he had witnessed the death of a friend and felt the whisper of his own mortality against his cheek. His body had been awakened to sensations and pleasures unimagined in Exeter. He had arrived in Japan a child. Now he was no longer a child. It was impossible that he could be. And yet he felt the same. He was still himself. Was this the way it should be? Did brooding Oscar regard himself as the same man who rode through the night streets of Yedo with the new student from England? No, that was impossible. Any fool could see how Oscar had changed.

But what of Peverel Fitzpaine? Did one only grow and age in the eyes of others? Would he ever gaze into the looking glass to find a man of maturity, a man whose wisdom he could respect?

He straightened on his hard chair and focused on the

black garden beyond the lamplit verandah. The orange pinpricks of fireflies danced in the velvety darkness. The night was moist, expectant. Thunder murmured in the hills. No moon. No stars. No sign of the samurai guards who nightly prowled the Tozenji grounds.

Sir Radley was still ebullient. 'The first Englishmen to travel from Nagasaki to Yedo since William Adams. Candidly I cannot but be proud of our accomplishment.'

Nicholson agreed. 'Your pride is quite justified, Sir Radley. After all, they tried all their usual tricks to dissuade us: the usual revolution and mayhem convulsing the countryside was promised, but we saw nothing of it. And at Osaka –' Nicholson poked a pudgy finger for emphasis – 'we were within twenty miles of their mysterious Mikado.'

'Shouldn't imagine the government johnnies were too pleased about that,' Foxwood muttered.

Sir Radley drew on his cigar. 'Apprehensive, most certainly. But we were discreet. Don't hold with meddling in religious affairs unless burning widows or human sacrifice is on the programme. Then, naturally, it is one's duty as a Christian to step in. However, this Mikado seems to be a harmless High Priest sort of chap.'

James Wilson woke from his reverie and asked suddenly, 'Is it not in the Mikado's name that the ronins attack us? When Abbé Phillippe was warned of a massacre was not the Mikado's name evoked?'

Sir Radley frowned, 'Well, yes, it was.'

Oscar said, his plump face grim, 'As far as we know, this Mikado has not yet signed or agreed to the treaties. And the government seems to think his agreement is vital.'

'Yes, that is true,' agreed Sir Radley. 'No doubt about it, the Governor of Osaka and our samurais did not wish us too close to his city. On the whole, although it will be difficult to justify to the Foreign Office, I have to admit that the Japanese are probably wise to demand a delay in opening Osaka and Yedo as treaty ports.'

'Not a popular view in Nagasaki, even though two more Dutch sailors were murdered last month,' Nicholson said. 'We of the Consular Service are seen as yellow-bellied cowards who stand by while the trading rights of true

Englishmen are trampled under heathen feet.'

'The same opinions are held in Yokohama,' Oscar said. 'Last week Fitzpaine and I were commanded to attend an assembly of merchants at the Consulate. Our reception was less than genial, was it not, Pev?'

The humiliation was still fresh for both of them: furious, selfrighteous citizens spitting contempt at the young diplomats. Faced with this determined mob, Pev, who had reasoned down Tilly and Donalds, was virtually unable to convince the irate traders that Sir Radley's restrictions on travel and poaching were aimed to protect English skins from samurai blades, not to destroy commerce. What little authority the diplomats were believed to have had been undermined by Morrison's victory in the Hong Kong court. Donalds had been the worst, almost as though he regretted his debt to Pev.

'It was that curio dealer who led them,' he said now, blurrily aware that the others expected him to contribute. 'He bellowed away, "Englishmen must needs eat meat and take exercise. What better way than shooting in the hills and be damned to the laws of heathen potentates!" Those were his words. I rather think we too heard about Englishmen's liberties being trampled.'

'I am afraid you would,' Sir Radley said. 'It is these newspaper writers in Shanghai and Hong Kong. Safe as houses there with the navy and marines in the Legations so they thunder away about iniquitous diplomats in Japan who kow-tow to yellow despots. Disgrace to Britain. Disgrace to Her Majesty. That sort of article is meat and drink to the dailies and weeklies in China. I have some in my baggage for you all to read. See what we are up against.' He shifted stiffly in his chair, looking tired. 'I had not intended to discuss such affairs tonight but as we have now begun – do they, in Yokohama, understand their possible peril? My restrictions are for their own safety.'

'Excuse me, please. I disturb the honourable company.' Tada Shoh bowed in the open doorway.

'Ah, Doctor, how d'ye do?'

'Welcome back to Yedo, Radley Sama,' Shoh replied in his slow hissing English.

'Will you take brandy?'

'Thank you, no.' He stood uneasily by the door. A constrained silence fell on the Englishmen. Sir Radley peered into his empty glass.

'Well, I am off to bed. Still, we shall sleep soundly with our hundred-and-fifty-some samurai at their outposts.' He rose.

Foxwood rose too, none too steadily. 'Prefer a company of marines myself.' He glared drunkenly at Shoh.

James said loudly, 'Come, Tada Sensei, shall we stroll in the garden? A storm is brewing, I reckon, and it may be cooler outside.'

Pev hovered, curious at what could have brought Tada so suddenly to the Legation so late, but James gently steered him towards the door.

'Off to your bed, Pev. There's a good chap.'

'Come along, Pev.' Oscar's brisk, sober voice guided him down the low, dim corridor. He had forgotten a candle but knew his way by feel along the smooth walls. As he passed Oscar's already closed door he sang out, 'Sleep well.'

His room was hot and under the mosquito net it would be hotter, so he left the verandah window open and the corridor door ajar in hope of a breeze. A splash of tepid water on his face, boots and dinner suit off and he collapsed on to the narrow bed.

Wilson and Tada walked out into the warm night. Leaves rustled uneasily in the gusts of storm wind. From the invisible lake came a croak of frogs mournfully busy among the creaking reeds.

'Something worries you. What brings you here so late?' Wilson spoke softly in his stiff Japanese.

'I have come from Shinagawa. I went to see my brother. It is necessary to inform him of my hope of visiting England and to discuss it. It is a family affair, of course. But he would not speak with me. There were other men in the house. Ronin. They have formed a brotherhood –' Wilson shook his head, puzzled. Shoh interlaced his fingers to illustrate connection. 'Tonight, I felt an excitement in that house – the excitement of men who joyfully approach their death. I felt it.'

'Your brother wishes to see us driven from Nippon. That is his life's work; you told me once.'

'So, né. The treaties bring dishonour upon Nippon and this dishonour of Nippon is the dishonour of my brother.' Shoh turned to Wilson, his face a smooth pale shape in the stirring darkness. 'It was wrong for Radley Sama to go so near to the Capital. My people are angry.'

'Your people feel insulted?' James asked.

'So, né. Those like my brother say the presence of outsiders in Nippon desecrates our islands. For them, for us all, one of the most sacred places is the Capital. It is unthinkable shame that a barbarian has breathed the same air, been touched by the same wind as the Mikado. It is the sacred duty of all true men to wipe out this shame.'

'But the government here in Yedo?'

'Yedo is unimportant to Masayuki and his brotherhood. They stamp with muddy geta on the Shogun and his ministers.' Shoh stared out into the rumbling night. 'Last week, at the tombs of the Tokugawa clan, the memorial statues of three Shogun were decapitated. This disrespect shocks me, but today, when I saw my brother, I understood that he would eagerly undertake such an act.' He saw Wilson could not understand so he said slowly, 'My brother is so certain of the rightness of his faith that he will destroy Nippon rather than endure its desecration by the Shogun's government and the outsiders.'

'Do you believe our presence desecrates Nippon, Tada Shoh?' Wilson asked softly.

'I do not know. But I fear you. You are like wood-eating insects infesting a great temple. Only a few at first, tiny channels in a mighty cedar pillar. Then more and more insects, more secret channels through the wood. The temple stands. To our blind eyes it looks perfect, whole. Until one day the temple collapses into dust and we see then that the pillars and the beams have been eaten, hollowed inside.'

'A temple is only a shell, built of dead wood, not living trees. If the spirit of Nippon is vibrant, alive, it will resist our gnawing.'

The wind sharpened through the foliage; a sudden flash of lightning illuminated the leaping trees, caught in a ghastly midnight dance. The thunder was close now, over the city.

Shoh thought of Akiko's death, of Shohtaro's pride. He heard Ohno's desolate moan. 'The Doctor now speaks my greatest fear. Suppose Nippon is just a shell. Suppose her spirit is dry and dead. Then she cannot escape the jaws of the outsiders or the cleansing fire of Masayuki.'

Wilson turned away. His friend's distress was too real. How could he, an Englishman whose temple was solidly constructed in granite and brick, share Shoh's agony over his fragile nation, teetering on the brink of the future?

After a moment he touched Tada's sleeve. 'It is too late to return to the clinic. The storm will be upon us soon. Sleep in my room.'

The two doctors turned their backs on the restless garden.

Shoh said suddenly, 'If it is possible I will go to England. I think Lord Okubo will help my wife and daughter. This idea will please him for he wishes Nippon to learn from the West.'

'Have you only the one child?' James asked, surprised. He had thought there were two.

'Yes. Only one now. I had a son but he is as dead as my brother.'

Pev woke with a start. Afraid. He lay quietly until the drumming of his heart slowed, listening to the darkness. A mettlesome breeze fidgeted at the window panel and teased the wind bell on the verandah. The garden rustled and groaned. Then a low vibrating murmur suddenly exploded into a roar of thunder. The storm. That was what had unsettled him. He relaxed, prepared to enjoy the drama, but his mouth tasted like the bottom of a pond and his bursting bladder reminded him of brandy unwisely consumed. Cursing his intemperance he pushed away the mosquito net and reached down for the chamber pot under the bed.

He froze, the hairs on the back of his neck bristling. Somewhere a dog snarled, a vicious challenge suddenly cut short by an agonized yelp.

Around him the temple creaked, moaning like a stiff old

251

man, but the sounds were not just the complaints of a settling building but of menace; of floorboards stealthily pressed. He groped under the pillow for his pistol. Not there. How could he have been so stupid? So drunk? For God's sake, where was his jacket? Struggling free of the mosquito net, his seeking hand rocked a chair. Something fell, thudding on to the tatami. His fingers closed on the leather butt of his riding crop. That would have to do.

He moved to the window. Silence. Instinct told him the danger was not outside but in the temple. He crossed to the half-open door and slid into the corridor. A black bundle of muscle and cloth thumped against him – a steel-hard, panting bundle with a musky animal odour of fear. Pev struck with his whip. The bundle sprang back, stretching out a very long arm. Something plummeted towards Pev's head. He too jumped back and lashed again with his whip. The bundle grunted. The arm and its sword rose and swooped down again.

Pev shouted. Holding the whip in both hands he slashed wildly at the man who plunged and struggled in the darkness.

At Pev's side a door swished open.

Oscar's voice cried, 'Who is there? What –' The words ended in a gasp. An enormous, ear-splitting crack in a blaze of orange deafened and blinded Pev for a moment. He heard a scream and then he rushed forward, colliding with a warm shaking body.

A dull length of steel flashed past his eyes and he felt a hot jolt in his side.

Men were screaming. He was screaming. The bundle had collapsed in a rattle of steel – a black heaving shape on the floor.

'Pev, help me! The dining-room. Help! Close the door. More men on the verandah. Help me. Take the pistol. I am dying.'

In the noisy confusion Oscar's insistent words were drops of sanity. Pev hauled him up and dragged him roughly down the corridor to the dining-room, trying not to hear his friend's shrieks of pain.

Sir Radley barked, 'Slam that door. Quick. Two more of the bastards behind you.' A pistol shot blasted the darkness. 'Fetch that heavy screen, Fitzpaine. Quickly. Push it in front of the door. I'll hold them off.'

Pev lurched at the screen, shoving against its unyielding weight. Fireworks exploded in his head. But he must go on trying. Hurling himself against the wooden frame, he inched its solid bulk across the door and then slid down the smooth, cool surface into a heap on the tatami.

'Faint,' he muttered.

'No. Drink this. Pull your shirt off. I'll bind that up in a minute but I must see to Sullivan first. Terrible wound. Where in God's name are the others?'

Pev spiralled down to a buzzing world of black and white and red circles. His stomach swirled into the floor and then charged violently up again. Something cold and wet splashed across his face. The circles disappeared and the world returned to black chaos.

'All right now? That brandy is better suited for throwing than drinking anyway.' Sir Radley was bending over him, tying something tight around his chest.

People crowded into the room from the verandah. Foxwood yelled orders. Terrified servants added chairs and tables to the barricades.

'Here. It's Nicholson. Let me in.' A voice outside squeaked over the gabbling servants. Round and pink in his nightshirt, the Nagasaki Consul crawled through the part-open rain shutter and clambered over the barricade. 'I have a pistol. I have a pistol.'

The rain shutters slammed shut and Sir Radley shot the bolts.

'Cannot take any more chances. God protect Wilson.'

Shouts spread from all corners of the compound. The fragile building shivered under thudding footsteps and banging shoji. Pev heard the tooth-jarring ring of steel against steel.

'The samurais! Our guards!' Foxwood cried. 'At last!'

'Is that the guards? And if it is, will they rescue us or join our attackers?' Sir Radley murmured under his breath.

Pev crawled over to Oscar. He was very still. His sodden nightshirt felt sticky under Pev's hand.

'We must help Oscar. He is bleeding away his life.'

253

'I have bound the wound as best I can. He needs Wilson but where is the man?'

'Oscar saved my life again. If he had not shot that man – The same thing as before. But this time the bastard got him first.'

An angry rending of wood screeched behind the screen. Nicholson cried, 'They are hacking the door down.'

'Well, then, pray, man!' Sir Radley bellowed. 'Pray those blasted guards fight for us. We have only three pistols and a handful of bullets.'

'Sensei. Sensei, wake up!'

The hoarse whisper dragged Wilson to consciousness. Shoh's palm was pressed against his lips. Thunder grumbled menacingly above the hollow.

'Men are moving around the temple and I heard a dog's bark cut short.' Shoh drew his hand away from James's mouth to make a stabbing motion at his own throat.

James sat up, surprised at his lack of surprise and his own coolness. 'My pistol is under the pillow. Have you your sword?' For the first time in two years, the absurd sword Tada carried in his sash made sense to him.

'Yes, but it is not enough. I fear this is a band such as Masayuki's brotherhood. Too many for you and me.'

'I must warn the others.'

A shot followed by screams tore the nervous night.

'Too late.' Wilson sank back on the pillow.

'Is this the Doctor's yukata?' Shoh held up an extraordinarily long garment.

'Yes, I had one made. They are comfortable,' he added in unnecessary justification.

'Put it on. Look more – native. No shoes. Lord Amida knows you stand tall as a young pine in your bare feet.'

Wilson slipped on the yukata, grabbed his pistol and joined Shoh where he watched by the verandah. The Japanese had pulled his sword arm free of his kimono and had the sleeve tied back. His naked blade gleamed dully. Shocked by these preparations for killing, Wilson suddenly tasted fear in his mouth. For an instant he thought he might be sick, but sternly he brought himself under control.

254

'Are you really skilled with that thing?'

Shoh looked down at the streak of steel. 'Once, I had skill. Now – Let us hope.' He peered out. 'The courtyard is empty. Glide as the serpent glides across the verandah, through the railing and over the edge. Crawl into the space under the house. Lie still. Wait. Do you understand?'

'That will not help the others. Listen to those shouts.'

'You will be murdered before you reach them. The Shogun's men must save the Shogun's guests.'

As if to prove Shoh's words, steps crunched on the gravel. A jagged flash of lightning illuminated several samurai, bent low, running across the courtyard, corselets and drawn swords gleaming steely blue for an instant. Anonymous figures of death.

'Pray to your Christian god that they are loyal samurai of the Shogun, for there were at least six of them,' Shoh whispered. 'Now. Quick. Quiet.'

After a silent angry struggle James Wilson managed to wedge himself in the small space between the floorboards and the earth. Stretched full length, wreathed in cobwebs, he lay rigid. Tiny claws scratched over his face, myriad legs crept up into his loose robe. His pistol felt cold under the fingers of his right hand.

The phrase 'Vengeance is mine. I will repay, saith the Lord' would not leave his head. 'Almighty God. You must lend strength if I find them all murdered,' he murmured.

Above and around him, in counterpoint to the rumbling thunder, shots, footsteps, screams reverberated in the inky blackness punctuated by long streaks of lightning.

James hidden, Shoh turned back towards the temple, but the sudden thought of dying in that honeycomb of strange rooms and dark corners horrified him and he stepped down into the courtyard. If he must confront his brother, let it be out in the open, under stormy heavens.

Just as he sensed Masayuki was present among the attackers, so now the same instinct urged him through the shadows at the edge of the white gravelled yard towards the back of the Buddha Hall. Its bulk, outlined by lightning, loomed over the sprawl of buildings. A gate in the

255

wall would take him into the gardens towards the other wing of the Legation.

Something, a solid pile of cloth, blocked the gate. Shoh touched warm flesh. Gently he rolled over the body of a monk. The shaven head lolled and blood from a slashed throat dripped into a smooth puddle of black satin.

Sickened, Shoh took his neck cloth to cover the empty eyes of the barbarians' reluctant host. The message was as vivid as a rock in a crystal stream: death to those who tolerate the desecration of Nippon.

The night was fading to a grey dawn. Men darted across the lawns to the central Legation block, their torch flames a puny challenge to the brilliance of the lightning. Shadows rippled along the verandahs.

Bewildered, unsure what to do or where to go but driven blindly toward Masayuki, Shoh moved awkwardly along the wall. A hundred paces away raged the torchlit clangour of the besieged dining-room, but at this end the darkened Legation was silent.

A man burst through a splintering door and clutched out at a pillar of the verandah. Shoh could hear heavy panting. The man groaned and threw back his head.

Shoh stared up into Masayuki's eyes.

'Hah! You! Here! The God of War blesses me. I feared that I would have to seek through Yedo for the barbarians' doctor that I might slay him.'

He jumped off the verandah and approached Shoh. The Chrysanthemum sword gleamed in his hand. 'Do you carry a sword?'

'Yes, as befits my birth and achievements but if I must die by the sword of the Tadas, the sword that should be mine, so be it.'

'If Akiko's sons must fight to the death, so be it.'

Shoh raised his weapon. The sword felt too long, unwieldy. Masayuki was already encircling him, as easy in his movements as Shoh was stiff. Desperately Shoh tried to summon up the training yard at Odawara castle, his sword-master's voice, the lessons of strategy, but these memories of his samurai past eluded him. He should become Masayuki, be a part of his spirit, but he could not.

They watched each other, waiting for any sign of weak-

256

ness. Shoh's blade might have been hewn from granite such was the drag on his arm. After an aeon of time, an eternity of silence, Shoh screamed and charged his brother, this stranger whose mind he could not understand.

Masayuki was surprisingly unprepared; he sprang aside but the Chrysanthemum sword met Shoh's in a jarring chime. Shoh's inferior blade tumbled from his vibrating hand on to the grass.

Before Shoh could think, Masayuki yanked out his short sword and ran at him. Helpless, Shoh threw up his hand as a useless guard against the brilliant steel. His brother's breath was hot in his face.

Shoh dropped his hand and waited.

'No. I cannot.' Masayuki fell back.

Exhausted, Shoh slumped against the wall. 'Do not spare me, Brother. I can die as bravely as you.'

'And die you should. You who betray everything. However, it will not be me that sends you to the Great Void. Another must do it.'

Shoh stepped eagerly towards him. 'Masayuki, can you not see how hopeless this struggle is? We cannot push the sun back into the sea. Nippon has need of men such as you, now when she struggles to the future.'

'The future you speak of is a future of merchants, not samurai. You dream of a Nippon where gold replaces honour. You, Tada Shoh, who always question, you are a man without faith in the spirit of Nippon. Empty as a dry gourd, that is Tada Shoh. It is the fire of bushido, of Nippon's spirit, that will forge the future.'

'That future will be a closed, airless world. Dark. What I speak of is unimaginable. Terrifying. But we must embrace it.'

Masayuki moved closer, his glittering eyes holding Shoh in feverish heat. 'Listen!' he commanded. 'Do you hear the sounds of fighting? Son of Nippon against son of Nippon. One fights for the Bafuku, one for the Emperor. I leave you to live in such a future.' He slid the swords into their scabbards. 'The honour of Tada Masayuki is the honour of Nippon. The honour of Tada Shohtaro is the honour of Nippon. Remember that – Elder Brother.'

He ran along the shadows of the wall and vanished through the gate.

Fat drops of rain cooled Shoh's sweating face. In a crack of thunder the heavens split wide, releasing a deluge.

From the Legation boomed Radley Sama's voice, shouting orders in bad Japanese.

The battle was over.

Despite the smoothness of the azure sea, friendly little waves rocked the dinghy and slapped at the black bulk of the frigate. Pev stood unsteadily and reached for the rope ladder, gasping at the piercing pain in his side. Eyeing his open shirt and bandaged torso, a sailor stretched out a muscular, ginger-haired arm to help the boy.

'Wounded at the Legation, were you, sir?' he asked kindly.

'Just some scratches and a slash across the ribs. Nothing serious but it can be dashed uncomfortable if I make a quick movement.'

'Nasty weapons, those Jap swords. Seen 'em for sale in Nagasaki. Terrible lot of damage those blades did to your friend. You'll find him in the cabin.'

Pev smiled his thanks and picked his way over the deck. The sailor watched him curiously: this latest of several bandaged gentlemen who visited the ship, survivors of the dastardly native attack.

A fresh sea breeze could not disperse the sour stink of dried blood and prickly heat. Pev stepped back quickly from the door, his handkerchief raised, but Oscar's blurry gaze had caught his retches.

'Sorry, old chap,' he said softly. 'Frightful, isn't it? Dressings encourage prickly heat. Beastly affliction, almost worse than the wounds.'

Oscar lay sprawled on the pillows. His freckles glared like dark stains against an unhealthily pellucid skin. A sheet lay over his legs but the top half of his body from neck to groin was wrapped in blood-splotched bandages. An angry scarlet rash swarmed around the bandages. Pev itched just to look at him.

'I brought you some broth. Lord Ando sent a brace of ducks as compensation. No, don't laugh. It will hurt you and me. The cook stewed them into a broth. It should be good for you.' He laid an earthenware crock on the table and sank into the one chair. 'You look fine, better than I feared,' he lied.

'The worst is over. Thanks to James and Tada Shoh. I shall never use my arm again, but then, I am lucky to be alive.'

That Oscar was only half alive was depressingly obvious. James Wilson had warned Pev, talking of blood loss, shock and possible gangrene, but he had also praised Tada's skill with sword wounds. He prophesied a future for Oscar, although as a cripple.

'The dinghy is waiting. I shan't stay long. You are weak. But I must thank you. You saved my life a second time.'

'No. I fired into darkness. It might have been you I hit. That haunts me. I might have killed you, not that ronin.' His voice faded weakly.

'Well, it was the ronin and I owe you my life.' Pev stood. 'I shall go now.'

'No.' A trembling hand grasped feebly at Pev's sleeve. 'No. Please, Pev, tell me what happened that night. Who were they? Tell me everything. Please. James always puts me off when I ask but I must know. I want to know. I *deserve* to know.'

Pev stared down at the hollowed pleading eyes. 'Only a few minutes,' James had said. 'Naturally you want to see him but he is seriously ill. It won't do to upset him and you are not very strong yet, either.'

Pev sat down on the edge of the chair. 'The assassins were a sort of brotherhood. Ronin from Shinagawa, of course, and sworn to kill all foreigners. Fourteen came to us but there were unsuccessful attacks on the British Consulate at Yokohama and then on the Americans at Azabu.' He grinned. 'No need to tell you how much Sir Radley enjoyed that!' He mimicked Ferrier's roar, ' "Where has Jessop's blessed patience put his successor? By Jove, I hope he learns about this. Almost feel tempted to pen the man a note myself." No, do not laugh or I shall leave.'

Oscar had tried a smile but it was a sad effort.

'Shall I go on? Are you sure?'

'Please.'

259

'They filtered one by one through those banks of trees. Remember it was a stormy night. No moon and the branches tossing. Perfect for their purpose. But –'

Oscar nodded.

'Two servants and a bonze were unlucky. The bodies were found in the morning: one in the courtyard, one on the back road and the bonze by the Buddha Hall. Oh, and a stray dog. That is what woke me.'

'The samurai guard?'

'Not one man saw or heard their approach or so it is claimed. But two gave their lives in our defence.

'As you may recollect, it was sultry. It seems not one of us closed his rain shutters so the Legation posed them no problem. Of course, they were not to know where we slept. When I woke and went into the corridor I met one of the brutes scouting around.'

'A brotherhood, you say? No traitors among us? No allies among the servants or guard?'

'Apparently not. I'll explain that in a minute. Anyway, mine – ours – struck at me but his sword hit a low beam instead of my skull. I think he was afraid and my whip confused him and in the dark he could not see what was stopping his sword. Thank God.'

Oscar pulled himself up. The freckles were even darker against his blanched face. 'Then I came out. He struck at me. I fired. Hit him and he struck at you as he fell. Is that right?'

'Yes. Lie back or I'll go. He turned on you, a good target in the doorway. He needed only the one vicious stroke to do – that to you.'

'He is dead?'

'Yes.'

'Two men. Oscar Sullivan who loathes violence has taken the lives of two men. Two men no longer breathe, laugh, eat, think because of Oscar Sullivan.'

'Oscar Sullivan defended himself and others from blood-thirsty aggression.'

'Nevertheless.' He stared at the open door, the creaking deck. Then slowly he said, 'Go on.'

'I pulled you into the dining-room. Sir Radley came from his room attracted by the noise. Others made their

260

way there – all but James – and we barricaded ourselves behind the doors and shot at them until the Tycoon's men rescued us. The fighting was terrible. Then warriors were milling about. It was all like something from the Middle Ages: torches, armour, swords. I was a bit groggy and quite honestly, Oscar, I felt for a moment that I was an actor in *Macbeth* or an opera. Of course, the Legation is wrecked.' He grimaced. 'Blood and bodies everywhere. It was beastly.'

Pev added hastily, 'So you see, it is as well you woke and fired. But this will not happen again, Oscar. We have a detachment of marines now. English voices in the night. Three rather jolly fellows came with me to the quay today.'

'James told me of the marines. How did he escape?'

'That was the quick thinking of Tada Shoh, who dressed him in a yukata and ordered him to hide under the house. After the fighting stopped he emerged covered in cobwebs and mud and insect bites. A giant in dirty Japanese dress. Really, it would have been funny if everything were not so awful and bloody and terrifying. But Tada saved his life. James has proposed that he join the first Japanese delegation to visit England. To study at a hospital, you know. But –'

'But?' Oscar was not to be denied any detail.

'I am afraid this is not very pleasant. His brother was one of the gang. Tada visited him in Shinagawa and suspected something was up so he came to warn James. That is why he arrived so late that evening. Do you remember? But he did not expect the attack to come immediately. He did his best, Oscar, and we must be grateful to him.'

'His brother?'

Pev pulled from his pocket a brocade cylinder. 'I shall come to that. Naturally Sir Radley has been at it hammer and tongs. The government shows no remorse – except for the ducks – and only claims that this proves Yedo and Osaka are not yet safe for foreign merchants. A delegation arrived, all exquisite in silk gauze, to potter about the wreckage. Most fastidious they were. Shuddering at the blood and sighing over that heavy standing screen slashed by swords. Apparently it was valuable. I thought it was hideous. Then, after endless niceties, they demanded, oh, so politely, that the opening of Yedo and Osaka as treaty ports be delayed. Of course, they are quite right and Sir Radley knows it but he let out a good, satisfying bellow that sent them scurrying off to their norimon like little silken mice. Made us all feel better.' He laughed at the memory and then gasped in sudden pain.

'But Tada's brother?' Oscar persisted.

Pev tapped the cylinder lying on the sheet. 'This was removed from a corpse. Each man carried one.' Oscar recoiled from the brocade letter case glistening like a serpent's opulent skin on the unbleached linen.

'This is a manifesto. Extraordinary blend of humility, dedication, patriotic mumbo-jumbo. But their bravery cannot be questioned.' The admiration in Pev's voice shocked Oscar. 'The attack was suicide; fourteen men against one hundred and fifty. They accept death eagerly. Await it. Welcome it like a lover his mistress. It is horrible, but powerful too.'

'Not quite what one expects from a class of drunken ruffians.' Oscar attempted a wry tone.

'By no means,' Pev agreed. 'These men are terrifying and yet humbling in the pure blaze of their belief. Two were captured – tortured – Sir Radley is certain. They have admitted that they killed Dirk. No, not admitted – boasted of it! Call themselves the Brotherhood of the White Cherry. It seems the cherry blossom is a symbol for a true samurai's life: fragile yet strong. Living only a short while before the wind blows the flower into oblivion.'

Oscar slumped against his pillows. Fatigue fought with curiosity. 'Who led them?'

'A samurai or, I guess, a ronin, from Mito. Or so the government said.'

'Of course.'

'Of course, the usual scapegoat for a maladroit government. But this Kojima does seem to be a Mito man. He was not captured or killed but the prisoners claim he will be dead by now. He will have cut his belly. They begged for the privilege of performing the same ritual.'

Oscar shuddered.

'Yes, it sickens one. All the three men who escaped will

disembowel themselves, it seems.'

'And Tada's brother?'

Pev answered slowly, 'He met Tada in the garden. Tried to kill him but could not bring himself to murder his own brother and fled. Perhaps in shame at his failure. Perhaps at his human weakness. Now Tada Shoh must live day by day knowing that any moment may be his brother's agonizing last.'

'Oh, my God. I am so glad to be leaving this blood-stained island. This pain is welcomed, yearned for, because it brings my release in its wake.' Oscar shrank into the pillows, sinking into his refuge.

Pev leaned forward eagerly. 'When you are stronger you will feel differently. The nightmare is still too real for you. But it is a fascinating city, you know. They are preparing for O-Bon, All Soul's Day. Everyone is doing something. Shop curtains washed; tatami out in the streets. The women are so charming in their aprons and headgear, even while they bang their mats and cover you with dust. The boats on the Sumida too. You can almost see the dusters flying. Even the coolies are good-tempered. The shops are full of decorations and good luck charms. Ah, now, I nearly forgot. I bought this for you at a toy-seller's.' He pulled out a bright paper monkey that clambered up its bamboo pole when Pev pulled a string.

Oscar's smile was one of courtesy, not conviction.

'Well, all right. It is a silly thing but, here, give that short string a tug.'

Oscar tugged. A scarlet tongue popped out of the monkey's mouth. Oscar laughed. 'Yes, they are a clever race.'

'You see. You will soon forget the ronins and their swords. James and I have already. In fact, there are plans afoot for a trip to Osaka in the autumn. Sir Radley is determined to gain something, some concession, after this attack. Now, Osaka will be an adventure, Oscar. And by October you should be hale enough to join us.'

'No. When this ship sails for Hong Kong I shall sail with it. Willingly. Joyfully. Never to breathe the violence of these islands again. But you will stay. And you will conquer. So will James. Perhaps the generosity of you both

263

will civilize them a little. But, Pev, forgive my weakness. Yedo has defeated me.'

To Tada Shohtaro,

A few hours after I, Masayuki, lay down my brush you will be the only surviving samurai in the Tada family. This great responsibility is placed on one as tender as a green willow shoot. But as the willow grows supple and strong, so grows Shohtaro.

Akiko, your honoured grandmother, entrusted your education to the care of Iwa family so that you might walk the ancient way of the warrior. When your feet are firmly set on that way, the sword of your Tada ancestors awaits you.

His Imperial Highness has declared that Nippon must remain free of barbarian outsiders. All true patriots live only to serve His Sacred Will, joyfully giving their lives in his service. So must Shohtaro live and die. The barbarians are the enemies of Nippon. It is the duty of the samurai to destroy these devils; to wipe them from the rocks and beaches of these precious isles.

This unworthy Masayuki has struck his own small blow in the service of the Emperor. Now the hour of my death approaches; like the white cherry I have blossomed and am ready to fall, but my heart is troubled for I know the outsiders are many. For each one killed, a thousand may replace him.

But as the sword of Nippon will triumph over their clumsy guns, so will the spirit of bushido conquer the outsiders' base spirit. Fired by Nippon's glorious history, Shohtaro must embody bushido as this unworthy Masayuki has struggled in vain to do. If the spirit of bushido is vanquished, then Nippon is nothing but a broken blade and the Imperial Majesty must bow his head in shame.

The tears of the sorrowing gods will then drown these islands and their undeserving children.

Revere the ancient deities. Revere His Imperial Majesty. Now, at this festival of O-Bon, cherish the memory of Akiko and treasure the dagger, her gift to you, as you will treasure the Chrysanthemum sword I leave you.

A samurai can achieve no higher glory than to die for Nippon.

Son-nō Jōi. Revere the Emperor. Expel the barbarian.

Inn of the Sunset Light
Eleventh day. Fifth Lunar Month
Fourteenth year of the reign of
Emperor Komei

A tall ginko stood as gracious sentry, its long boughs scraping gently against the tiled roof of the cemetery gate.

Granite grave columns glowed golden warm in the sun. O-Bon offerings of gleaming rice or lilacs nestled in the thick grass. A warbler sang from a gnarled mesh of hydrangea swarming over an untended corner of broken stones under low-drooping pines.

While he had walked the straight streets of the ancient capital, monks had laid Akiko's newly cut tablet into the raw ground by the Tada monument. Now moss crept over the sharp stone edges, ragged tendrils curling into the chiselled characters of her name: Autumn child.

He knelt and pulled away the intruders, breathing in their sweet scent. The earth was warm, welcoming after his hard flight down the Tokaido. As a boy he had loved to crouch down on a hot day in the high weeds against the wall foaming with morning glories to watch insects scurry about their affairs. This fragrant, drowsy heat carried him back to the Tada house and he almost expected Shoh's teasing or Akiko's clear call to pierce his daydreams.

The ginko's cool shadow nudging across the grave roused him.

Carefully, he arranged the setting. The letter to Shohtaro and the Chrysanthemum sword he placed on the Tada monument, high, where his blood would not spatter them.

With a quick cut he released his top-knot. His hair spilled down in wild array. But there was no white cloth, no tall candles, no screens. Only the soft grass, the mountains blue and gold against the sun, birds as witnesses, the cicadas' prayers.

He held out the short sword towards his mother's grave, a glinting scarlet tribute in the setting sun.

*   *   *

Together Hanae and Kimi wrestled out each tatami mat and beat it free of crumbs and soot. With steaming cloths Kimi rubbed every board and bead of aged cedar. Bamboo brooms darted over the kitchen, stepping stones, the vestibule. The gardens were raked, shrubs trimmed, the bathhouse and storerooms aired and scrubbed. The tea pavilion and its few precious contents were lovingly dusted. While Kimi pasted fresh paper on the shoji frames Hanae reverently wiped the carved shrine and its bronze Kannon. Pungent sticks of incense went into the polished vessel. The familiar tablets of Tada ancestors were arranged around the newer ones: Teruhiko's, darkening now; Akiko's; Masayuki's, the ink as fresh as the offering apricots on the sacred lotus leaves.

Finally, cleanly sweet as a rain-washed evening, the house lay open and welcoming to twilight. Lanterns of white paper swayed like ghostly fruit from the dustless beams.

Flint and steel sparked. The candles, one by one, flared into celebration. A little fire blazing between the posts lit the open Tada gateway for returning souls. Glowing lanterns guided the spirits back to the waiting family altar.

The garden stirred, whispering. Dark shadows of camellia, peony and maple spread in the deepening dusk. Beyond the rustling screen of willows the tea house lay silent.

All over Nippon the flames of the living welcomed the dead.

Tada Shoh stood by his gateway, protected by the warm moist night of Odawara. Beyond the walls, the invisible fields singing with insects, the Tokaido stretched to Yedo.

And in twelve months, when once again the lanterns of O-Bon glowed in the night, where then would be Tada Shoh?

266

Becoming a doctor is just the beginning . . .

VITAL SIGNS

a dazzling new novel by

BARBARA WOOD

Sondra, Ruth and Mickey are three girls with very different
backgrounds who met on their first day at medical school.

They are passionate women whose pioneering dreams and
desires would become dramatically intertwined in the years to
come.

Yet each in turn would find – as perhaps only a woman who
seeks a special challenge can discover – how her vocation made
her look for the deeper, richer meaning of life, how through
love, devotion and sacrifice she could find her own place in the
world . . .

GENERAL FICTION   0 7221 9201 0   £2.95

Also by Barbara Wood in Sphere Books:
DOMINA

You'll never feel closer to your dreams

a ravishing new novel by

Caroline Gray

Orphaned, penniless, destitute, Wilhelmina Doberley
arrives in New York armed only with an aching ambition
to make her dreams come true.

Dreams that seem a million miles away when she starts
work as a lowly chambermaid in the spell-bindingly
glamorous Hotel Superb. There she discovers a world of
champagne and oysters, ease and elegance – a far cry
from her own life of drudge and poverty.

But Wilhelmina is determined to succeed. And when the
outrageously attractive heir to the Superb begins to fall
for her beauty, she knows where her destiny lies . . .

GENERAL FICTION   0 7221 41041   £2.95

Also by Caroline Gray in Sphere Books: FIRST CLASS

FROM A FORGOTTEN AGE OF ELEGANCE – A STORY
OF GLAMOUR, PASSION AND WILD EXCITEMENT

ORIENTAL HOTEL

Janet Tanner

Just the mention of his name . . . and for Elise
Sanderson the years simply rolled away, taking her
back on a sea of bittersweet memories to those heady,
dangerous days before the flames of war had ravaged
the East.

Then, in the golden days of her youth, she had swept
through the doors of the Orient's great hotels, into a
world where bell-boys ran to answer every whim, where
the champagne was permanently on ice, where elegant
men in tails and women in exclusive *haute couture*
danced to the endless music of orchestras.

It was then, she recalled, that she had first seen him,
lounging languidly in a rattan chair, already in uniform,
cigarette smoke curling lazily around half-closed hazel
eyes. It was a dangerous face, she had thought in that
first startled moment. A face to be reckoned with . . .

GENERAL FICTION   0 7221 83372   £2.50

A SELECTION OF BESTSELLERS FROM SPHERE

FICTION

DUNN'S CONUNDRUM	Stan Lee	£2.95 ☐
GOLDEN TALLY	Pamela Oldfield	£2.95 ☐
HUSBANDS AND LOVERS	Ruth Harris	£2.95 ☐
SWITCH	William Bayer	£2.25 ☐

FILM & TV TIE-IN

BOON	Anthony Masters	£2.50 ☐
LADY JANE	Anthony Smith	£1.95 ☐

NON-FICTION

THE FALL OF SAIGON	David Butler	£3.95 ☐
THE AMBRIDGE YEARS	Dan Archer	£2.50 ☐
THE SUNDAY EXPRESS DIET BOOK	Marina Andrews	£2.50 ☐
THE PRICE OF TRUTH	John Lawrenson and Lionel Barber	£3.50 ☐

All Sphere books are available at your local bookshop or newsagent, or can be ordered direct from the publisher. Just tick the titles you want and fill in the form below.

Name _____

Address _____

_____

Write to Sphere Books, Cash Sales Department, P.O. Box 11, Falmouth, Cornwall TR10 9EN

Please enclose a cheque or postal order to the value of the cover price plus:

UK: 45p for the first book, 20p for the second book and 14p for each additional book ordered to a maximum charge of £1.63.

OVERSEAS: 75p for the first book plus 21p per copy for each additional book.

BFPO & EIRE: 45p for the first book, 20p for the second book plus 14p per copy for the next 7 books, thereafter 8p per book.

Sphere Books reserve the right to show new retail prices on covers which may differ from those previously advertised in the text or elsewhere, and to increase postal rates in accordance with the PO.